Good Woman

Vanessa Russell

Good Woman
Copyright © 2003 by Vanessa Russell

Fiction

ISBN trade paperback: 0-9744938-0-5

All rights reserved. No part of this book may be reproduced or transmitted in any form or by any means, electronic or mechanical, including photocopying, recording, or by any information storage and retrieval system, without the written permission of the publisher, except in the case of brief quotations embodied in critical articles or book reviews.

This book was printed in the United States.

For inquiries or to order additional copies of this book, contact:

Gardenia Press
P. O. Box 18601
Milwaukee, WI 53218-0601USA
1-866-861-9443 www.gardeniapress.com
orders@gardeniapress.com

For Amy and David, my own precious gems.

Acknowledgements:

Writing my first book gave me some days of self-doubt, worry about others reading my words from the heart, this exposure of one's underside. I wasn't sure my story was credible until others read it and encouraged me to keep at it. I owe a big thanks to the following folks who helped me along the way.

To my aunt Phyllis Delong who read my first 30 pages and believed enough in my seed of an idea to sew books with Ruby's name on a library quilt. Her inspiring words kept me writing.

To friends Natalie Eggeman, Lynne Mielke, Laurel Cook, Karen Wonneck, Deb Courtney (editor), and Annette Foster who each read different drafts but all had the same understanding. Thanks for your insightful critiques, ladies, and for the illustration on the front cover, Laurel! You represent womankind very well.

To my grandma Bess and my dad, Roger Osborne, from whom I inherited the love to write. And to my children, Amy and David, both of whom I passed this same love on down to.

To my husband, John, who helped me build that bridge to the other side. It's hard to believe such a liberal thinker gave me pointers that steered me to write the Letter from the Editor in Part II. For someone who cooked all the meals while I wrote, he sure can write sexist. Thanks, Babe!

To Gardenia Press for making it possible to say all this in the first place.

Prologue

Ruby's memories of her wedding ceremony are little more than blurred images of crowding, gawking spectators, Robert perspiring around his forehead and upper lip, and his hand shaking as he slipped the wedding band on her finger. She was surprised to realize he might be as nervous as she. Men slapped him on the back as if he had accomplished some great deed while women gave her teary-eyed hugs. Her mother-in-law's loaned light blue silk wedding gown was scratchy around the high-necked lace collar. Mama had teased her as she took in the seams around the small bust, saying that a few children under the belt would fill in above the belt.

What Ruby remembers most is the wedding night. She is struck numb by the thought that they are alone for the first time when they pull up in front of her mother-in-law's house. Robert assists her from the unsteady buggy and this is appreciated because she feels as if she has become one with the buggy and doesn't think her trembling legs can remove her on their own. He takes her small canvas bag from the backbench, which is all she has with her. Ruby hasn't moved her things here, as his mother thought it best they wait until after the wedding. Neighbors might talk, she explained. He hurries toward the front door with her trailing in his steps. He waits with his hand on the doorknob, his eyes on the windows of the neighbors' houses as if an unwelcome audience is watching.

The house is quiet when she enters, the ticking mantel clock sounding louder than usual and demanding more time. How dark and cool it is, the darkness surrounding her as if she is submersed in murky waters, vision and hearing subdued by its density, heart beating in her ears. The dongs of the clock only count seven times as she watches him walk up the stairs with her bag. The ineptness within her is born from uncertainty of what to do next.

He only speaks when he reaches the top of the stairs. Looking down at her, he clears his throat. "Well, you don't wish to have tea with Mother, I hope?"

Face flushing hot, she can only shake her head.

"Then come on up the stairs. Mother is not here, I assure you." His tone becomes cajoling, as one offering a present to a child. "You will get to see the *upper floors.*"

Ruby grips the stair rail and takes one step at a time. He backs away when she reaches the top.

"There now, Ruby. That wasn't so bad was it?" He gestures around the hallway. "So, what do you think?"

There is a window at the far end, its outside light barely visible at the end of its day, and two closed doors on the right and one on the left. Another shorter flight of steps behind her leads up to the third floor. Nodding, she pulls at her scratchy lace collar.

Robert opens the two doors on the right, one being a sewing room, the other a small bedroom. Remaining at the doorway of the bedroom, he nods toward a closed door across the hall. "Mother's room is over there." He turns and points up the stairs. "A large room is up that way, currently used for storage. Mother said it could be made into another bedroom someday." Taking a handkerchief from his back pocket, he wipes the perspiration from his forehead.

She wishes they were on the cooler first floor having tea with his mother. Maybe he does, too; he is fidgeting more than usual.

"This is my bedroom." His laugh sounds uneasy to her. "I guess this is our bedroom now, isn't it?"

Without warning, a wave of homesickness rises in her and she longs for the familiarity of her own bedroom. These rooms are strange and Robert seems a stranger to her. How can she possibly share a bed with a stranger? Never in her whole life has she slept outside her own home. Never again can she go back as part of that family. Today's ceremony has cut her away, cut the umbilical cord for good. This realization of its vows and the profound change on her life floods over her and she grips the doorframe to keep from falling. He is already in the room taking off his jacket and bow tie. He hasn't noticed that her life has changed in that moment.

Opening a window, Robert then rolls down the Venetian blind, pulling the room from dim to dark. He notices her still standing there at the door as he is turning on the gas wall sconce. He sighs. "Really, Ruby. Why do you look like a scared rabbit? I won't bite." He nods toward the hallway. "Your bag is there. Take it into the sewing room and change. You don't plan to sleep in my mother's dress, do you?"

No, and I didn't plan to sleep in your mother's house either, but here I am. His tone makes her feel sassy.

Hesitating with bag in hand, she turns to ask if it isn't a little too early to go to bed, and sees him taking off his trousers. Her cheeks burn with mortification and she hurries away to the next room. She believes she has blushed more times than not today. If her face continues to flush hot in the heat of these rooms, she will surely faint.

Perspiration rolls down her stomach from her breasts as she unsnaps the corset in nervous jerking motions. The room has only muted light from the curtained window so with some difficulty she rummages inside her bag of belongings. She shakes out the white cotton nightgown her sister, Opal, had made for her. To think she'd worried about the wrinkles when she is only going to bed. The nightgown will be expected to wrinkle there. Panic grips her again but she keeps moving in preparation because the stifling heat in the tiny sewing room is worse than the fear of going into his larger bedroom. The gown now on, she sees it stops short at her knees where one of her petticoats is ruffled and damp with perspiration. Off come her nightgown and the two layers beneath. She hugs around her breasts feeling ashamed of her nakedness. She desperately longs to wash. Where can she find a washbowl? She is at a loss as to how to ask Robert for water and soap.

What in the world is she supposed to do? Why didn't her

mother prepare her for this? All her life she was told not to show so much as her ankle. Now she is to — she hears the bedsprings squeak through the wall.

Mercy, he wastes no time!

Once again donning the nightgown, the unease is no better. Her nakedness underneath feels as exposed as if she is walking outside in the sun without a stitch on. She shuffles to the doorway and happens to look down to her stocking feet. With her hand over her mouth, she stifles a hysterical giggle. As she rolls down her white stockings she thinks of his raised eyebrows if she came into his room like that. "Yes, Robert, I always sleep in my stockings, don't you?" Being silly lightens her up a little.

"Robert?" she calls from the door.

"Ye-" he clears his throat. "Yes?"

"May I wash?"

There is a pause, then the bedsprings squeak a release. She can hear the porcelain pitcher click from its bowl and return with a louder scratch.

"There is no water here, Ruby," he calls out. "You can do that tomorrow."

The bedsprings squeak again.

She folds her arms and leans against the doorframe of the sewing room. Work and effort was ahead of her in living with a pampered son, an only child of an overprotective mother. Well, it is too late now, she resolves. I must take him as he is, and he must take me as I am, sticky body and all.

As she enters his room, he tells her to turn off the gas lamp. But not before she sees the hair on his chest and thinks it is possible he might be naked.

When the room is turned to darkness, he tells her to take off the gown before getting into bed. "It's too warm in here," he explains.

She can't dispute that, but is glad of the darkness. How cool and different the sheets feel on her naked skin. How odd his hairy leg feels as he moves closer to her. She lies on her back, bringing the sheet up to her chin. His arm comes across her stomach and he kisses her cheek for the first time since being pronounced man and wife. A hairy patch brushes her hip as he lies on his side, and a question forms in her mind of growing hard flesh moving against her. His breathing is erratic in her ear.

Lying there like one big question mark while he is moving his fingers between her legs and inside an opening she herself does not know exists, her knees clam together and her hand grabs his wrist.

His arm becomes ridged. "Don't," he says.

He continues to probe until a pleasant tingling takes her by surprise. She tries to remain still but finds she cannot relax her knees. Her womanly odor rises. Can he smell it? The tingling stops as soon as he removes his hand. He looms over her and now he is flattening himself on top of her, his male underarm odor surrounding her. Something large and hard is trying to push and enter between her legs. Feeling like a small, trapped animal, she stiffens.

"No!" she whispers. "You are hurting me!" She tries to move from under him but she is pinned.

"Shh." He pushes harder. "Help me. Guide me in."

"I don't know what you are doing!" She is suffocating under his weight.

Lifting himself, he grabs her hand, forcing it down to his hardness as he raises his hips. Smooth skin feels so strange as her fingers wrap around it. Her touch suffices to spur him on. His hardness jerks in her grasp for a few seconds. He gasps. Warm thick liquid oozes onto her pelvic area. He collapses on top of her for a moment before rolling onto his back.

Her body is still, but her mind is racing. Why didn't Mama tell me about this? Her mama's only advice the night before was a reference to the Bible that Ruby must be submissive to her husband. "As God ordained it, as nature planned it. We have all seen it enough with our own farm animals. Your husband will teach you what you need to know." If so, then why does Ruby feel so helpless and stupid? She makes a silent commitment that when this at last results in children, she will prepare her daughter for her own wedding night.

Ruby isn't sure if they have just mated or not. Could pregnancy occur this way? She wishes to wash but she knows the answer to that one, so she quietly wipes her pelvis with the sheet. Is it over? Is this it? She can just about make out the outline of him lying on his back. He appears to be asleep.

From the darkness, he speaks. "You are a virgin. So am I. But I do know that I am to enter you. You must not resist or I am forced to release my seed where it does not belong. I cannot provide you children this way. This I know for sure. Next time you must relax and open yourself to me. Never move my hand again or close your legs to me. Can we agree on that?"

He is blaming her, the sting of his words biting at her guilt. Tears burn her eyes. "I am sorry I have disappointed you, Robert. I was frightened."

"Have I ever hurt you?" he asks.

"No."

"Did you not promise just a few hours earlier to love, honor, and obey me?"

"Yes."

"Do you think your way of behaving tonight showed me love, honor, or obedience?" His chastising tone makes her feel again as a child.

"Please be patient with me, Robert! I'll try to do better next time, I promise." Her voice sounds like someone else. She had become a stranger in a stranger's bed.

"We'll see, Ruby." Robert rolls to his side facing her. "Remember. Relax."

With purpose, he places his hand between her legs. His foot pulls her leg to him. His fingers search and probe. Ruby takes deep breaths to relax as he asked. Her legs tense, relax, and then tense again as his finger enters her. She reaches for his wrist.

"No, no," he warns.

She drops her hand.

"I'm ready now," he whispers. Lifting himself above her, his knees force her legs further apart. "Open yourself to me, Ruby."

She swallows hard, easing her knees apart. He lowers his hips, his hardness replacing his fingers. She feels herself being spread apart and an opening enlarged as he pushes. Her no-longer-private area burns with each thrust.

"No!"

"Yes!"

Something gives way and the burning becomes very wet. He grunts with each lunge, forcing himself deeper and deeper.

Her knees grip his hips. He pauses. "You promised," he says.

She knows he is challenging her, testing her. She obeys. He moves freely, unrestrained now. The burning intensifies and fluid runs down between her buttocks, onto the bed. She is reminded of her friends whispering, *Virgin's Sheets*.

The bed squeaks without shame and the headboard is hitting the wall in rhythm. Their sweaty stomachs make sucking noises as he moves on top of her. She is so thankful they are alone in the house.

He finally stops in mid-air and gasps. A few smaller thrusts and then he pulls out, collapsing beside her. The burning remains, as if he is still inside her.

She remembers him saying, for the second time that day, "There now, that wasn't so bad, was it?"

PART I
Spring's Seed

Trapped. Without shackles, nor ball and chain, no cuts from metal teeth, but the grip was there around her heart. Ever present was the heavy load as were the invisible bars. Ruby looked out the parlor window, walked to the front door, opened it, but didn't go beyond. She closed the door and paced, trying to rearrange the stays of her corset, pinching into her side.

Ruby surveyed the parlor, trying to imagine her own visitor in here. She hadn't invited strangers into the house in ... well, never. The parlor had been sanctioned for the limited occupancy of her husband and his mother.

She spotted white as her boot stepped forward from under her ankle-length brown skirt, realizing the ruffle of her petticoat was protruding.

Which to do first? Either rearrange her skirt and petticoats, or pick up that saucer she saw under the chair, likely hidden the night before by one of her two boys. Aimee was due any minute, to notice both her dress and dish.

"Mercy," she whispered, as she rushed toward the kitchen carrying the saucer, her free hand pulling at the worn elastic of the petticoat. A needle and thread would mend the blessed thing, but that required time and a trip upstairs to the sewing room.

With her frayed nerves, Ruby was in a perfect frame of mind to learn about women's suffrage with these ladies. She had asked Robert if she could walk with Aimee to a tea. Tea was innocent enough. Why would he forbid such a harmless and socially acceptable bit of entertainment? Those prison bars could almost be heard clanging reinforcements when he reminded her of her responsibilities at home. As if she didn't know well enough, indeed.

Well, there was little choice in the matter now. She had already accepted the invitation from her next-door neighbor Aimee, only yesterday.

Peering around the parlor's lace-covered window panels for any approaching visitors, she saw only the streaks on her window. She walked to the front door but resisted the urge to open it. Instead, she leaned her back against it, facing the staircase to the bedrooms. Nothing lay on the stairs. Good. Walking through the dining room, her eyes darting here and there for out-of-place things, she opened the door-hung drapes into the kitchen (*they are called portiere, my dear, please remember!* her mother-in-law's memory reminded). Walking past her worktable to the back wall's sideboard and sink pump, she reached for the soap to wash the saucer, drew back, reached again, and then waved off the saucer. The kitchen was given one more glance, the corset one last tug. Her lungs took in as deep a breath as her corset allowed and blew out slowly. What an invention to torture, these whale-boned spikes. They squeeze in the waist but the resulting lack of oxygen squeeze the mind.

Her nostrils twitched and she wished the house didn't smell from coal heat and gas lighting. When the weather was warm enough, would be the time to air out the winter and wash down the coal grime on the walls.

The tree beyond her window, with its sparrows fluttering from branch to branch, held her in place. Ruby watched them, longing to be one of their kind. Nailed to earth with many duties rushing at her like tireless ants, there was little room to move.

"Mercy, I have all this work to do!" Ruby muttered to the glass pane, her mind making a mental note to wipe the steamed circle she was creating with her breath. "Why am I reminded that the house is not mine but the duties are?"

She folded her arms across her chest and rested her forehead against the cool glass. Good thing Robert and the children weren't here to witness this. One more duty, one more request would be enough to see her burst at the seams. Perhaps that wouldn't be so bad. Her eyes closed to envision the sudden release this would bring; her bondage of whale bones, petticoats, heavy wool, menstrual belt, straps, snaps, and buttons spinning off in all directions while her inner being vaporizes through the wall, lift toward the heavens, and fly the freedom flight to the light.

The mantel clock chiming half-past-the-hour brought her back to earth.

Aimee was late. She was due here thirty minutes ago.

"Did I misunderstand the date and time?" Ruby asked the clock. After a moment, she shook her head. No, the invitation came only yesterday and Aimee distinctly said the gathering was today. "Perhaps I was supposed to go over to her house?" She paced the parlor again. "Oh, I don't know! Well I can't very well stay here and just wonder, now can I? I'll cross over to Aimee's." She stopped and shook her head. "No, I can't do that."

Walking to the dining room window that faced Aimee's house, Ruby pulled back the red flannel drapes. No, no one was out there. The front door was closing behind her before she could say *no* again.

* * * * *

Freedom. Ruby felt a surge of energy, of elation. Elated the moment her boot hit the boardwalk outside her home, beyond her verandah. An outing. She stood for a moment to appreciate the fresh spring air. Walking out here was like going from dark to light, like being turned inside out. Her three-story dwelling cast a shadow behind her. The brown scalloped-patterned shingles reminded her of day-old fish scales at the market; the brown and green painted railing, thick posts and abundant scrollwork were too dark and overbearing. Those walls could not hold her in try as they may. She smiled, feeling the same freedom as a once-upon-a-time little girl heading toward the candy store. She could go wherever the moment took her. Chores could wait for her return. As long as she was home prior to her children's return from school, everything would be fine. Ruby had a sudden desire to run and skip, but ever conscious of her mother-in-law's teaching of watchful eyes in neighbors' windows, she kept herself in check by pulling her heavy woolen shawl around her a bit tighter.

Ruby attempted to dress properly for the outing, as much as was possible within her small wardrobe containing three sets of outerwear. The black dress Ruby now wore was once brown, but she had soaked this in a vat of black dye last year for her mother-in-law's funeral. The mourning period was but a few months, unfortunately the heavy wool with its full skirt and tight bodice was to last much longer and was now her day dress for the market. She had hemmed it to the instep length, just touching her boot, allowing her to wear it outside where it wouldn't drag through the mud and grass. Practical, without loose sleeves that might catch and snag on baskets. Bone buttons decorated the front. Black cotton gloves without so much as a frill.

Regardless of practicality, she believed her appearance drab and dreary. While brushing dust and lint from her dress this morning Ruby decided to ask Robert if some light-colored cotton fabric could be purchased for a summer dress. She was so tired of the dark colors her mother-in-law had always insisted she wear. She nodded in memory that yes, it was logical that darker colors disguised the dirt. The heavier wool could be brushed instead of laundered. Yes, of course, laundering was backbreaking work ... ah, but a light green cotton frock would be perfect for afternoon teas with her newfound acquaintances. Hot summer weather would be a good reason to ask Robert for the money. He might agree, if she promised to keep the dress simple, not too ornate. Her only ornate accessory today was a gift from her sister, Opal. The small-brimmed hat made of white straw was trimmed around the rim in black velvet ribbons and small silk red roses.

Her first thought that morning upon rising was her invitation to tea received the day before. Ruby was surprised to be asked by someone she was not acquainted with. She had kept within her boundary, as had Aimee. But speaking to another woman older than her eleven-year old daughter was too tempting. Ruby was rushing about the laundry on the line before a rainstorm, when Aimee invited her over to the fence and gave her a calling card to Cady Pickering's home. Aimee's description of the group was sketchy, but enough was said to know they were called *Ladies of the Lost Legion* and used terms like "women's inferior status".

Ruby silently agreed that the frustrations she'd dealt with in this household were less than desirable. She had not questioned her duties before. At least not out loud. No woman had told her before that she was permitted to question this. Her mother, then her mother-in-law told her she was a wife and mother first, a woman last. Was it wrong to want more? No, there had to be more than endless chores, with no time for thoughts of her own.

All she knew was that she wanted to know more. What do these ladies intend to change and how, being only women? Do they ever feel like sinners, or that they were doing something wrong, since Robert said men oppose so strongly to their cause? For the first time, Ruby had skimmed through Robert's newspaper this morning, hoping to find clues, but found no articles on this subject.

She was amazed at herself for wondering such things. How inspiring it was to realize one's own sentiment! Life was accepted as it came - until now. She had no idea what other women thought, except perhaps her mother, sister, and mother-in-law. Even then, their discussions never touched intimate feelings, or questioned their role in life. She knew her mother-in-law's beliefs best through ladies' books of etiquette, from which she used to quote often to Ruby. Her favorite was from a copy of *Godey's Lady's Book*: *Hair is at once the most delicate and lasting of our materials, and survives us like love.*

No wonder I feel unaware, she thought at breakfast. I was born, raised and married within a ten-mile radius.

Born and raised on her parents' dairy farm just on the outskirts of town, the school Ruby attended literally grew as she did, up to grade ten. The remaining grades of eleven and twelve were academic or technical, designed for the boys' furtherance to college or to learn a trade.

Ruby met Robert in the same shoe store he now owned. She had just turned sixteen. He was twenty-four. In that one Saturday trip to town, she had splurged a month's savings on an adorable pair of red velvet slippers, accepted his company for a coffee in the diner next door, and ended the visit by being so bold as to invite him out for dinner the next day, Sunday. She loved his eyes, warm chocolate drops was her description to her sister. That Sunday was his first – and last – courting.

Ruby viewed the following year, up to their marriage, as a series of callings. Every Sunday afternoon, Robert arrived on their front porch, hat in hand, asking her papa if he could call on Ruby. His mannerism was quiet and courteous, winning the parents' approval as a decent young man with good intentions. He joined the family for dinner, joined Ruby for a walk in the evening, but alas their lips never joined as she so often dreamt. There was only a brush of his lips across her cheek as he said goodnight at dusk.

On many Thursdays, she walked from school to his home where he lived with his mother, for afternoon tea. On those days there was still no departing kiss for Ruby, because his mother never left them alone longer than a trip to the kitchen, reckoning it only appropriate that she chaperone faithfully, reminding the young couple of the neighbors' constant vigil.

Ruby walked away from the house with this last thought, looking back at her three-story dwelling with a puckered brow. This same house was where they met for tea, once his mother's house, built by his father's own hands. Rarely a living day went by for his mother, that she didn't remind Ruby the house was still hers. On her wedding day, Ruby moved from one parents' home into another. And just as Ruby's own mother told her what to do for the first seventeen years, Robert's mother told her what to sew, what to wear, what to cook, and how to clean, until her dying day eleven years later. Ruby glanced up at her bedroom window, the same bedroom where Robert was born, and then his three children.

Life is an endless cycle, his mother had said over a new grandchild. *Birth, death, rebirth.* She had pointed to her ringed finger.

This wedding ring, this circle, symbolizes this cycle, you know. Endless. A year ago, on the day she died, she reached a trembling hand to Ruby and dropped her thin band into Ruby's hand. *First time I've taken this off,* she whispered. *Pass it down to Bess.*

Back then Ruby, so quick to nod, always nodded, always wanting to please. Now she was not so ready to nod. She surmised that this last year had helped her slowly evolve into a woman. A woman who had developed her own thoughts. Surely there was more than a ring to pass on to our children? She forced her memories away and knocked on Aimee's door.

The knocking had created quite a stir from inside. Padded feet could be heard running, a dog was barking, and children were calling out to their mother. Ruby looked through the chipped screen door toward the commotion, and then stood back, embarrassed by her ill manners. Her visit was perhaps not expected.

Remember how to present yourself in public, her mother-in-law's memory whispered. *You do not wish to become a blot upon nature.*

She turned to walk back down the porch steps when the front door opened. Only slightly. Aimee remained in its shadow. The screen door stayed closed. Her head peeked around the edge of the door.

"Oh my ... Ruby! I had no idea. I thought it was another peddler, was going to send him away."

"Hello Aimee. I must apologize - but your invitation for tea - was it today or ..." Ruby felt dreadfully uncomfortable by now. She was not accustomed to visiting outside her home and now on her first social outing in years, she had already made a discourteous move. She almost fled. Instead she stammered. "I-I will come back another ... or p-perhaps you could come over—"

"Oh no, the tea, of course! You just caught me in an inopportune time is all. A sick child, you see." Aimee waved her arm toward the interior of her home. The curtains were still drawn and the inner room appeared gloomy. Just then her door was opened farther and Ruby saw it was a young toddler pulling it while reaching toward the screen door. Aimee stepped forward, clearly clad in her nightgown. She snatched her toddler up, scolding "no, no" and retreated back into the shadows.

But not soon enough. Ruby saw the bruised eye and red swelling on Aimee's right cheek.

Her stomach twisted. The houses on this street were only ten feet apart; windows were opened often year-round to air the coal and gas, the smoke from the fireplaces, and the cooking smells. Several times, a man's shouting voice, loud slaps, and a woman's cries were quite telling sounds urging through Ruby's bedroom window. On one such night, Ruby rose from bed and asked Robert if they may go next door to offer assistance. He refused and forbade her to go.

"This is strictly between a man and his wife," he had insisted. "It is none of our business how he sees appropriate to manage his home."

Aimee held tight to the child who was unsuccessfully trying to get down. "Another time perhaps. I really should get Anthony out of this draft." Her tone was subdued. Without waiting for an answer she closed the door.

Ruby felt her face blush, decidedly rejected and helpless. There must be something she could do but she wasn't sure what. She raised her hand to knock again, to offer assistance this time. After all, Robert wasn't here to hold her back. But then she lowered it. Perhaps she was intruding. Aimee was embarrassed enough already. With reluctance, she turned away.

The sun had come out, but Ruby now felt as gloomy inside as Aimee's living room. For lack of knowing what to do, she returned home; at least here she had some control.

Ruby stood inside her entranceway. A longing from deep within surfaced and bubbled in her ears like the soapsuds in her wash water. As much for herself as for Aimee, was the desire to reach out to a friend. The secretariat desk against the back wall of the parlor gave her an idea. A note! She would write Aimee a note and slip it under the door.

With shawl and boots still on, she rushed over to the desk, pulled off her gloves, pulled out the paper and pencil from their cubby-holes, and wrote carefully in her schoolgirl penmanship,

"Dear Aimee, I wish to be your friend. I am only a moment away, if you wish to talk. I've decided to come out into the sunshine. Please join me. Ruby."

She read it twice and hesitated. Before losing her nerve altogether, she folded the paper, and walked back to Aimee's door and slipped the paper under. Aimee's parlor windows faced the front, her house being in a similar design to Ruby's. Ruby guessed that Aimee could see her through the windows so would probably spot the note at once. At any rate, hopefully Aimee would find it before her husband arrived home from his employment.

Ruby walked back to the boardwalk by the street. She felt lighter somehow for at least making an attempt.

She looked down the length of her street on both sides. To the right, past Aimee's house, the cobbled street stretched into a dirt road which if followed for about eight miles led to her family's dairy farm. On her left, the street eventually reached the center of town. At the end of her block was the blacksmith's shop, which was slowly converting into an automobile garage to repair those "mechanical beasts that were invading the town" as Robert expressed it. She noted very few other changes here the last twelve years. Five houses across the street with empty fields on either side; ten houses on her side of the street. There was a mixture of dark red brick and wood siding with trim. All had wide front porches or covered verandahs, some which wrapped around one side, as Ruby's did. Although designs were similar, the decorating tastes varied greatly. Some owners had added a considerable amount of woodwork in gingerbread scrolls and borders. A few of the wrap-around verandahs were painted in bright yellows, pale blues, creams, or baby pinks. Other owners preferred to decorate in flowers and shrubs, leaving the architecture of the house plain. Construction on these homes had begun some thirty years before, during the building boom following the Civil War. Many who lived here were the original owners, as were her mother-in-law and father-in-law, Margaret and Jonathan Robert Wright. Jonathan had been a cabinetmaker in his living years, and had built all the cabinets and staircases on this street. Ruby's staircase, with its intricate scrolling on the landing post, was the finest in the area, or so her mother-in-law used to tell her. She had not seen the inside of the neighbors' homes.

"If I've come out into the sunshine, I can't very well go back into the shadows, now can I?" she said out loud. She found herself walking past her house toward town.

Her brow puckered in deep thought. Cady's home was only a few miles away, the Beauchamp Manor. The address was on her calling card.

Why not go to the tea on my own? I will reach out to these ladies as I am asking Aimee to do with me. They may well be the light at the end of my tunnel.

The sun touched warm on her face and urged her forward into the daylight.

"Ruby, wait!"

Ruby turned to see Aimee running down her steps toward her, her hat in hand, her cape unbuttoned.

"Thank you for the note," Aimee said when she stopped beside Ruby. She began tucking blond flyaway curls under her floppy hat, her crystal blue eyes shining. "It was what I needed to get me going. I can't stay hidden forever. And it is a warm sunny day!"

Ruby looked at the hastily applied face powder highlighting the blues and purples.

The sun may be warm, but it can be harsh.

* * * * *

Ruby stopped abruptly, outside the white gate of Cady's home. The vast elegance of this estate was overwhelming. The white colonial brick house gracefully adorned acres of lawn and gardens. A red brick walkway winded its way to the whitewashed porch, its landing armed on each side with a large white column. Two white wrought iron chairs sat to one side, separated by a matching table displaying a potted geranium.

Ruby swallowed hard. "Aimee what is the proper etiquette for a tea nowadays? It will no doubt be a formal one, from the looks of this place. I'm not suitably dressed!" She touched her cheeks and hair with nervous fingers. "Mercy, I'm so pale! Do I still have dark circles under my eyes? I tried this new hair design this morning, from *Harper's Bazaar* magazine, a Gibson Girl hairdo I think it's called, some sort of pompadour, but my hair is too thick and long, and oh dear, look at the straggly ends coming down!"

"Oh Ruby, you mustn't worry about such things," Aimee said, moving her own frizzed hair away from her eyes. She was slightly out of breath from their fast walk and constant talk about children. "If these women worried about such trivial matters as appearance, they would be society's proper ladies clinging to their own homes, serving tea to other properly behaved wives. That is not the purpose of this tea. Why, I see them as hardy soldiers prepared to fight for their rights as women!" She linked her arm with Ruby's. "Besides, we are all pale this time of year and you have such pretty blue eyes and shiny brown hair, nothing else matters."

This image of soldiers charged Ruby. What all these rights were, Ruby wasn't quite sure, but she was willing to risk appearing ignorant and ask. One thing she knew for sure; Aimee and her friends would surely understand her own invisible prison. She felt her jaw and neck muscles relax and the down turned lips slowly turn up into her own defiant smile. She lifted her chin and walked up Cady's walkway ready to right her world.

* * * * *

The ladies were assembled in somewhat of a circle so that one could see all. Ruby couldn't say they were unattractive, but there was a certain austerity that seemed to infiltrate into a statement of take-me-as-I-am. The various shapes and design of white blouses and simple black skirts established their uniform of mixed travels, yet all roads led them to this unity. The air about them sang out with a mission. One on the outside had to fight hard not to feel intimidated. Ruby wiped her clammy hands on her skirt.

Although hosted in various homes, they obviously had an orderly routine that they adhered to. Ruby heard one say to the others that their time together was hard earned and precious and must not be squandered. The meeting had come to order when she entered the front parlor. As unassuming as possible, she sat on an overly stuffed sofa, colored in rich hues of flower patterns, and sank deeply into its upholstery. It was not so easy to sit comfortably in her tight corset. She straightened her back and from there, she could see the high tin-plated ceiling, stamped in diamond patterns. A colored woman delivered to their center table a shining silver tea tray laden with cookies and small cakes, before joining Ruby on the sofa.

Soon the sweet tinkle of chatter mixed with teacups was replaced with one voice. That of Cady Pickering. Ruby recognized Cady as a teacher at her children's school, and wondered why she was not teaching today.

She knew this lady and Aimee by name, but couldn't recall the others' names given during introductions, her only thought being, I hope they don't notice my clammy hands, as they shook a how-do-you-do. Their extended hands took her off guard - she had never been offered a handshake before. Was this socially acceptable now among women? It seemed so manly.

With teacups quietly resting in their laps, Cady quickly captured the attention of the others. Ruby was awed by Cady's self-confidence. Her tone was not loud nor overbearing, yet its soft consonants filled the room. She controlled the agenda as a teacher would control her classroom. One who was accustomed to leadership and authority. She read from a paper the topics of discussion from their last meeting.

Ruby could not be attentive for long, not with these elaborate surroundings distracting her. The two vast windows took her breath away. The window dressing was layered in royal blue brocade satin with white sheer under-panels. The matching blue valance was draped and trimmed in tassels and rosettes. The chairs placed under each window were in the same fabric, a marble table and a golden oblong mirror between the two. From her vantage point, she could see beyond the two open doors of the parlor to the main hallway's winding staircase. Midway up the stairs, above the landing, was a stained-glass window throwing in rainbows of colors onto the lightly stained wood of rosettes, beading, wainscoting, and spiral spindles.

Ruby's head was fairly spinning, consumed with the overwhelming peculiarity of having tea with these infamous ladies right here in a manor house.

Cady handed the paper back to its originator on her left. "Thank you Sarah. Your minutes are accurate as usual."

Ruby's attention returned to Cady and Sarah, shoulders back, erect, their backs not touching the backs of their chairs. Sarah was as thin and straight as the pen she held poised over clean paper, ready to record today's discussion. Her black hair was parted down the center and brushed back into a tightly rolled bun, her spectacles on the end of her nose giving her a young granny look.

The others waited expectantly as Cady slowly took off her spectacles and rubbed her eyes. She had generous sprinkles of freckles on her hands and face. The small streaks of gray through her light brown hair only added to her persona of wisdom. Her hair was loosely knotted at her neck, threatening to unfurl. It mattered not, for she obviously was considering more important things at hand.

Cady took a deep breath, eyeing each lady with purpose. "Ladies, we have a dilemma. I must be frank here and say we will be required to gather our strength from within, and from each other. We must move forward from the shadow of our meetings, to the light of open scrutiny. Wrapped in the warmth of camaraderie, we must take a stand."

Her eyes rested briefly on the lady across from her, her white hair further highlighted by the sun's patched rays coming through the parlor windows. She was sitting on the edge of a wing-backed chair, her carriage tense. Her eyes did not waiver but her face had paled slightly. She appeared to know what was coming next and was readying herself for the blow. Cady's eyes shifted to the window behind, looking beyond all of them, to the outside. Ruby thought she recognized the yearning in Cady's eyes; that longing to push forward, beyond the walls.

Cady continued, her voice shaking with conviction. "But we must stand united, or else we all fall. And we must stand publicly, or else we all stagnate in our stillness."

The colored woman next to Ruby began rocking her upper body slightly, humming ever so softly, her dark brown hands resting on her knees, weathered to leather. Ruby made out the tune, *Shall we gather at the river?* No one else seemed to notice. This colored woman's name was ... ah, yes, Lizzie.

Cady paused, clasped her hands together in her lap, and then she smiled slowly. Her tone raised in an announcement. "Ladies, the Women's Rights Convention is now set!"

The humming stopped, the pen stopped. The rocking chair across from Ruby, occupied by Aimee, stopped.

"When? Where?" Aimee blurted out, her pink cheeks pinker, a furrow deepening between her eyes. Her finger froze on her temple, where she was absent-mindedly twirling a loose blond curl.

"July eighteenth, in the year of our Lord, 1900, right here in our little town of Annan, New York. We shall begin the new millennium with new rights! I feel it in my bones!" Cady answered with what Ruby thought was a forced optimism.

Ruby discretely eyed the others who appeared frozen in time.

Cady forged ahead. "Seven in the evening. I have spoken yesterday with the principle of the Parkdale High School, Mr. Whiting. He has graciously agreed to our use of the school auditorium. The school will of course be closed for the summer holidays. We discussed the afternoon, but as we all know, the auditorium can become very warm. An evening hour should bring us a cooler temperature."

This detail seemed to trivialize the impact of such a convention and the room relaxed a little. The rocking resumed.

The lady in the wing-backed chair cleared her throat. Her white hair appeared to be premature against her tanned and youthful complexion, but her hands were roughly weathered with chipped nails. Ruby guessed this lady spent a great deal of time outside.

She addressed the group in a singsong resonance. "Mr. Whiting is a very kind gentleman. He was my history teacher – a number of years ago." Her smile came and went. "I'm not the least surprised that he would support our cause. His mind is academic and he questions any society that allows oppression of any kind."

Cady nodded. "You are so right, Phyllis. He is an extraordinary man. As one of the leaders of this community, he is willing to risk his popularity by vocalizing his support to our cause. Herein lies our dilemma."

Placing her left hand on the back of Sarah and her right hand on the shoulder of Lizzie, Cady leaned forward toward the others as if to bring them closer into a huddle. "If he, as opposite gender if you will, is willing to take such risks, how much more should be expected of us, as the women whose rights we fight for? We are called to arms, ladies! We must each go forth openly and publicly; even to the point of speaking before an assembly. This convention will permit us to bring our lights out from under our beds and into the open where we may shine and show others the way. We can do it, ladies! You each have unique talents to share!"

At this, Ruby suddenly felt she was outside looking in. She stared down at her hands, slightly shaking her head.

If they are expecting unique talent, then I cannot participate.

It did not go without notice. Cady looked directly at her as if looking into her heart. "You are *all* hard-working women who have learned to work hard with your hands, but long to work hard with your minds. Now here is our chance!"

Cady returned her hands to her lap and leaned back against her chair. She lowered her voice. "I also know that to work toward this convention publicly, may create tremendous hardships in your homes. Our battles are not only public but also private. Our husbands and family all voice various levels of opposition to our quest for women's rights; either from a religious perspective where they say women are subservient. Or from a political perspective where they say the Constitution states only men were created equal. Or yet again, from the personal perspective that the man's position as head of the household is being threatened ... " Her voice tapered off here. She sighed, forcing a smile. She waved a hand at the group. "I don't need to elaborate. You have heard it all, I'm sure. I shall retreat off my soapbox and turn the meeting over to you for discussion." She opened her arms to all. "Please. Open your thoughts."

Phyllis raised her hand timidly. Cady grinned and nodded to her. "Yes, the little girl in the back. You have a question?"

Phyllis giggled. "Well, teacher, I have been doing some soul-searching. We have been meeting in homes for two months now but we knew that the day would come when, as you say, we must shine our light. But I expect there will be adverse repercussions. I have already heard criticisms. Not all will appreciate our brightness." She added this last sentence with a smile and effort toward humor but it hung heavily in the room. "Therefore, it is important to me that I believe and understand why we are doing this, with all my heart." She placed her hand over her heart to emphasize. "Joan of Ark I'm not, but if I am to be burned at the stake, figuratively speaking, I wish to have a first-rate reason for my martyrdom!"

Lizzie waved her hand toward Phyllis. "That's right, honey, you got to *believe*!"

"Will repercussions really be that bad?" Aimee blurted out. She looked around the group for help. Ruby's heart went out to her - Aimee's husband was enemy enough.

Phyllis raised her hand. "I am exaggerating to make my point." Then she added, "I hope" and placed her hand to her mouth to stifle a giggle. She glimpsed at Cady and straightened her face. "What I recommend is, we test the waters. See how much support we have, before going out into a den of lions. To test I mean to petition. To go out and canvas other women, explain our cause, and ask for their support, their signatures. I've started writing a mission statement to carry door-to-door and I'll bring it to our next meeting."

"Oh, I could do that!" Ruby cried. She raised her hands to her cheeks, embarrassed for being so out-spoken.

Lizzie patted Ruby's knee and chuckled. "I said to myself when I saw you there at the door, now here is a little lady who is on a mission!"

"A mission? Well ... " Ruby's eyes darted around to the others, their return stares making her nervous. She decided to look only at the colored woman's moist brown eyes. "I did come here wanting to make a difference in my life. I am tired of watching others suffer and yet ... I am helpless. I am tired of working all day and yet remain ... dependent. I am tired of sending my children to school, yet *I* feel ignorant. I am only a spectator."

Her face felt hot but she didn't want to stop, relieved she could express her heart-felt thoughts out loud to someone. She swallowed hard and continued. "For some time now I have questioned so much in my life. Why must I always be told: Do as your father says, do as your husband says, do as your preacher says, keep quiet, know your place, do your duties. As if I have no mind to think, no right to question! I have felt trapped somehow, and blamed myself for feeling that way. I was standing still while everything else moved around me. Now I believe I have met my kindred spirits. So I guess my mission is, I am offering my services to the Ladies of the Lost Legion, be as they may. I am not talented nor am I much educated. I have no particular skill. But I work hard and cook favorably. I-I can no longer remain inside and watch life through my window!"

Cady's head went back in a delighted laugh, and to Ruby's surprise, Cady's hands tapped together in applause. "That was a touching speech and one we must write down to convey at the convention. You have talents, Ruby. Please do not under-estimate yourself. Women can be their own worst enemies." She tilted her head and studied Ruby's face, as a teacher might read a student's. "You have talents that only need to be dusted off—"

"And aired out!" Ruby finished. They all laughed together and Ruby felt bonded to other adults for the first time in her life. Most of all, she admired Cady and the way her spectacles enlarged her intelligent blue-green eyes slightly, eyes that were fully focused on what Ruby had to say and that what she was saying was important.

"Now that I have your pledge, Ruby, I wish to explain our purpose," Cady said. "First, we must work effectively and in a peaceful manner for our cause in the suffrage movement. Secondly, to inform ourselves of our history. If we better understand where we came from, we may have better foresight into where we are going. Our weekly meetings are committed to both.

"Before the American Revolution, a woman had some limited rights, particularly if she was a landowner. Landowners had a right to vote in the villages and towns. After the Revolutionary War, with the drafting of the Constitution, the states were given the decision as to who would vote. Voting rights were eventually given only to all-white adult males and then after the Civil War, all adult males.

"The first Women's Rights Convention began in 1848 with the Declaration of Sentiments. The twelve resolutions in the Declaration, one being the right to vote, received endorsement from those delegates in attendance, and the women suffrage movement began. These women were no different than we are yet they stood up and insisted they be heard. But these resolutions and the women's fight for freedom were lost to the fight against slavery in the Civil War, and to the attention it required in its aftermath.

"So here we are in 1900, fifty-two years later, and we continue to fight for those same rights: to vote; to be allowed to enter the profession of our choice; to be allowed to further our education; and to have equal rights in our marriage. What few rights single women have, such as owning property, we lose to our husbands, because in marriage wives have no right to own property, to divorce, or to child custody. Men have the absolute authority. Unfortunately men are not required to prove they are fit to be trusted with absolute power in marriage, as they might be in other institutions. There are different grades of good and bad men and if a woman marries a good and loving man, she will not suffer abuse of power. But if she marries a bad one, she has no escape from his brutality. Law does not punish for domestic oppression.

"Yet marriage is the only choice for so many, for without our own education and profession, we remain dependent on a man's income, whether that be our father, brother, or husband.

"So we must go into battle again, with another Women's Rights Convention on our horizon. We owe it to the women of our past to carry forth their sacrifices. First, we must fight for the right to vote. But we must make people aware of this. Gathering signatures for petitions is an excellent way to reach out to housebound women. I also propose a parade where we march with banners and hand out leaflets. Most importantly, we should attempt to influence the pulpit and the press with well-worded positive statements. For *there* is where people form their opinions and decide to support or oppose."

"Why won't men let us vote?" Ruby asked. "It seems harmless enough."

"The main challenge is our politicians. Many oppose women voting, for it simply complicates their agenda and here is why. To win a vote, they must address issues that the voters are concerned with. Women are concerned with issues that can be quite different than men's, such as better education and cleaner schools for their children, purer meat and food processing, and child labor. Women are the ones who make the choices in raising children and preparing food, so naturally they are the experts. But men do not know enough about these issues to lobby for them so they treat them as trivial."

"That's why we're here, honey!" Lizzie said. "To speak out for what we believe in! When Lincoln freed the colored folk, he forgot about the women folk!"

Cady turned to Lizzie excitedly as if she had given Cady a great idea. "Lizzie, would you consider performing as Sojourner Truth as part of the convention? It is such a moving speech and truly speaks for *all* women." She leaned toward Lizzie and squeezed Lizzie's hand gently. "What do you say? Would you do it?"

Ruby was more confident now to ask her next question. "May I ask who is Sojourner Truth?"

Good Woman

"She is a colored woman from way back in…" Lizzie's forehead furrowed deeply and her mouth protruded in thought. "1851. She dared to speak out at a Women's Rights Convention somewhere in Ohio. Here's what she done." Lizzie stood up slowly and entered the center of the circle. Aimee and Sarah quickly moved the table and its tea tray over to the side. Lizzie turned her head and Ruby noted several black braids meeting in a bun at the back. Lizzie straightened her thin shoulders, as if releasing a heavy burden from her slightly hunched back. It did not seem possible to Ruby that such a small woman could have such a deep booming voice.

"Well, children, where there is so much racket, there must be something out of kilter, I think between the Negroes of the South and the women of the North – all talking about rights –the white men will be in a fix pretty soon. But what's all this talking about?" Lizzie pointed her finger at Phyllis. "That man over there says that women need to be helped into carriages, and lifted over ditches, and to have the best place everywhere. Nobody helps *me* any best place. And ain't I a woman?"

Lizzie stood up taller and raised her right arm. She slapped its forearm with her left hand. "Look at me! Look at my arm! I have plowed, I have planted and I have gathered into barns. And no man could head me. And ain't I a woman?

"I could work as much, and eat as much as any man – when I could get it – and bear the lash as well! And ain't I a woman? I have borne children and seen most of them sold into slavery, and when I cried out with a mother's grief, none but Jesus heard me. And ain't I a woman?"

Lizzie turned and pointed to Ruby, with eyes glazed with a past life of someone Lizzie understood completely. "He talks about this thing in the head. What's that they call it?" She tilts her head and puts her hand behind her ear, pretending to listen. "Intellect? That's it, honey. What's intellect got to do with women's rights or black folks' rights? If my cup won't hold but a pint and yours holds a quart, wouldn't you be mean not to let me have my little half-measure full?"

Turning again, Lizzie faced Cady and pointed to her. "That little man in black there! He says women can't have as much rights as men. 'Cause Christ wasn't a woman'." Lizzie outstretched her arms and bellowed, "Where did your Christ come from? From God *and* a Woman! Man had nothing to do with him!"

Ruby gasped and quickly brought her fingers to her lips, staring up in wide-eyed awe at Lizzie.

Lizzie lowered her arms and looked fiercely over Cady's head into the late afternoon's darkening room, at the unseen spirits of the white man whose chains of slavery were released from her father, but forgotten on her.

"If the first woman God ever made was strong enough to turn the world upside down all alone, these women together ought to be able to turn it back and get right-side up again. And now that they are asking to do it, the men better let them!"

* * * * *

"Women, women, women, why I am surrounded by them!" A slender, tall man, with careless blond hair falling onto his forehead entered the parlor smiling broadly.

Cady turned toward his voice and returned his smile. "Hello Thomas darling. You are home early."

Introductions were made and the guests prepared to go. Ruby had little to say and much to absorb. Believing in her ignorance, she felt miniaturized by it all. She wondered how she could possibly make a difference.

Cady's husband, Thomas, offered to drive Ruby and Aimee home, since they lived farthest away. He explained that the water boiler in his new steam automobile was adequately heated from his drive home and would be a cinch to restart. Aimee hastily declined stating she had other errands to run, and ran down the walkway. Ruby was thankful for the offer, now conscious there was insufficient time to walk the distance before the children arrived home. The sting of a blister on her heel from her worn out boots made her all the more grateful.

Her next thought brought her worry. Robert would totally disapprove if he knew she was alone with another man, and he would be outraged to discover the drive was in a steam carriage. He was convinced this new invention was a wheeled cannon, likely to explode at any given moment, killing its unfortunate travellers. They themselves had no means of transportation, excepting their God-given legs. Not since their old mare, Blacky, was retired to pasture on the dairy farm. Blacky was employed on the daily milk run, first by her father and then by her brother. After many hard years of labor, she was replaced by a younger mare, and thus given to Ruby and Robert to hitch to their small old buggy, another remnant from Robert's mother. Blacky was kept in the stable behind their house, accessed by a dirt alley in the back that ran parallel to their front street. The horse and buggy were rarely used. Robert walked to his shoe shop, the children walked to school, Ruby walked to the market. Holiday visits to Ruby's family farm required the buggy for the eight miles, but the two wood seats were cramped with three growing children and Blacky trudged slowly under the weight. Robert decided the cost of the feed did not equate to the need of the horse. Blacky was given tearful goodbye hugs from the children, and Ruby was given promises of new transportation by Robert. That was two years and many walking miles of shoe leather ago.

Thomas ran ahead of her to his car, obviously eager for an opportunity to drive his carriage again.

He patted the hood of the big black machine as he waited for Ruby. "I named her Fizzie," he stated proudly, "because of the hisssing noisssse the boiler makesss".

He chuckled at his use of words as he opened the door for her, and then he disappeared under the hood. A moment later he trotted around to the driver's side. His well-suited tall frame easily moved in behind the wheel. He clutched the large metal steering wheel and looked over at Ruby with green eyes and a big grin.

His exuberance was contagious, and she burst out laughing, in spite of her worries. His own laughter joined hers. "Isn't she a beauty?" he asked.

"Yes indeed!" she nodded, looking around the interior, inhaling strong scents of oil and leather. The two tiny round dials meant nothing to her, but the heavy frame and padded seat made her feel quite safe. She would explain this to Robert. She settled her handbag in her lap and folded her gloved hands on top, prepared for the adventure.

"This is my first ride in an automobile!" she declared.

"Well, then, we shall take the scenic route!" He released the brake and the automobile jerked forward.

Worry and regret came rushing back to Ruby. She wished she hadn't said that; now she would really be late. She forced a smile. "Oh, well, thank you, but, umm, I must be home soon ... the children."

He patted the dashboard affectionately. "This lovely lady will have you home in moments - under the control of these steady hands!" He raised his leather-gloved hands as proof of his strength.

As he pulled out onto the bricked street, Ruby turned and waved at Cady. She was still standing on the front porch, her home's slate blue shutters and warm inner lighting framed around her, the potted geranium beside her. The soft dream-like colors etched into Ruby's memory.

"You ladies must have cheered the ol' girl substantially!" Thomas said as he slowly maneuvered around a plodding horse and carriage. "She was feeling quite poorly when I left this morning. I came home early to check on her and here she is having tea, smiling brightly."

Ruby looked at him in dismay. "Oh I had no idea! She never mentioned any such thing."

Thomas waved it off. "Nor would she. She rarely complains."

"Nor does this girl." He patted the steering wheel. "She has an astonishing performance going as fast as forty miles per hour when I can find a long paved road. I hope the roads improve soon, but I recently did some research and wrote an article in the paper saying there are only about eight thousand automobiles out there and only about one hundred miles of road so far. She can go ten in town though which is good enough for now."

Take out the word automobile, and you would think he was talking about a winning racehorse, Ruby thought and smiled. She felt quite comfortable watching the houses and people go by at such a steady pace. The engine was loud but she liked its vibration and sense of mechanical power. Although he took a longer route to her home, they arrived too soon for her fancy. He pulled in front of her house and stopped.

Ruby reached out and patted the dashboard approvingly. "Good girl! Thank you so much. It was quite delightful!"

"My pleasure, my pleasure!" He was still grinning like a Cheshire cat.

She found the door handle and pulled it gingerly but not enough. He reached across her and pulled the handle harder, pushing the door open. His arm brushed across her breast and she held in her breath, as if to suck in her breasts, her face feeling hot. He appeared not to notice. She quickly turned her back and lifted her skirt above her boots to step out onto the cobblestones.

As she straightened, she saw her husband walking toward her, still a few houses away. They both froze as one spotted the other. Before she could gather her thoughts enough to ask him to wait for introductions to her husband, Thomas had closed the door behind her and drove off. She listened to the engine fading away, longing to be back inside its safety shield with someone with happy thoughts. Robert was not happy. He adjusted his tie and then resumed his approach. Ruby did not take her eyes from him. She stood very still and waited. To shift away would appear guilty and she knew she had nothing to be guilty of.

So why do I feel so guilty? Because I knew he would be angry! But I have done nothing wrong!

In spite of her will, her face felt hotter than before. She attempted a smile as he came up close but he did not return it.

He glanced around at the neighbors' homes to see if anyone was peering from their windows. "Come inside now!" he hissed. He turned on his heel and headed toward their front door.

Ruby followed his brown suit silently; sorry to leave the warmth and laughter behind her and enter the dark anger Robert would fill the house with.

*****

He loosened his tie, but did not take it off. Instead he paced the parlor. Ruby tried to show a calm composure but her hands were shaking as she hung her shawl on its hook in the entranceway. It was best to say nothing so she headed toward the kitchen to begin supper. She tensed as she walked past him.

In the kitchen's doorway, he grabbed her arm.

He jerked her to him and brought his face close, nose almost touching hers, eyes as hard as dried mud. "I will not give you the courtesy to explain yourself, woman!" he spat between clenched teeth.

With his other hand, he reached down and unbuckled his belt and pulled it from around his pants. Ruby instinctively pulled back, trying to get out of his steel grip, but the grip only tightened. She was surprised at his strength, he being only a few inches taller than her five-foot frame.

"Oh, Robert, please, the children are expected home any moment!"

He eyed the parlor window with slanted eyes and for the first time ever, he looked like a mad man.

Ruby was truly frightened of him. He punished the children in this manner and she had seen their bruises. Once when they were first married, he had slapped her face hard which successfully "put her in her place" and it had not happened since. But then, she rationalized, she had never ventured out on her own before without his permission.

His hesitation allowed her to try again. "Robert, please don't let them see us like this!"

There were no children visible through the window and he looked at her accusingly, as if she was trying to trick him. He swung out the belt and brought it back hard against the back of her legs. He struck again and again, emphasizing with each strike, each word, "Don't….you….ever….disobey….me….again!"

Each time she stifled a cry, each time she tried to break free of his grip on her arm, but it did no good. The folds of her skirt and undergarments prevented serious pain, nonetheless she felt her body shrinking inch by inch with each strike, until she became very small and worthless. She could barely breathe. He pushed her away then, and she collapsed onto the floor.

He treaded heavily into the dining room, clenching and unclenching his hands. The belt landed loudly on the floor. He stood there for a moment, breathing deeply through his nostrils, and then returned to where Ruby sat in a small heap. She involuntarily flinched when she felt his hands come under her armpits from behind. He lifted her up to her feet. She kept her back to him as she wiped her eyes with the back of her hands. She straightened her spine and walked silently into the kitchen to return to her duties.

* * * * *

"Maaaamaaaa!"

Ruby need not announce her whereabouts; she was where she always was this time of day so she said nothing and simply waited. By the tone of Jonathan's wail, this would be a tattletale on his older brother. When Jonathan found her, he ran to her, looked up at her imploringly, and tugged at her skirt. She absent-mindedly moved the hair out of his eyes.

Eyes so much like his father's, big brown chocolate drops, except these were soaking in salt water. Something she had never seen his father's eyes do. Now what would make Robert cry? "—so then he punched my arm for no reason. Make him apologiiiize!"

"How old are you now, Jonathan?"

"I'm six years old - hey you already know how old I am!" His smooth face creased into a scowl – an expression seen often enough on Robert.

"I do, but I think you need to be reminded once in a while. You are a little too old to be crying like this. Why, you are a big boy now! Big boys don't cry!"

Hmmm...why don't big boys cry? Could it be that Robert was told the same thing when he was young? Do their tear ducts eventually dry up from discipline? Why do we never say, 'big girls don't cry'? Come to think of it I have never said that to Bess. But certainly to Victor, and now to Jonathan. Do all mothers treat their boys so differently from their girls? Is that the reason they grow up different? She smiled at her newfound curiosity of such things.

Her hand was still on top of his head and as she looked back down, he was wiping away his tears with the back of his hand. She squatted and gave him a hug. "Sorry, sweetheart. It's fine to cry once in a while. Keeps your eyes clean. Just...just..." she was searching for the right words to say about his relationship with his big brother. Should he stand up to Victor and fight back? Or would that compel physical fighting with others? Should he make peace and risk her older son calling him a sissy? Should he come to her when his brother begins sparring? Definitely not, she decided. Jonathan must not be a tattletale, nor depend on others to defend him. She mussed up his brown mane and kissed him on the cheek. She held his chin so he would look her in the eyes. His eyes now were red, but dry.

"You are the smartest six year old I know. I bet if you go back to your bedroom, you will find a way to work this out with him. You know, sometimes I suspect he just wants your attention, because deep down he loves you - in his own brotherly way. Now go get on his good side by telling him supper is ready."

"Oh, all right," he said, pulling his chin away. He didn't look convinced.

She turned his shoulders toward the door and gently nudged him away, nudging away as well a thought that perhaps she should take some of her own advice when it came to Robert.

* * * * *

Supper was leftover potroast from the night before and supplemented with boiled potatoes. In her haste, Ruby had stoked the stove far too much, and the kitchen was an oven in itself. It was a continual struggle to achieve the correct internal temperature in its belly to boil, cook, heat water and heat the house. The oven seemed eternally hungry for more coal. The kitchen was so hot, she was pretty sure if she sat dough on the worktable, it would bake to a golden brown. Luckily baking was not required. Cookies with lavender flower buds mixed in had been baked earlier in readiness for Aimee's supposed visit. Cookies for dessert would satisfy the children enough to end the meal.

"What did you do this fine day?" Robert asked.

Ruby glanced across the corner of the table to where Robert sat at the head. She made a mental note to trim his bushy brown sideburns creeping down the side of his face and his neck hair growing over the back of his shirt collar. Also the button-holes on his shirt were stretched more now from his belly and she would have to enlarge his shirt pattern before sewing another one – he wouldn't have this problem if he were bound up in her corset. She smiled at her own absurdity.

He did not meet her eyes. He looked intently at his beef, knife and fork in hand, slicing it into bite-size pieces. As was his habit, he would continue to do this until all the beef was cut and then he would lay his knife on the upper left-hand corner of his plate before proceeding to eat. The tone of his question was one of politeness in front of the children so she felt comfortable in being vague.

"Some baking. This morning I fertilized my lavender beds with wood ash. I hope to have a larger harvest this year to make linen sachets. And of course I must make more lavender oil. It worked well to stop the itch of your insect bites last year, remember children?"

Whether they acknowledged this or not she did not notice, for her head remained bent toward her plate in silent prayer that there would be no more questions about her day. The less Robert knew, the better.

"Oh!" said Bess. "Did you iron my blouse, Mama? I've already worn this one two days and—"

"I will tonight after supper," Ruby interrupted. She did not look at Bess as she spoke, feeling some remorse for her negligence to duties today. She diverted her attention to her oldest son. "Please stop making that pesky noise and allow your little brother to eat in peace!"

Victor stopped his low growl and looked at her in exaggerated surprise. "It wasn't me, it was him!" He pointed his fork at Jonathan to clarify which "him".

Jonathan looked genuinely surprised and cried out, "No it wasn't me! It was hiiiim!" He pointed his fork in retaliation.

His brother accepted the challenge. "Wanna sword fight, do ya?" A fork duel began.

"Boooys!" Robert continued to focus on his plate, but they received the message and turned their forks toward their food. He paused, gave the boys a side-look, and a low growl of his own. The three children giggled.

Ruby snorted through her nose and shook her head, hiding her relief. He was in a playful mood, thank goodness. The day's events were making her uneasy.

There were a few moments of quiet eating but her potato stuck in her throat. The heightened emotions of the day had taken her appetite, so she gathered some dishes from the table and left the dining room. She reappeared with a plate of cookies. Dessert was a good diversion to keep the conversation light.

She returned to the kitchen and set in motion heating the water and pouring this into the dishpan for washing. Robert appeared in the doorway and watched her for a moment.

"You seem rather distracted," he said.

At least he cares enough to notice, her mind snapped back. She added lye soap to the water and swished her hand around to mix. She kept her back to him. "No, no, I'm a little tired is all."

He leaned against the doorframe and folded his arms across his chest. "Then you do understand why I forbid you to have tea with that lady next door and her friends? It is not as innocent as you were led to believe. Today I made some enquiries and heard some disparaging comments about the ladies' motives that go beyond idle gossip. Criticisms these women are dealt with stretch far beyond their code of behavior, to an outcry of warning. This group is nothing more than men-haters and their intentions are to destroy the home and family. Did the next door neighbor not explain their motives to you?"

She closed her eyes in frustration.

What does he want me to say without bringing about a further argument? Should I continue to press the point, and what would be the point of that? Does he only wish to reiterate?

She reached for the towel and turned to him, drying her hands. She shrugged her shoulders, attempting to appear nonchalant.

"It was a brief discussion and nothing more." She veiled her thoughts and returned his gaze.

"Very well," he said slowly, nodding once. "So do you understand you're not to engage in any sort of social events if approached again?"

Swallowing hard, she nodded in return. She turned back to the dishpan, hidden from his knowing gaze, and closed her eyes again. The light she envisioned brought in by her new friends, dissipated into darkness. With it went her newfound aspiration for belonging to something beyond her door. She suddenly felt exhausted, spent.

He turned to leave. "I'm going on up to bed. Come on up now."

Was that a request or a demand?

"I have ironing to do but I'll be up soon afterwards." He didn't appear to notice that her voice was shaking.

"You have all day tomorrow to do those sort of things," Robert said and walked away. When she heard his steps complete the flight of stairs to the bedrooms, she leaned over her worktable, head in hands. Why are his words so cold? One warm touch, one kiss on the lips …

Her daughter entered the room with dishes from the dining room table. Looking at them made Ruby nauseous.

"Do you think you could be a sweetie and begin washing these dishes while I heat the iron?" She knew the argument would be limited since Bess wanted a pressed blouse for tomorrow.

Perhaps unfair tactics but I need help tonight.

"I suppose so, Mama, but — " Bess cut short her rebuttal, looking more closely.

"What's wrong, Mama, are you ill?"

"No, no," she quickly replied and then realized she had heard that word *no* enough times for one day.

* * * * *

Ruby extended her bottom lip and blew up in an attempt to remove the hair that had fallen into her eye. The perspiration kept it in place so she tried again with her forearm. The kitchen was unbearably hot. The stove was stoked sufficiently to keep the alternating irons hot and she had been at the ironing board for what seemed like ages. Bess's blouse had been pressed long ago but many more damp garments had been rolled on wash day, in preparation for ironing. Too many to finish yesterday.

Absent-mindedly, she reached for the glass jar, its lid punctured with holes and filled with water, and sprinkled more water onto the pillowcase. The monotony and mindlessness of the work allowed her mind to wander beyond the body tied to chore, to the light and airy memory and imagination. Images and conversations, real and imagined, kept her entertained while levelling the raised wrinkles, the heavy black iron going back and forth, back and forth. At times like these she thought of writing a story for her children but Robert's likely response that she was wasting her time would squelch such a silly notion.

She looked down at the basket – were the garments multiplying while she worked?

Robert will be angry I didn't come up sooner. And I would have followed him, too, with just a touch, just a kiss. Why must I fantasize what should be reality?

But sometimes she felt she needed an escape and her prose allowed her to do that. Her mind wandered once again into her song, a song she had created years ago but dared not write down.

> I visualize you kiss me tenderly,
> On a mountain, in a cove, or by the sea.
> Starry eyes, secret smile, my quiet mood,
> I realize I am fantasizing you!
>
> Well I guess you'll never know
> What a woman needs, to grow,
> But truth be known, I know you'll never be
> Half of what my dreams of you will see.
>
> In my dreams you hold me oh so dear,
> Don't wake me up for I'll see that it's not real.
> I dream sweet dreams that I know you'll never do,
> But I can live on the fantasies of you.

Or can she? She closed her eyes for a moment. What was the point in living in dreams? Longing...lonely...mercy! It was time to wake up! It was time to move out into the light and away from the constant darkness of her dreams. Tonight Robert may have closed the door on today's enlightenment but he cannot shut out the light. In her mind's eye the light was flowing out from under the door and she liked this image. He wasn't going to keep her down, even if he whipped her again. She opened her eyes and saw that her flat iron had scorched Robert's linen shirt.

No matter. Today's tea had brightened her spirits. With a renewed vigor, she finished this last garment and raked the coals in the stove. She walked up the stairs ready now for a new day, the gas lamp she was carrying lighting her way.

* * * * *

She climbed the two flights to the boys' third-story bedroom. Trying to catch her breath within the grasp of her corset – she had loosened the stays for her evening's work but obviously not enough - she opened their door. She glanced in to witness the blessed stillness and crumpled sheets, legs and arms scattered over the bed, their dreaming faces angelic. Victor reminded her so much of her brother, Jesse, with his curling locks falling on his forehead and that endearing dimple. Jonathan was the shorter version of Robert, with his square jaw and long dark eyelashes. She opened the door wider to allow unusual sounds to travel down to her second floor bedroom. She particularly feared fires and she feared the worst might happen while she slept. Her mind had played grim scenarios of burning children since the children were born. The innate need to protect them seemed to come with the afterbirth. She guessed this need wouldn't go away until they grew up and were married.

Her nightly vigil continued to her daughter's bedroom on the second floor, across from her and Robert's room. Her eyes followed the trail of light into the room. Its cluttered walls reminded her again of how desperately a wardrobe was needed for a soon-to-be woman. Hooks on the walls were not enough anymore. The necessities of women were many and would require privacy away from teasing younger brothers. The boys would not be bothered with the modesty and self-consciousness a growing lady would endure. Soon Bess must bear the menstrual curse. Robert could possibly build such a wardrobe if she could convince him that Bess was not a little girl any longer.

She sighed, thinking of yet another conflict with her husband over another required change in the household.

The light illuminated Bess's sleeping face into a spiritual glow, long strands of dark hair strewn over her pillow like a wild headdress. For the first time Ruby noticed that her round doll-like face was becoming more oval in shape, more like her own. Not far from becoming a woman now. Ruby leaned against the doorframe, pulling at her corset, wondering what kind of marriage would be in store for Bess. Ruby recalled how, in her own young years, her friends gave their worldly counsel that marriage was the only way to independence. Now, many ages later, she believed she had only gone from her father's demands to her husband's demands. How could she have a woman-to-woman talk with her daughter, to explain her own experiences, without sounding negative and contradicting what was meant to be? Thank goodness Bess had pretty enough features to someday attract a man. Marriage was inevitable for a woman.

She remembered that Robert recently announced at the supper table his plans for a savings account for college education for the boys, for they would be heads of their own households someday and must earn a decent living. He reached across the table and patted his daughter's expectant head as if bestowing on her a gift too, as he announced that some lucky man would make her happy someday. Her trusting eyes lingered on him as she waited for more, but he returned his attention to his plate, ending the conversation.

Before that someday, Ruby silently promised the sleeping face, you and I will resume that conversation, just woman-to-woman. I will learn what else is out there, so you will know there may be other choices for you. We will work this out together, I promise you. She closed the door to symbolize her daughter's recognized maturity. It was time to start making preparations for her future.

* * * * *

Ruby turned the knob and opened the door to her shared bedroom with her husband, trying to be as quiet as possible. As was his habit, Robert had turned the gas lamp down to low so that she could make her way in the room. She tiptoed over to the washbowl and emptied leftover water from his nightly wash into the collection basin on the bottom shelf of the table. She poured fresh water from the pitcher into the bowl and began the tedious process of unbuttoning the many buttons on the front of her blouse. The blouse off, she then worked the snaps on the front of her corset.

As her hands tugged and pulled automatically, she looked in the mirror above the table at her reflection. The low lighting behind her silhouetted her shape, reminding her of an hourglass.

The corset finally came off and her small center visibly expanded. She sighed in relief, thinking, small waists weren't everything – breathing was important too. In this lighting, her skin tone smoothed and tanned and her blue eyes became a mysterious dark velvet. She decided she looked pretty tonight but as she leaned closer to the mirror she was reminded of the dark circles under her eyes and she touched these lightly with the tips of her fingers.

She felt she had less energy these days, these long, repetitive days. She thought wearily of her six days a week schedule. Monday wash day (sometimes spilling over into Tuesday), Tuesday ironing day, Wednesday baking day, Thursday sewing day, Friday scrub floors, Saturday bath day and marketing, a schedule just like her mama taught her. If let go, the chores doubled the following day. In between, she beat rugs, cooked two to three meals a day, emptied and cleaned chamber pots. In the spring, summer and fall, there was the large vegetable garden that required planting, weeding, watering, harvesting, canning and preserving. She shrugged her shoulders in an attempt to cast off the sudden burden of endlessness this thought brought, but her shrug only reminded her of the stiffness in her arms and shoulders from the ironing.

What was the silly poem her mama made up to cheer Ruby's chores when she was a little girl?

> Monday wash my sins away,
> Tuesday iron out my wrinkles,
> Wednesday knead my cares all day,
> Thursday mend my crinkles,
> Friday cook a pot of love,
> Saturday buy more trinkles,
> Sunday pray to God above,
> That Monday I don't stinkle!

Not even the silly poem could bring a smile tonight. She dipped the washcloth into the water and gritted her teeth against the cold cloth on her face and neck.

It could be worse, she warned herself. Her mama, Garnet,

had known worse hardships, carrying nine children, eventually losing two babies to whooping cough and pneumonia, two were born dead, two she miscarried. By the time her three remaining children were grown, her husband had become an invalid and remained so for several years. He passed away two years ago from heart failure and Ruby could have sworn that her mama's face had become smoother after he died, somehow more relaxed, from the relief of no longer being an around-the-clock caretaker. Garnet continued to live in the family farmhouse with her only living son, Jesse, and his wife and six sons, dairy farming still their principal income. Garnet put a pot of pinto beans on the stove every day and baked pies and bread to help out. She didn't want to be a burden on anyone, she was always saying, waving away her own aches and arthritic pains with her customary expression, "It could be worse."

Ruby stopped midair with her washcloth and thought, so that is why I use that expression; I'm sounding like Mama!

She shook her head, wondering if her future would be the same as Mama's. Was growing old the only light at the end of the tunnel? Was all the hard work of mother and wife only rewarded with someday simply sleeping alone? Did Mama feel her life was worthwhile?

With washcloth in hand, she hurriedly rushed behind the screen in the corner and squatted low onto the chamber pot, flinching at the cold rim. The chamber pot was almost empty and her urine sounded a loud sputter that couldn't be helped. Her mind still questioned why people believed indoor flush toilets truly spelled disease. She saw one in a Sears catalogue so they must be suitable. They would be so much more convenient – and cleaner – than emptying these bloody chamber pots.

She raised her hips and looked in the pot. Good, her menstrual bleeding had stopped so there was no need to apply more clean rags layered with cotton balls. Behind the privacy of the screen she continued undressing, then washed between her legs, and next grabbed her cotton gown draped over the screen's frame. The oversized fabric went over her head and shoulders and fell to the floor.

Breathing in deeply, Ruby stretched her arms above her head, appreciating the ability to expand her diaphragm without the tight bony squeeze of her corset. All the daily bindings that daytime clothing brought to her body were gone, and in its place her loose breasts and unwrapped flesh gave her a sense of freedom. She would now be able to recline comfortably. The fatigue from the long day was now able to seep from her bones. She wished to end her day once and for all.

But there was still more hygiene to do. Returning to the washstand, she opened the tin of baking soda, rubbed some onto her teeth with a rough cloth, and rinsed with a glass of water. No loose teeth yet and they were still reasonably straight, thank goodness. There were others who had lost their front teeth at an earlier age than Ruby's twenty-eight years. Mrs. Jones for example. No wonder though, since the poor thing had eight children by that age.

She reached back and released the comb and hairpins from her bun. Her hair snaked down her back and stopped at her buttocks. Her fingers separated her twisted hair and brushed without pause, without thinking. She then splashed cold water on the roots around her forehead and ears and on the part in the middle, rubbing her roots with a cloth to clean. In the morning she would add lavender water to the roots to freshen.

As was the routine since the children were born, she turned the gas lamp down a bit lower but not off. Her memory was always tweaked by her mother-in-law's lecture that gas lighting in the bedroom posed as a health risk. But if one of the children needed her, she must be able to see herself quickly to the door without taking time to light a candle. On her way to the bed she spotted splashed water on the floor by the basin but any further cleaning was waved away for the morning light. She lifted her side of the quilt and sheet with caution, so as not to disturb its snoring inhabitant. Crawling in carefully, she stretched out, feeling the comfort of the feathered mattress giving her a welcoming hug. As always, she closed her eyes and mutely thanked God for her family's health.

She turned onto her sleeping side position facing the window, away from him.

His arm came across her waist. She tensed, sensing its next move. The snoring had stopped earlier but it hadn't registered until now. The hand came up to her chest and began kneading her breast.

"Is your womb still weakened?" Robert asked, his voice still coarse from sleep.

Tempted to scream out *Yes!* she set her jaw and shook her head, *no*. Denying him would only create a worse stiffness than his body held now. Not just in one part but also in his whole countenance, and a coldness in his attitude toward her to suffer through for several days.

Robert scooted closer to her back while tugging at her gown several times until it was up to her knees. He pressed on her hip then, a signal for her to move onto her back. She did so, raising her hips at the same time to allow him to pull her gown further up to her hips. Lifting himself over her, he spread her legs with his knees. She looked up at him, trying to relax, hoping for soft words to soften her, but his eyes remained closed. Supported on one elbow, his other hand worked between her legs, opening the front of his long-johns. She felt his hardness then against her thigh, and could only wish this would be over briefly.

Positioned on his elbows, Robert moved his hips to guide himself between her legs. He pushed repeatedly against her dryness until their bodies' lubrication began to emerge and mingle. To ease the discomfort, Ruby placed her hands around his forearms and spread her legs further. He groaned at her motion and plunged deeper inside her. She was grateful yet again that three childbirths had stretched her opening enough to ease his abrupt entrance.

Robert placed his chin on her shoulder, barely supporting himself, and his weight was too much. Thinking she would surely suffocate, her hands pressed against his chest to signal he should rise a little. He momentarily paused to move his elbows in closer to her body, and then resumed his movements inside her. He continued to face her shoulder, moving only from his hips.

Ruby experienced a tingling rush that too quickly subsided, so she made no sound. She focused on the familiar twisting crack in the ceiling over the bed and began counting the number of days until her next menstruation, counting in rhythm to his bumps. Then she thought how the blood could be considered a long-term blessing - *I am not with child!* - yet a short-term curse.

His body suddenly froze in mid-air and he sounded as if he caught something in his throat. With relief she watched his face contort and then relax.

The wet stickiness smeared across her leg as he moved over and collapsed beside her. He reached over and patted her stomach in the same way he patted their daughter's head; it felt condescending to Ruby. He didn't move again. In a moment he would be snoring. She moved her legs slowly back together, raised her hips pulling her gown back down to her calves, and stared again at the crack in the ceiling. Did it matter to him if she was awake for this? Or even alive? The release of his substance inside her slowly spread from her groin, throughout her body dispersing fatigue to the very tips of her fingers.

Thank goodness I won't conceive.

To rise again to wash was out of the question. She rolled back over to her side, her back to him, with her last thought of the day:

Finally this day is over and my duties are done.

* * * * *

For the next several days Ruby worked without stop, without thinking. She focused on the spring cleaning; airing out the feather bedding, beating the large rugs, turning up the soil in her garden plot, washing the walls, anything to prevent her from questioning. As soon as a quiet moment would allow her mind to wander, she would hastily move to the next large task. She fell into bed well past midnight, unwashed and exhausted. If Robert heard her come to bed, he made no move toward her. He remained on his side, his back to her. She knew he considered this silence as further punishment to her, and she was grateful for this one small blessing.

She and Robert only spoke to each other when necessary, primarily in front of the children. Finally on the fifth night she heard his voice in the dark, just as she was drifting off to sleep.

"Thomas Pickering. I have made some inquiries and you were in the horseless carriage of Mr Thomas Pickering. I have one question that only you can answer, however. Why did the gentleman feel privy to kiss you before your departure from that ... steel cannonball of a contraption of his!" His voice had begun calmly enough, but the last part was filled with emotion. Ruby was exhausted from a very long day, but this question gave her a jolt. She tried to remember that fateful day. It suddenly came to mind - Thomas' arm across her breast as he leaned toward her to open the door. From Robert's vantage point, it easily may have looked more intimate.

"Mercy, Robert! Is that what you assumed? He was simply assisting me in opening my door. I had only been introduced to him within that same hour! And by his wife at their home, no less!" She sighed loudly and shook her head to signify the absurdity.

He was quiet then. After a while, Ruby thought he had gone to sleep. She tried to do likewise. His voice opened her eyes again.

"You will not permit yourself to be in that type of situation again. I forbid it. Your place is at home and you are perfectly aware of that. You were always an obedient wife." *Until now*, was left unspoken but she heard it nonetheless. He moved to his back and folded his hands on his chest, fixing his eyes on the ceiling. "I sense a change in you somehow. Only recently."

Ruby held her breath in anticipation. Please ask me, her heart cried. How she longed to open up and tell him her hopes and dreams, if he would only permit it!

"Perhaps it is the weather," he continued. "Cabin fever, spring has sprung, and all that." His tone was of one who had heard it all before.

    He clicked his tongue and nodded as if the answer had suddenly been written on the ceiling paint. "What you need is a visit with your mother. I shall ask your brother to pick you up upon completing his milk run this Saturday. You will remain on the farm until Sunday. On Sunday morning, you will attend church with your family, and I shall meet you there. The boys will go as well. Fresh air on the farm will do them good. Bess will remain here to prepare my meals."

    Having thus resolved another family crisis, he promptly reached over and patted her arm, as if to say *all is better now.* He returned to his side.

    Ruby remained motionless, staring at the same cracked ceiling he did but her search saw no answers there. It only seemed to move lower, the walls to move in closer. Everything around her was shrinking, suffocating, clutching her; the room, her nightgown, even her own skin felt drawn tight. The door was closed and she could see no light from under it. Her eyes closed, searching for the dreams again.

*****

    The next afternoon, rain clouds threatened her laundry on the line. Ruby and Bess rushed outside to bring in the sheets and shirts. Bess had stayed home once again to give Ruby the needed second pair of hands to boil laundry in their scullery, a small room off the kitchen. It took all the strength they could muster to agitate the round disc of a wooden dolly stick within the copper pot, built in brick over a coal fire. It took both of them again to feed the laundry through the wringer while the other turned the crank. The dolly stick and wringer were again required for the rinsing. By the time the rain clouds came, their promise of cool air was a welcomed sight because the scullery was too hot to tolerate any longer. Ruby's arms were aching and her hands red and cracked as she piled dried sheets and quilts over her arm. Her mind set on bringing this in before the rain, she was startled when she

Good Woman

heard a "You-hoo!" from Aimee's yard. She patted down the pile of laundry she held to allow her sight to see over to the owner of the voice.

Aimee was waving from her back porch steps. "Don't forget our meeting tomorrow. Cady will host again since Sarah had to cancel, and she and Lizzie are so inspiring! Shall we walk over together?" She sounded light-hearted, as if she had not a care in the world. Aimee obviously had left her former self inside, the one Ruby last talked to. Without walking closer, Ruby peered at Aimee's face but she saw no more bruises. She suddenly realized that the empathy she felt for Aimee last week had now turned to sympathy. They could compare notes, she thought bitterly.

She had made a decision that morning during breakfast. Robert was in better spirits than she had seen in weeks, and the children reacted accordingly, absorbing and enjoying his teasing and conversation. He announced they would all go on a picnic the next Sunday afternoon after church, where the boys might fish. Bess clapped her hands and the boys drummed the table with "hurrahs!" Eating out of doors and dealing with tangled hooks and repeated worm baiting with active boys were not activities Robert would relish, and Ruby recognized his valiant effort.

Fishing then reminded Victor of a joke. "Hey Papa, how do you communicate with a fish?" He paused for affect and his little brother answered by sucking in his cheeks, and moving his puckered lips up and down. Victor ignored the fake fish. "You drop him a line!" he declared loudly and proudly, his dimple deepening with his grin.

Robert actually laughed out loud at that one and patted his son's head affectionately, which was rare. Ruby watched this exchange and determined to work harder at ensuring her family's happiness. To seek her own was selfish. She would not attend any more meetings; she would silently withdraw from the Ladies of the Lost Legion. Its sacrifice was too high, her hopes too extreme, only to fall back down to reality and its ensuing battle. Best to live in this gray cocoon. Its familiar casing could be comforting at times, this she knew.

But she would have to lie. She hated having to do that, especially to one she had once hoped to be her friend. Well, she had made up her mind and it had to be done. She squared her shoulders now and shook her head at Aimee.

"No, that would be impossible," she answered, as firmly as she could muster. Her mind went blank.

Aimee looked visibly surprised and walked toward the fence asking why.

Why?

That word seemed to echo through Ruby's mind. Why indeed? "Because my husband…because I…well, *we* do not approve, that's why!"

She was saved by the rain. One drop hit her nose, and she quickly wiped it on the sheet she was holding, vaguely appreciating its fresh smell.

"Really, Aimee, I must go in before these are wet yet again. I really do hate to repeat my work; there's enough to do without duplication!" She forced a laugh. The most artificial laugh she had ever heard. She hated standing here doing this, and her dreaded blush always revealed her discomfort.

Ruby rushed to her back door, ignoring Aimee's call to please wait a moment, to please talk. She stood safely inside.

The tears came quickly and dripped unnoticed onto her fresh dry sheets.

* * * * *

The clanking of the large aluminium milk cans and the clip-clop of his two horses announced her brother's arrival on Saturday morning. He was tying the reins to the hitching post by the street when Ruby walked out to greet him.

"Good morning, Jesse!" she called out. She surprised herself at how happy she was to see him. He reached around her for a light hug.

"And good morning to you, too, Ruby" he said. He lifted his cap, smoothed down his thick brown hair, and replaced his cap, smiling shyly, thus reminding her of his dimple. "I received a note from Robert asking that you be taken back to the house?"

She nodded.

"You ready to go, then?" he asked.

She nodded again and headed back inside to gather the weekend's necessities, and round up the boys, who were still eating breakfast.

Bess and Robert joined them outside as they prepared to go. Robert and Jesse shook hands but said little else. Robert assisted Ruby up to the front seat of the wagon and handed her the basket of jarred jam and bread loaves. The boys clamoured noisily into the back seat with the canvas bag of over-night clothing and stern instructions from their father to behave themselves.

Ruby looked down to Bess's upturned face and saw the longing in her blue eyes to go with them. Bess had gone to the trouble of braiding her own hair before breakfast; probably hoping her father would change his mind. Ruby opened her mouth to ask Robert to reconsider allowing Bess to come, but then closed it again. To embarrass him by questioning his decision in front of Jesse would only backfire with more duties for Bess. Ruby secretly considered Bess too young for this responsibility. As a result, Ruby baked feverishly the day before. Several bread loaves, Bess's favorite maple syrup pie, and a large pot of beef vegetable soup would ease Bess's weekend meal preparation. That was as much as Ruby could do for her in the situation.

She smiled at Bess instead and told her to be a good girl.

Jesse hopped up next to Ruby and grabbed the reins. He tipped his cap to Bess and Robert and clicked the reins and his tongue to the horses. They rolled slowly away. Ruby purposefully focused straight ahead, away from Bess and her wave, away from Aimee's figure watching from her own parlor window.

The day was the perfect spring day; warm sun, birds chirping in the budding trees. The leather covering over the buggy provided sufficient shade, the light breeze fresh and soothing. It all had a calming effect on Ruby. She watched the horses; ears up, harnessed to their load pulling them forward, and she listened to their steady clip-clop on the stones. Childhood memories rushed back; her early morning rides with her father during his milk runs and she missed him.

She glanced over at her brother. His round face and short nose were just like Papa's. Only Jesse had the added sweetness of a dimple and thick curly hair that stuck out around his cap. And he was quiet and self-assured, like Papa. He was accustomed to spending a great deal of time alone with his own thoughts. At dawn every morning he delivered his farm-fresh milk to the local dairy in the large aluminium cans. In exchange, they gave him cleaned empty cans and several cases of fresh bottled milk that he would then deliver to assigned homes on his milk run. Ruby's street would end his deliveries for the day, on his way back to the farm.

Communications between Ruby and her family were primarily through Jesse via hand-written notes tied to a milk bottle with string. Every morning his footsteps could be heard on the wooden planks of her porch with the clink of milk bottles, as he replaced two empties with fresh bottles. She could set her clock by his timeliness.

"You must have had a pleasant run this morning, yes?" she asked. She glanced back at the boys to make sure their legs were inside the wagon, away from the wheels. For once, they were sitting in quiet anticipation, engrossed in their own thoughts and scenery. She smiled at their bright eyes. They loved petting the farm's jersey cows, and never grew tired of climbing the rafters in the barn and jumping down onto the hay. At the farm, she only saw her boys at mealtimes.

Jesse rubbed the back of his neck, as was his habit when spoken to. "Yes" he answered. He cleared his throat. "Great to have spring here, after that harsh winter. Lost two jerseys."

"Mercy! Are you going to replace them?" She knew the loss meant less income.

"Got to. May have to wait until the county fair. The market brings in good jerseys then."

"I do wish you would accept payment from Robert for our

milk."

"Nope. Family."

"Temporarily then. Until you can buy more jerseys."

He shifted on his seat. "We're doing just fine. Edith's egg business is doing well. We sell them for twenty-two cents a dozen. Now we're going to combine egg deliveries with the milk. You'll start getting eggs next week."

She turned to him in surprise. "What a marvellous plan, delivering eggs with milk!"

He shrugged. "Edith's idea. She can tell you all about it when you get there."

It was like pulling teeth getting information from him. She wished his words were as generous as his heart. With him being her only means of family connection for several months at a time, his clipped sentences always became an annoyance to her after a few minutes.

She sighed. "Fine."

A long stretch of silence ensued, eventually leading to restless boys in the back. Their fallback position for entertainment was to aggravate the other. This prevailed until Ruby sent back threats that they would walk beside the buggy if they didn't behave. This worked and human silence resumed. They all listened quietly to the occasional snorting and jingling of harnesses and the sounds of the horses' hooves plodding over the road that had become hard-packed dirt outside of town, the wheels creaking over the deep pits and ruts.

"How is Robert?"

"How is Mama?"

They asked at the same time and this made them laugh. She had forgotten how similar their minds worked when together. Siblings shared that mystery she guessed.

"Robert is fine, thank you. He is very busy of course at the shoe shop. He spends as much time mending shoes as he does selling them."

Robert and Jesse had nothing in common and at times Ruby detected a dislike between the two. Neither voiced this to her but she sensed it just the same. She thought of the permanent stain on Robert's slender fingers from the dye he used on the shoe leather. She looked over at her brother's hands holding the reins, large-knuckled and heavily callused. Yes they were as different as day and night. And they say you marry your father's likeness. Must just be wishful thinking on some poor woman's part.

* * * * *

Jesse stopped the wagon by the front of the house rather than going on to the back as he usually did. He was giving Ruby the same subtle formal welcome as company who only goes to the front door, rather than family who only goes to the back door entrance.

The squeaking of the screen door was music to Ruby's ears, her nose twitching pleasantly to the familiar smell of baking cornbread wafting out of the entrance. Edith came out onto the front porch, drying her hands on her ever-present apron. She was two years older than Ruby, but Ruby looked at her as being much older. Her once-thin figure had thickened permanently in the middle from carrying a child almost every year of her marriage to Jesse. Her hair was already graying, but more than that, it was those penetrating brown eyes that held ancient wisdom.

Garnet, Ruby's mama, trailed behind, the arthritis in her hip causing a slight limp, her height shrinking a bit more to Ruby each time she saw her.

Edith gave Ruby a hasty hug. She was always in a hurry. "You are just as pretty as you ever were," she said, as she looked Ruby up and down. She was looking too close, with scrutiny. What Edith said and what she was thinking could be two very different things. Her eyes were asking, *Is everything all right?* as she patted Ruby on the back.

Her mama was more to the point. "Now what do we owe this visit to? Are you hungry?" She hugged the boys. "Now where is Bess I wonder?"

Jonathan piped up. "Bess had to stay *home* and we have to

behave!" His last words deepened in tone to mimic his father. He was a little feistier when away from his father's stern eyes, and in front of his grandmother.

"And I am certain you will, Johnny boy!" Garnet laughed.

"*Really* Jonathan!" Ruby tried to sound stern, but it came out sounding like she too was mimicking Robert. She changed the subject. "Victor, please take our bag upstairs and then you boys go play."

That was all the direction they needed and they were gone. Ruby turned to Garnet and Edith. "I hope I'm not coming at a bad time for you. With this time of the year, getting your garden planted, spring cleaning —"

"Why, Ruby, I'm surprised at you!" Garnet said. "You know any time my children are at home, it's a good time! Why, Edith and I were just talking about you yesterday while we were making soap."

"Oh I forgot about the soap making at spring cleaning. Do you still do that? Why, you can find wonderfully fragrant hard soaps now in town, in all sizes and shapes, even heart-shapes, for only pennies. And soft soaps you add directly to your washtub. Making soap is such hard work!"

Edith shook her head. "Pennies go a long way toward feed and farm tools. Making soap costs nothing and uses up all that ash and grease from the winter. That's what we were talking about yesterday. Your Mama was saying how that was your job, to collect the ashes from the stove and fireplace, and to save the animal fats in buckets. And how you hated handling the animal fat."

"Do you remember that, Ruby?" Garnet asked. "How you would wrinkle up your nose when after we would render the fat and grease and let it cool, and then boil it, your job was to skim off the floating debris and dirt. You never could understand why we would use dirty ashes and greasy fat to clean our bodies and clothes. Goodness, you would make a fuss!"

They headed toward the porch. Edith touched Ruby's arm. "Ruby, remind me before you go, and I'll give you the sweetest smelling soap of any in town. I got the idea from Opal, who loves sweet smells like you, so I crushed some lilacs and some dried herbs, and started experimenting. I think even a town girl like you will be impressed!"

Garnet placed her arm around Ruby and squeezed. Ruby sensed her mama was now concerned she had hurt Ruby's feelings in saying Ruby made a fuss over soap. She studied Ruby's silence closely. "It is so good to have my oldest girl home! You don't have any bad news for me, I hope. We weren't expecting you 'til Easter."

"No Mama, as you so often say to me, 'things could be worse'. We are all healthy. Robert sends his best. And then he sent me," she added lightly.

Garnet grunted as her heavy frame took the porch stairs slowly, and finally chuckled as the play on words sunk in. "Well, not for good I hope! We are already bursting at the seams here with Jesse's children." She opened the screen door for Ruby. "Honey, we are definitely blessed with children; no one can argue there." She followed Ruby into the well-worn living room.

The same furniture was where it had always been, down to the scalloped lace doilies over the back of the brown cotton sofa, and on the arms of the green velvet chair, worn smooth in patches. There was something about its sameness that was comforting to Ruby. Somehow this homeplace was still her root where she could return for nourishment. As she accepted the cold milk Edith handed her and sat down on the sofa, she wondered if Robert didn't know her better than she gave him credit for. Then another thought came to mind. Was Robert sending her home for some parental conditioning because he was having trouble handling her?

Garnet limped over to her rocker and sat down slowly, holding on tight to the arms for balance. "And speaking of children," she continued, "looks like there is potential for more."

Ruby looked at Edith expectedly. Edith read Ruby's face and waved her hands at her. "No, Ruby, I've done my share of

Good Woman 63

birthing babies!"

Garnet raised her voice over Edith's giggles. "I'm talking about Opal!"

Ruby's eyes opened wide in shock. "Mercy, don't tell me! Opal is…is…" she lowered her tone to a whisper. "…*with child?*"

Edith and Garnet laughed long and loud at this.

"No, no! Listen to me, honey!" Garnet paused to wipe at her eyes with a handkerchief from her dress pocket. "Of course, you may not take this news any better, when I tell you." Her fingers played nervously with the handkerchief. "Well, she has accepted Jacob Penn's proposal to marry!"

"The *Amish* Jacob Penn?" Ruby looked at her, disbelieving.

"One and the same," Garnet nodded.

"But…but, he is so…*Amish*! Is this union even permitted in his church?" Ruby still couldn't believe it.

Garnet's face had turned somber now. "So I'm told. Well, of course she must convert to his religion. And live the way they do…" her voice faded away. She looked out the window. "I don't know all the details." Her eyes focused on Ruby. "Perhaps she will talk to you. She seems distracted and quiet. You two were close before your marriage. Do you think you could have a heart-to-heart talk tonight? I admit I am worried."

So many questions were running through Ruby's mind, she could only nod. What was Opal getting herself into? What was the Amish life like? She had so hoped to someday become close again to Opal. It suddenly occurred to her that, in the back of her mind, she intended to someday bring Opal to the Ladies of the Lost Legion meetings. She reminded herself that she was no longer participating, but then Opal could, on behalf of both of them. She was single. Without the obligations to a husband, Opal would have the freedom to attend. With this marriage to Jacob Penn, Opal would be impossible to reach. Although his family farm was only a few miles down the road, Opal might as well move to Syracuse, Ruby thought sadly. Obligations to an Amish husband may be greater than to a town man like Robert. She saw her sister's life slipping away, slowly fading down that dirt road.

* * * * *

"Would you walk with me?" Ruby asked Opal.

Supper was over, dishes were done, but as was tradition here, this was the time of day when everyone remained around the long wooden kitchen table, telling tidbits of hearsay. Especially when company was there. At least for the adults. The boys had eaten with gusto and headed back to the barn with biscuits in hand. Ruby watched them go, trying to block out the thought of them petting the cows and munching biscuits with the same hand.

"I would love to." Opal stood up, smoothing down the full skirt of her pink and cream-colored dress.

Another new one and this one matched her complexion perfectly. Forgive me Lord for jealously.

"Where would you like to walk to?" Opal asked. She smoothed back the braids of her dark-blonde hair and checked the pins in her knotted bun. She winked at Ruby and grinned, her round face reminding Ruby of a cherub. "Want to take your and Robert's favorite route? Should be a path worn down by now!"

"My legs would know no other way!" Ruby sighed dramatically.

"Is Robert still such a creature of habit?" Opal asked.

Garnet turned around from the sideboard in surprise. "Opal, that's not very nice!"

Ruby laughed and leaned toward her sister. She placed her hand to the side of her mouth, as if pretending to tell a secret. "Well, let's just say, if I moved the furniture he'd be lost."

"I knew it, I knew it," Opal said.

"Oh you girls. Shame on you Ruby for criticizing your husband!" Garnet waved her hands at them, shooing them through the mudroom to the back door. "Here, Ruby, wear my poncho." Garnet took it off one of the many hooks on the back wall and threw it over Ruby's head. "It's still mighty cool outside after the sun goes down." She brushed it down around Ruby. "I feed the chickens in this, but it doesn't look any worse for the wear." She looked knowingly at her. "You two have a nice talk now." She gently pushed them out the back door.

Garnet followed the country pattern of raising a large family. A large family was needed around the farm. Once the older children were partly raised, they, in turn, helped raise each other. Talking, learning, watching out for each other. Until death, Ruby guessed.

Opal and Ruby walked out into the dusk and when they heard the back door close, Ruby chuckled. "Mama's a good soul. I suppose we will always be children to her."

Opal put her arm around Ruby's waist. "Especially a child she rarely sees. It's so good to have you back home again, Ruby! It's been since Christmas, last time you visited. I've truly missed you…especially recently."

Ruby knew her little sister well enough to hear an opportunity to bring in the news.

"Only recently? Why, I'm hurt!" Ruby dabbed at her eyes.

"Well, I need your advice," Opal answered matter-of-factly. They were habitually walking toward the apple orchard. "You are the wise one, the married one, the *older* one," she added, teasing.

She paused, collecting her thoughts. "I'm certain you remember Jacob Penn. He went to school with me up to grade eight. Do you remember how he used to come over and offer to help with the chores, only to end with chasing me with little creatures in hand, showing off? If I was outside even close to his vicinity, he would pull cartwheels, or jump over the fence, or leap on to one of the horses, bareback." She sighed loudly and shook her head at the memories, as if they were nonsense.

"If I recall correctly, Opal, you made certain you were…how do you say…'in his vicinity'," Ruby teased.

Opal appeared shocked. "Why, I never!" She stopped to take a new growth of leaf off a near branch. "He has grown into a decent man since then," she said softly. "After eighth grade, he worked on his family farm full-time as all Amish boys must do and I only saw him the odd time, on the road into town usually.

Until recently…" her voice faded off as if she weren't sure where to take this.

Ruby picked up a branch from the ground and began breaking off its twigs, to give her fingers something to do. She felt her sister's awkward moment but could think of nothing to say.

Opal squared her shoulders in determination. She continued walking, talking more rapidly. "Recently, meaning after Papa passed away. He came around offering to help Jesse. Jesse was short-handed with the dairy business growing like it is and gladly accepted. He worked for several hours a day for a week. Jesse then attempted to pay him a week's wages, but Jacob would not accept payment. He asked that instead he be permitted to call on me and begin courting. Can you imagine?" She again shook her head.

"Had he yet approached you to ask how you felt about this?" Ruby asked.

"Not a word." Opal answered. She was quick to add, "He was very shy you see."

"Let me understand this," Ruby said. "He worked into the good graces of Jesse in payment to court you? What about *your* good graces?" She squeezed Opal's arm. "What do *you* feel for Jacob?"

"I am sincerely touched by this, Ruby. And naturally he would go to Jesse for permission. After all, Jesse is head of the household now that Papa is gone." Her tone was defensive. "Furthermore, since we are not Amish, Jacob was concerned that Jesse would forbid it."

"What does Jacob's family say about this? Does he have their blessing?"

"Yes. Of course I must be baptized into the Amish faith and join their church. I am now reading the Ordnung, which is their written set of rules for daily living."

Ruby could cry hearing this. There was not one word of love mentioned yet. This was all being worked with Opal on the periphery. She stopped walking and turned to Opal. She tried to speak as gently as possible. "You haven't answered my question yet. What do you feel for Jacob? Your heart matters here, too, you know."

Opal licked her lips and focused on the tree trunk next to her, following a crack in the bark with her finger. "Ruby, I am twenty years old. I am lonely. No other has courted me. I've told you that Jacob is a decent man. He is also hardworking." She leaned against the tree and folded her arms. Her misty blue eyes finally met Ruby's. "What would you have me say? That I love him? Love, I believe, comes with time and ... and ... children. Living with one another, learning one another. How do you know a man before marrying him?"

She looked down at a shrivelled apple that had somehow survived winter and kicked at it with the toe of her boot. "Ruby, please don't worry about me. After all, I've known him longer than you knew Robert. Our courting is no different, and look how well you faired!"

Oh, mercy! If Opal only knew! But Ruby could not bring herself to confide in Opal and betray her husband. Opal would only pity her, or worse yet, simply not understand Ruby's ...unhappiness...frustration? What *was* she feeling anyway, she asked herself. Yes, she decided, Opal would only think her demented. And ultimately it would not change Opal's plans for marriage. But perhaps there was something to say to at least prepare Opal for this commitment.

"You are right, Opal. I am in no position to question your decision. But you did say I was the wiser one, remember?" They smiled at each other, the tension passed. "May I just say that a wife's obligations are many. I admit I find these difficult at times. A man's needs..." She blushed, having said this and not meaning to, but decided since she had already said it, to continue, "... are often. And you worry when he is meeting his needs, that conception will occur. And conception means childbirth. And childbirth could mean death, for you, for the baby. And then, if you are blessed to have a healthy child, you must breastfeed, wean, clean, and make his clothes. And then conception begins again, and you worry again. And it repeats itself. And the worries and the work grow. And sometimes, it seems...there is no end..."

She realized she was crying then and she walked at a faster pace, hoping the wind would pick up her tears and blow them away. Opal followed quietly behind her. After a few minutes, Ruby turned her head and looked at her from the corner of her eye and saw Opal's brow knitted together in concern. She slowed down her pace and took in deep breaths to calm herself.

She felt Opal's arm come around her shoulder and her voice was soft in Ruby's ear. "In the Bible, when Sarah was told by the Lord that she was with child, she said, 'God hath made me to laugh, so that all that hear, shall laugh with me'. She was so happy and she wanted everyone else to be happy with her! As I would be! And, Ruby, you are *so* right to say you are blessed to have a healthy child. You have t*hree* blessings! I am so envious, Lord forgive me! I only want the married life that you have and no more! And I want you to be happy again, Ruby, so please smile!"

Ruby dabbed at her eyes with the handkerchief Opal handed her and forced a smile as bidden. "So much for being the wiser one," Ruby said, sarcasm etched clearly. "Is there anything else I can help you with?"

She glanced toward the house, now only outlined in the darkening sky, windows warm with yellow light. "Mama would be so pleased to hear my advice. I was supposed to be counselling you."

"Really? Mama has said very little to me." Opal thought for a moment and then shrugged her shoulders. "Oh well, I am her youngest and last to go. Since Papa died, she worries more about being alone. I think she is as lonely as I at times. And as for you, my dear sister," and she gave Ruby a hug, "you may indeed be blessed for a fourth time!"

"Mercy! Opal, why would you say such a thing?" Ruby was sincerely dismayed.

"Well, you do seem a little more emotional this visit." Opal's voice now had a I-know-it-all tone that irritated Ruby.

Ruby felt foolish now for confiding. She had sincerely wanted to help her little sister, and now it appeared as if she her-

Good Woman

self needed help. Her pride moved forward. Turning toward the house, she grabbed Opal's arm and pulled her along.

"Look, little sister. I only wished to prepare you for the worst. I only wish you the best. There are some scary moments ahead of you that you should know about. It will not be only happiness and laughter, regardless of what Sarah said." Her tone sounded harsh in her own ears and this was not the way she wanted to end the conversation. She squeezed Opal's arm. "But you are strong. This I know more today than ever. You will endure. And you must promise me that, no matter what, you will laugh!"

And so they both laughed to prove that they could still do so.

As Ruby lay in bed that night next to her sleeping sister, she still felt a little foolish and exposed as if she had walked through the orchard in her petticoat. To reveal her inner feelings was to reveal her dark side. A dark side but also her practical side. Why didn't women speak more openly? There was nothing one had done that another had not done or at least would do after marriage. She rehashed the conversation in her mind, but could only conclude she had no alternative. Her sister must be made aware of this submission to her husband. This total vulnerability to his body and needs. To give yourself to him was to lose yourself to you. To be totally exposed to his eyes and touch, and while he sees and touches you, you only see and feel the pain of the eventual child labor this act will bring. Will Opal still laugh after her wedding night? What was expected of a woman on her wedding night was no laughing matter. No wonder women never spoke of it.

* * * * *

Early morning sounds brought her slowly up from sleep. Jesse's voice could be heard outside, calling commands to his boys. The crow of the rooster was reminding him that he must get a move on to his milk route. His voice sounding so much like Papa's, Ruby let her memory pretend it was Papa's. Papa would be knocking on her door any minute now.

"Ruby, if you are going with me, better get down here now."

"Coming, Papa!"

She would grab her britches off its hook on the wall, and love the feel of them on. Free movement. The only time she was allowed to wear them, hand-me-downs from her brother, was on the milk routes with Papa, so that she could help with the lifting and climbing without snagging her skirts and showing her ankles.

She would run outside and grab milk cans to load onto the back of the wagon, or do whatever Papa said to do. Moving quickly so that he would not loose patience and threaten to take her brother tomorrow. She didn't want that; she loved these runs with Papa. This was the only time he would talk to her, just the two of them. She loved the physical labor this outside work called for, making her feel strong and alive. She loved the early morning sounds of the milk slosh-sloshing into the buckets during milking; the stillness of the fields around her; the dew along the side of the road catching the light of the lantern hitched on the side of the wagon. She remembered their last ride together, on the way back home after just such a run. Her last fatal question to him.

"Papa, can I run the dairy business someday?"

Papa turned and looked at her with that one eyebrow raised in surprise.

"Why would you want to do that?" he asked.

"Because, Papa, I know how!" She counted off her gloved fingers. "I can milk the cows. I can feed the cows. I can harness the horses. I can fill the cans with the fresh milk. I can clean up the barn. I do all that –well, with a little help from you and Jesse Junior. But I'm getting stronger as I get older. I can do it!"

"Don't you let your Mama hear you say that! She already gives me a hard time for letting you go with me in the first place." He rubbed his stubbed chin with his callused hand, sounding like sandpaper against wood. "How old are you now? Fourteen?" He saw her frown. "Fifteen?"

"Sixteen, Papa, I'm sixteen now, and old enough to know

what I want!"

"Life will teach you that what you want is not always what you get. You're closer to womanhood than I realized. Hmmm. Time you started actin' like one. Dressing in those britches is starting to make you think like a boy. My fault I admit and your mama will hold me accountable, I'm sure." He took off his cap and scratched his head.

"Papa, what is wrong with working with you? I like it a lot more than house chores."

"It won't be long 'til you are getting married, Ruby. What good are you as a wife, if doing man's work is all you know? What kind of man are you going to catch, if you smell like manure?" He reached his hand over and affectionately flipped under her chin. "Smile, my little gem. How can you shine like the deep red of a ruby if you are covered in calluses like these?" He opened his rough palm in front of her face to show her.

She said nothing. She had some of her own. Did he think rubbing, pounding, boiling, and squeezing laundry was any easier?

He looked over at the sunrise coming up on the far field's horizon and nodded toward it, its pinks and purples softly tinting a gray-sided barn, as their wagon passed slowly by.

"God has his own gem right there in the sun. And then He said to me, Jesse, I'm going to give you three gems of your very own. Yep, I'm a lucky man, with three gems of my own, to brighten my world. Garnet's blush, Ruby's red, Opal's cream. You three are my most precious possessions."

He clicked at the horses and flicked the reins to move a little faster. "The farm goes to my oldest boy. You should know that, Ruby. No more silly talk."

He never knocked on her bedroom door again. Now it was Jesse Junior's door. Only he was given the key. The hurt finally subsided and went away. Or so she thought.

She climbed out of her sister's bed and went to the window and opened the curtains to the sunrise, God's gem. Still there bringing in pink and lavender rays as if nothing had changed. She saw Jesse climb onto the wagon and ride slowly away, milk cans clinking, harnesses jingling, and she felt the longing of the sixteen year old all over again.

*****

> A-maz (clip-clop) ing Grace (clip-clop)
> How sweet (clip-clop) the sound (clip-clop)
> That saved (clip-clop) a wretch (clip-clop) like me! (Clip-clop, jingle, Clip-clop)
> I once (clip-clop) was lost (clip-clop)
> But now (clip-clop) am found (clip-clop)
> Was blind (clip-clop) but now (clip-clop) I see!

Ruby hummed and bobbed her head back and forth to the rhythm of the horses' hooves, their horseshoes on the cobble stones in perfect rhythm to *Amazing Grace* sounding out of the church windows. As Ruby reined the horses into the front yard, she heard her mama sigh loudly. She knew Garnet was regularly dismayed at her children's tardiness to church services. She considered this a sin right up there with blasphemy. But she would say nothing to her adult children, for the power of her parenting was over, she believed.

Ruby glanced over at her mama's solid figure next to her in the buggy, framed by the church with its steeple and cemetery to one side. It was the perfect image of how Ruby pictured her mama in her mind. Always in her forest green wool church dress with its high collar, garnet brooch given to her by Ruby's papa many years ago, black lace shawl, and black bonnet. Ruby remembered no other dress worn by her mother to church. Always with the church in her background. Living to go to church and dying to eternally rest in the church cemetery, next to Ruby's papa. Garnet treated Sundays different than other days; more quiet and subdued, singing hymns to herself, her misty eyes looking beyond the movements of the day. At times like these Ruby believed that her mama was simply waiting to die.

Ruby maneuvered the buggy to the shade of a tree to cool

the horses. Opal and Edith climbed off the backbench and walked back to assist Jesse and the boys, bringing up the rear in the wagon. Ruby helped her mama's bulky frame climb down from the buggy.

The commotion their arrival created in the churchyard was discomforting to the women, but tolerated silently. Their early morning chores with the farm, breakfast, and dress-up always made for a challenge in arriving on time. Ruby thought that bringing so many rambunctious farm boys into town and church, to sit still on a pew for two hours, was like trying to saddle a pig; you were going to put a lot of effort into something that wasn't practical in the first place. Reading the Bible to the boys at home seemed more practical, but Jesse married someone who believed much like his mama. Edith was a staunch church-goer, and so would be her boys.

The church congregation was singing their last verse and glancing sideways at the latecomers. Ruby, Garnet, Opal, and Edith, heads down, attempted to walk discreetly down the narrow center aisle to their accustomed pews. Robert was in their pew with Bess. Bess's eyes lit up when she saw Ruby and she immediately slid over to make room for Ruby to sit between Bess and Robert. Ruby could hear her two boys and Edith's boys thumping into the last pew several rows behind her.

Victor and Jonathan weren't sitting in front of Robert and Ruby, where they were normally under watchful eye and a flick to the ear by their father when they misbehaved. Robert clicked his tongue and shook his head. He was not going to correct the situation by arising in front of the congregation's watchful eye, so he brought out his handkerchief instead, and blew his nose in frustration, while staring straight ahead.

And a good day to you, too, Ruby said silently. Did Robert remember he had promised a picnic after church? She breathed in deeply the ever-constant smell of musty wood, mingled with the earthly bodies of these church souls, and tried to relax. Only in church was she around so many and always became unsettled by their many curious eyes. To help her focus on the sermon, she brought out her small Bible and pencil, ready to take notes.

The song ended and the church quieted except for a cough here and there, and the horses' snorts coming in through the open windows. Preacher Paul ever so slowly arose and walked forward, appearing to expect pain when he reached the pulpit. He raised the waist of his trousers that had slid beneath his protruding belly. On the front of the pulpit was carved in the wood: *The lion hath roared, who will not fear? The Lord God hath spoken, who can but prophesy? Amos 3.8*

The pulpit beheld a very large Bible, and he began turning its pages, as if each one was heavily weighted. He cleared his throat.

"Welcome to our out-of-town brethren who have come nigh on 50 miles from our affiliated church in Masontown." He turned around to where three gentlemen were sitting behind him in large high-back wooden chairs. "Welcome" he said to them as he shook each one's hand. They nodded solemnly.

He returned to the Bible and cleared his throat again. He found his page and then placed his thumbs on his chest behind his suspenders, and read loudly as if emphasizing reverence to the command of the verse.

"'And God said, Let us make man in our image, after our likeness: and let them have dominion over the fish of the sea, and over the fowl of the air, and over the cattle, and over all the earth, and over *every*" and here he raised his index finger toward the heavens "creeping thing that creepeth upon the earth'."

"What we are talking about today my brethren is *Man's Dominion.* Dominion, in other words, besides the sacred words of God," he patted the Bible and then opened his small black book of notes.

Preacher Paul pulled his spectacles from his chest pocket and placed them on the end of his nose. He looked above his spectacles at the congregation. "One would think I would learn to write as large as these Holy Words. Pray for me that I would gain the wisdom, or gain larger spectacles." The congregation, familiar with his movements at the pulpit, laughed softly. One of the gentlemen behind him, shouted "Amen!" and the congregation rumbled laughter again. A smile moved across the preacher's face quickly and then disappeared. He brought his black book even with his eyes and held it out a foot or so and read down his nose.

"Dominion, in dictionary words means...to rule, to tower over, to have absolute authority." He lowered his book to face the people. "To have absolute authority," he repeated. "Brethren, this is God's command and we must ensure we take charge and have complete control. IT... IS... OUR... DUTY!" He bellowed these last words and they seemed to bounce off the walls and high ceiling and fall down around Ruby's ears.

"And what is our domain, brethren? What are we, as modern men, to have dominion over? What is our sphere of influence? It is our household, brethren! Whether you have sheep, cattle, horses, wives, children, they must have a master. And the master must rule and protect. What are sheep without a shepherd to shelter the fold and lead to feed, and to shear to give us clothing? What are cattle, without the farmer to feed and in turn to feed and clothe man? What are horses, without the cowboy to tame it for our means to travel and to till the fields? What are wives, without the husband to procreate, and to provide for and protect? What are children, without their father's rule and teachings? They would be aimless, brethren, without a purpose! And men are not without a master. What are *men* without our heavenly Father and His Holy Word? We would also be without purpose, or promise of ever-lasting life. Folks, we all have a master. It is the natural pecking order.

"Matthew, chapter 4, says, 'Man shall not live by bread alone, but by every word that proceedeth out of the mouth of God'. That is men's absolute authority. It is our duty then to provide this spiritual food to our subordinates in our domain. Do you see its design? Its natural order of descension?"

The preacher moved his hand to indicate steps down. "Every living creature has a role in descending order. Here on this top step is our Almighty God. Next step down is man, next step down is woman, next step down is children, on the next step are animals, then fish, then crawling creatures. To step outside what we are designed to do under God's rule, is to disobey God. Men, you are to obey God; wives you are to obey your husbands; children, you are to obey your parents. Our domain is our household! Amen?"

"Amen!" brethren shouted.

He stepped from behind the pulpit and walked to the edge of the platform.

"Look around you and you will see God's design." He pointed to the front pew. "There sits Brother James Preston and his wife, Claire. They own the farm out at Willow's Bend. Five beautiful children. All God-fearing folk."

Preacher Paul held his hand out again, indicating stairs. "So here is Brother James on this top step, sister Claire on the next step, their children right below them, their horses and cattle here on the next one, the fish he catches in his own trout pond on the next one, and on the bottom are the worms on the end of his fishing pole!" He chuckled and looked over at the family and nodded, then smiled appreciably when they responded with a nod and a chuckle of their own.

"Over there is Brother Ernest Campbell. His wife, Sarah, just had their eighth child. Hope to see her and her new one next Sunday. Good people." He pointed this time to Jesse and Edith. "Brother Jesse Johnson and his wife Edith have six boys. And none would argue that they are big healthy boys." Some chuckling rippled through the pews. "His sister, Ruby, and her husband Robert Wright are here with three fine children. Their mother, Garnet, and her husband, may God rest his soul, helped build this church with their own hands some thirty-five years ago. Right after the Civil War. And of course I can't go on talking about family without mentioning my own dear wife of thirty years, Sister Joan, and that handsome strap of a boy of mine and his three sisters."

Joan smiled and waved her handkerchief at him to go on.

"Family. God's design for Christians. This blessed America was built on Christianity. Christianity was built on God's word. But let me say this and listen carefully: The number of Christians is only the sum total. What affects the units, the individual family, influences more slowly than the whole."

The preacher returned to his notes. "The Bible says: 'God setteth the solitary in families.' It also says: 'And thy seed shall be as the dust of the earth, and thou shalt spread abroad to the west, and to the east, and to the north, and to the south; and in thee and in thy seed shall all the families of the earth be blessed'."

He looked above his glasses at his attentive group.

A foreboding gnaw was working on Ruby's stomach and she placed her hand on her belly to attempt to soothe.

"If you do not believe this, here is what is prophesied in Deuteronomy: 'Lest there should be among you man, or woman, or family, or tribe, whose heart turneth away this day from the Lord our God, to go and serve the gods of these nations; lest there should be among you a root that beareth gall and wormwood'."

He paused and took a deep breath. He moved his eyes down the rows of pews.

"As the preacher of this church, as the shepherd of my flock, I also have my own duties. And right now, my duty is to warn you of a dangerous wormwood, right here in our own beloved town. A plan to talk heresy. Heresy, I say, because there is a group of women who wish to proclaim certain rights that are not of God's purpose. To step outside their intended place. A plan that is intended to drive our families apart!"

He shifted his pants up around his belly and cleared his throat. He raised his right hand as if to swear.

"Now I just want to say that the women of this church are a blessing indeed. The meals they prepare for our church socials, the cleaning of this sacred building; its floor and windows. Always bringing food to the sick. They are a valued member but I feel led to say this to you."

Preacher Paul shook his finger at the congregation.

"Sisters of the church, take heed, for the Bible says, 'No servant can serve two masters; for either he will hate the one, and love the other; or else he will hold to the one, and despise the other'. Sisters, it is your duty to serve your husband and no other; to work for your husband and no other; to submit to your husband as God commands."

Walking back to the three gentlemen, the preacher shook their hands again, as if needing to gain strength through their touch. Each one nodded with affirmatives, "Tell it, preacher!", "Amen, brother!"

He returned to the pulpit. "Word came to me from a God-fearing sister of our church that a meeting will be held this summer by a group calling themselves…" He read from his black book "…Ladies of the Lost Legion."

Ruby sucked in her breath, and then prayed that Robert nor others noticed her reaction. She glanced sideways at Robert, where he remained staring straight ahead, watching the preacher intently, the scowl between his eyes deepening. Fear seized her with a vision of the preacher turning to her, eyes glaring, finger pointing, shouting *we have one in our midst, stand up!*

"These *ladies*" he emphasized, "are wanting to *vote*, and to own *property*. And why, I ask, unless they want to be a *man*! Wife-hood and motherhood are women's God-given profession! Imagine if this were turned upside down! Imagine the deserted firesides, neglected children, and forlorn and hungry husbands. Frayed clothing and loose buttons. The babies crying while your wife and the mother of your children is sallying forth to do her duty at the polls. I don't wish to go into politics here, but what if I stood here on God's Holy Ground and said to my brethren to be pure, and to the maidens of the church to be brave? Nature itself teaches you that I would be wrong."

Preacher Paul shook his head in disbelief. "Let me just read you what the 13th century Christian theologian, Thomas Aquinas, said: 'Woman was created to be man's helpmeet, but her unique role is in conception…since for other purposes men would be better assisted by other men'.

He took off his spectacles and walked to edge of the platform. Shaking his spectacles at the group, he shouted, "These Ladies of the Lost Legion and their so-called suffrage movement will only make our women unwomanly and thus will destroy our homes!

"And if that isn't enough to make you run home and lock

your doors, listen to what the Bible says about legions."

He returned to his Bible and turned pages. "Look at St. Mark, chapter five. This is where Jesus met with the maniac of Gadara. This maniac had an unclean spirit and verse four says, 'Because that he had been often bound with fetters and chains, and the chains had been plucked asunder by him, and the fetters broken in pieces; neither could any man tame him'. But Jesus said to him, 'Come out of the man, thou unclean spirit'. And then Jesus asked him, 'What is thy name?' Are you reading with me, brethren, for look what the maniac answered in verse nine, 'My name is Legion; for we are many'. Now it goes on to say that these many were *devils* and they besought Jesus saying, 'Send us into the swine', and Jesus did, 'and the unclean spirit went out, and entered into the swine; and the herd ran violently down a steep place into the sea, and were choked in the sea'. Now think about this; not even a herd of pigs wanted to live with the legion in them! And people heard about this and in verse fifteen it says, 'And they come to Jesus, and see him that was possessed with the devil and had the legion, sitting, and clothed, and in his right mind and they were afraid'. The man who was possessed wanted to go with Jesus but Jesus said, here in verse nineteen, 'Go home to thy friends, and tell them how great things the Lord hath done for thee, and hath had compassion on thee'.

"And folks, that is what I want you to do; go home and tell everyone that this legion of women is of the devil, for it says so right here, as clear as day, in the Holy Word.

"Brethren, we are in perilous times when we see mothers, wives, and daughters who no longer wish to abide by the Holy Word. We must, as masters of our domain, fight this venomous opposition, and protect what is rightfully ours. I promise, as protector of my flocks' souls, I will do what I can to stop this so-called women's rights convention and these *men-haters* … which is to say … *they … hate … God*!"

He brought out his handkerchief and wiped his mouth and brow. He sighed heavily. "Those who wish to join me in this crusade, please join me for a meeting after church."

He supported his arm on the pulpit and concluded with scripture Ruby heard him use many times to end his sermons.

"Ecclesiastes, Chapter 12, says 'Let us hear the conclusion of the whole matter: Fear God and keep his commandments: for this is the whole... duty'" and he shook his finger at his attentive audience, "'of man'. Let us pray."

Ruby exhaled slowly. Holding her breath for so long had made her dizzy. All she could do was close her eyes and pray silently, *please God, protect me and forgive me if I did indeed sin, because I don't believe my men-folk will. Amen.*

* * * * *

Garnet was fanning her flushed face with a small cardboard fan, compliments of the church. A small number of these were stored in the pockets in the back of the pews. One side of the fan portrayed Jesus, children gathered at his feet; on the other side was the Lord's Prayer. The colors on the fan blended into a solid brown as she fluttered it back and forth quickly. The room was to become very warm by the end of church.

"My, my! The spirit of God was speaking through Preacher Paul today! The way he described the natural order of things! I do believe he was preaching to someone in our midst, do you? I haven't heard anything about any such group of women, have you?" She looked at Opal, then at Ruby. "Ruby, you're a town girl, now. Have you heard of such talk?"

"A little...from my neighbor," Ruby answered vaguely, thinking she certainly wasn't going to lie, standing here on holy ground, but she wasn't going to tell all, either. She glanced around and saw Robert up on the platform with the preacher and other men, in a huddle. They all looked so serious she wanted to laugh. Those so-called men-haters were not of the devil; they were harmless! Peaceful, even. Just looking for their own rights and here men were, acting as if they were going to save the world from the women's wrath. Really, what were these men afraid of?

She changed the subject. "Let us move outside, Mama, where

it is cooler. The men should be along directly."

Once outside, she saw Jesse carrying hay from the wagon to the horses. She guessed Jesse would agree that the men were worrying about trivial matters, when there was more important work at hand. He never stopped working. Edith was gathering her boys around her as a hen would gather her chicks. They were preparing to head home.

Opal turned to Ruby with a scowl. "Why do some women want to vote? It is ridiculous! What business would I have at the polls, talking men's politics when my place is in the home? Where I want to be! If I voted, I would simply vote the same as my husband, anyway, to support him. I would certainly value his advice on such matters, more than mine. Just as I would expect him to value my advice on matters, such as, well, canning tomatoes, or birthing babies!"

Garnet shook her head adamantly. "I just can't imagine! Sinners they are! If this group of women thinks like men, what's next? Will they start dressing like men as well?" She fluttered her fan before her face and then added, "Mark my words. We are nearing the end of time, girls, when we see the devil at work in women! Another Eve in our garden."

Ruby could be quiet no more. "Really, Mama! From what I've heard, they are simply asking that all women have a right to be heard and counted."

Opal shook her head adamantly. "I hear you, Ruby, but it makes no difference in the end. The results are the same, for the wife should follow the husband in what he does!"

"You might not think so idealistically, once you are married a few years," Ruby snapped back. She immediately bit her lip in regret. She was hinting at problems in her marriage, showing disrespect to Robert, and worst of all, she sounded like a know-it-all to someone who looked up to her as having it all.

Garnet frowned and sighed. "I was worried when you moved into town, Ruby, that you would be forever contaminated if exposed to city ways and radical thinking. Remember Sodom and Gomorrah? You need to come to church more!"

Now it was Ruby's turn to be flushed. "Yes, Mama, but—"

"Are you coming out to the house for dinner?" Jesse called out. "Or do you want a ride home, Ruby?"

Ever vigilant, aren't you brother?

"No, Jesse, I am waiting for Robert, and then we plan on a picnic with the children," she called back. She waved to him, and quickly gave a hug to each of her women kinfolk standing close by. Her way of saying the conversation had ended as far as she was concerned. This was neither the time, nor the place.

"Ruby, don't stay away from church so long, and come out to see us more. Robert, too. Jesse will bring you out anytime you want. You know that. You are in my prayers." Garnet's misty eyes looked at Ruby sadly. She hated disagreements and she hated good-byes.

"Of course, Mama." Somehow her mama made her feel guilty when she talked that way. She heard herself making excuses. "I am tasked 'til the end of the day, every day! Honestly, where does the time go!"

Ruby watched them ride away, wondering if she should have invited them on the picnic. Perhaps then she could have better explained the purpose of the women's convention. She owed both sides at least that much. Preacher Paul meant well and was sincere and she wasn't angry with him, not really. But she also believed the Ladies of the Lost Legion were not sinners. She felt torn between. Deep down her allegiance remained with her newfound friends and their cause, yet her heart questioned the Biblical sense of it all. She would study the Bible, she decided. All in all, she wanted to do what was right. Ah, but what did it matter, her mind asked her? You can put your hand in the bucket and splash it around, but when you take your hand out, the bucket looks the same.

Besides, Robert would have been furious if he overheard any such discussion about the women's convention, and at the very least, would have frowned on all her family and children visiting their home. *Too much noise, everyone talks at once*, the-only-child-in-his-family often grumbled.

Victor and Jonathan tugged on her arms.

"Picnic, picnic! Fish lots, eat quick!" Victor chanted.

"Let's go, let's go" Jonathan joined in. "I'm huuungry!"

Bess joined them and leaned her head against Ruby's arm. "Mama, Papa told me to tell you that we are to go on home," she said sadly. "He will be home in a little while."

Ruby looked inside the doorway to the church but it was so much darker than out in the bright sun. She couldn't see much. Must still be fighting demons, she thought, her sarcasm winning over her Christian tolerance.

"Sh-sh boys" she said to the boys' repeated desires to fish. She was disappointed, too. If she had spoken to Robert herself, she would have asked for some coins to buy ice cream, to temper their disappointment. How could he be so thoughtless?

"How about a picnic in our very own backyard?" She attempted to sound excited.

They were not to be fooled. "Mama, Papa *promised*!" Her children's down-in-the-mouth was turning her frustration to Robert.

She sighed loudly. "Well, he must have a good reason for it. We'll have to make the best of it, is all."

"But we can't fish in our backyard, Mama!" Jonathan advised.

"Ah, no kidding, dummy!" Victor chided, and shoved his brother.

She recognized the signs of them taking their disappointment out on each other. She placed her hands on their shoulders. "Enough, Victor. How about an ice cream on the way home?"

"Yay, yay, the ice cream parlor, the ice cream parlor!"

She left them outside talking about the flavors they would choose, while she walked back into the church and approached the platform. The men ceased talking and eyed her suspiciously. They obviously did not approve of her intrusion.

"Forgive me, gentlemen. Robert, may I speak with you a moment?" His puffed stance told her he felt quite important in participating in these men's discussion. He nodded solemnly and stepped down from the platform and escorted her by elbow to the back of the church.

"I told Bess to tell you to go home. What is it?" he whispered, sounding irritated. He squeezed her elbow hard.

"The children are so disappointed, Robert, I thought I would buy them an ice cream treat on the way home."

"Disappointed about what?" His eyes darted to the front, looking afraid he was going to miss something up there.

"The picnic, Robert! Remember?"

He turned and took a moment to focus on her and what she was saying. His eyes squinted in exasperation. "You are interrupting an important discussion for *that*? Must I deal with such trivial matters?" He leaned to her and whispered. "Ruby, do not be so childish. Now go home as you were told. Dinner at three o'clock." He squeezed her elbow harder and turned away.

She walked back out into the sunshine and to her children's upturned faces waiting in anticipation. Waiting for her good news, depending on her to bring them joy in their day. She felt empty and yes his word, trivial; so little to offer them. She smiled her best false smile.

"Anyone for home-made maple syrup pie?"

* * * * *

Out in her backyard, contending with the wind amid the bread, sliced ham and pie, she watched her children play.

They are so forgiving. They accept life as I give it to them and question little. To have the faith and trust of a child again! No wonder Jesus said, 'come to me as little children'.

But I am not a child, and I question a great deal, her mind argued.

She couldn't help herself from repeatedly glancing over to Aimee's back door hoping to see her. When Aimee finally appeared, her tall frame crowned with long blonde braids walking toward the fence, Ruby felt she was witnessing an angel. Her loneliness was keen for a kindred spirit. She had been around no one who understood, for what seemed like ages. She almost ran to the fence.

"Aimee it is so good to see you! I cannot begin to tell you!"

Aimee reached down and picked up her little boy who had followed her outside. Her long, blonde braid fell forward, and she moved it to her back and positioned her child on her hip in one smooth motion. She smiled at Ruby. "You seem in better spirits than last time we spoke. How are you?"

"I do apologize, Aimee. I have done some thinking since then. Please forgive me."

Aimee waved off the apology. "No need to apologize. I understand more than you may realize." They looked at each other knowingly. Bess and the boys shyly approached the fence.

"I would love to join you for afternoon tea, Aimee." She winked and glanced down at the little ears surrounding her. "Next Wednesday? Is it possible then?"

Aimee raised her eyebrows in surprise. She smiled broadly now, a beautiful smile to Ruby. "Next Wednesday is perfect! Phyllis is hosting the tea and she is quite a character!"

The wooden fence was no longer a barrier then, but a meeting place and they easily chatted about their children and spring gardening, until Robert's return from his church meeting. Ruby returned to her family, light and refreshed. The wind was no longer a hindrance to her picnic, but a breath of fresh air. Breathe in deeply, she told the children. Let's play Ring around the Rosy, now let's play Duck, Duck, Goose. Life was sunny. She had a friend again. She had a purpose again. A means to somehow gain some control in her life. Suddenly it was all so clear to her. A seed had been planted and she would allow it to grow in fertile ground, an open heart, for nothing would grow in a heart of stone. Somehow she would make it all work. Somehow.

PART II
Summer's Rapid Growth

Aimee offered her buggy as means to travel the several miles' distance to Phyllis' home on the other side of town. This was a blessing, for to walk there would require leaving earlier, which would not have been possible. There was hardly enough time to prepare as it was, what with this being baking day. Ruby rose earlier, at the hour of four, to give herself more time, but time ran out at any rate, as did her flour supply, so she reduced her loaves to four.

Ruby could only remember Phyllis having white hair and chipped nails, and a strong handshake at Cady's tea. Any uneasiness about going to a strange home was immediately dispelled when finally Ruby and Aimee arrived at the home of their hostess. This quaint little white-sided cottage had two second-story dormer windows which stuck out noticeably because the first level was almost hidden by the bright varieties of shrubs, flowers, and climbing ivy. A birdbath, birdhouse, and small statues of dwarfs and fairies competed for space amongst the flower garden covering the small front lawn. Aimee's delighted laughter blended with the birds chirping their arrival and the tinkling hello from the wind chimes hanging over the landing. Bells hanging from the Welcome sign jingled as the door opened.

Phyllis shook hands firmly with rough, callused palms, reminding Ruby of Jesse's hands. Two walls of her tiny living room were covered in quilts, with complicated patterns Ruby didn't recognize. She herself had only attempted the logcabin pattern. The makings of yet another quilt was on a large spool against a wall and

Phyllis explained she was in two quilting bees.

"Where do you find the time?" Ruby asked.

"I married my children off early!" Phyllis answered, her hearty laughter bouncing her white bun and un-corsetted belly. She clicked off her brown fingers, "My first two boys were married at sixteen, next went my two daughters at fifteen, my youngest son at seventeen, and my youngest daughter at seventeen. And *she* was afraid for a year that she would die an old spinster!"

She continued talking as she walked into her kitchen and returned with a plate of tiny iced cakes that she passed around to the little group now sitting. "There is of course my Andy, may he rest in peace, who died when he was six of pneumonia. So, you see, little feet no longer trample my garden, and for a time, I only had my husband's big feet to look after, bless his heart, until he passed on last winter. For the first time in my life I'm free to do what *I* wish to do and no one can bid me do otherwise unless I choose to. I've nothing to lose. So I garden to my heart's content, keep my idle hands busy quilting, and march these legs beside my dearest friend, Cady, in her quest for all women's freedom. How are we doing so far, Cady dear?"

Cady smiled in appreciation for the lead-in to her agenda. Ruby understood that Cady did not like idle chatter, especially in light of their limited time together, but moving to the purpose of the meeting was not easily managed when the ladies first congregate.

"Don't sell yourself short, Phyllis," Cady said. "You are an excellent midwife. The best there is. You have saved many lives, I'm sure." Cady addressed the group. "Phyllis is a midwife but her dream was to become a doctor. Phyllis, you have given me a wonderful idea. I wish for each of us to briefly describe why we are here. A testimony, if you will. Phyllis, would you please begin by continuing your story?"

Phyllis perched on a footstool and rolled her eyes around to the group. "Oh my, I guess I got us into trouble, girls, sorry. Me and my big mouth!" She laughed and then thought a moment. "Well, let's see. My first memory of wanting to become a doctor was hearing my first heart beat. My uncle was a doctor and he let me hear his heart through his stethoscope. I can still recall how fascinated I was – hearing an organ in someone's body! Something you couldn't see or touch or smell, but you could hear it and knew the heart was right there!" She put her hand over her heart.

"The questions I would ask! My uncle finally shooed me out of his office after several visits, saying he was too busy – but not before I *borrowed* one of his medical books that I still read to this day. I was foolish as always and told him he was only afraid of losing patience with me. Do you get it? Losing patients? Haha!" Phyllis clapped her hands together and cackled.

She shook her head and her face settled in thought again. "Well, he smiled but would not address any more of my silly notions of becoming a doctor. He said I would grow out of it but I never did. So I began looking into medical schools and found that there was one Female Medical College, in Pennsylvania. I asked my uncle for assistance. He spoke with my father but not in support of my education. He, instead, read to him and then to me, an excerpt from a book called 'Sex and Education', by Dr. Edward Clark. I'll never forget the book. Dr. Clark wrote that a girl could learn, but not without uninjured health, and could suffer from uterine disease, hysteria, and other diseases.

"My uncle had a tremendous influence in my family and told my father I must be married soon, before I thought of any more foolish things to do. He said next thing they would hear, would be me joining the petticoat rebellion of women wanting to vote. He was wiser than I gave him credit for at the time! My father, ever conscious of criticisms, introduced me to a long time friend of his, whose wife had died and left behind eight children. He told me I would be Frank's new wife and added that I was fortunate in that Frank had agreed to do so; otherwise, with such manly ideas, I could end up an old maid, or worse, a bookworm – a dire threat to any chance of ever attracting a husband. I was fifteen and Frank was more than forty, so his children were already half-grown, half of them older than me! They were not going to listen to a child-mother, and oh the struggles I had! But...well, the

Good Woman

short story is, his children were about all gone in the first six years of our marriage for one reason or another, and in the meantime, I had seven more.

"But as Providence would have it, having children was a mixed blessing because I had a wonderful midwife during my pregnancies and I learned so much from her! She was a wise old woman who had a healing touch and gut instincts that were more successful than any educated man I knew. Her eyes looked right through you to what ailed you, *without* a stethoscope. She taught me all she knew about midwifery and then because I still wanted to go to medical school, she suggested that I ask for assistance from the Civic Hospital.

"The doctors there knew and respected my work as a midwife. But the hospital told me that medical school would do me very little good because the American Medical Association barred women from membership, so I would not be recognized as a certified doctor at any rate. So I asked if I could start off in nursing there at the hospital and move up. The hospital board advised me that women nurses there were rare to none. They hired primarily men because the hospital board believed it was not proper for ladies to feed and bathe men - and in men's beds no doubt! A lady seeing a man's nakedness would only add discomfort to an already sick man and could hamper wellness. Now think about that! An art that for centuries was considered a woman's domain was now considered for men only!"

Phyllis paused, thinking for a moment. "It seems that the more education is required for medicine, the less need there is for healing." She scraped at her cuticles, saying no more.

The room became quiet.

"Let us take a break," Cady said, "and while Phyllis serves the tea, I shall read the Minutes from last week."

Ruby's mind raced for the right words to say in her own testimony. What would she say? Why was she here? She wasn't quite sure. Her reasons were not as justified as those of Phyllis and would only sound shallow. She was here because she needed friends, an outlet, a brief reprieve?

"—and it was unanimously agreed we would march in the Fourth of July parade, carrying banners and signs, announcing our July eighteenth convention—"

"Pardon?" Ruby blurted out. "Did you say, *march*? My goodness, in public?" Her eyes darted around to everyone. "I'm sorry to interrupt. I wasn't here last week. Forgive me. A march? Everyone will know then, won't they? I suppose that is the perfect opportunity. A freedom march right along with the Declaration of Independence. But my husband, you see, he will know then, and my children. Shouldn't they come first? And my husband forbids me...well, he thinks...well, this is why I stopped attending! My participation seemed to be creating more problems than resolving any. But once I knew of your group, I couldn't stop – there is so much to learn and be done! I suppose that my decision to join is like - like cleaning your stove, isn't it? Once you get started cleaning, you get dirtier and dirtier, and you wonder why you didn't leave well enough alone. A stove is black anyway; who would know it was dirty? Only you do, and that is enough and so you start cleaning and finally you work through the grease and the grime, until your arms feel as if they will fall off with the effort and the time. Finally you stand back, and you say, yes, the stove does shine! It will work much more efficiently now! And you feel better for your efforts, and you know deep down you've done a good day's work, the best you know how!"

"Thank you for your testimony, Ruby! I like that metaphor," Cady said.

"Is that what that was?" Ruby asked.

They all laughed around her and Aimee patted her shoulder.

Ruby felt flushed for rambling on so. "Well, I do apologize for disappearing awhile. My family—" her voice trailed off.

"Ruby, my dear," Cady spoke up quickly, "I am sure I speak for the others when I say we do not sit in judgment of you. On the contrary, we completely understand. Your first priority is to your home and family. You are first a wife and mother and nothing should interfere with that. That is what we all hold dear and what brings a lady out into the streets, calling to arms.

Good Woman

There is no creature fiercer than a mother protecting her cubs. If it were not to defend her rights to her home and children, what would give her the reason? None other can provoke a woman to fight! This primal instinct is deeply cored within us. Why, the reason that brought us together in the first place was this very thing! A wrongful decision that adversely affected one of our dear members and her children. This member's child was a student of mine, so I saw first-hand the child's withdrawal and despondency. And then, her rebellion and lack of emotion. And what this separation did to her mother—"

"You may say who it is, Cady." Sarah spoke softly. "Let this be my testimony."

This took Ruby back in surprise. To her, Sarah was the studious spinster, one void of emotion. Instead, she looked like she might cry any moment. She turned to Ruby.

"It happened rather quickly, really." Her voice trembled as she continued. "My husband of eleven years told me one day last year he wanted a divorce. I was shocked, hurt, frightened. I knew no other life. I asked to remain in our home to raise our children, ages ten and six. He said I was no longer required to do so, because he had made other arrangements. *Other* arrangements, I asked? He answered that he had a housekeeper moving in who would look after the children. I informed him I was not leaving without my children. He showed me how wrong I was. That same evening, a lady appears on my doorstep. Young, well put-together, she introduced herself as the new housekeeper. While she takes the children upstairs to their nursery, my husband enters our bedroom. He threw a few things into my dress case, set the case outside. He takes my cloak and wraps it around my shoulders. I watch all this, shocked beyond belief. He says to me ever so calmly, 'You will now leave quietly, so as not to disturb the children. You will walk to your mother's home. She is expecting you.' He turns my shoulders to the door, opens the door and nudges me outside. I hear the door close behind me.

"The next morning I walked to the sheriff's office and explained what my husband had done. I was in tears and could barely speak. I clutched the arm of the deputy and begged him to help me. I obviously was a nuisance to him because he brushed me off and said any divorce was for the courts to decide. He asked if I had been beaten, and I said, no, then he stated there was nothing he could do. This was a domestic problem. I asked if I could go back home, and he shook his head and said, no, not without my husband's consent. What about my children, I cried to him. He would not tolerate my outcries in a public place, he said. He nudged me out the door, same as my husband had done the night before.

"I walked around town in a daze, for hours that day. I walked by my home several times looking for life, for I felt dead, but saw no one. My life, as I knew it, had ended. I craved for the arms of my children, as a drunk would crave for his wine. I was inconsolable for weeks. My mother tolerated me in silence. Somehow she blamed me. Then one day she said that if I had been doing everything for my husband, then he would not have seen the need to replace me. My God, how could she have said that? I was his slave!"

Cady placed her arm around Sarah's trembling shoulders and continued the story for her.

"The court ruled that the home and children would remain with the husband as his sole property. The court also ruled that a divorce would be granted because the wife was the one who departed the marital home, and left behind her children. It was all obviously well planned but Sarah has no recourse. The law does not protect her. She came to me during class one day soon afterwards, and asked if I would permit her to see her daughter after class. She told me the story then. I have since arranged visitation twice a week at school during lunch hour with her children. Otherwise she is not permitted to see them, because the judge decided home visitations would be too disruptive for the children.

"Many of us are not aware of the law until we are affected by it. Its realization can be quite frightening, particularly to a woman. I have been affected by it as well. I have my own story to tell, my own cross to bear. My cross is not nearly as heavy as some others, nonetheless, I shall tell you mine.

"I have loved going to school since I was a little girl. I remember sitting in that one room schoolhouse for so many years, trying to listen to not only what I was being taught, but also what other grades were learning. I cherished books, down to their very scent and feel of the leather coverings and pages. I was in awe of the classroom and of the knowledge held inside its room and inside my teachers. Naturally my dream was to become one. I wished to share the knowledge my teachers gave to me, with others. As I neared grade ten, I decided I would go on to a university. I wasn't yet ready to leave the classroom as a student; I had so much more to learn! I wished to teach at a higher level, perhaps high school, or even college. How naive I was! I wish I had a penny for every time I heard someone say that it was impossible for a woman to be thoroughly educated without loss of womanliness. If not for my dear father, who was also a schoolteacher, I would not have graduated from high school. He wrote several letters and appealed before the board of education to allow my continued education. He won because he believed in me, and he taught me a valuable lesson in that I, too, must carry on and take a stand for what I believe in.

"It wasn't long before I had to stand on my own. The local college set up their own difficulties, stating they had already met their quota of three per cent women, and had no space for me. By then, my father was terminally ill and I wished not to disturb his last days in doing battle for me. Just as he had before, I wrote my own letters and made my own appeal, and was finally granted sufficient courses to earn a teacher's certificate. And not in 'Domestic Science', as was recommended for all women to make them better wives and mothers. The courses I completed were academic in nature and I was the only woman attending such classes. Fellow male classmates, for the slightest naive question I might ask, constantly ridiculed me. Ah, but they did not know that I carried my mother's stubborn stock. It was a most happy day when I received my certificate!

"Unfortunately my education did not carry me to where I

wanted to go. I soon found I was only allowed opportunities to teach young children. One school principal advised me that women's nurturing ways were only suitable for children, and that higher learning can only be taught by men. Men's minds, he said, had evolved further than women's minds, and could better grasp lofty ideas. I must be patient, I was told, for evolution of this nature took hundreds of years! Imagine!" Cady shook her head, as if still not hearing it correctly and sat back quietly contemplating this.

After a few moments silence, Lizzie patted Cady's knee and spoke. "Well, now, my testimony is short and sweet. I don't talk much about my past - it becomes too real, too dark. I'll just say this: I was born into slavery in Virginia. When my papa found out that our master was selling him to another plantation, he ran off and escaped on the Underground Railroad up here. Mama told me after the war that he had gone to a station here in the town of Cicero, to the home of Matilda Joslyn Gage. Mama said Mrs. Gage was a brave woman with four children of her own who signed a petition saying she would face a six month prison term and a $2000 fine rather than obey the Fugitive Slave law. This law made criminals of anyone assisting slaves to freedom. I wanted to go there, too, but Mama said Papa was supposed to come back for us...but I never saw him again.

"My mama and I had no where else to go, so we stayed on the plantation long after the war set us free; free from cleaning for the white folk for free, but only free enough to earn small wages cleaning for the white folk. You see, that was about the only difference, because schooling was not provided for colored women. And without learning you find yourself right back where you started.

"I just want to say, I thank the Lord for Cady taking me in the way she did. She taught me to read and to write, and showed me how to stand up for myself, or else I'd never know how. That is why I am here today."

The room became quiet once again.

Only Aimee had not spoken now. Ruby noticed Aimee

tugging her blouse sleeve down to cover the bruised wrist and folded her hand over top of the bruised hand.
"I am happy to be here," was all Aimee would say.

* * * * *

It was Thursday sewing day. The basket of garments waiting for mending was ignored this day. Instead Ruby was making a white blouse. Ruby needed a uniform. White blouse, black skirt. Cady said that white represented the woman's non-violent and nurturing soul and all white women shackled in slavery. Black stood for all Negro women shackled in slavery, and black also stood for all women's oppression for hundreds of years. Cady said they represented opposition to oppression without aggression. Ruby decided if she was going to march with the Ladies of the Lost Legion in the Fourth of July parade, heavens be, she was going to look like one!

She tediously cut out the stitches of three white pillowcases, and using a shirt pattern, sewed together a respectable blouse. Plain, yes. No lace, no puffed sleeves. A bit baggy, perhaps. Small bone buttons from an old shirt of Robert's – or so it was old now that she needed the buttons! She smiled at her thriftiness. She was being clever too! No suspicions were raised by asking Robert for money. He probably would not notice the blouse, once she had it on.

Only the morning was available to sew it. Today, she had agreed to gather signatures on a petition for public support. Cady and Phyllis had come up with what they called a mission statement, written in Sarah's pretty and precise penmanship. Ruby loved its simple message. She read it again as she headed down her boardwalk toward Aimee's house, now donning her uniform. The petition read:

We aim to build a path that will allow women personal, educational, and professional growth. A path to allow a say in her children's development. To allow a say in her community's development. To be heard. To be given a voice. To be given the Vote!

The Ladies of the Lost Legion ask for your support. Your signature will not only support this group of women, but all women from all walks of life. Your signature will support our Seven Reasons Why We Fight For Our Rights:
1. We have no right to the law giving freedom to all.
2. We have no right to vote for others who rule over all.
3. We have no right to our land we work for all.
4. We have no right to our property but we pay tax for all.
5. We have no right to our bodies, which gives life to all.
6. We have no right to our children, the next generation for all.
7. We have no right equal to our husband, who has power over all.
Will you help?

"How can anyone say no?" she asked Aimee as they headed downtown.

Ruby and Aimee had agreed not to petition those living on their own street. Word may get to their husbands quickly. Best to canvas homes some blocks away. They avoided Main Street and one of its occupants, Robert's Walk Wright shoe shop. They avoided First Street's National Bank and one of its bank tellers, Aimee's husband. They walked first to Cady's street, feeling somehow sheltered there, as if Cady's spirit would be amongst all who lived close by. They had consciously decided that petitioning during the day was best. Not only because their time away from home was limited to the afternoons, but that husbands would be away, therefore other wives may be more likely to talk freely.

"Ruby, we are in public!" Aimee cried, slapping Ruby's hand gently. They were approaching Cady's street.

"I don't care. This corset is killing me, I do declare! They're restricting enough when in good shape, but my seams are wearing apart, and an inlaid bone is sticking into my inlaid rib! I think the two are becoming one."

"Really, Ruby! Some things you say! Must we discuss such things in public?" Aimee exclaimed, her hand over her mouth.

Ruby pulled again at her side with pinched lips. "I am sorry, Aimee but perhaps we women should speak more openly about such things. Isn't that the beauty of our little group? Really now,

Aimee, these corsets are so tightly laced and so rigidly constructed, only to pull in our stomachs and push up our breasts. Whatever for? I wear these feeling as if I'm being punished for something. Don't you find these blessed bindings an imprisonment?"

Aimee lowered her voice as if telling a secret. "Well, I heard once of a lady whose liver was punctured by her stays. But I have to admit that on some days these blessed bindings, as you call them, are the only thing that holds me up. So, they are blessed. Otherwise, I would fall straight to the floor, in a heap. Looking somewhat like the laundry I have left behind me this sunny day! As an added bonus, I lace mine snugly enough to allow wearing dresses that I made before the children came along." She displayed her hands on each side of her waist. "Why, I can squeeze down to a twenty-eight inch waist. I can't breathe, I see spots, and I feel faint. Pretty much disintegrates my five senses, but I look fine!"

"Well," Ruby said, with a chuckle, "you at least have your *sense* of humor! Get it? Sense? Ha-ha, I sound like Phyllis!"

They laughed merrily down the street.

Ruby was having the time of her life. Each meeting with the Ladies brought her more understanding of what was happening around her, in what she knew now was called her community. She was amazed at how different other women's lives were, some she could not imagine. How different they were and yet somehow the same.

They all believed in three basic principles: the institution of marriage, protection of the children, and a firm belief in God. They simply wanted to be able to stand up for these beliefs and be counted. As Lizzie stated more than once, "Ain't we people, too?"

More surprisingly, Ruby learned she was not alone in her frustrations as a wife and mother. She had looked inward before knowing these ladies, only to find her thoughts sometimes dark and aimless. The group brought light into her mind and a purpose to go outward. Each woman had been brought to this meeting place through calamities of her own, where her rights as a woman had somehow been violated.

There was an openness among these women that intricately wove a connection in and around them that was as delicate as lace; durable and colorful as needlepoint. Each life, each story, brought a different color, another scene to the mosaic.

Ruby suspected that Aimee was taking physical risks in attending the meetings and that other members were dealing with family criticism. But this was not discussed - time did not allow their gatherings to become a pity party. Knowing though that they were all in this together made Ruby appreciate all the more, the time she spent with Aimee and the others. Their afternoons together were hard earned which enhanced every meeting into a joyful experience.

This was their first time to go door-to-door gathering signatures for their petition. Ruby could not have done it alone. Walking up the brick walk to their first house suddenly became terrifying – to the point that she linked her arm through Aimee's for support. Her mind went blank and could only focus on the grass growing in between the bricks, rather than to what she would say when someone opened her door.

Please dear Lord let it be a 'her', she prayed.

Her prayer was answered. Through her own heartbeat banging in her ears, she heard Aimee say, "We are representing a group of women who believe women should have equal rights with men. We are asking for the right to vote—". The door slammed shut.

They avoided each other's eyes as they carefully stepped back down the steps. Ruby glanced briefly at Aimee's blushing cheeks and gathered some strength to address the next house. Her eyes focused on the high grass and chrysanthemums as her mind plotted what to say. She resolved to say something that women could immediately relate to and understand.

The door opened to another 'her'.

Ruby took a deep breath and spoke. "We represent a group of women who wish to see law changed, whereby we, as women, do not have rights to our children and to our homes. Would you please read our mission statement?" She handed their petition to the lady of the house, the paper shaking noticeably.

The lady glanced at this and handed it back. "I cannot read this. Would you please read it to me?" Children were collecting around her. She placed her hands on little heads peeking from her skirt, but was seemingly unaware of them as she continued to stare curiously at her visitors.

"Of course!" Ruby answered. She noted to herself that, in the future, she would ask if she could read out loud the mission statement, to avoid any embarrassment. She read the statement slowly, speaking her words distinctly. When she finished, she looked up at the woman at the door and waited.

The woman seemed to be in deep thought. Finally she said, "Hmmm, to be allowed a say in my children's development. I see. I have seven children and another one on the way." Her ample frame did not reveal a pregnancy to Ruby, but ... after seven ...

She invited them in. Ruby and Aimee had not predicted inside visits that would eat into their short afternoon but they wished not to be rude. They followed the waddled step of their hostess into a cluttered front room, consisting of a mixture of parlor chairs, kitchen chairs, scratched tables, and a small bed draped with a large fabric, pillows against its back wall as if trying to disguise it as a sofa. She asked them to take a seat and then breathlessly reentered a few minutes later with two tin cups of coffee for her guests.

She sat down heavily into the rocker and leveled an expectant gaze on them. "What can you do for me?" she asked bluntly. She reached down and picked up one child and put him on her lap. It seemed to pull the other children back around her as if all were attached on a string.

Aimee had regained her composure and spoke first. "Well, Mrs...?"

"Mrs. Henry Watkins," she answered, rocking slowly and still staring.

"Mrs. Watkins, we are asking for women's signatures on this petition because we believe that women do not have the same rights as men." Aimee counted off her gloved fingers. "We do not have the right to vote, we do not have the right to our children—"

"Pardon me, madam? What do you mean, we do not have a right to our children? Do you not see them here and around me? Do you not see one on my lap, two at my feet, three at my arm? Are you saying someone would take them away? Who would dare do such a thing?"

Ruby decided to be as blunt. "The law states that if your husband decided to divorce you, he could choose to take his children with him. Or, worse yet, take this home as his own, and you would be required to leave – without your children. One such lady in our group has experienced this personally. We are simply asking that women's rights be equal to men, particularly when it comes to our children. That the law be changed to give us that right. We should not be so vulnerable!"

"I suppose...though I have never worried about such a thing with my husband." Her pudgy face crinkled with a chuckle, the first sign of color coming into her face. "Can you imagine my husband taking on such a brood by himself? They would all simply sit here and go hungry!"

Her expansive frame moved up and back down in a heavy sigh. She moved back wisps of faded sandy-colored hair from a frazzled bun.

"Would you believe I am only twenty-three? I feel much older. My husband is Catholic and large families are expected. I have had a baby a year since I was married at sixteen. I do not have the luxury of concerning myself with problems outside these rooms. I wish to help other women, though, truly. I have seen others trial through some terrible times...how do I sign this petition. Remember, I cannot read nor write."

"I will write your name on the line and then you can put an 'X' beside it. Yes?" Ruby asked.

"Perfect!" Mrs. Watkins exclaimed.

"What is your first name?" Ruby asked.

"*My* first name?" Mrs. Watkins seemed incredulous to this question. "Why, my first name is Suzanne!"

"Suzanne Watkins" Ruby said out loud as she wrote the name.

"There! You are entered as our first signature!"

Thereafter, with each home's door they approached, their introductions were improved and they became more confident. If women were curious enough to ask questions, they would conclude the discussion with signing the petition. The difference in their stature in saying yes or no was as different as day and night. Those who signed, did so eagerly and two asked to join their group the following Wednesday. Admiration and compliments. Other women looked on them as evil and frightening. Fear and name-calling. Ruby and Aimee tried to shake these names off as they walked quickly away, but some of the insults hung onto their shawls as cold water would cling to wool. Was it a fear of change, they asked one another. Even if a woman chose not to vote, why would she wish to take this right from other women? Some doors were slammed in their faces. Others were opened only slightly, only to have the wives shake their heads sadly. Ruby and Aimee were called angels, they were called devils. They tried to decipher what they were saying to cause the difference, but could not. Their petition and its mission statement were the same for everyone.

By the end of the afternoon, they had only fifteen signatures. They returned to their respective homes realizing their steep uphill climb, with questioning minds.

* * * * *

It was the day of the parade, July Fourth, 1900. Town businesses and shops were closed for the holiday. Robert was home. He was not interested in parades. Ruby would need an escape route. She and Aimee hatched a plan. Each told their respective husbands that they were asked to bring food downtown to the park, and prepare picnic lunches for the needy.

Early departure was necessary, before the boys arose. Or else their unrelenting requests to go with her would only raise suspicion.

She was so nervous; she had barely slept at all and was up before the crack of dawn. She tiptoed around the bedroom, washing and dressing as quietly as the old wooden planked floor would allow.

School was out for the summer so she woke up Bess to help with baking and breakfast. Only Bess habitually woke up slower than the boys, sitting up rubbing her eyes, her long brown hair fuzzy around her head.

"Come on, sweetie, rise and shine! Mama is in a hurry!"

"Why?" Bess asked, still sitting, still rubbing.

"I have to go on an outing today, downtown." Ruby answered as she grabbed Bess's housedress from its hook on the wall. She threw it over Bess's head. She hunted around the room for stockings and found some on the floor. She quickly rolled these up Bess's legs to above her knees.

"Come on Bess! Stand up now so I can brush your hair. You are moving slower than a snail!"

"Sorry, Mama. If I help really good, can I go with you?" Bess stood up and smoothed down the brown calico dress, falling to below her knees. Ruby tied the waist at the back.

"Not today, sweetie. Mama needs you at home to fix breakfast and look after our men." She relied on Bess a great deal here lately and felt guilty about it. She consoled her conscience by rationalizing that she was working for Bess's future.

Ruby took a hair comb from her own hair and began combing Bess's hair. Tangles were inevitable in this thick brown mass, but Ruby didn't want to go back into her bedroom for the good brush and possibly disturb Robert.

"But I will tell you, Bess, that when you get a little older, I want you to come with me. It is important that you someday get involved in – in helping other women."

"Help other women do what, Mama? Cook?"

Ruby laughed, shaking her head. Naturally Bess would think that. Most of Ruby's waking hours was spent in the kitchen. "It does appear as if that is all we do, doesn't it? Not that there is anything wrong with that, mind you. Women keep their families alive and happy with good food. But there are a few women out there doing a great deal more. Someday, you'll see."

Together, they baked cornbread and a strawberry pie for the family, and a strawberry pie to take with her. The bowls and pans were piled high in the wash pan. Ruby had no time for clean-up. As she was taking off her apron and exiting the kitchen, she turned to see Bess dragging a small wooden bench over to the wash pan. An old cricket bench Ruby had made when she was a young girl. She watched Bess step up onto the bench and then look down at the work before her. She sighed, removing wisps of hair from her face with the back of her hand. She looked like a miniature woman doing that, and Ruby wondered how often Bess must have seen Ruby doing just that same thing.

The mantel clock chimed seven times as she hurried to her entrance way and slipped her shawl around her.

"Mama, where are you going?"

Ruby closed her eyes for a second before turning around. She looked up to the top landing of the stairs to see her youngest son. Jonathan was rubbing his eyes with one hand, and scratching the front of his shorts with the other. His knobby knees gave him a pitiful look that squeezed her heart a bit. She placed her finger to her lips. "Sh-sh, you will wake your brother. Go back to bed."

"May I go with you?"

"No, I am going to prepare food and will be very busy. Please go back to bed!"

To prevent further dialogue, she blew a kiss and walked out the door quickly. Aimee was waiting out on the boardwalk looking as jittery as Ruby. A clearly defined red handprint was on her cheek. She smiled and said nothing, so Ruby did the same.

They walked at a clipped steady pace the two miles downtown. The exercise released some of the tension of the morning. They walked through small clouds of fog, giving everything a dreamlike appearance.

The group was meeting at City Hall Park, under a cluster of gnarled oak trees. Cady and Lizzie were already there with supplies of large white cardboard and black paint. Ruby and Aimee immediately went to work preparing their signs. They were all subdued and kept busy with the task at hand. The parade was a big moment for all of them and they had done much preparation for it. Ladies of the Lost Legion were finally coming out into open scrutiny. Repercussions were inevitable. They prayed fervently that the reaction would be positive.

Ruby printed large black letters, trying to keep her jittery nerves from wiggling the letters. The sign finally read:
Equality for Women
    Rights for All
    Change the Law!
    Others printed signs that read:
    Give us a voice –
    Give us the vote!
    and
    Come hear 7 reasons to fight
    for Women's Rights!
At the bottom of all the signs was advertised: 'Women's Rights Convention, July 18th, 1900, City Hall Park'.

City Hall Park was a last-minute change to their plan. Cady announced at their last meeting that the Parkdale High School auditorium was no longer available. Mr. Whiting, the principal, apologized with a vague explanation that the auditorium had already been booked, before his commitment to the convention. Cady believed there was more than he was telling, behind the cancellation. There were rumblings among the school staff that the school should not be associated with a controversial political agenda. Parents opposed to the convention may believe that its influence would seep into the children's education, and would not present the proper ethics of a learning institution. Cady heard through the educated grapevine that there were supposed threats of children being pulled out of the school, if the Women's Right's Convention was held there. She did not wish to create a dilemma for her colleagues, or be at fault for hampering the children's education. Thus, to prevent further conflict, Cady moved the location of the convention to the park grounds outside City Hall.

The large white gazebo centered in the park was used as a stage for public outcry every Friday and Saturday night, from various male citizens who wanted to be heard when injustice rained on them. People out for an evening stroll would gather around the gazebo to listen, some to learn of current issues, some to be entertained, some shaking their fists, some shaking their heads, some wandering off with disinterest. Orators protested the fall of corn prices, property taxes, job loss from the local paper mill, or a gripe about a neighbor's wildstock. Anyone was allowed to speak, as long as he waited his turn with respect to the speaker before him. When he finished, he handed the megaphone over to the next, and exited the platform. Only one speaker at a time was permitted on the stage. A mounted sheriff's deputy was usually close by in case the complaint erupted into a fist-fight. Freedom of speech also permitted those "not quite right in the head" to ramble about their own views, whether that be sightings in the sky, or the government being seized by some foreign entity.

Never had the ladies witnessed nor heard of a woman walking into the gazebo to speak. It was normally considered loud male buffoonery. Cady realized that the Ladies' credibility would have been much stronger if supported by the school's institution. But they were left with little choice. On the bright side, Mr. Whiting pledged his continued support by promising to speak at the convention. He was an excellent orator and they drew encouragement from his pledge.

Cady paced around the women bent diligently over their signs, offering suggestions and encouragement. She finally tapped her hands together rapidly.

"May I have your attention, please! Ladies, please stand up and hold your signs in front of you…let me read them now…excellent! Now shoulders back, stand tall…yes! Now I want to see you smile! Beautiful! Remember as you walk two by two, stand proud of who you are and what you represent!"

Cady clasped her hands together at her chest and continued pacing in front of ladies whose signs were visibly shaking from trembling hands. "Do not worry about the crowds! Do not hang your heads! I believe our march will receive the attention we need. To be heard! To bring in more audience to our convention!

Remember why we march! As we gain support, we gain strength!" Cady pounded her hand with her fist. "Our government can no longer ignore us!"

Ruby suddenly felt she was going into battle. Panic seized her. She was thankful her shaking knees were hidden within her full skirts. The thought of her knees reminded her of Jonathan's knobby knees in the early morn, and she felt more remorse for lying to him. Please God, she prayed silently, tell me I am doing the right thing. Not only for my sake, but also for my children's sake.

The thought of her secure home holding its familiar tasks, was sounding mighty comforting at the moment.

Then the marching drum began its beating rhythm to sound the beginning of the parade.

"Ladies, formation please!" Cady called out loudly.

Their group consisted of ten women now and they were all here. All were in their uniforms of white shirts and black skirts. Two by two they formed a line. They stepped in rhythm to the drumbeats and marched into their assigned place behind the school band.

Behind their group was a wagon pulled by a team of four horses. The wagon was covered on the sides in chicken wire and many carnations of red, white, and dyed blue, were strategically placed in the holes of the wire to depict the United States flag. Four people were standing in the wagon, dressed to look like George and Martha Washington, and Abraham and Mary Lincoln, each one waving their own small flag. Ruby saw several clowns join in behind the wagon, some on bicycles, and another on a unicycle. The town sheriff and his ten deputies led the parade on horseback, each carrying a large American flag. The mayor and his wife in a buggy colorfully decorated in flowers and streamers followed them, their horse draped in an American flag.

The parade moved slowly away from City Hall while the band played *All Over This Land*. It was a rare treat for Ruby to hear music and she was thrilled and inspired by it.

The procession snaked right onto First Street where spectators were beginning to form.

Ruby looked from the corner of her eyes to each side to see the smiling waving onlookers. There she noticed some faces form into frowns, some were pointing their fingers at her group, two heads were shaking. She blushed crimson when she heard a woman from the sideline call out "Shame on you!" She heard "Men-haters!" from an angry man with a clenched fist aimed at them. She swallowed hard and focused on the straight narrow back of Cady, and the slight hunched back of Lizzie, leading the group. They held a six-foot long, three-foot high banner between them. Printed in large bold letters on white silk were the words:
Take the Shackles from Women!

They marched for several blocks and then slowly gyrated onto Main Street, the longest street in their little town of Annan. The sparse gathering of spectators had flowed into crowds. The band was now playing *The Star-Spangled Banner.* Flags were waving everywhere. The noise was getting louder. The drums seemed to be beating from within Ruby's chest. The ground was pulsating. Ruby hadn't prepared herself for all the many eyes and panic seized her again. She looked over at Aimee, walking at her side. She was appearing confident, smiling, returning waves. Three teenaged girls joined in beside Aimee, and began waving cheerfully to the crowds, their brightly colored ribbons and calf-length dresses adding rainbows to the little black and white group. She heard one shout clearly, "What is right for the goose, is right for the gander!" A few women on the sideline laughed and applauded. As if brought over by a breeze, their confident exuberance flowed over Ruby. Her fear dissolved to her feet. She kicked her feet up higher and higher, to kick off fear's burden.

The sounds were undulating between applause and booing. The response was amazing. Far more outcries and applause than the Ladies ever supposed while in the confines of their disciplined, peaceful parlor meetings. To be able to create such a stir made Ruby feel so strong! She moved her sign up and down, up and down, chanting, "Fight for women's rights! Fight for women's rights!" to the rhythm of the band's song, *America the Beautiful.* Aimee looked over at her, obviously surprised and delighted. She joined in the chant and raised her sign up higher. The three teenage girls yelled the chant too. Ruby could easily imagine Bess doing this in a few years. She could no longer feel the ground beneath her feet, so high was her energy.

They chanted down the street as the parade snailed past the bakery, the shoe shop, the shops of the dressmaker and the tailor, the flower shop. Booing no longer bothered Ruby. She only noted the smiles of their supporters. What fun it was to represent something so large that could evoke emotions from opposite ends of the spectrum! She felt elevated, protected in their righteous cocoon of black and white. And then the cocoon slipped away, and for a brief and beautiful moment, she had the sense of a butterfly, weightless, free to fly. For a brief and beautiful moment, nothing else mattered.

She looked over to the crowd on her right and saw Robert and her children. Her mouth froze in mid-chant. They had a clear view, a perfect shot. It was too late to hide behind her sign. Bess had her hands to her mouth in surprise and then was jumping, pointing, leaning to the boys, still in the housedress of early morning. All three children waved frantically, shouting, "There is Mama! Mama! Mama!"

Robert did not wave. He only stared at her hard and long. His eyes were large in surprise and then slowly became smaller until they were slits in his face. Ruby saw all this as she walked slowly by. She flapped her hands to them as broken wings. She pasted on a smile and nodded to them as if she always marched in the Fourth of July Parade.

Marching on down the street, she wondered how she could have been so stupid in thinking she could join a march such as this, without Robert knowing about it. Her feet became heavy and leaden. The band sounded like a blare of noise. She became terrified again, but not of many eyes, only of his.

She tried to focus on Aimee's eyes, eyes who were looking at her, her mouth saying, "Ruby, are you alright? You've grown so pale! I saw Robert, too!"

Ruby pasted on a smile and shrugged her shoulders, more to

brush off Robert's angry stare on her back, than to show indifference.

On down Main Street the parade continued. It now seemed to go on too long. The sun that was bright one moment ago, now felt hot and burned into her straw bonnet. Her face felt flushed, her heart was racing. Was she going to faint?

Ruby had not known before that so many emotions existed. She felt fear. Then she felt foolish. A lady waved timidly at her, and she felt comforted. She remembered her husband's stone face, a face two blocks behind her by now, and suddenly all men in the crowd had that hard look. Fear returned.

Aimee looked at her oddly again. "What did you just say? Did I hear you say, 'Fight for my life?'"

"Mercy!" Ruby muttered. She looked ahead saying nothing; Aimee's chant of "Fight for women's rights!" sounding too loud in her ears.

The band was playing, "Daisy, Daisy, give me your answer, do!" The shops and bank were behind them. Another block of homes slowly went by, fewer spectators on the sidelines.

Next was an empty field, followed by the steel fencing of the paper mill. Two newer members of the Ladies of the Lost Legion practically screamed the chant as they passed the mill's entrance gate. They both worked there and had informed the group of their twelve-hour days in the intense heat of the machinery. The scale of meager wages was entirely dependent on the whims of the owner and the level of tolerance to his groping hands. Ruby felt goose-pimples rise on her arms as she marched by, hearing the women's anger behind her, and seeing, before her, the dingy dark windows of the mill.

Main Street, at last, ended at St. Mark's Catholic Church. The parade slowly disbanded and streamed out onto the church's expansive grounds.

As she walked onto the grass, Ruby felt the sting of another blister on her foot. She was relieved the parade was over, yet dreaded the walk home. She had no regrets about participating and yet regretted that her family was there to see her. Was she being a hypocrite? Why had Robert brought them down town? Where are they now? She looked around but saw no sign of them. What was Robert thinking now? Oh Lord, please don't let him vent his anger onto the children. Or would he soothe all questions by perhaps treating them to an ice cream cone? Small chance he would think of that if she weren't there to ask.

She let her sign drop to the ground and dragged it behind her to the shade of a maple tree. She dropped herself onto the grass in exhaustion. Back and forth, up and down her emotions had run all the livelong day and she was quite literally spent.

Aimee sat down next to her and said nothing for a few moments. She finally patted Ruby's crossed leg.

"Do you want to walk home now?" Aimee asked. "I'll walk with you. I should be getting back too. Come, let's let Cady know we are leaving."

Ruby felt too numbed to answer.

Aimee sat quietly for a moment and then stood back up, determined to remain cheerful. She displayed a smile back down at Ruby and reached out her hand. "Come on, girl! I'll give you a lift!"

Ruby looked up at her friend, and slowly returned the smile, feeling sheepish. She waved Aimee's hand away and raised herself back onto her burning feet. "I am behaving like a child. If Robert had done this, I would have called it a pout!"

They laughed, brushing the back of their skirts off and looking around. Some of the other women in their party were preparing a picnic lunch from the dishes each woman brought that morning to City Hall. Thomas, Cady's husband, had kindly transported the dishes from the City Hall to the church. Ruby saw her strawberry pie prettily displayed on a white tablecloth surrounded by china saucers, utensils, and a vase of daisies. The cloth was on the ground but somehow looked elegant.

Some women just have the touch. The sight of the food brought some life back into Ruby and her stomach called out in a growl.

They found Cady amid a group of women and men. Thomas

had his arm around Cady's waist. He looked very cool and comfortable in his off-white linen suit. Envy swept over Ruby. To have this support from your husband! I am coveting your husband, she silently said to Cady.

They joined the group as a gentleman's voice was asking, "Thomas, do you agree with your wife? Does she have your permission for such a display of outlandish women's politics?"

Ruby looked closely at the gentleman. She didn't recognize him. He had puffy cheeks and a full beard that miniaturized his eyes. His mustache was waxed on the ends and curved upwards into handlebars. His rounded stomach was pulling hard at the buttons of his vest. His fat fingers held each side of his coat lapels. Ruby decided he was quite full of himself.

"Yes and no," Thomas answered. He laughed good-naturedly.

The questioning man remained serious and persisted. "Yes, you agree your wife should be off to the polls, playing politician? And no, meaning that she has disobeyed her husband? Isn't this a contradiction?" His tone was one baiting for an argument.

"Yes and no," Thomas answered, appearing unraveled by the provoking. "Yes, it is a contradiction, I suppose, because I see both sides. I see myself as somewhat to blame, since I am of the same gender that directs these hardships that my wife and her group speak out against. Yet I understand some reasoning behind our laws. I believe many of the laws were designed to protect our women - they have enough on their plates as it is. Yet those men who wish for more power have abused these same laws. Our government might benefit from women's higher moral standards. But men do not like to change, and so they resist. And no, she has not disobeyed me. Any married man knows that husbands and wives learn by discussion and argument. If I told her to be silent, truth between us would no longer exist. She has my unabashed respect for her beliefs. She has a sound mind and excellent control of her faculties. I'll not stand in her way."

He raised his index finger and tilted his head. "However, I do not stand too far away because there are those, I understand, sir, that vehemently oppose the ladies' sentiment in women's rights. Why this anger, I do not know." He looked down at the ground and shook his head. He did not look directly at the gentleman but the accusation was directed, nonetheless. He continued. "I am concerned for my wife's well-being, so I admit that I asked her not to partake in such an active role. This was the same as asking these birds in the trees not to fly. Or like asking you not to question. You both have the right, am I right?"

The gentleman was red-faced. The ladies were smiling and nodding. Cady looked at her husband gratefully. Ruby noticed for the first time, how tired and pale Cady looked. Dark, recessed circles had formed under her eyes. She noticed that Thomas's arm was holding her waist quite firmly, as if for physical support.

The gentleman cleared his throat and spoke loudly. "Sir, surely you are not upholding women's rights to vote! Most are unversed in political or financial affairs. Many are not even educated."

Thomas raised his head and confronted the gentleman as if accepting a challenge. "To say that a woman cannot vote because she is uneducated is a mute point. First of all, a voter does not make the rules but simply votes for those men who can, hoping that his own personal interests are regarded. Secondly, women are uneducated through no fault of their own but are oppressed by the very men who criticize them for what they are lacking."

The gentleman shook his head at the applause of the ladies circling around them. "You make men sound as tyrants. I am a married man who provides well for my wife, my mother, and my daughters. Men are perfectly capable of representing women. They take their beloved's best interests to heart. Regardless what legal position may be out there, women's actual conditions are quite good. We are not barbaric, inflicting misery and suffering!"

"Yes, this is true for many but not all," Thomas said, "If he so chooses, he has the power to subordinate her will to his whenever they argue. You must admit that, at the very least, if you exclude her from being heard then she is in danger of being overlooked."

Thomas looked down at his wife, concern showing on his brow. "I must interrupt and excuse my wife and myself. She has *agreed* to go home for a rest. She has had a very tiring day. Good day." He tipped the brim of his panama hat to the circle. With his arm steadfast around Cady, they walked away.

Ruby saw the gentleman shake his head and whisper to the gentleman standing next to him. She took pleasure in viewing his fat form as more deflated now. She wasn't sure if she understood everything said, but her heart went out to Thomas for supporting women's woes. She and Aimee left the group and fell in behind Cady and Thomas.

Outside the earshot of the others, Ruby called out, "Cady, is anything wrong?"

Cady stopped and turned around. "Only fatigue, my dear. May I ask you for a favor? Would you be a sweetheart and collect the signs and bring them to our carriage? It is parked right over there." She pointed to the steam automobile that Ruby had the pleasure of riding in earlier that spring. Ruby thought briefly of the whipping she received because of it. She tensed in the sudden realization that a whipping could happen again today.

"And one more thing," Cady was saying. "Would you please lead the group through the picnic on my behalf? Give them some encouraging words. You all did beautifully today! Would you do that?"

"Of course!" She gave Cady a hug. Cady had made a request and Ruby felt whole-heartedly honored by it. Robert's wrath would have to wait.

Ruby and Aimee walked quickly around the grounds, collecting signs from the ladies who were standing or sitting on the grass. They were all in good spirits. Could she be the only one with trouble brewing at home like an overheated teakettle? She remembered Aimee's marked face that morning and decided not. She would have to forget herself for the afternoon.

She smiled brightly at each woman with renewed strength and respect for each. She thought of what Cady would have said if she were still here. "We have achieved much today!" she exclaimed to all. "You did a beautiful march. Well done, ladies!"

"We will read about this in the paper tomorrow!" one

exclaimed.

"Right is might!" another shouted, her fist in the air.

"The convention can only be a success!" another cried.

But at what cost, Ruby wondered gloomily as she, with Aimee in silent tow, finally headed back home in the late afternoon sun, her empty pie plate clutched in clammy hands.

* * * * *

The best part of an hour had passed in their walk as Ruby stepped slowly up her steps to her verandah and front door. Her feet were aching from their extra exertions of the day, the blister protesting painfully. Perspiration soaked the back of her shirt and ran down behind her ears and more ran down her sides, collecting inside her corset. She looked down at the pie plate and decided she would need a crow bar to separate her fingers from the plate she still clutched.

The house was unusually quiet for this time of day. The boys should be outside playing on a sunny day like today. She turned the doorknob. It was locked. She tried again, thinking it was stuck. It wouldn't turn. Walking over to the parlor windows, she sat the plate down on the wicker rocker under the window and shielded her eyes with her hands. Her eyes adjusted to the room's inner darkness but neither saw nor heard anyone. Could they still be downtown? Perhaps Robert took the children to the Rose Café for dinner! Her heart felt uplifted. She would just have to wait for their return.

Sitting down on the wicker settee relieved her feet. She stretched out her legs in front of her. To allow air to reach her sweaty limbs, she stretched out her legs and fluffed her skirt and ruffled petticoat a few times. Comfort prevailed over modesty and she raised her skirt to her knees - thank goodness there was only one petticoat on today! Her black ankle boots were scuffed and so worn that they formed around her toes, indicating their descending shapes distinctly. She could visibly see the bulge of her corn on her little toe. She thought of taking off her shoes and stockings but knew Robert would disapprove of this in public. She didn't wish to tweak his nose any more than she already had today. Thinking of his scowl, she lowered her skirt back down to her ankles.

She looked around at the other houses. Why did Robert view the neighborhood as an audience to their home, as if their house was built on a stage? No one was looking, no one was around. To prove the point, she rolled her stockings down to her ankles.

She closed her eyes and rested a moment. A question suddenly came to mind: Why would he lock the door? She only saw him lock when they were going away overnight. Robert did not think it necessary otherwise so Ruby was never given a key. Of course, if he knew that her daily excursions now extended longer than a visit to the market, he might think differently.

What she would give for a drink of cold water! Perhaps the back door is unlocked. He very likely would have forgotten to lock that door. Her thirst moved her off the settee, off the verandah and around the house to the back. It was so still here, too. Something was different but she couldn't quite put her finger on it. She walked up the few wooden steps to the back door. It was locked. She stood there for a moment pondering what to do. Drink was her predominant thought. She ran over to the water pump and pumped its handle. The rusty hinges squeaked loudly from little use. She had a similar pump in the kitchen, so she only used this one for watering her garden on dry days. She pumped repeatedly, finally using both hands, until the blessed water came out of the faucet. She continued to pump for a short time to clean the inner pipe of bugs and dirt. She cupped her hand into the water flow over and over, drinking from her hand and then splashing her face and neck. There, that felt much better!

She walked over to the outhouse and relieved herself there, glad for once that they did not have an inside toilet with a flushing water tank.

Refreshed, she looked around her yard and counted herself lucky that she had a well and water pump. Some people closer to town had to have their water delivered in water-hauling tank wagons, and must collect rainwater in rain barrels.

She pumped water into the watering can and walked over to her vegetable garden. The cucumbers were rapidly growing to the point of preparation for her twelve-day pickle recipe. She would give them three more days, she decided. The beans were abundant and she noted that she would have many to string on lines to dry and enough to can for winter consumption. Some tomatoes were reddening nicely and she pulled two off the vine to take in for supper. She breathed in deeply the tangy smells of the green leaves and earth. Gardening was the one chore she enjoyed above all others. Here she could see her labors come to visible fruition and could proudly display her labors as eventual sustenance for the family. It wasn't monotonous and repetitive like washing and ironing was. Each year her garden was a learning experiment of when to plant, what to plant, how much to plant for canning and preservation.

She noticed weeds here and there and decided to make good use of her time while she waited for her family's return. Weeding absorbed her thoughts.

Next time she looked up, it was close to dusk. She raised herself off her stiff knees, shaking the dirt off her skirt, and looked back to the house with concern.

"Where could they be?" she said out loud.

She wiped the perspiration off her forehead with her arm, picked up the two tomatoes, and walked slowly toward the house. Something caught her eye in the third-story bedroom window. She thought she saw movement there. She stopped and looked up but saw nothing there. This was all very odd. The sun was setting quickly and the house took on a quiet gray gloom.

She walked around to the front verandah and saw a lamp on in the front parlor window. She was so relieved!

Why, they must have come home while I was in the garden! Why didn't I hear them? It will be good to get inside and wash up.

She tried opening the front door. It remained locked so she knocked. No one answered so she pounded louder. She heard

Good Woman

footsteps on the stairs inside and muffled voices. Still no one answered. She walked back to the parlor window and saw Robert sitting in his chair, gas lamp lit beside him, reading the newspaper. She tapped on the window.

"Robert!" she whispered loudly, hoping the neighbors did not hear her. How embarrassing to be standing outside while your deaf husband cannot simply answer the door!

He looked up from his paper slowly and deliberately and focused his eyes on her. No, she decided, he was boring his eyes into her. So, he was still angry. Well, they would have to talk it out. She had decided in the vegetable garden that she would tell him everything. No more secrets. She wanted a relationship like Cady and Thomas had. Perhaps Thomas could come over and talk to Robert … she flinched as he threw his paper to the floor and rose from his chair. The front door opened and he came outside. She met him as he was closing the door behind him. He folded his arms across his chest and stared down at her.

"Robert, I am sorry. I can explain everything!"

"No need. I wouldn't believe you." His voice was low and calm. "You lied to me. You lied to the children. Worse yet, my mother would turn over in her grave if she saw the state of this house. Dishes, dirt…look at this shirt, Ruby. Look at it! Two buttons are missing from it. I came downstairs this morning to find little Bess standing on a bench trying to wash pots bigger than she is. We had strawberry pie for breakfast *and* lunch. I had to take the children downtown to actually *buy* something to eat and that is where I found the disappointment of my life! My own wife marching with men-haters! Which can only mean that you must hate men, too. Which can only mean that you hate your own *husband*! Worse yet, I will be the laughing stock among my customers – if I have any left now! But you are not concerned with my life, are you Ruby? Nor my children. You are not a good wife. You are not a good mother."

He purposefully eyed her up and down. "You are also a poor seamstress with that cheap blouse you are wearing. And it is no longer white - you are also filthy. Look at the dirt on your hands and skirt for all the neighbors to see. My own mother and father built a decent home and reputation in this neighborhood, only for you to tear it down! Such a wonderful example for a mother, aren't you?"

His words bit her heart with cruelty. Her eyes welled with tears, retorts jammed in her throat. His cold eyes met hers and did not waver. "My children do not need this sort of upbringing. They deserve better, Ruby." He pointed to his chest with his thumb. "*I* deserve better, Ruby."

He took a deep breath. "Filthy liars are not welcomed here. This has always been a Christian home. It will remain so. You are to leave my home and these premises!" He made his final statement through clenched teeth, his voice shaking. He turned his back to her and opened the door.

She reached out her hand and clutched his shirt. "Robert, what are you saying?"

"Is that Mama? Where is Mama?"

"Go to bed!" he yelled around the door to the inside. "I already told you to stay in your rooms and away from the windows! Now GO!"

Ruby came up close behind his back in an attempt to step around him to get inside, but his arm shot out and he pushed her back. He did not look back at her as he quickly stepped inside and slammed the door hard. The click of the lock echoed over and over in her ears.

She could only stand there.

Don't move; just let me think, her mind said over and over.

She knew what being in shock truly was now, for she was in it. What do you do when you are in shock? You get a blanket, that is what you do. She looked around the verandah. But I don't have a blanket.

She heard more shouts and cries from within and it knocked some sense back into her. She ran back to the parlor window and peered in.

"Oh my God, please Robert don't take this out on the children!" she cried in a loud whisper to the window glass. She tapped

Good Woman

on the window. She ran back to the door and banged there. She heard more cries, more shouting. She stopped banging. She realized she was causing her children's hysterics and whippings, by an angry man who would vent his anger out on them.

She wrapped her arms around herself and started crying. Harder than she had ever cried in her life. "Oh, please dear God, tell me what to do! What to do!"

She collapsed into the rocker and landed on something hard. She reached under and brought out the pie plate. She stared dumbly at the crumbs in the plate, not registering what it was. The recognition brought on a new wave of sobbing and the pie plate fell to the wooden floor with a loud rattle. The parade and the picnic seemed like years ago.

It was all her fault. She banged her knee with her fist. "I hate you, I hate you!" she whispered to herself through tears. "You are a bad woman, a bad, bad woman! How could you be so selfish! How could you do this to them? To your husband, to your children? You do not deserve such a loving family! Opal told you how fortunate you were but you wouldn't listen! How will you face Opal and Mama now?"

They all seemed so far away. Everyone who loved her. Such loneliness gripped her that she choked and cried again. Finally the tears subsided. She would have to get a hold on herself, she thought, as she wiped her face with the sleeves of her streaked blouse.

The light coming through from the window showed the dirt on her clothes and she realized what a mess she must look. Where would she go now? She couldn't walk out to the farm looking like this. It would frighten them to death. And she didn't think the blister on her foot would permit any further walking tonight. She sat still for a moment, trying to think. Then, the light went out in the parlor and left her in darkness. Only the fireflies came around her to offer her their meager light. She hoped for one brief moment that Robert would open the door on his way up the stairs. The house had become so still that she could hear the creaking of the inner stairs as he climbed to his bedroom.

Fresh tears came as the impact of his words began soaking in. His intended cruelty in leaving her outside, in the dark. She wrapped her arms around herself as the cool night air breathed its arrival around her. She leaned back and began rocking slowly.

"I hate you, Robert," she whispered. "How could you do this to me when I have obeyed you every day of our married life? Well, at least until this spring! I cooked you hot suppers every day. I boiled and scrubbed your soiled underwear, I ironed your shirts, I cleaned your house, like the servant I am to you. And never once did you thank me or tell me you loved me! You, your mother, you both only made me feel that *I* am the one who should be thankful. Well, your mother is dead, Robert, and you need to bury her once and for all. She is starting to stink around here!"

She tried to calm her mind of its storm of hateful words, tides of anger rising and falling. She hugged herself tighter and took deep breaths. She had to think clearly about where to go, what to do. She looked over at Aimee's dark house. She had not heard nor seen anyone, even while working in the back garden. Her mind drifted back to times when she thought how cruel Aimee's husband apparently was, by the many bruises seen on Aimee, and she wondered, did Aimee hate her husband, as Ruby hated her own right now? Aimee's mother lived with them and helped look after the children, so maybe Aimee's absence today was not quite so noticeable to her husband. Aimee said little but from what Ruby had gathered, his violent tempers seemed to be ignited by minor inconveniences, mixed with too much whiskey. Asking for Aimee's aid any evening, with her husband there, was out of the question.

Her tears were drying again, mixing with the dirt and sweat on her face and hardening. A hardening that was penetrating through and through. It reached her heart and she made a resolution. She would eventually find her way back in. Here was where she belonged. Mama and Opal and Edith would tell her the same thing. She had nowhere else to go. He was her husband, who, whether she liked it or not, she took an oath to love, honor and obey. He made an oath, too, to love, honor and keep her, though he needed a little work on the keep part. These were her children, her own flesh and blood.

They were her responsibility. But she would take more control of her life, and of her children's lives, than she had in the past. She had been too trusting of her security within these walls. She would make sure she was never so vulnerable again.

Suddenly it dawned on her what women's rights were all about. Now she fully understood for the first time what she was marching for. What she was petitioning for. Before this, she was only a student going through the motions of class participation. Now she was living it. Now she fully understood what the other women were saying in their testimonies, and the scars that brought them to the place to fight back. How law must be changed to protect women from the anger of men. In such an exposed state, she saw what they were fighting for so clearly. Robert's cruelty only strengthened her resolve to support the Ladies of the Lost Legion, all the more.

"If he is attempting to teach me a lesson," she whispered, "he will be surprised at what I've learned."

She would take it one step at a time. First step tonight is to find a place to sleep. She stopped rocking and looked over at the wicker settee, its thin cushion offering little comfort.

"Mercy," she muttered.

She walked over stiffly to the settee, sat down and then laid down, slowly drawing her body into a fetal position. She smoothed her skirts down over her shoes, and for the first time today, was grateful for its heavy layers. She raised her head slightly and removed her hairpins. She loosened her hair around her back, shoulders, and arms, appreciating her hair's thickness and warmth. She crooked her arm for a pillow.

Once back in the house, her mind continued, the first thing she would do is have another key made. Yes that was it.

Take it one step at a time.

Her exhausted body finally pulled her mind down into sleep.

* * * * *

She walks down a very long street. It is very cold. It begins to snow, the snow blowing around her, through her, blowing up her skirts, billowing them out like a storm-swept sail.. Her teeth chatter. Her fingers and feet are frigid with cold. She bends her uncovered head against the wind and pushes forward. The snow is getting deeper against her legs, as she pushes through. Her stockings become wet and stiff. She lifts her feet higher and higher to trample through the rising white but she is moving so slowly. The wind chills her lungs as she breathes in heavily. She is losing strength. She plows her body through again and again, the icy flakes escalating to her knees. I must keep moving, she repeats over and over. If she stops, she knows she will become buried in these cold drifts. No one will ever find her. She must not stop. She pushes on, the snow now up to her hips. She looks beyond the white mounds to the endless street. There is no end in sight. She brings in her shoulders and pushes herself forward. The snow is now at her chest and she uses her ungloved fingers to claw it away from her. It is of no use. The snow is only mounting higher. Her body is becoming numb to the cold. She is getting sleepier. It does not seem to matter anymore, this struggle. Why do I struggle so, she asks herself. Doubt causes her to stop, for only a moment. A moment that she immediately regrets, for the snow quickly covers her ears, her eyes and then her head. She can only see the white crystals before her eyes. She can no longer be seen. She is suffocating. Why did I stop, she cries. Her tears freeze on her face. She will die here. No one will find her, now that she stopped the struggle. She is so angry with herself. Why did she stop, why did she stop?........out of the distance, she hears Papa's voice. "Ruby, Ruby, get up! Get up!"

"Is that you, Papa? Papa?"

"No Ruby, it is Jesse!" He was shaking her shoulder hard.

"Jesse?" she mumbled, trying to climb out of her dream. She tried to open her eyes, but they were crusty and hard to open.

"Ruby, why are you out here!" Jesse's voice sounded troubled, scolding.

The night before came rushing back and with it more tears to soften her eyes. She rubbed her eyes hard as she tried to raise her stiff body into an upright position. She tried to focus on Jesse who was leaning over, looking intensely at her face, his hand still on her shoulder.

"Ruby, what happened?" His voice was softer now, filled with concern.

Good ol' Jesse, she thought, steadfast and true. He was always there when she needed him. The love she felt from him broke through the crust and she burst out crying. She couldn't speak.

"Did Robert do this to you?" He shook her shoulder again. "Did he?"

She could only nod.

"Why?" Jesse asked. He raised up straight and said, "Well, it doesn't make any difference why, anyway. No kinfolk of mine is left out in the cold like some barn animal! No, not even if you marched with the Confederates!" He took off his cap and slapped his leg with it. "This ain't right, Ruby!"

He paced in front of her, obviously in question as to what to do. His mind made up, he stated matter-of-factly, "Well, you are coming home with me!" Without waiting for a reply, he reached down and picked her up as if she weighed as much as a pillow.

"Jesse!" she protested feebly but had no more strength to argue. His warm arms felt so comforting around her cold exposed body. He carried her down the steps and out to his wagon. Ruby looked at his face as he did so. She had never seen him at such close range before. His lips were pinched together and his nostrils flared, whether it was from her weight or anger, she couldn't tell. Yes, just like Papa.

He sat her carefully onto the bench. "Whoa!" he called to the startled horses. "I'll be right back!" he said to Ruby. "Don't you move!" he commanded.

Ruby rubbed her eyes again and tried to gain composure. She was going to have to face her Mama and the rest of them, looking like death warmed over. She gathered her hair at the nape of her neck and found a clinging hairpin. She attempted to twist the hair's heavy mass into a rope and pin back into a bun, but the one hair pin could not hold its burden alone and her hair fell into a downward spiral that she could feel move down her back and land on her seat. She felt like she was performing all her movements in slow motion.

She looked up startled, as she heard Jesse knock on the door. In the gray early light, Ruby noticed the milk bottles sitting there by the front door and realized it must be around six in the morning and Jesse had delivered their milk as usual. Jesse's morning deliveries had not occurred to her the night before. Jesse banged on the door this time. Ruby was surprised when Robert finally answered. He must have noticed the wagon out front. Ruby could not hear what Jesse said, but she could hear the punch from where she sat. She saw Robert fall back against the door, clutching his face in shock. Jesse simply turned away and walked back down the steps, rubbing the knuckles of his right hand. Robert was holding his jaw as he closed the door again.

Ruby could only stare open-mouthed at the scene. Her first thought was she hoped Robert remembered to come back for the milk, for the children's breakfast. Her second thought was that now Robert would know what it felt like being on the other end of an angry hand. In her exhausted state, it all seemed like a gray nightmare.

Jesse climbed onto the bench next to her and clicked his tongue to the horses. He looked straight ahead, saying nothing.

As the horses plodded slowly away, heads bent down to task, Ruby looked up at her home of twelve years. The memory of her daughter pulling the bench up to the wash pan, and the memory of her son's knobby knees came flooding back to her. Was that only yesterday? They both had asked if they could come with her that morning. Oh what she would say to them if they asked now! What would they do without her now?

She stared at the bedroom windows, starving for a glimpse of their faces. The blinds were drawn shut, like closed eyes shutting her out.

"Oh my babies!" she whispered through choked tears. She clutched the bench to keep from jumping off and running to the door again. But Robert wouldn't open the door again now, for certain. And she couldn't very well stalk around the house until someone came out. She didn't want her children to see her like this. Yes, Jesse was doing the right thing.

She folded her arms and shivered against the chilled morning air, against Robert's cold eyes, against the frigid snow in her dream. Cold pierced through to her soul and she needed the love of her family to bring warmth again.

Jesse silently handed her the reins and reached back behind him to the backbench. He pulled out a coarse woolen horse blanket and draped this around Ruby's shoulders.

Ruby wiped her face with a corner of the blanket. "Jesse, you are God's gift, did you know that?"

He scratched the back of his head and straightened his cap, in his way of shyness. He gave her his lopsided smile and his beloved dimple. "Do me a favor and tell that to Edith. She won't be too happy when she finds out I just punched Robert." He glanced over at her quickly as he took back the reins, and then looked ahead again. "You alright?" he asked.

"I have more explaining than you do, Jesse. You had cause to do what you did. Robert had it coming and I-I am glad you did it! But ...do you mind if we don't talk any more about it, Jesse? My mind is in a fog and I need to collect my thoughts."

"Don't mind at all," he answered.

This time she was thankful for Jesse's quiet ways.

"Jesse?"

"Hmmm?"

"Thank you for looking after me."

"Papa would turn over in his grave, if I didn't look after his girls."

She remembered Papa's voice in her dream, and what Robert said about his mother turning over in her grave the night before. Well, there are two dead ones I've disturbed in short order, she thought grimly. How can I bring peace back to the living and to the dead?

* * * * *

By the time they finally reached the farmyard, Ruby's heart felt squeezed in two. There was an invisible clothesline attached there and the other end was attached to her front door. The farther away they plodded, the tighter the line became. She could barely breathe from the pull when they stopped between the dusty red barn and the weathered-gray backdoor of the farmhouse, the scattering chickens and dogs announcing their arrival.

Edith, Opal, and Mama would be putting breakfast on the table by this time, expecting Jesse's morning return. She ran shaky fingers through her hair again, in an attempt to smooth it around her head. Returning the blanket to the backbench, she climbed stiffly down the step from the bench to the ground. The sun's morning rays were flowing through the apple orchard and onto the ground around Ruby, drying the dew on the grass and giving warmth to her hands and face. She took a deep breath, trying to gather strength to face the concerned - or possibly critical - eyes and questions from inside the house. She smoothed her skirts down around her and was reminded of the dirt and streaks on her white blouse and around the knees and hem of her skirt.

"Mercy," she muttered. "What will they think?"

Jesse was already lugging a large aluminum milk canister toward the barn, and would not come in until the wagon was unloaded. She was left to face them alone. The rusty hinges on the screen door announced her arrival as she stepped into the mudroom. Smells of fried bacon and biscuits soothed her discomfort. After all, this was home too.

Edith came through from the kitchen and met her there. Ruby's appearance startled her and she flinched a little.

"Why, Ruby, what on earth!" She placed her hand on her chest, as was her habit when at a loss.

"Ruby is here?" came her mama's voice from the kitchen. She came limping into the mudroom, followed by the sound of chairs scooting on the wooden floor, and six boys on her heel. The boys stood crammed into the doorway as if caught there. Garnet came forward with her arms out to Ruby.

"Ruby, what is wrong, child?" She gave Ruby a quick hug and then purposefully looked at her up and down. "Has one of the children taken ill?" She smoothed Ruby's hair down her back and squeezed her arm, as if making sure she was alive. She wiped at a dirt smudge on Ruby's sleeve. "There hasn't been a fire at your place, has there? Did something catch fire in your kitchen?"

Ruby couldn't help but smile at this last question. "Well, Mama, I knew I looked a fright, but I had no idea." She waved it off but her hand was noticeably trembling.

She didn't quite know what to say and she cast a helpless glance over at Edith. Edith simply continued to watch, as if she were studying tea leaves in her tea cup. Ruby always thought Edith's kind, intelligent eyes penetrated, straight down to the heart and stay there until she knew what to do. She seemed to have honed in on reading action, not words, as her boys' story-telling of who was right or wrong became increasingly keen. The boys had an unprofessed competition to see who could tell the most convincing argument that might sway their mother.

Without wavering her watch, she finally said, "Boys, say hello to Aunt Ruby and then go back to your breakfast." Reminder of food replaced their curiosity and they obeyed.

Ruby breathed a little more easily now, without so many faces staring at her. She felt dazed, as if the wind had previously been knocked out of her, and breathing was just returning.

"Child, are you hungry?" Garnet asked softly. She was ready to wait as long as Ruby took to tell her what was wrong. One thing Garnet knew for sure was that good food soothed the heart of anyone.

Ruby was very hungry. She realized she hadn't eaten since the picnic the day before with the ladies. Another time ago.

But she couldn't eat with the others, looking like this. The dim illumination coming through the screen door was bad enough, but the kitchen was bright with window light.

"Could I wash first? Maybe by then, the boys will be done eating? And then we could talk?" She felt so unsure of herself, so low, she wasn't sure what to do, or where to go. She was also ashamed for giving them the expressions they wore now; the worried brow.

As Garnet led her up the backstairs, she wondered what they

would think of her when she told them what happened. She very well remembered what Garnet and Opal's opinions were of the Ladies of the Lost Legion, from their conversation after church services.

Will they think I'm of the devil, too?

Garnet tapped on Opal's bedroom door. "Opal, are you dressed yet? Ruby is here –". The door opened immediately to Opal holding her light brown hair to her head with one hand, the doorknob with the other.

"Ruby!" Opal's smile quickly became an o-shape shape of dismay, her eyebrows raised, when she saw Ruby's disheveled appearance. She recovered quickly and brought back her smile. "Ruby, your hair! My goodness, I haven't seen you wear your hair down since we were in school! You look so young!"

Quick thinking on your feet, little sister, Ruby thought. Out loud she answered, "Yes, it is the latest fashion, along with wrinkled clothing."

Garnet waved her hands at both of them. She never quite understood their level of teasing. "Opal, go fetch your sister some fresh water for washing. And give her a clean dress to wear."

Opal returned to her oval mirror hanging over her dresser and bent her knees a bit to see the top of her head. She was still holding her hair in place. "Just give me one second, while I pin down my hair...there...and there... now, all done." She let go her hair slowly, her hand suspended expectantly, in case the braided knot came tumbling down.

Ruby admired her sister's hair techniques that could braid and curl, and spring ringlets around her face. Today the top half was braided separately from the long lower braid and then intertwined in the center and pinned with a comb trimmed in opal stones, a comb Ruby recognized as a gift from their Papa a number of years ago.

Opal walked over to her wardrobe and opened its doors. "Help yourself, sister," she said to Ruby.

A mixture of colors, lace, and ruffles displayed themselves prettily within the wardrobe. Opal was known in the area to be an excellent seamstress and made good money at it. For herself, she designed dresses that distracted the eye from her large bosom and thick waist. Today, she was dressed for an outing in a cool silk taffeta day-dress, colored in light rose. Long, laced sleeves matched lace sewn around the neck and shoulders and long lace strips were sewn in even intervals from the waist down to the hem. Its full skirts rustled and swished the floor as she grabbed the pitcher from her water stand and walked out of the room, leaving a scent of lilac behind.

Without meaning to, Opal diminished Ruby to a lump of barn dirt brought in by the boots of the boys. Ruby watched her, envying Opal's cleanliness, her pretty dress, her outright perkiness. Opal seemed to take life in stride, without question. Life was black and white to Opal, contrary to her name. A name that conjured up changing hues of shimmering grays and pinks.

Garnet's hands seemed at a loss and finally landed on Ruby's shoulder. "Honey, now you wash up and then come down and eat a good breakfast. You'll feel better," she said and then followed Opal out the door, closing it softly.

She peeled through her layers of dirty, smelly outer and under garments, imagining her family meeting downstairs in a cluster, shaking their heads in whispers.

Someone knocked on the door and as Ruby snatched her blouse to her bare chest and ran to the door to hide behind it, it opened only a little and a hand holding a pitcher came through.

"I haven't forgotten your modesty, Ruby," Opal called out from the other side. "Here is your water."

"Thank you."

"You're welcome! See you downstairs!" Opal answered gaily.

What is she so happy about, Ruby wondered grudgingly, as she poured the water into the washbowl. My whole world is falling apart, just as hers is coming together. It is no wonder we have trouble understanding each other. With our age difference, she was interested in animals while I was courting. She was interested in school while I was having babies. Now that she is interested in marriage and babies, I am rebelling against the woman's married predicament! Worlds apart, indeed! Will we ever understand each other?

*****

She worried needlessly about how to tell them of her participation in the 'devil's work'. When she came down to the kitchen, clutching the skirts of her baggy borrowed dress to keep from tripping over its skirts, she saw a newspaper placed in plain view on the table. On the front page, was a picture of the Ladies in the Fourth of July parade. As if that wasn't enough, it was taken from her side of the marching group, and she was clearly displayed. She looked determined in the photograph, almost angry. Her mouth was open, her sign was lifted above her head, one knee was lifted high, showing her white petticoat and scuffed boot. Headline above the picture read, 'Evolution: Girl, Government, or God?'

Jesse must have brought this home, Ruby thought. He must have already seen her picture ... which means he already knew ... that was what he meant when he said 'not even if you marched with the Confederates'! And he never said a word about it! He only brought her home to look after her.

Her three female family members sat silently at the other end of the long wooden-planked table, coffee cups in hands, looking at her with shock, confusion and yes, she believed with some awe. Now it was their turn to be at a loss for words.

She lowered herself heavily onto the first chair she came to and pulled the newspaper over to her with both hands, as if it weighed much more than the paper it was written on. She rested her elbows on the table, involuntarily bringing her hands up to her forehead to shield the oncoming stares and began reading. Below the picture was a short paragraph describing the parade, its participants and its path. The text then referenced an editorial on page 6; one was from a Mrs. Cady Pickering.

She had to read this. She could not continue the day without reading this. The rustling of the pages as she turned to page 6 seemed to bring Garnet out of her frozen state. She jumped up, muttering something about Ruby's breakfast. A plate of scrambled eggs, biscuits, and back bacon slid into Ruby's peripheral view. Next came a cup of coffee and then a pitcher of milk. The hunger for food met with her hunger for words from her friend and she read and ate with equal appetite.

'Cady Pickering, leader of a women's group speaking out for the women's suffrage movement, has submitted the following article. We uphold the constitutional right to freedom of speech and thus have published said article with the understanding that the opinions of the author are not those of the publisher.

'Cady Pickering writes: I wish to thank Mr. Edward Jones of the *Town News* who allowed my first opportunity to articulate in writing the mission of our women's group, Ladies of the Lost Legion.

'Our march in the 4th of July parade was our first public appearance. The courage of these ladies and the sacrifices that they made in being there did not go unnoticed. I wish to give them my public heartfelt gratitude and appreciation for their stand in such a worthy cause as the Women's Suffrage.

'There are questions addressed to me that ask if women have changed; have evolved into something more than they were. I can assure you that we are the same steadfast and dedicated wives and mothers and sisters of always. We do not wish to *be* more, but simply *do* more. We wish to have an active role in our community, our town, our government. We have much to contribute. An evolution of women is not required, but an evolution of government is required. Enfranchisement of women is the next logical step to improve government thinking regarding domestic life. Our government must be brought up-to-date to harmonize with the present social conditions. Government must recognize the competence of women who are asking for enfranchisement.

'Enfranchisement has two meanings in the dictionary: It is either admitting a person to electoral franchise, or it can mean to release from bondage. In the women's suffrage, it means both. To not allow women to vote means to keep her in social bondage.

'Today, July the 4th, we as a country, celebrate freedom and independence. The American Revolution was fought more than 120 years ago to win the patriots' freedom from tyranny. Only thirty years ago, in 1868 and 1870, the Civil War won the 14th and 15th Amendment to the Constitution, granting freedom and suffrage to the Negroes. Although women made equally tremendous sacrifices through those dangerous wars, they did not win this freedom or independence.

'We remain patriotic women. Our devotion to God, country, and fellow man remain strong. We simply wish to participate in equal roles with men in improving our government. The first step government must take is to keep the promise that *all* men and women are created equal.

'Once we are granted the right to vote, we wish to improve our government through reform. Reform is needed for women. In marriage, she gives up her name, her identity, and all her property goes under her husband's control. In divorce law, the husband keeps legal control of both children and property. Reform is needed for women and children who work in textile and paper mills, and garment shops. They work twelve-hour days in over-heated and overly crowded rooms. Thus, legislation should be passed to allow a woman equal rights in her marriage, and to improve working conditions in industry.

'The most basic American civil right is to vote for our leaders. Yet we women meet staunch opposition. We ask why? What does our opposition fear? Every Congress since 1878 has failed to pass an Amendment to the Federal Constitution asking for women's enfranchisement. Only in the State Constitutions of Wyoming, Colorado, and Utah, are women allowed to vote. The eastern states have resisted. Why?

'The National American Women Suffrage Association of which we, the Ladies of the Lost Legion, are affiliated with, are struggling hard to deal with this opposition. We need our local leadership to bring our petitions forward, to speak on our behalf.

'We are in a powerless position. We are a non-violent gender. We are wrongly accused of being men-haters. We love our husbands, fathers and brothers. We live and die for our children. We simply wish to have a public voice in our lives, in our children's lives. We believe that wifehood and motherhood are our most important role in society. It is for these reasons we ask to be heard. It is for these reasons we will hold a Convention on July 18th. This Convention is our public and peaceful way of asking for your support. Support for our movement toward legislative change in enfranchisement for women. Winning the vote will allow women to achieve these reforms.

'The Convention will address the life and rights of the woman. What her social, civil, and religious roles are in our modern society. What we propose to do to improve those roles. Please come in peace.'

Ruby wiped her mouth with the back of her hand. Her plate was now empty. She was starting to feel inner warmth again and relaxed a little.

"Beautiful, Cady," she whispered. Where did Cady find such strength and understanding? How did Cady know to submit this letter in today's paper – did she somehow guess that their picture would appear? Cady's grasp of government and law, the town's inner workings were way beyond Ruby's grasp, and she felt Cady was way above her, far beyond what Ruby would ever be. She prayed a silent thank you to God for Cady as their leader. She was honored to know Cady and made a mental note to say just that to her next time they met. Which, she suddenly realized, it was going to be more difficult to attend the ladies' meetings, as long as she remained here at the farm. The group would need her more than ever, to prepare for the Convention. It was only two weeks away! Panic squeezed at her stomach again at her predicament. Well it won't be long. Robert will cool down eventually.

She glanced up from the paper and met the three pairs of eyes. Her mama's forehead was furrowed with worry. Ruby smiled with returning confidence. "You must read this letter from Cady Pickering. She can explain to you what this is all about, better than I ever could."

Opal winced a little and forced a return smile. She stood up suddenly from the table. "I apologize, sister, but I must leave. I hear Jacob pulling into the yard." In answer to Ruby's raised eyebrows, she quickly added, "Jacob and I are meeting at his parents' home, to discuss the wedding." She patted Ruby's shoulder as she passed on her way out. "We have much to talk about when I return." She stopped suddenly at the door and turned to Ruby, giving her full skirts the appearance of a large swinging bell. "You will be here this afternoon, won't you Ruby?"

She looked the prettiest that Ruby had ever seen her, in her light rose dress and pink glow.

Of course she is happy! I'm only thinking of myself, while my own sister has one of the biggest events in her life coming up! Shame on me! I should feel happy for my sister and this fresh new slate that she has in front of her to write on.

"Yes I most likely will be here. Perhaps I can help you with your wedding plans?" Ruby asked.

Opal waved her hand at Ruby nonchalantly. "What little there is to do. Amish folk have a very simple ceremony, from what I understand. I shall know more today. Bye-bye!" Her rustling layers of fabric faded as she exited the back door. Her bright chatter could be heard above Jacob's low tones as she met him in the yard.

Edith had arisen and was pumping water at the sink into a large washtub filled with fresh-picked green beans. Her task seemed to remind Garnet of their day's work.

"I'll go outside and have one of the boys help me start the fire to sterilize the canning jars," she announced to Edith. As she stacked jars into a large wicker basket, she called out to Ruby to finish her breakfast. She waddled out slowly, under the basket's heavy load.

Edith followed her and called out to one of the boys to come here quickly and help grandma with these jars.

The day had begun, as every other day here in Ruby's memory. Ruby knew its routine's hard work. What she would do to make herself useful, she knew all too well. An extra pair of hands was always needed. She sighed. She felt exhausted and out of place slumped here in an oversized dress, like a half-sack of year-old apples that no one quite knew what to do with. She folded her arms on the table and settled her chin on her forearm. She listened to the many sounds around her; the ticking grandfather clock coming from the front room, dripping water from the sink pump behind her. The outside voices of the living; of boys, dogs, chickens, horses, commands from Jesse to his boys – keeping them busy doing their chores during the summer months was always a challenge. Underlying it all was the softer resonance of her mama and Edith, tones of harmony, working the summer-long task of food preservation.

She didn't belong here. Her place was in her own home, with her own chores. She had her own garden and her own children to look after. Everyone, everything around her seemed distant, she didn't feel part of the living. In her exhausted state, she was only a ghost wandering old places where she once belonged, longing to feel alive again. How long must she wait before Robert called her back home? Hours? Days? Weeks?

Words on the newspaper in front of her blurred and a tear plopped onto the page, highlighting the word 'legion'. Other words came into view, 'Fight for Women's Rights'.

Ruby sat up, drying her eyes with her skirt. She scanned the article back up to its beginning. This article was a full page and not written by Cady. It was titled *Evolution: Girl, Government, or God?* By Edward Jones, editorial staff.

'4th of July. Celebration of our Independence. Independence that granted us freedom. Freedom of religion. Freedom of speech. Freedom from being subjects of a king, from monarchy, from burdening taxes to royalty. Celebration of the spirit of man. Of self-government. Celebrate the men, the real soldiers who fought for our liberty. This is a time to celebrate democracy as we know it: the best government, the best society in the world.

'Yet, best is not good enough for some amongst us. We, in our peaceful town, were abruptly confronted with a group of women, marching like soldiers in uniform, carrying banners of protest through our serene streets, as if marching to war. Banners that tell us to 'change the law', 'give us the vote', '7 reasons to fight',

'fight for women's rights'. Such angry demands!

'While the band played *America the Beautiful*, these female fighters of disruption seized the opportunity to sew strife amongst us, to turn us against ourselves, man against his wife, to attempt to divide us so as to tear at the fabric of our families, to divide us, to conquer us back to the era of cave men. Evolution of Girl? I think not. Devolution, perhaps.

'This legion of women carried a banner saying 'give us a voice'. America the beautiful already has the best system of governing in the world. Our democracy is a vast improvement over any former system of government. I thank our forefathers who struggled tirelessly to prepare our constitution. I thank our fathers of today: state governors and our mayors, who work to provide us with effective government. The issues of the day are complicated and difficult. It is foolhardy to have female fighters voicing opinions to further complicate today's issues and delay governmental proceedings. Why, with such angry female voices in our legislature, we would not get any laws passed! They ask to change the law in the institution of marriage, and in women's labor in the mills and factories. Yet women have the choice to accept or deny a man's proposal of marriage. When she says yes, she is accepting the rules that protect this institution. And our textile mills and garment shops are the most modern in the world. The old adage applies here: 'If you can't take the heat, stay out of the kitchen!' Evolution of Government? Not required. I say 'If it's not broke, don't fix it!'

'This legion of women asserts to change the order provided by our God, but I ask you, who are they to improve on God's work? They advocate that men and women are created equal. Have they not eyes to see? Do they not know that the contents of men's britches differ from the contents of women's petticoats? Do these female fighters not see that men naturally carry the seed of life, women naturally carry the child, and women naturally nourish the child at their breast? Can they not see that men and women are not created equal, but are complimentary? Do these women pretend that they will fight to defeat nature? Evolution of God? Read your Bibles, ladies: 'He is the same yesterday, today, and always'.

'These legionnaires carried a banner saying 'give us the vote'. We already have one vote going to the head of the family, the husband. A second vote in the family would simply the double the number of votes and double the costs of our elections. God knows we already pay dearly for our democracy. A second vote in each family would be wasteful. In addition, if the wife were permitted to vote, it may serve to nullify the vote of the head of the family, if the wife ever decided to vote differently from her husband. Are these female fighters trying to take over the position as head of the family?

'It is unnatural for women to fight. Women who fight against our established order, God's order, against good government and good family, are fighting against our children growing up in the images of their parents. It is right that a son should grow up in the image of his father, and a daughter grow up in the image of her mother. It is right because it is God's plan, it is the natural order of God's creation. From an early age our children start to assume their proper roles. If this legion of female fighters is successful in their battle against government and God, then our whole order of society will be tossed upside down. Our children will not know what is expected of them. They will not know what path to follow through life.

'Why the Ladies of the Lost Legion have chosen to fight Our Father, our forefathers, our fathers, and to fight the natural order of hierarchy of family and state, I will never understand. They must think their battle plans through a little more clearly.

'Mrs. Pickering, if you wish to use words like 'fight!' and 'change!' and question the rules we live by, then don't expect those of us who proudly live by those rules, to 'come in peace' to your convention. We will fight your proposed change of disruption! I suggest that your Ladies of the Lost Legion stay lost.'

"Poor Cady!" whispered Ruby. She must be devastated, if she had read this by now. Most likely she had, since her husband, Thomas, was part of the newspaper staff. Cady must feel betrayed by this, perhaps Thomas, too. She obviously trusted Mr. Edward

Jones to publish her article without malice, but he only used it as fuel to vent his own anger. It had to be anger because Ruby's face felt flushed from the heat of his words. She wished she could somehow reach Cady, at least let her know where she was, and offer some kind words of support. Perhaps Jesse would agree to drop off a note to Cady tomorrow morning.

And the convention! Mercy! Would it become some sort of conflict? That was not the intention at all! Would she have the courage to participate, knowing all its opposition? First her husband, and now this! And what would her contributions be to the convention?

She gripped her belly, to hold in the stomach that was twisting. Her digesting food was working far too quickly and the outhouse would have to be reached immediately. She rushed out the back door, trotted past the surprised faces of Edith and Garnet stooping over a boiling kettle, and down a short path, to the two-seater - as the tiny gray wooden structure was referred to - hidden behind two maple trees.

As her mind settled with her body on one of the seats, and the flies settled around her, words came to her in the form of a rhyming poem, as so often happened in her quiet moments. She whispered the words as she thought them through.

> I've cried for my babies,
> I've cried for my soul,
> I've cried for my kinfolk
> I've cried for more coal
> I've worked for my husband,
> I've worked for my home,
> I've worked and I've cried
> On my own, all alone.....

Ah! That was it! She would write just such a poem and read it at the convention. She could surely do that without too much terror.

She joined Garnet and Edith at the fire, and spent the rest of the day washing and hanging boys' clothing on a clothesline that seemed eternally to suspend the same apparel. In silent moments when there were no instructions at hand from Edith, or strings of worry from Mama about children and grandchildren, Ruby created and memorized her poem. She would write it down that evening with a note to Cady, to let her know she was still there, somewhere, and still working toward their big day.

It wasn't until the three of them were walking in to start supper, did Ruby realize that no one had prodded her as to why she was there.

* * * * *

Opal quietly took her seat at the supper table. She did not meet Ruby's eyes, her own looking tired and distant. Her pink glow had faded into cream.

Ruby was having her own difficulties swallowing her food past the lump in her throat. Sitting there with the boys around her silently shouted to her that her own children were not present. She longed to see them there cajoling with their cousins, forgetting their manners, talking loudly with their mouths full. Ruby missed Bess's presence. Bess always watched the boys attentively, only to roll her eyes in mock disgust when their teasing was directed toward her. Without them Ruby felt like a limb of her own was missing.

"Why didn't Vickur and Jonny come with you?"

Hearing their names jolted Ruby back to the voices around her. Six-year old Thomas, but called Tommy, was looking at her intently across the table, his fork clutched in a fist. He was lined on both sides by his brothers, all Biblical names, but cut into handy nicknames of Joey, Davy, Tommy, Timmy, Sammy, and Jesse Junior who was called Juney.

"His name is Vic-*terrh*," corrected Davy, his face leaning in close to Tommy, spitting the last syllable onto Tommy's cheek.

"Stop that!" Tommy cried, wiping his cheek with the back of his hand. Being the youngest, he was always the easiest prey.

"Aren't they coming?" asked Timmy, looking around as if noticing for the first time their absence.

Ruby scrambled her mind for an answer. The table became quiet, with less on their plates and the evening settling around them. They would want to talk now she knew. Judgment day was falling upon her.

Jesse signaled the end of his meal by scooting his chair away from the table. He pulled out his small leather pouch of tobacco from his shirt pocket. He met Ruby's eyes briefly and then cleared his throat. He concentrated on the small white paper within his fingers as if tending to a delicate insect. Ruby watched him sprinkle crumbled leaves into the paper's fold, anticipating the aroma of the smoking tobacco. She often wondered what this smoke tasted like. Men obviously became relaxed and derived pleasure from its inhalation.

Right away, Edith removed his plate and brought him a cup of coffee and a battered tin plate he used for tapping his ashes.

"Boys, your Aunt Ruby is staying here awhile, and her boys and Bess may show up any day now," Jesse answered.

Ruby understood his logic. Robert could not afford to stay home with the children and they were out of school for the summer, so were home all day. Bess was too young to prepare meals for any length of time. By now they would need fresh bread baked and fresh vegetables from her garden. Robert understood the kitchen to be a hallway exit to the back yard outhouse. And he had never planted nor picked a vegetable in his life. He may have to bring the children here! Her spirits lifted at the possibility.

Jesse's response seemed to satisfy any further curiosity, and the boys one by one left the table as they finished their meal, evening chores assigned to each by their father.

"Ruby, really, what is going on?" Opal asked, agitation in her voice. She seemed in low spirits and in no mood for mystery.

"Robert left her to die on their front porch," Jesse answered.

"My goodness!" Garnet exclaimed.

Edith turned around from the sideboard where she was scraping plates into the dogs' bowl. Her hand went to her chest, her

Good Woman

eyes moving back and forth between Ruby's pinched lips and Jesse's squinting eyes.

Ruby couldn't tell if he was squinting from anger or from the smoke. She felt a light cool hand rest on her arm, and she turned to Opal's light blue eyes.

"Ruby, please tell us what happened. We are here to help you any way we can," Opal said softly.

Ruby had planned to start from the beginning and explain her way to the parade, but now she would have to go backwards, from the night before, thanks to Jesse's dramatic opening.

"It is not all Robert's fault!" she blurted out. "He was quite upset when he saw me in the parade. He-he didn't know I would be there, well, I told him I was going downtown for another reason. He was quite upset, you see, and for a good reason."

"So he leaves you to sleep outside, like some cat?" Jesse asked. "And that was the right thing to do?" His voice was challenging her explanation.

It was coming out all wrong. Why was she covering up for Robert?

"You lied to Robert? Is that what you are saying?" Opal asked. She removed her hand from Ruby's arm and placed it with her other hand in her lap.

Ruby sighed audibly. This was going to be so hard to explain. She would just have to jump in and hope for the best. They were all going to be upset with her for their own reasons anyway, no matter how she explained it. Perhaps they would ask her to leave, not wishing to harbor a liar, and then she *would* become some stray cat.

"Oh, please understand. I was so afraid to tell you because of what the preacher said about our women's group, speaking against them because they are asking for women's right to vote. Please don't judge me but I really believe in what they do! They wish to protect women, through better law. And I have met women out there who need protection!

"My friend next door is often beaten by her husband – where does she go? Another was kicked out of her home and divorced, and her husband brought in his mistress to raise their children. Others cannot have professional careers because they are women. And I've seen women terribly afraid to come out of their homes or even open their doors, because their husbands tell them to stay in, stay put. Where do they go for help? There are no laws for abused women, so our sheriff will not help. The husband is the law, period."

"Ruby, these women you speak of, are they Christian women? Because I don't think this would happen if they went to church," Garnet said.

"Mama, that is unfair! You don't know what it is like to be mistreated. You were fortunate to marry Papa. He was a good man. He protected you," Ruby said.

Garnet's weathered hand, bumped with arthritic nodes along its fingers, smoothed down the tablecloth in front of her as she thought about this. Her eyes of light blue film, looked up at Ruby finally, eyes that were looking into her own past and it pained her to do so. "He was a good man because I was a good woman to him. I carried his children. I fed him three hot meals a day. I worked by his side and I prayed by his side every day of our married life."

This stung. Was Mama implying that Ruby deserved what Robert did, because *she* was not a good woman? Ruby blinked back tears. Why was it the burden of the woman to make the marriage work?

Opal leaned toward Ruby. "What Mama is saying here, Ruby, is that God is the law in a Christian home. And we know our places in our home. Why, without God in a marriage, I suppose the woman could dress in knickers and rule the roost! What is this group of women going to do next – ask that the *law* be changed, so that men would bear children, too?" Opal shook her head and smiled.

Ruby hated Opal's superior tone, talking down to a stupid child. "Really Opal, I asked for your understanding. But to you it is either *your* right, or wrong!"

Opal sat up stiff and sniffed. "Right is what the Bible says—"

"Girls, girls" Edith said. She had a way of soothing and reproving at the same time, Ruby noticed. Edith clicked her tongue, drying her hands. She had continued cleaning since Jesse's meal ended, and now the dishes were washed and stacked for drying.

Jesse uncrossed his legs and stood up slowly. "I have only this to say, Ruby." He ended the smoking of his tiny paper cylinder by squashing it into the tin plate. "My home is your home as long as need be. But when you go back to town, be careful. I've heard talk in town, and men don't like it – they say these women are getting all womenfolk riled up over nothing. So just be careful, is all I'm saying." He put his cap on by the door, tipped his cap rim to his own womenfolk, and headed outside.

Fatigue came back to completely wash over Ruby, so much so she felt she was drowning in it and could barely breathe. All this for what? Was she only 'riled up over nothing'? None of her loved ones were listening to her and perhaps it was because she didn't have anything really to say. She didn't have a cause for complaint. Her problems with Robert didn't begin until she started holding the cross for other women's woes. Was it worth all this? This judgment? She could see disappointment in her Mama's eyes, disapproval in her sister's eyes. She remembered Robert's eyes the night before, burning with condemnation. She closed her eyes to it all and lowered her head into her hands.

She decided to give it one last feeble attempt. She raised her head and looked around her for the newspaper. There it was on the sideboard tucked between canisters of flour and sugar. Bracing her hands to the table, she stood up with effort and walked over to the newspaper.

She opened it to Cady's letter and laid it out on the table in front of Opal. "Please permit me this one courtesy. Read this out loud to Mama, Opal." She pointed to the article. "Cady Pickering is a good Christian woman, married to a fine man, all the qualities you speak of. Now let her speak. Let's open our hearts and minds to something other than what we know. We owe it to others, we owe it to ourselves. As for me, I must retire. I can't go on without some sleep. Please forgive me."

She wasn't sure if her request for forgiveness was for retiring early, or for everything she represented tonight. Either way, they simply nodded, said their goodnights, and as Ruby slowly climbed the stairs to the bedroom, she heard Opal's soft voice reading Cady's words.

* * * * *

"Sister, may I wash your hair for you?" Opal asked. She gently took the brush from Ruby's hand and began the long strokes down Ruby's back to her buttocks to cover the length of hair.

"Opal, there is no need now, you must be exhausted, too. I hope you don't mind I'm in your nightgown."

"I have another. You do look so much more comfortable than I. Let me wash and also get into a nightgown. Then I'll bring in the small wash tub, place it here on the floor. I will sit you here next to it with pillows, towels, and wash this heavy blanket of yours. My, Ruby, your hair is growing so beautifully! My hair has stopped at my shoulders and refuses to go further. Really, what do you do?"

"Not much, really. Other than the monthly wash, I massage the roots each night with cold water, and freshen each morning with lavender water. Could it be the lavender, do you suppose? At any rate, it is far too heavy now and difficult to pin up. Do you think you could cut some length off for me?"

"Oh no, I would never! Why, Ruby, the Bible says the woman's hair is her glory! You must pray thanks! I will pray as well for forgiveness in envy and jealousy. I would love to have your hair. There are women in town who would pay good money for three feet of real hair, just like yours!"

"Really? Now that is something to think about, isn't it? Well, as far as envy we are even, because I would love to have your dresses, and even more so, your talent as a seamstress. Opal, it is no wonder you are so sought after by others. Your dresses are lovely! So there!"

Opal paused in her brushing and looked over to her wardrobe, where the door was slightly ajar. "Well, then, you shall have my dresses," she said softly.

Ruby watched Opal resume her brushing through the bureau mirror, Ruby's eyes arched in surprise. In the dim light she could not read Opal's face.

"Mercy, Opal, I can't take your dresses! I only meant—"

"Ruby, I no longer have a need for such elaborate...costumes."

Ruby turned to her and their eyes locked, Ruby's silently questioning.

"I'll explain upon my return with more water and the tub," Opal said and quickly left the room.

Ruby sat on the bed and resisted from lying on its soft feathers. Opal needed to talk. She talked best when her hands were busy doing what she loved to do best: laboring over hair and clothing. She spoke often of the sensations in her fingers when touching the diverse textures of smooth silk and coarse wool, and considered hair much the same as fabric, its texture differing depending on its owner. Opal's creativity in shaping long lengths of hair was endless. Layers of hair could be molded into a pompadour or a chignon of curls simply held with clasps. Layers of fabric could transform into a prismatic gown magically held by a thread. She once told Ruby she imagined she was creating a princess when she fabricated wedding gowns of satin and lace, and arranged the hair into gardens of flowers, of those so fortunate to become queen. She had worn thin the pages of an outdated Godey's Lady's Book, always there on her bedside table, that recommended different fashions of dress, hat, and gloves.

Ruby picked up the book and thumbed quickly through it, uninterested in what dress was suitable for different activities and times of day. Why so many rules to govern what one wore?

If she were to write the rules, it would be a short book: Be charmingly careless. Be comfortable. Wear at all times what is appropriate for the market. Therefore, clothing resembling men's apparel is allowed: ankle length britches of comfortable cotton, with waist bindings that stretches, of course, and a bodice that doesn't require a tight fitting. High neck collars aren't required, and an open-neck blouse is permitted. And oh yes, one more rule: No bloody corset! She smiled at the absurdity of it.

Opal returned soon afterwards, walking like a penguin, the weight of the filled tub obvious in her rigid arms. Ruby jumped up and assisted in setting the tub down.

Opal rubbed her hands together. "I'm going back downstairs to get some eggs for egg whites. A shampoo recipe I recently read in 'The Ladies' Home Journal' calls for egg whites. Edith just came in from gathering eggs for the milk run tomorrow. Have you noticed she runs continuously? I don't know where she gets her energy! She is now heating bath water for Jesse's evening bath." Opal lowered her voice. "He insists on having one *every* night because he believes cleanliness is next to godliness when dealing with eggs, milk and customers every morning. I'm certain his customers agree but poor Edith..." she shakes her head. "She walks up and down the stairs filling the tub with hot water. And she bathes him like he is a baby—"

"Pardon?" Ruby was shocked that Opal would know such a thing.

Opal seemed unashamed of the impropriety. "Well, their bedroom is by the stairs and the tub is in the open, and they don't always close their door." She waved her hand. "Anyway, every evening they must both lug the heavy bathing tub down the stairs and outside to dump the water and then carry it back up to the bedroom for the next evening's bath. The boys all bathe in the mudroom but Jesse needs his privacy - away from Mama and I, I guess."

"Why doesn't Jesse bring in plumbing pipes to drain water from the tub? Build a separate room for it," Ruby asked. She had asked Robert to do the same thing but money was always the obstacle in his reply.

"No space!" Opal answered. She puffed up pillows and placed towels on the floor around the tub. "The boys have the attic, the three bedrooms here are occupied by Mama, Jesse and Opal, and myself. Oh, you've just given me a great idea! They can have my bedroom then! And I shall buy them one of those claw-footed large white bathing tubs – have you seen one? They're not made of wood or tin but something else entirely. It will be my wedding present to them, for taking care of me all these years!" She clapped her hands together in delight and exited in a rush.

Ruby sat back down on the bed tiredly. She wished she could just go to bed and go to sleep. Opal's enthusiasm was not contagious. She dozed sitting up until Opal re-entered beating egg whites in a bowl with a fork.

"I have added honey...and now for some rose water...there! I'll wash with lye soap, and then rinse with this, and you will feel wonderful again! Light another candle, Ruby, so I can see what I am doing. Then sit here on these pillows please while I change into my nightgown."

Ruby obeyed and waited quietly while Opal changed behind her. Soon they were both gathering Ruby's hair from behind. Opal placed a pillow on the tub's rim and Ruby laid her head there. She remained quiet a few more moments while Opal worked the many strands into the water, Opal's expression intense on her task at hand. Finally Ruby could wait no longer.

"Opal, may I intrude for just a minute? When you left this morning, you looked happy, when you came home, you looked...sad. Now you say I am to take your dresses. Is there some bad news I should know about? You are not departing this world at such a young and...uhmm...virgin age?"

Opal laughed easily. "*Really*, sister! No, but...well...I am, I suppose, departing *this* world" and she pointed toward her bed, her finger unknowingly dripping water onto Ruby's face. In a lower tone, she said, "I will be sleeping in another bed, in his parent's home, come October. Then we visit his many relatives throughout the winter months, who then help us in building our own home next spring. You see, the Amish world is quite different from our own. Odd, isn't it, when you think about it, we only live a few miles apart. I learned today, it might as well be a thousand." She was silent for a few moments, collecting her thoughts as she collected water in the tin cup she was using to wet Ruby's hair around her forehead.

"The Amish believe they should remain separate from society. So they hold their worship services at home, not in a church. Which means, I will be married in Jacob's parents' home and not in a church."

Ruby looked up at Opal, hearing resignation in her voice. For years, Opal talked about her dream of her own wedding in her own church.

"Silly me was concerned about how much time and money needed in order to sew my lace and pearl wedding gown. No need to worry. My dress will be of blue cotton – I can choose the shade. Don't you think sky blue would go best with my eyes?" Opal talked on quickly. "I also make my newehockers' dresses. Newehocker means sidesitter in Amish. That dialect of German they speak. You know — bride's attendants. Which will be Jacob's sisters. And you, if you want to be ... if you are permitted. Anyway, it won't take long because the dresses are unadorned, without trim or lace, or train. How simple! Jacob's sister told me this dress would also be my Sunday church dress. I will also be buried in the same dress! Isn't that practical? Assuming of course, my weight doesn't accumulate by then!"

She laughed, but the laugh was not easy this time. "And do you remember how much trouble I always have making button holes for buttons? Well, never again, because all Amish clothing only have hooks and eyes. Simplicity at its best!" She took a deep breath as she lathered her hands with the soap. "Which means, of course, there is no longer a need for these costumes of colors filling my wardrobe. I don't mind really. It is a small sacrifice."

Ruby looked over at the pink and lace chest of Opal's nightgown. Even her sleeping garments were adorned with pearl buttons. "Oh my then, were their eyes strained by the bright pink candy that walked into their *simple* abode today?" Ruby meant for it to sound funny, but it sounded rather mocking.

Opal blushed and forced a smile. "Well, yes, unfortunately that *was* a problem, because his mother looked at me as if I had arrived in my petticoat! So Jacob asked his sister to take me aside and explain what is expected of my attire. Jacob said afterwards that it wasn't his place to talk of such things. He said he resisted asking me to return home and change into something more fitting as a soon-to-be Amish wife. He was quite uncomfortable about the whole thing so naturally I apologized profusely."

"Well, how would you know, Opal? Jacob has only courted you here at home. That was your first visit to his home, yes?" Ruby asked.

Opal nodded.

"Well, then, your apology is not required. He should have prepared you for it first."

"He speaks well in English but he believes he communicates better in German," Opal explained. "He is a shy quiet man. He had great difficulty asking me to marry him. I didn't think he would ever get the proposal out of his mouth. And do you know what he gave me with his proposal? A mantel clock!"

Ruby laughed out loud at that. "Was this symbolic? Did he mean that time is quickly marching by on your way to being an old spinster, and that you must accept and get a move on?"

"Ha-ha, very funny," Opal answered. She had soaped the hair through and now began rinsing it. She frowned down at Ruby. "One thing troubles me, in my commitment to Jacob. You may think it's their traditions in dress and living but with time I can accept their traditions. Their life on the farm is not so different than ours. It is the worshipping part I'm struggling with. I must join the Amish religion, be baptized again under their faith, learn the Ordnung, which are the written rules and some unwritten rules, and ... and" she took a deep breath and here Ruby noticed Opal's chest was shaking, "I may not attend my own church again."

"Never?" Ruby asked.

"I must show complete faith in my new faith, Jacob said," Opal answered.

Ruby blinked back tears. She couldn't imagine going to church without her sister sitting there in her customary pew. Her absence would be sorely missed, as if she died. She wondered again why it must be that the woman must make the sacrifices.

"Opal, no one else I know loves our church more than you do, except maybe for Mama and Edith of course. And you must know that Mama is troubled by this conversion to Amish. Are you willing to make such a sacrifice?"

"Yes!" Opal cried. She stopped rinsing and clutched the tub with both hands. She looked down at Ruby, her eyes brimming with tears, her large chest heaving with the unfairness of it all. "Time *is* marching by, Ruby. Is it not part of God's plan that we marry and have children? And here I am twenty-one years old, for goodness sake! You were married at seventeen! And God will know me in that church, as well as mine...won't He? There are good in all faiths, who believe in Jesus Christ as their Savior!"

Ruby attempted to raise her head in order to address her sister's tears with a hug, but her hair's weight in the water was too much. She rested her head again and patted Opal's shoulder instead. "Do what you believe is best, Sis. You must follow your heart, of course. I am in no position to preach good marriage, nor how to be a good wife. In fact, I would say right now, that I am a poor example of a good wife. Just ask Robert."

"Which reminds me of why I'm here. The newspaper article, Opal - what did you think of Cady's letter?"

"I think," Opal said slowly, "that she also is from another world, a political world I know nothing about. Nor care to. But Ruby," Opal paused, capping her hands around Ruby's head, "although we are different, you and I, we are sisters and I love you. I want to understand you. Where is your own heart leading you?"

Ruby closed her eyes and looked into her heart and spoke words she did not know were there.

"I want to go beyond my doors. I want to run in the sun with nothing on but my nightgown. I want to feel loved and feel love." She folded her arms tightly across her chest. "I want to embrace and be embraced. I want to walk in this world with a sense of freedom and make a difference, not just exist. I want to work with my mind, not just with my hands. I want to feel money in my hands I have earned myself.

"I...I feel suppressed, somehow; smothered. Instead of an embrace, I feel gripping hands. Instead of love, I feel ridicule.

Rules of what I must do and what I must wear in doing it have me so tightly bound to the earth that it reminds me of a raccoon I saw once caught in a trap. It was chewing off its own leg for release. I, too, am making sacrifices, yearning for that sense of freedom."

She paused and listened to the chinking sounds of fork in the bowl as Opal mixed the recipe. Opal began slowly pouring it onto Ruby's scalp and massaging it in. Opal's fingers seemed to stir up imbedded thoughts in Ruby's mind. Since she opened the door, she might as well let it all out.

"At times, going through my household chores, I want to scream and run out of doors, looking for more. My days are filled with serving Robert. Robert reminds me that it is his home, his children. So I clean my husband's home, care for my husband's children. But I long for more in my life. Something of my own. Friendship for one. A skill, for another. Something I can learn, to earn money. Because of my duties at home, though, I have been forbidden friends, and only domestic skills are allowed.

"When I did find friends, in the form of the Ladies of the Lost Legion, I was inspired beyond what I had learned with my kinfolk. There is so much out there to experience, so many others to reach, to talk to. Robert forbade me to get involved with such a group. But my desire to participate was stronger than my fear of Robert. So I agreed to march for women's suffrage in the Fourth of July parade. To really belong and be part of this group, marching for a common purpose; it was an experience I shall never forget nor regret. What I do regret is that Robert found out about it at all. I can't say I regret lying to him, because telling him the truth would only have led to strict orders to remain in the house. But I regret seeing the anger, and now as I think back, I believe there was hurt in his eyes but I was too frightened to see that. He is only human, after all, but I have difficulty in talking with him. He sees life as a set of rules that all must follow or suffer the consequences. Somewhat like you, Opal, in that it is either right or wrong. Only he shows no mercy to the wrong, nor wants to hear the other side of the story. And there always is, Opal. I've learned that, with listening to other women out there. Life to me is colored more gray, than black and white. I must sound rather negative here, but that is where I am right now.

"I will say something on the bright side, though, that will please you, my faithful sister. I made a vow to Robert when I married him and I belong nowhere else, even with its chains that bind me. After all I am blessed with children who brought light into my life and bring me out into the sunshine. I will try harder to be a good wife and a good mother. But I've had a taste of life beyond my doors and I love it. To stop now would be like taking a bowl of ice cream from me when it is only half-eaten. So just a word of warning in case you see my picture in the paper again. I will be in that convention if I have to drag my ball and chain every step of the way! And one more thing. I would love for you to participate with me."

Opal was twisting Ruby's hair into a long rope, to squeeze water out. She nudged Ruby's back to sit up. Ruby supported herself on her elbows. "Ruby, no. But if I see you there, I shall smile and say, 'there is my sister who is following her own mind, her own heart!' Thank you for opening your heart to me. I will try not to criticize so. It is a fault of mine. 'Judge not, lest ye be judged', the Bible says. Agreed?"

Ruby reached up and patted her sister's wet hand.

"Agreed." Ruby answered. "Now let us see if this new egg recipe will give me shiny clean hair. I must be presentable in case my own husband comes courting!"

* * * * *

Jesse came in to breakfast the next morning, with words of thanks from Cady's housekeeper, Lizzie, for the kind note from Ruby. Cady could not come to the door, Lizzie said, and when Jesse was leaving their house, Doctor Hughes pulled up his buggy behind Jesse's wagon. Did Ruby know if Cady was ill? Jesse asked. Ruby could only shake her head. How would she know anything going on in town, all the way out here? She felt isolated and restless.

She shooed the other womenfolk out of the kitchen after breakfast and washed the dishes alone, wanting time to think on her own. Afterwards, she decided to take a walk. To avoid the questioning eyes in the back yard bent over their chores, Ruby walked out onto the front porch. She stared out onto the road. If she walked out there and turned left, the path would lead her directly home. The children would be outside playing by now. She could join them and then Robert would see her and want her to come back. Or he could make the children go back inside and close the blinds again.

Resigned to remain, she turned left off the steps, walked over the sparse grass of the barnyard and into the red barn. Its massive size was necessary to house the thirty or so dairy cows. She thought it unfortunate that animals were given more space than people. Why, they could fit three farmhouses in this place. She looked around at its high loft. But of course to heat a house this size ... never mind – smaller is warmer. The visit here and its acrid smells brought back memories of helping her papa here feeding, milking, sweeping, hands red from the cold mornings. Ruby guessed from the number of cows and the cleanliness of the barn that Jesse was well organized and running a more profitable business, than was Papa. Jesse's larger family of boys working here enabled him to increase the milk production, and buy more chickens for Edith's egg selling business. Ruby walked through to the other side and out by the smoke house, almost empty except for some beef jerky and back bacon. The fall would find it filled with fresh smoking pork and beef for the winter.

Back a little farther was the tool shed. This was her favorite hideaway as a child. A gigantic spruce tree lived behind it, its branches reaching around on one side affectionately, some of its branches draping over the top of its tin roof. Thick lilac bushes snuggled up to it on the other side. Green moss covered much of its low tin roof. Some pieces of tin and wooden planks dangled from the roof's corner. Grasses and low brush had grown up around it. Yet with all of nature's protection, the wooden structure still continued to buckle. One day it would fall in on itself, but for now she felt safe in going inside. Only one window existed and it took a moment for her eyes to adjust to the dimness. She spotted wooden planks of board next to the heavily nicked wooden workbench, always kept on hand for mending the barn and sheds.

Ruby remembered the cricket bench Bess had scooted over to the sink and how Ruby had made that bench with her papa right here in this shed as a young girl. There were enough wooden boards here to make several of these benches. One for each of her children as a gift!

Sleeves rolled up, she propped open the window and door, found the measuring stick and small hand saw and went to work. By early afternoon, boards had become three benches with twelve inch by twenty-inch seats, twelve-inch wide legs. In the boards she had cut for legs, she had sawed out an upside down V in each. She stepped back and looked at them, proud of her handy work. They weren't perfect but they were her own. Now all they needed was color.

She walked back outside and breathed in deeply the fresh air. Wild blueberry bushes were spotted over to the side of the smoke house, on grounds that Jesse had not cleared. Birds had eaten many of the blueberries but many more stubborn ones were hanging on. Ruby picked these into a rusty tin container and walked back toward the house.

As she came around the barn, the scene in the backyard and beyond to the garden stopped her pace and brought a smile to her face. The women working there looked like a scene from a painting; one Ruby wished she could paint to capture the moment. Opal was off to her right in the distant garden, her large pink bonnet shading her face from the bright sun, walking, bending, stooping, basket on her hip. Edith was in the center of the scene, bent over the large black iron kettle, a hungry fire licking around its grate. She was dappled in sun and shade from the trees behind her, her face flushed, her bonnet dangling on her back. Mama was on the left of the scene, sitting on a bench in the shade by the back door, churning butter, her hand moving the thick handle up and down inside its clay crock without notice. Her attention was on Joey who was chasing a chicken.

"Now grab its neck, Joey," Mama was calling out. "That's it. Now hold on tight to the neck and spin it in the air, like I showed you. That's it!" She cackled loudly at Joey's beaming expression as he looked down at the severed head and neck in his hands. The chicken's body was now running in circles back down on the ground.

Ruby placed her tin container on the grate next to the boiling kettle holding canning jars, nodding and smiling to Edith. The heat rising from the fire was intense and the berries quickly began to bubble. Ruby mashed and stirred until the berries were cooked down into mush.

"Now what are you up to?" Edith asked, peering into the container.

"I am making cricket benches for Bess, Victor, and Jonathan," Ruby answered. "A way of reaching out to them, I suppose."

She patted Garnet's shoulder as she stepped up to the back door. How many times had she seen Mama sitting there churning butter? Countless times. That faded red chair with the cane bottom was her mama's favorite place to sit. Ruby stepped inside and waited for her eyes to adjust, appreciating the cool, musty smell of this old house. Her father and grandfather had built this house a long time ago, sometime before the Civil War. So many memories for one place, but she didn't want to look back. She wanted to move forward, toward town, walk to her own home carrying her three cricket benches if she had to.

She poured some milk from the icebox into the blueberries. The milk looked so good, she poured more into a glass to drink. The cold heavy liquid soothed the heat on her face, and smoothed the knots in her stomach.

She returned to the tool shed through the sounds of thunk, thunk of the butter churn, the snapping fire, male voices calling out in work and play around the barn, cows and chickens and dogs echoing around her.

She found lime powder in the tool shed, her father's words of long ago drifting around her. "One part lime to twelve parts milk.

So twelve is in all your measurements of wood and paint, easy enough even for a little milk bucket like yourself to remember!"

"Yes, Papa, I remembered, just like you said," Ruby whispered, stirring the mixture with a piece of wood. Papa's old shaving brush - her makeshift paintbrush from long ago - was still here hanging on a peg. Amazing, not much changes here. Its stiff tips were still covered in blue. The paint loosened the brush bristles and soon she had cricket benches colored in a mottled bluish-purple. Her heart swelled with the thoughts of her children's expressions when they saw what she had made for them. She hoped it would let them know how special they were and how much she missed them. The memory of their cries that last night came back, bringing with it stinging tears.

She wiped away the tears and perspiration from her face with the skirt of Opal's calico housedress. Thank goodness the bagginess of the dress didn't require the corset – she felt loose as a goose, wherever she heard that expression. She hadn't put hers back on since she had arrived. Of course she would have run upstairs to squeeze into it, had she seen Robert coming up the lane. He would have frowned at her unkempt appearance.

The longing to go home was getting stronger by the hour. She had barely eaten, wondering how much longer would she have to be patient and wait for Robert. She prayed that somehow he would see that he needed her.

* * * * *

Her prayer was answered the next morning. A note was on an empty milk bottle by Robert's front door, addressed to Ruby, Jesse said, as he handed her a folded paper. His face looked sad. He walked back outside. Ruby read the note and then ran to the back screen door, calling out to him.

"Jesse, can you take me home today?"

He continued his walk toward the barn; his only sign of hearing her was his nodding and waving.

"When, Jesse?" she called out again, more anxious this time.

"Robert says that Bess is ill and I'm needed at home!" She waved the paper at him, as if he hadn't seen it already.

He stopped and looked back at her. He took his cap off and scratched his head. Mercy, that is just what Papa used to do - the spitting image.

"Well I guess we better leave directly then," he said. "Just let me finish unloading the wagon and water the horses."

Ruby nodded and went back to the kitchen entrance. "I must get my things together!" she called out to the kitchen group, and ran up the back stairs. She was excited, worried, and nervous all at once. It was unusual for Bess to be ill. She resisted colds and viruses that the boys caught.

Opal was in her bedroom sewing at her machine, her feet moving rapidly up and down on the black iron pedal to keep the sewing steady.

"The clothing you wore here is cleaned and hanging in the wardrobe," Opal said without looking up. "Fresh water is in the pitcher for washing. I'm taking in these other dresses to give you a better fit. And my ruffled and lace petticoats, too. I have one petticoat you are going to love. Eleven inches from the hem are three rows of beautiful white lace. The other petticoat is cotton with a silk ruffle at the bottom. Wear the two together and your skirt flares beautifully and your waist shrinks like magic. You could use some flare - you look like a poor orphan girl wearing my housedress."

She stood up with a measuring tape in her hand. "Now take that dress off so that I can measure you."

Ruby quickly obeyed, forgetting her modesty for a moment, in a hurry to head out. Opal measured her length of arms, and around her waist, chest and neck.

"Why is it that you got Mama's small waist, and I got Mama's large breasts?" Opal asked.

"I've heard it said that Mama was a beauty in her younger days. Farm life and babies take their toll," Ruby said.

Opal seemed not to hear the intended warning toward her upcoming marriage.

"Well, she is past fifty years of age, Ruby. We can't stay young-looking forever." She patted Ruby's hair. "Your braid is holding nicely. It is best to do it after it is washed like that, to hold in place. Should be good for another week, I would think."

She sat back down at the sewing machine. "I'll continue sewing while you wash. I promise I won't look. Now I need to know what length you prefer in your skirts. The instep length is appropriate for shopping; the clearing length is one inch longer for general street wear; then there is the round length, for visiting with the ladies for tea, or whatever else you do for women's ... suffrage, is that the right word? And then, if you host the tea, you'll require skirts that actually trail the ground. Makes a lovely *swi-i-ishing* sound! Now when it comes to evening attire, I have never been anywhere in the evening that required a train, so you must do without, when it comes to me—"

"It doesn't matter to me," Ruby interrupted. Even though Opal had her back to Ruby, Ruby turned her own back to wash her breasts and between her legs. "Make it easy for yourself. Give me all the ... which length is it for street wear - clearing or instep? Give me one of those. I wish for my feet to be free and clear." She reached for her corset in the wardrobe. It had been brush-cleaned and aired outside, by the smell of it. She slipped her arms through it and began the tedious job of sucking in her stomach and squeezing together the many hooks and eyes.

"Ruby, you are a walking contradiction," Opal said irritably.

Ruby stiffened at the words and tone. "Whatever do you mean?"

"You wish to socialize with the ladies of the town, yet you wish to dress like a farmhand. You wish to be free as a bird, and yet you can't wait to get home to the very chains that bind you."

Ruby stared at Opal's back for a moment. Could this be true? She watched Opal gently handling the sleeves of a light green frock trimmed at the sleeves and neck in dark green velvet, its many yards of fabric flowing over the side of the table onto her lap and onto the floor.

"Perhaps you're right," Ruby said softly. "Perhaps we both

are contradictions. Or perhaps we both are willing to make sacrifices to do what is right. Or ... perhaps we have no other choice?"

Opal's movements stopped, her head remaining down. Then slowly her head nodded, and she resumed her work.

Ruby buttoned her skirt, her last layer of apparel, and looked hurriedly in the bureau mirror. She didn't wish to leave under this somber note, so she went behind Opal, bent down and gave her shoulders a tight squeeze. She noticed Opal's hair was in a uniquely braided bun clinched with her comb of opal stones. Dear Sis, better wear these things while you still can. "I'll have the shiniest hair in town, thanks to you. It was so good to spend time with you again, despite my own difficult circumstances. Come and visit with me soon, would you?"

"I will. I'll deliver these dresses myself. Poor Jesse must feel like a mailman and a taxi at times," Opal said. She paused and turned her head to Ruby. "Be good!" she said and smiled.

Ruby returned the smile and called out behind her as she left the room, "I might have a better chance of *looking* good anyway, credit going to the generosity of my sister! Farewell!"

Garnet was waiting at the bottom of the stairs in the mudroom wearing a worried frown. "What is wrong with Bess do you think? Send me a note tomorrow with Jesse, if you need anything. We've packed up some eggs, butter, soap, and a fresh-killed chicken for you. All you need do is pluck it," Garnet said. She patted Ruby's back. "Remember, you are in my prayers."

"Thank you, Mama. I'll write you tonight, I promise." They hugged.

Edith came in with their basket of goodies and her own hug. She, too, looked worried and sad.

"Thank you for everything," Ruby said. "Hopefully the scene I made here won't happen again. Now it is your turn to visit."

"Well maybe someday, if we ever finish canning and preserves. Can't leave right now, honey, there is too much to do!" Edith answered. She looked deep into Ruby's eyes, her own large brown ones moist. "You need us, you come right back, you hear?"

This gave Garnet the opportunity to say what was on her

mind. "And Ruby," she said, "I don't want to interfere, but...well...Robert shouldn't have done what he did. You tell Robert to look after my little girl!" Her eyes had filled with tears and she continued to pat Ruby's back.

Ruby didn't know what to say except to tear up, too. All along she had imagined Mama silently scolding her.

Jesse pressed his face to the screen door from outside. "Edith, put some bacon in some biscuits and hand them to me. I'll eat on the way. Ruby, your blueberry seaters are on the wagon. I'm ready when you are."

Jesse and Ruby pulled away, Ruby waving back to the womenfolk, Opal joining them as well. Ruby felt her heart tug with gratitude and love for them. They were always there, solid and true to their own. Such hearty, strong women.

Why can't I be so strong?

* * * * *

Ruby climbed down from the wagon bench with Jesse's last words ringing in her ears. "I won't stand for you being treated badly. If I see you sleeping outside again, I'll do more than give ol' Robert a punch. Let this be a warning!" He handed her the benches and basket from the wagon, tipped his hat to her and rode off, without once glancing at the house.

The door opened then, cries of "Mama, Mama!" came tumbling out with the children.

Ruby ran to meet them halfway, her arms open wide. "My babies!" she cried. She had never been so happy to see their little faces. They came headlong into her, forcing her to lose her balance and fall onto the grass. They all shouted, laughed and tickled each other.

"Children," came a stern voice from the doorway, "please let your mother come in."

This public display was making Robert uncomfortable.

I have made a muddle of my welcome already, and hadn't yet even spoken to him.

She stood up quickly, brushing her skirt off. With Jonathan and Bess in hand, and Victor towing behind, she walked up the steps and to the door where Robert remained standing. It was good to see him and she thought of giving him a warm hug, until she saw his eyes. They were cold. She noticed his untidy clothing and those of the children.

"Robert?" Her voice was soft and tentative, her eyes were pleading.

He stepped aside to let her in. The parlor was cluttered with newspapers and dishes. To her left she spotted dirty dishes on the dining room table.

She reached down to Bess and felt her forehead for fever. Her forehead felt cool. "Bess, how are you feeling?"

"Better now, Mama! Last night I wasn't feeling well at all and I asked Papa to get you home to look after me. You would know what to do!" She was looking up with eyes that were longing for affection.

Bess clung to Ruby's skirt, as were the boys. Ruby stooped down and hugged all three again. She looked up at Robert, knowing he was seeing in her eyes the same longing she saw in the eyes of Bess. He was watching them all closely, yet staying a distance apart. Their eyes met and held, his turning into warm chocolate drops once again. He cleared his throat and finally looked away, folding his arms across his chest.

He missed me!

Ruby straightened up and timidly approached him, her ducklings walking in step with her. She tiptoed up and gave him a lingering kiss on the cheek. She noticed the slight bruise on his jaw. Jesse would be pleased with himself.

"And how are you feeling, Robert?"

"Very well, thank you," he answered, nodding. He wouldn't meet her eyes at such a close range. He cleared his throat again. "I am going to the shop now. I have been home with the children since you, er ... well, at any rate, I'll be home at suppertime." He looked down at the children, blinking a few times. "I'll bring home something fresh from the bakery for dessert."

Amid the claps and cheers from the children, Ruby sent a warm smile up to him. He was being extravagant! Bess wasn't ill. Bess knew it. Robert knew it. They all wanted her home and they were each showing it in their own way. Tonight she would prepare the best supper ever. Make it festive. And top it off with a shop-baked dessert! Extravagant indeed!

He reached over to his hat on the hook in the entranceway where they all still stood. He placed it on his head and wished them a good day. He paused at the doorway as if remembering something. "Oh, by the way, could I possibly have a shirt washed and ironed by tomorrow? I am really looking unruly in this one. Quite embarrassing, with customers and all."

"Certainly, Robert. Washing will be my first task of the day!" she answered, trying to smile brightly.

He nodded solemnly, as if expecting that to be her answer and walked down the steps. She heard him whistling as he turned left and headed toward downtown. She watched him walk until she could see him no more.

Victor pointed toward the street. "What are those things, Mama? Want us to bring them in?"

"Oh, yes, please do. I've made a cricket bench for each of you. I'll grab the basket. Let's go!" They all ran to the front yard and returned inside with their gifts.

Ruby closed the door and turned toward her children. Their sweet faces were looking up at her expectantly.

"Now, children!" she exclaimed, bringing her hands together with a clap. "Let's take our cricket benches to the backyard. Last one out back to play 'Duck, Duck, Goose' is a rotten egg!"

They all clamored through the house to the back door, Ruby grabbing her own cricket bench in the kitchen on her way out. She winced and closed her eyes to the battered kitchen. She paused on the back stoop, watching her children tottering with their benches to the center of the yard, sun shining down to unashamedly expose their unwashed heads and wrinkled, spotted clothing. They sat down on their benches in a semi-circle and called out to her.

"Ha-ha, Mama, you are the rotten egg!"

She laughed loud and deep, clutching her tight stays. Yes, God did have a sense of humor.

* * * * *

Darkness was settling in around the house, and brought with it blessed cool breezes. Ruby raised the kitchen window higher and took a moment to enjoy the fresh night air flowing through her cotton dress. She pulled herself away and stoically faced the heat of the black iron stove to stoke and provoke for more heat. The irons and the basket of washed and rolled laundry waited patiently.

Where is the maid when I need her most? What a luxury that must be to have someone to help clean. Edith is fortunate to have Mama and Opal there. They will surely miss Opal when she marries and moves away.

As she moved the iron back and forth over Robert's shirt, she ticked off in her mind what must be done. Early tomorrow morning, first thing she must gather flower spikes from her lavender plants and spread on newspaper to dry overnight. Then she would bring in the many small cucumbers to begin the twelve-day process to pickle. Then all the rugs must be taken outside to beat and rub with salt to clean. Once the rugs were out, the wooden floors would need scrubbing to rid of that constant coal dust. Then the washing must be caught up, which brings about more ironing. And she needed to find time to bake bread, but that would have to be late in the evening, too, because the heat of the stove was too great to bear during the summer days. It was unfortunate the house was not built with a summer kitchen. Maybe someday. What day was it anyway, because she needed to get back on schedule or —

"Ruby."

She jumped at the voice and looked up startled to see Robert leaning in the kitchen doorway, arms folded.

"Mercy, Robert, I thought you had gone to bed!" Ruby laid her hand over her heart to settle it down. "Your door was closed when I was tucking the children in and –"

"I was washing up," he said. "When are you coming up to bed?"

"Oh my, Robert, I have hours of ironing –"

"You have all day tomorrow."

"Well, yes, Robert, but you need this shirt tomorrow, and it is cooler in the evenings to iron."

"Finish my shirt. Then come up to bed," he said and then he was gone.

She heard him going up the stairs whistling. Why did he take on whistling? Darn, the stove was just getting worked up to produce sufficient heat for the iron! Well, she would have to obey him. Better the stove being left unattended, than Robert.

He had earlier expressed disappointment in that the parlor remained in its untidy state upon his return home. And supper was late. But she had arranged her own priorities into children, garden, supper, in that order. Although the children assisted in hoeing weeds and bringing in freshly picked green beans and cucumbers, and had gathered in a circle with her to pluck the chicken, they still ran out of time. Ruby had forgotten how town life had spoiled her in that she now bought her chickens already dressed for cooking from the butcher.

Robert appeared at the backdoor to witness Victor standing on his cricket bench, blowing a handful of feathers over his mama's head and announcing, "It is not raining cats and dogs, but chickens!"

Ruby was hunched over the balding bird, cradling it in her hands, crying, "Don't rain on my baby! Not on my baby!"

They all had a jolly time until Jonathan pointed to Robert. They quickly became somber, parading into the house where Ruby held out the bird to Robert, declaring, "Behold a feast!"

He only raised his eyebrows and said, "A feast indeed? I prefer mine cooked."

She only smiled and said, "Coming right up!" and chopped it into several pieces for dredging and frying.

"Well, it took several days to get the house this way, and it will take me several days to return it to normal," Ruby stated matter-of-factly at supper. She would not allow Robert to upset her homecoming supper of fried chicken and fresh picked green beans. The boys were gobbling her hours of effort down in moments in order to get to the chocolate cake Robert brought home.

Bess stopped chewing at her mama's statement and her eyes darted from Papa to Mama. Her large blue eyes looked at fault. "I'm sorry Mama," Bess said. "I tried to wash the dishes but I couldn't keep up. The boys kept eating all the time. And they wouldn't help me. Victor said dishes are women's work."

"There is no need to apologize," Ruby told her.

And she meant that for herself, as well as for Bess.

She finished ironing the shirt and then put a large pot of water and chicken bones on the stove to take advantage of the heat. It would simmer into broth by morning.

She paused at the staircase, holding on to its ample and ornate landing post and her eyes followed the stairs up to the closed bedroom door. She closed her eyes and attempted to find some inner strength. Her body ached from exhaustion but it would still be some time before sleep was permitted. It had been about three weeks since their last intimacy.

She slowly climbed to the door and it opened to a brighter bedroom than normal for this time of night. Usually the light was turned down low. Instead, the gas lights on the wall were turned up, and the gas lamp by his side of the bed was lit. Robert was lying on the bed, arms propped behind his neck – oh mercy, he was completely nude! She reached up instinctively to turn the gas light down.

"Leave it alone!" His command was deep and sudden.

Her hand jerked back. He had never displayed his nakedness like this before. Even his weekly bathing was done with some modesty, requiring her only to wash his back and then exit the room. Try as she may not to look below his stomach, her eyes went there of their own accord and she was reminded of a nest with a baby bird in it. There was an unusual tangy odor in the room - whiskey? What was she to do?

"I want to watch you wash," Robert said.

"Wash what?" she asked, confused, feeling like she walked into the wrong bedroom. Excuse me but have you seen my husband, she wanted to ask. He sounded as casual as if she were standing at her clothing tub.

"I don't need to explain. I am your husband. Now undress." His tone was level, without emotion.

Ruby walked hesitantly over to the washbowl and took the pins from her braided bun. Two thick braids fell like ropes down her back. She began unbuttoning her blouse.

"Take the braids out," said the voice from the bed. Her fingers obeyed, plucking through the inter-linking locks, and slowly Opal's fashion dissolved into kinky strands. Sadly Opal's handywork fell away; Ruby would never be able to duplicate the style. She fluffed her hair to separate, peeking out of the corner of her eye toward the bed. He hadn't moved; only his head was turned to watch her.

Again she tackled her blouse buttons and then her corset, moving more quickly this time. She wanted to get this exhibition behind her. Off went her skirt and petticoat. Apparel she once considered her enemy was now being laid aside with misgivings, as if losing a friend. She fluffed her hair again, now thankful for its unbraided mass to shield her. The long strands fell forward to hide her breasts as she poured water into the bowl and soaped a cloth. Trying to keep her emotions as calm as he appeared to be was not working, her hands were shaking so.

"Wash slowly," the gruff voice came again from the bed.

Inside her, she imagined throwing the cloth down, stomping her foot and yelling, "Now Robert, you are being ridiculous!" Outwardly she made an effort to control herself. This was intimidating, if he really cared. He seemed a stranger to her, the bright room out of place, and this was alarming. She closed her eyes in sheer embarrassment when she moved the cold cloth between her legs. It was met with a groan from the bed. Ruby peeked over there again and saw what had once appeared as a bird, now had taken the form of a serpent's head and neck.

Robert was touching it! Oh mercy, how vulgar! Vulgarity, indeed! Now what must I do?

No need to wonder.

"Come here!" he commanded.

She walked over to the bed, thankful to sit down before her knees buckled from trembling. The sheets felt oddly cool to her buttocks. He took her hand and laid it where she most feared.

"Now stroke it," he said. She had touched it before, of course, but only to help him guide it in. He folded her fingers around the smooth neck and moved her hand up and down roughly to demonstrate. "Your hands are cold, woman!"

She could only watch in horror, her hand feeling detached somehow. He closed his eyes and groaned again, moving his hips in rhythm. His breathing was in rasps now. She wanted to withdraw her hand but his hand remained firmly over hers. Suddenly the serpent spit its venom, and milky liquid dripped down her thumb. His movements slowed and he gradually let go her hand. She silently walked back to the washbowl and washed her hand.

She walked over to the nightgown on its hook and took it down.

"Don't put that on, Ruby."

"I thought we were—"

"No we are not."

"Really, Robert, it is getting –"

"I will not listen to resistance any longer!" he shouted, raising himself up into a sitting position. "I did not take a firm stand as master of this house, and look what happened! Now I make the rules here, understand? And you will do as I tell you, if I have to beat it into you!" He slammed his fist into the mattress with these last words.

Ruby clutched the gown in front of her. "Robert, I have always been an obedient wife. I made an error in judgment—"

"Then obey me now!"

"What do you wish me to do?"

Robert closed his eyes and inhaled slowly. He was struggling with some emotion, but she didn't have a clue what it could be. He opened his eyes and they moved down the length of her steadily, with intention.

"Return your gown to its hook and come lie down." His voice was calmer now. He patted the spot where his fist had been a moment ago.

Will this night ever end? She approached the bed. Her hair was concealing her breasts, but did little to cover its curly shorter version remaining exposed between her legs. Just like a sitting duck waiting for the firing. She sat down and swung her feet around onto the bed. She laid down stiffly, her arms straight to her sides. Not even her doctor, in all his humiliating examinations during her pregnancies, made her feel as exposed as she did tonight. Even he, as his hand would search for the baby through her opening, would ensure her gown remained at her knees, in the name of propriety.

If Robert would only let her turn down the light. She focused on the ceiling and its ever-present crack in the plaster.

His hand crawled across the distance between them and moved away her shielding hair from her chest and stomach. Her nipples rose to the touch. Why were they doing this? They only hardened when they were cold, and this room was certainly far from cold this evening.

Her eyes followed his hand as it moved over her white stomach, over her white mounded breasts, topped with rounded brown circles, and then slowly down to her small mound of boldly contrasting black hair. He cupped his hand over it and squeezed, his middle finger slipping inside, touching, touching, sliding lower, deeper. Ruby felt a familiar sensation, as if her nerve endings in her skin had come alive. Ever so slightly, her hips reached to him, something inside her black mound betraying her, its own heartbeat asking for more.

Instead, he removed his hand and grabbed her own, still at her side, and laid it where his hand had been.

"Touch yourself," he whispered hoarsely.

Her eyes opened wide to him and her legs closed together. "Pardon?" she whispered. His eyes remained on her hand, his lips red, his nostrils flared, breathing as if on a fast gait.

He demonstrated, moving her hand down between her legs and up again, down and then up. Her hand was limp. What did he want her to do? The heartbeat died. She only felt awkward and foolish in this light.

The act sufficed for him. "Ahhh," he said. He brought his foot over to her ankle and dragged her leg toward him, thus separating her knees, opening their union to him. He removed her hand and forced several of his own fingers inside her.

She stiffened in discomfort and by reflex grabbed his wrist and removed his hand.

Her resistance spurred him on. He rolled over onto his knees, between her knees. He placed his hands firmly on her knees and pushed them further apart. His hands slid up her thighs, opening, examining, prodding. His breathing was erratic now, his strange lack of control disconcerting. She kept her eyes closed tightly, afraid to look, afraid of him, afraid of what he was seeing down there.

"Ahhh!" he gasped. "I love seeing your body like this!" His speaking only added to the strangeness. He normally said not a word during their intimacy.

Grabbing her wrists and raising them to the pillow above her head, Robert fell forward on top of her, pressing himself on her, between her, over and over until he found her opening. He raised himself up on his elbows and thrust completely into her, moving with short rapid jerks.

Now he was in a routine she was familiar with. She tried to settle to wait this out.

He pulled out and returned to his knees. "Go over onto your hands and knees." He attempted to pull her hip over to the other side.

"Pardon?" she asked.

"Hands and knees, I said!" Her confusion seemed to irritate him. He pulled her arms up to force her to sit up and then roughly pushed her over onto her stomach. He raised her hips up, bringing her to her knees, and then separated them with his own. He held on to her hips and jabbed from behind until he was moving inside her again.

She had only seen such a thing from farm animals during mating season. He certainly was grunting like one, she thought with repulsion. This seemed so primitive, so uncivilized! Ruby tried to turn her mind away from her behind. Suffer-in-silence, suffer-in-silence, she chanted in her mind to the rhythm. He was banging her buttocks with a resounding flap, flap, flap. She felt pressure on her bladder and tried to focus on remembering to go to the chamber pot when it was all over. She found a little comfort in thinking of this routine, this normality. But of course as this lighted night would have it, he lasted longer than was his routine. His grunts continued to alert her that he was indeed enjoying this in some beastly way. Just when she thought he would release, he would only slow down, and then move faster again, pinching her hips in his clutch, as if he would fall down if he let go. Her knees began to ache, being held in this barbarian position. It forced her mind to question: Was this a sin? Was this her fault? Was he trying to teach her a lesson? She listened to the squeak-squeak-squeak of the bed springs until she thought surely she would scream to stop. Finally, he thrust inside her hard one, two, three times, lurching her body forward each time. He made a sound somewhat like a cry. Everything about him that was hard now relaxed. He released his grip on her hips and fell to his side.

She lowered her knees to where she was lying face down on her stomach. If she moved, he might touch her again, so she did not move. The chamber pot was out of the question. Her half-closed eyes saw the bright light dim as she heard him lowering the gas light. Very soon she heard him breathing beside her in his familiar sleep pattern, and she ever so slowly reached down to the rumpled sheet at the foot and pulled it over her. She moved to her side, into a fetal position, hugging her arms for comfort.

The heartbeat was a throb now that only subsided in sleep.

* * * * *

The early morning alarm tinkled softly to start the day, as it always did. Ruby was facing the window, focusing on the early morning light as she always did. But something seemed to be out of the ordinary, with only this cool sheet lying lightly on her skin. Then memories of the night before flooded over her with crimson shame. She was afraid to move once again, and disturb the sleeping beast she heard snoring behind her. But her bladder insisted otherwise so she slipped off the bed in slow motion without looking back, and tiptoed behind the screen to relieve herself on the chamber pot. Sitting down fully on the thin cold rim, she hoped to muffle her bodily functions, wondering how to get to her gown and robe, out there in plain view. She did not want this animal she was sleeping with, to awaken. Something about a nude body, was it? She shook her head. And here she was, sitting naked as her plucked chicken from yesterday. She wiped and winced at her soreness, spotting three purple bruises on her hip the size of fingerprints. Merciful Lord, there was her robe hanging over the screen. She was never so happy to see any object. The robe went on quickly before someone could stop her, hugging her sleeved elbows in the robe's generous protection. The gown would have to wait.

As usual, she would not wash and change until Robert had done so, had eaten his breakfast and left for the shop, so she tiptoed lightly to the door to prepare the morning meal.

"Ruby."

Her hand froze on the doorknob. She pressed her forehead to the door. Please dear Lord, he is not going to make me—

"Yes, Robert?"

"Tonight," Robert began, and then cleared his morning throat, "tonight Preacher is coming by. After supper."

Preacher Paul?

"Why?" she asked, turning toward the bed. Only his face was

visible, thanks be to the sheet that now covered him. The window light had not yet reached his side of the bed and he lay in shadows. He rolled from his side to his back and placed his hands behind his head and stretched.

"Because I asked him to. He stopped by the shop yesterday afternoon. Discussions led from one thing to another, including an invitation here."

Why now? Preacher Paul hadn't been here since the birth of their last child, six years ago. Ruby's labor had been a three-day long dark passage. She remembered thinking she might die, right here in this room. Garnet had asked Preacher to come in and say prayer. He kindly had done so, and Garnet attributed Ruby's recovery to the miracle of his prayer.

Robert sat up and ran his fingers through his hair. "Please heat some water for my bath. I wish to bathe before breakfast." Laconic as always, Ruby thought irritably. He moved his legs over the side of the bed. Ruby did not wish to view the sheet slipping altogether from his body so she hastily exited, without further questions.

What a day I have in store for me!

The cluttered parlor looked bleak regardless of the sun coming through the windows. Its bright sunrays only highlighted the dust in the air, the dirt on the floor. And now a visitor! And Robert would expect the house and children to be washed clean of their sins before the Preacher's arrival.

The kitchen was very warm, the stove still heated from the night before, bubbles popping through the lid of the kettle of simmering chicken bones broth. She shoveled red-spotted gray ash from the stove's belly into her ash bucket, fed it more wood pieces, and newspaper to start a large flame, and then added coal. She pumped water into the kettle and placed this on the stove. She walked out to the small scullery between the kitchen and backdoor and pulled out the large round gray bathing tub she stored beside the bricked and copper laundry tub. She sighed, hearing the grit of coal dust move across the floor under its heavy weight. She wondered once again if her mother-in-law and Robert had done the right thing in installing the sink pump in the larger kitchen. This room was once used as a back kitchen for washing dishes, and a sink pump would have been handy to wash both dishes and laundry. She started a fire in the grate under the laundry tub to begin the chore.

As she was pouring boiling water into the bathing tub followed by cold water, he entered the room behind her. She flinched involuntarily. She silently handed him his soap and scrub brush from the shelf above her, draped a towel over the tub and exited. He pulled the cotton curtain across the kitchen doorway and she heard the robe land on the floor.

"Now he is being modest!" she muttered under her breath.

"More cold water, please," she heard from behind the curtain.

She pumped more water into the bucket and carried it through to the tub. He was sitting on his haunches in the tub, his knees drawn up to his hairy (beastly!) chest, his buttocks not yet touching the water. She didn't wish to see more. She drew back the curtain at the backdoor window to look outside while she continued to pour. There was Aimee out in her garden! It was so good to see her! She was bent over, appearing to attack the dirt viciously with her hoe, in between her rows of green leaves. Her one long yellow braid had fallen over her shoulder, its pointed end bobbing up and down, threatening to lick the dirt.

"I said, that is enough water!" Robert said from below. "For the love of decency, would you close the curtain? What are you looking at out there?"

She closed the curtain. "Oh, I see our next door neighbor, Aimee."

"Oh yes. She called to me from her fence one day," Robert said. He was soaping his hands now, his knees still at his chest, his buttocks submerged.

I see there are no bruises on *your* hips.

Robert continued, "She asked me where you were. She wished to speak to you. Why would that be?"

"We've become friends and visit occasionally," Ruby answered. Was that casual enough?

"Yes, I am *perfectly* aware of your friendship," Robert said.

Yes, all-knowing, all-seeing, Ruby thought, sarcasm dripping like the water from his arms as he washed.

"A friendship that has led you right down the main street of town, parading yourselves in front of God and men alike." Agitation was returning to his voice as he spoke.

She didn't want to discuss this any further. She must get him bathed, fed and out of here, so that she could talk with Aimee. Ruby's day had brightened, just seeing her out there in her bright yellow frock and large white apron. She exited to the kitchen, cracked eggs into the skillet, and returned.

She held her hand out to Robert. "Hand me the brush, please, and I'll scrub your back."

He consented and leaned forward. As she lathered his back, he said, "Ruby, you will not remain friends with Aimee. She is an angry woman and her husband is having difficulties enough as it is. I heard her shrieking again, only two nights ago. She will not spread her disease to her neighboring home and into my wife. I will not allow any more of this nonsense." His skin flinched, as she scrubbed a bit too hard on his lower back. "Do you understand me, Ruby?"

"I'm right behind you, Robert," she answered softly. She dropped the brush in the water behind his back and left, drying her hands on her robe. Just let him try to squeeze around in that narrow tub to reach the brush. If he says one more word, I shall surely shriek myself.

They spoke no more. Finally he was gone. Unfortunately, by that time, so was Aimee. Ruby watched for her during her many trips to the clothesline and garden. It wasn't until the late afternoon, while Ruby and Bess were beating rugs, and the boys were pushing the rusty grass cutter through thick grass, that Aimee reappeared. They met at the fence. Bess followed Ruby and remained shyly hidden, in part, by Ruby's skirts.

"I'm so happy to see you—" Ruby's voice caught in her throat. Aimee's left eye was swollen and purple, her lip puffed on the same side and bruised. A tiny cut was on her right cheekbone.

Facial powder had been applied, with futile efforts.

"Oh, Aimee, not again! This is the worst yet!" Ruby cried, reaching out to squeeze Aimee's arm. Aimee quickly turned her right side to Ruby and shrugged. She squinted at her back garden as if watching something significant going on in her tomato plants.

"I apologize, Aimee. I spoke without thinking. I don't mean to embarrass you."

Aimee smiled a lopsided smile. "Naturally you would notice," Aimee said, now concentrating below her, the toe of her boot kicking at a stubborn weed. "The lavender here along your fence row smells lovely!"

Ruby could not divert to another subject. This was just too much, to see her friend like this. She leaned forward over the fence, longing to hug and comfort, but Aimee only backed away a little. "Aimee, why does he do it? What drives him to such – such violence?"

"I say it is because he is drinking hard liquor. *He* says it is because I am not obedient. But this last one ..." she shook her head. "I deplore you not to be angry with me. I hesitated all day to come out to speak with you. But I had to come out eventually because I have an invitation for you. But that is the good news. First the bad." She paused and reached for the fence for support. "Two mornings ago, I was bringing in some laundry, when I spotted your husband walking from your ..." she thumbed her finger toward their outhouse, "your privy. I hadn't seen you since our march, so I was worried. Silly me ran over to the fence, in a hurry to catch him. I was only asking him where you were. I suppose I shouldn't have been so forward but..." She looked back toward her garden, refusing to look at Ruby.

"I don't understand the connection. Why would I be angry?" Ruby said.

"I was talking with a man, other than my husband, and was dressed unsuitably, to boot." Aimee explained, her tone parrot-like, like she was quoting another's words. She kicked the weed harder and its roots became exposed. "*Your* husband, Ruby!" she emphasized, as if wanting to bring home the point that Ruby would understand, and perhaps would then understand Aimee's husband. "Look, it was morning and I was still in my robe. I was being far too bold." She folded her arms and kicked the weed some distance away from her. "Do you suppose he was jealous?" Her tone to Ruby sounded of hope for some understanding, her own understanding.

"Humph," Ruby answered, also folding her arms across her chest. She turned toward her own garden, not willing to see Aimee struggling so. Ruby could not, would not, justify his drunken temper, no matter for what reason. "Jealous, indeed! Mercy, Aimee, why aren't *you* angry?"

"I was ... I was, but not anymore." She focused her attention on the fence, her fingernail chipping away at the cracked white paint on the fence rail. Her hand was red and chaffed.

Ruby looked down at her own hand, folded across her opposite arm. No different, she realized.

"Yesterday morning," Aimee was saying, "when he sobered and drank enough coffee to rid of his headache, he then noticed my face. I was pouring his coffee and he grabbed my wrist and just *stared* at me. I am a fright, I suppose. I backed away, spilling some, but it was he who apologized. He reminded me that it is partly my fault, for I *do* provoke him and do not always do as I'm told. Which is true ... of course." She attempted a little laugh, but it sounded more like someone had pressed on her stomach and forced air out her mouth. "The ironic thing about it all was that if I had been advancing toward your husband with illicit thoughts, it would have been all for naught."

"What do you mean?"

"Because your husband was rather ... un-neighborly. He stopped at your stoop there, and, I believe, *glared* at me! Then he answered, 'Ruby has gone to her mother's for a few days. When she returns, I suggest you remember that the fence is there for a reason. Please keep on your side of it!'"

Ruby waved her hand and shrugged her shoulders, trying to appear nonchalant. "Oh, he didn't mean it!"

"Oh, but I think he did!"

"Then, neither one of our husbands mean to misbehave, and we all shall live happily ever after." Ruby said.

They both chuckled without mirth. It was a fine line from crying.

"Let us change the subject, then. Gratefully I have good news." Here, Aimee lowered her voice and moved her side closer to the fence. "My husband will be out of town assisting at another bank tomorrow, so I am able to host our ladies' tea! Isn't that wonderful? You *will* be there, Ruby?"

"With bells on!" Ruby blurted out without hesitation.

"Wonderful! I can't wait! Tonight will move so slowly!" Aimee said, reaching out and patting Ruby's hand.

"Oh, tonight...Preacher Paul's visit," Ruby said, suddenly noting the lateness in the day. She clicked her tongue in dread. She had a sinking feeling about the purpose of his visit. "If I live through Preacher Paul's fire and brimstone tonight, I'll be there," she said. She laughed and shrugged. "Oh well, if I *don't* live through it, I shall *still* be there with *wings* on!"

* * * * *

"Well! Sister Ruby! Shall we have prayer first?" Preacher Paul said, hiking his rain-damp trousers at his knees and sitting down in Robert's chair in the parlor.

Robert seemed at a loss as to where else to sit, that chair being his only resting place. Ruby sat in her rocking chair and he finally sat stiffly on the settee.

Whatever else this visit might bring, Ruby decided it would be well worth the rest off her feet. Finally, to sit! Not even supper allowed more than a five-minute rest, for as the meal began, so did a rainstorm, and Ruby ran outside to bring in the sheets before the rains came to diminish her efforts. The others were finished eating by the time she returned. She ate her meal walking between kitchen and dining room, clearing up the dishes. Preacher was due soon after.

The rain was pouring by now. The children, previously told

they must play outside, were now sent to their rooms. Why they couldn't remain here after their preliminary how-do-you-dos, was beyond Ruby. Robert found their giggling chatter a nuisance during adult conversation so they were promptly sent away. They knew by heart their father's favorite expression that children should be seen and not heard. Oh well, they might be better off, she thought, keeping her eyes respectfully closed during Preacher Paul's prayer. The Preacher was a sincere man, but he talked loudly and long, as he was doing now, as if his congregation sat in the wings of the room.

"And dear Heavenly Father," Preacher continued, "I come to you today, asking that you give me your holy word. Righteous words, Lord, to say to our dear Sister Ruby. Dear Lord, guide me to show Sister Ruby the error of her ways, so that she may be a light to others, so that she may bring love to her family. Dear Lord, help me in delivering the message that a woman's obedience is a virtue and one required by law, by God's law. Dear God, show Sister Ruby that as Christ *is* head of the church, so *is* man the head of woman. I ask this in the name of the Father, the Son and the Holy Ghost. Amen and amen."

Ruby felt flushed with...anger, embarrassment, shame, hurt? She wasn't sure but when she opened her eyes, they welled with tears in being treated as if she were naughty; somehow ill behaved. Her chair had become uncomfortable now, for it was the judgment seat. Error of her ways. Indeed!

She blinked back the tears and eyed them both and waited and rocked, her hands appearing docile, folded in her lap. If she spoke, she would surely cry, and she would not give them the pleasure of pointing to her emotional womanly ways as another error. Preacher was leaned over in his chair, arms on his legs, his small Bible in both hands, looking at its worn black cover as if waiting for words to appear. Robert would not meet Ruby's eyes, but folded his arms and looked away, pretending a keen interest in the framed embroidery on the wall over Ruby's head that read, 'Learn to do Good'.

In a slow purposeful motion, Preacher put on his spectacles and opened his Bible to a page marked by a red ribbon.

"Sister Ruby," Preacher began, "Hebrew, chapter 13 says, 'Obey them that have the rule over you, and submit yourselves; for they watch for your souls, as they that must give account, that they may do it with joy, and not with grief; for that is unprofitable for you.'" His head raised from his reading, his watery, tired eyes beseeching Ruby's.

To Ruby, he often looked as if he had just finished crying or was getting ready to.

"This verse is talking about your preacher," he said. "For God's Word tells me to watch over your soul. To rule over you, to guide you in God's Word. And that is why I am here, Sister Ruby. For I believe you are going down the wrong path and only grief can come to you if you continue. I want to account for you with joy, Sister Ruby, not grief."

He can certainly project his voice. The children will hear from where they are, no need to be here. And no need to hear of their mother's sins, either.

"I wish now to take you to Titus, chapter 2." He opened to a page marked with a slip of paper and moved his finger down the page line by line until he found his place.

"Could you give me one moment, please?" Ruby asked. She jumped up and walked to the back of the room, to the secretariat, where her own Bible lay. She returned with it in hand. "I wish to follow along, if that is ... permissible?"

"By all means!" Preacher answered, his head cocked to one side, looking at her Bible in surprise. "I'll give you a moment to find Titus, chapter 2 ... very good. Now let's read verses three, four, and five. 'The aged women likewise, that they be in behavior as becometh holiness, not false accusers, not given to much wine, teachers of good things. That they may teach the young women to be sober, to love their husbands, to love their children. To be discreet, chaste, keepers at home, good, *obedient* " here he raised his finger to emphasize, "to their own *husbands*, that the word of God be not blasphemed."

What was he insinuating? "I understand I'm being chastised

here, but for what reason may I ask?" Ruby found her voice and it was shaky.

Preacher took off his spectacles and rubbed one eye. He sighed the sigh of a burdened man, his hunched back telling of a heavy load. Accounting for souls could not be easy.

"Sister Ruby, let me be frank with you. Ever since July fourth I have been praying for you. You have been on my heart and I believe that is God's way of telling me, 'Preacher, pray for her for she has been led astray.' Why, I was shocked and deeply wounded to see one of my own Christian soldiers, one of my own souls, marching with she-devils! Yes, Ruby, she-devils, marching against God and God's word. Onward Christian soldier, not with the cross of Jesus, but with a banner of bad tidings. My poor wife was crying and praying for you, too. I tried to block it from my memory, saying, no it can't be so, not our little Ruby, who has been going to church, faithful and true, since she was a baby. But then God said, 'Wake up, Preacher!' and He showed me your picture on the front page of the newspaper. Sister Ruby was marching, as part of a God-forsaken women's march. These women dressed in black skirts, are no more than black widow spiders, going against God, the church, venom to poison their own homes and families. Somehow you got tangled up in their web, Sister Ruby. But as the Lord forgives us of our sins, He teaches us to forgive others. I forgive you, Sister Ruby. I am not here to condemn you. Why, on the contrary, I am here to set you free! I prayed to God to forgive you as soon as I saw it, and I walked over to your husband's shop as soon as I could."

"Why not come directly to me, Preacher? As you said, I have been attending your church since I was a baby."

"It is my obligation to know first, if you had your husband's permission in doing such a vulgar public performance. He assured me he had forbidden you to meet with these ladies at all. He was as shocked as I was! Why, Sister Ruby, you outright disobeyed your husband! Since you have been attending my church all these years, have you not listened to my preaching of God's Holy Word?"

Disobeyed. There was that word again. First Aimee was beaten

Good Woman

for it, and now she herself was in danger for it. She looked down at paper tucked in between pages of her Bible, notes she had taken from his sermon on Man's Dominion. She had written 'men have the right to master over all living things. Master must rule and protect.'

"To obey my husband would mean my husband is my master?" she asked.

Preacher nodded happily. "Yes, he is the master of his household. I see you *were* paying attention in church," He sounded relieved that he had gotten through to her.

"Then I am his slave," Ruby stated matter-of-factly. "And of course it wasn't long ago that we fought a very bloody Civil War over that very thing. Do you know what Abraham Lincoln said on the subject? Let me find that quote for you."

"Well, now, Sister Ruby, there is no need—"

But she was already walking over to the secretariat and soon returned again while reading out loud from a newspaper clipping, one of several she had saved on the assassinated president. She found his life and speeches fascinating and was sorry she had missed his presidency by less than a mere forty years.

"Mr. Lincoln is quoted as saying: 'As I would not be a slave, so I would not be a master. This expresses my idea of democracy.'" She stopped in front of him and looked at his bent head, his thin threads of gray hair, his pink scalp. "Surely, you believe in democracy?" she asked. She knew she was challenging a Man of God, but she found strength in Mr. Lincoln's words.

He did not look up but continued looking down at his Bible, his finger still on the Word. "Yes, of course, democracy is a rule of government, for all *men* that are created equal. But God's Word presides over government, Sister Ruby." His tone was of one talking down to a child and losing his patience, although she was the one standing there looking down on him.

"But you just read that we must obey them that have the rule over you. This can certainly be interpreted to also mean our democratic rule of government? Our laws? Laws which include freedom as a right to us all, men *and* women?" She knew she was blushing at her boldness in adding 'and women' but continued. "Mr. Lincoln is also quoted here as saying: 'Those who deny freedom for others deserve it not for themselves.' How far must obedience go before we are denied our freedom?"

Speaking these words of freedom somehow gave her courage and from deep within she felt a release of her own words. Preacher opened his mouth to speak, but she forged ahead, sitting back down on the edge of her rocker, her arms on her legs, leaning forward in earnest. Her corset pinched her side as she did this, but she paid little mind to it - or to Robert and his pinched lips.

"These women you saw me marching with, are all good Christian women. But their freedom has been denied. Take Aimee, my next door neighbor, for instance. Her husband, in the name of obedience, beats her. Would you beat your wife into submission? Of course not. But what about the men who do? Must she obey a drunken husband? What if, in his drunken stupor, he told her to rob a bank? Must she obey, and break a government law, because God's presiding law said she must obey her husband first? You read here in Titus ... let's see ... here it is ... that women should be 'teachers of good things'. Well, women are not permitted the schooling they need. How can they teach the good things to others, if they themselves are not permitted to learn? How can an aged woman teach young women, when they are forbidden by their husbands to leave their own homes, forbidden to talk to strangers or even their own neighbors? How can I teach my children of life's lessons and struggles, when I myself am not allowed to experience it beyond these walls!"

She clutched her hands together as if in prayer and gave both gentlemen her pleading eyes. "Please forgive me, but I see 'obey' as another word for control or slavery. I see the democratic law not protecting women. And I see husbands not protecting their women." She tapped her fist into the palm of her other hand. "Where are these women's rights, Preacher?" She did not wait for an answer. Her thoughts were tumbling over one another in an effort to get out and be heard.

"And what else does God's law say? Why do you only read to

me what women are supposed to do? Look here! It also prescribes what men are supposed to do. Let us read on here in Titus. 'That the aged men be sober, grave, temperate, sound in faith, in charity, in patience ... young men likewise exhort to be sober minded. In all things shewing thyself a pattern of good works; in doctrine shewing uncorruptness, gravity, sincerity.' And does the Bible not also say, in Genesis I believe, for the man to cleave unto his wife? To love her as Christ loves the church? Well, I say that if man *obeyed* the commandments and did all these things, then women would be happy to *obey* the man! Because to obey a sober, patient, loving man would not require obedience at all, but many returns of love and honor. She would stand beside him happily and willingly, both man and woman teaching the young good things!"

She was out of breath with these last words, her face feeling hot from her audacity. She swallowed hard and her mouth was dry. In the pursuing silence, her boldness slipped away. "May I offer you something to drink, Preacher?"

Preacher Paul seemed to be at a loss. He shook his head. His cheeks had turned a bright pink. His finger had not moved from his open Bible. His eyes darted over to Robert and then back to Ruby. Clearing his throat, he returned to the verses. "Well, now, Sister Ruby, you may be right in some things you are saying there, but not being a minister of God, you have misquoted. You see," he shifted in his chair and began tapping on the page of his Bible as if he were trying to keep the words down, "the verses you are reading are commandments for the pastoral work of a true minister. If you studied your Bible more, you would know this chapter does not apply to all men." He said this last sentence sounding rather relieved at finding a rebuttal.

Ruby looked down at her own verses and nodded as if she suddenly understood. "Oh, yes, of course, I see...then that means that the quote about women being teachers of good things, only applies to women ministers?" She put her hand to her mouth as if struck by a revelation. "Oh my! Does that mean that women can preach? For truly, what is the difference between teaching and preaching? And does this mean, then, that only women ministers must obey their husbands?"

There I am challenging him again, perhaps even mocking him, but what can I do? Does he think I am stupid and cannot read?

Preacher sat up straight, shaking his head emphatically. His eyes were dry now, heated in anger. "God did not call women to preach!" He shook his finger at Ruby. "Jesus chose only men as his twelve disciples!"

Ruby's eyes went wide in surprise. "Surely you are not saying that this chapter only applies to all women, and not all men?"

Preacher looked truly confused, and helplessly directed his glares to Robert.

Robert uncrossed his legs and then crossed them the other way. He looked reluctant to take charge. He cleared his throat. "Ruby, are you questioning a Man of God? And, I might add," he said in appeasement to the Preacher, "you are being disrespectful in our own home."

Ruby drew in a deep breath and let it out slowly. She sat back in her rocking chair, attempting to settle, rocking to soothe. She was both amazed and a bit disconcerted at being so outspoken. Where did all that come from?

Well, I started this petition and I will surely have to finish it.

"I do not mean to be disrespectful," she said cautiously. "I am only asking that Preacher Paul, as the true minister I know him to be," and she read again, "be 'sober, grave, temperate, sound in faith, in charity, in patience' when preaching to me. Preacher, please, in charity, listen to me. I have done nothing wrong! You see me marching for women's rights and neither one of you have asked me why. Without a fair trial, I am judged and on my way to fire and brimstone. And for what? For speaking out for downtrodden women! I *can* speak my own mind, which surprises me as much as it may dismay you."

She stopped rocking and looked at Robert. It occurred to her that Robert had said 'our home'. He was certainly on his best behavior in front of the Man of God. His hypocrisy made her angry. "And Robert, while I have the courage to be so outspoken, I wish to add that I am happy to hear you call this," and her arm swept around the three walls and windows of the parlor, "*our* home. I had heard quite the opposite from you only a few days ago. I don't remember you cleaving unto your wife as she slept on the front verandah."

She turned away from his reddened scowl.

Well I've said it all now so I had better excuse myself before the counterattack. Two against one is hardly fair.

She stood and extended her hand to Preacher Paul. "Forgive me but I must beg leave."

Preacher half-stood, nodded his head, and sat back down. He ignored her hand. He looked dazed and a little upset.

Ruby continued. "I must get the children tucked in to bed. I am so happy we talked." She placed her hand over her heart. "I feel so relieved I have gotten this off my chest. More and more I find, I have my own mind! As a Christian woman in a democratic society, I should be able to speak it! Good night, gentlemen!"

She nodded toward Robert and left the room, her skirts rustling noisily in the silence that followed. She walked up the stairs feeling like she understood the word 'liberated' for the first time in her life.

Bess was sitting on the top step, chin propped in her hand, evidently eavesdropping.

"Your mama actually spoke her mind!" she whispered to Bess with a hug.

Bess returned the hug and smiled. "That's good, Mama," she whispered back. They walked hand-in-hand to Bess's bedroom.

Bess sat on her bed and looked up at Ruby. "Mama, why does Aimee's husband beat her? What does women's rights mean? Could we talk about that sometime?"

Ruby looked down at Bess, her sky-blue eyes looking up in praise to her mama, so innocent, so trusting. Would Bess understand? Would hearing adult reality taint her childish belief in her parents? Most likely. Bess was yet too young.

Ruby smoothed the hair around Bess's face. "I think my little girl has heard too much already. There is more though to talk about some day. Lots more. Perhaps some day soon."

Ruby kissed her daughter good night and walked to her room. She would have preferred, instead, to run across the yard and tell Aimee about tonight. But of course, she would have to wait until ... tomorrow! Yes - the tea at Aimee's! She had walked through the fire and brimstone and came out the other end a stronger woman. Finally had something to contribute to her tea with her legion of friends.

* * * * *

The door slammed hard behind her. She jolted from the washstand, her camisole clutched in front of her breasts and turned toward the door. Robert approached her in three long strides and grabbed her shoulders.

"How dare you be so rude to a guest of our home, or, no, of *my* home, as you so eloquently reminded me! I am ashamed of you!" He slapped her face hard with his open hand. "Is it not enough you flaunt yourself in public parades, carrying my name? Now you must do so in my home and give me the blame?" He shook her hard.

She began to cry and her tears were only fuel to his flame.

"Not so high and mighty now, are you?" He pushed her hard and she fell halfway onto the bed, her camisole falling to the floor, her breasts exposed. She crossed her arms across her chest, afraid to rise.

He placed his hands on his hips and looked down at her smugly. "Preacher's last words, before he left were, 'You better get control of your wife, Brother Robert, better bridle her and break her in or she'll just buck again and run off.'" He pulled his suspenders off his shoulders and unzipped his pants. They fell to the floor and he fell on top of her.

He pinned her shoulder down with one hand as his other hand jerked at her pantalets. Somewhere in her mind she knew they were tearing, but the sound was muffled by the sound of her sobs. Each time she tried to raise, tried to struggle, he only pressed his weight down harder on her, until she was gasping for air. He was whispering names in her ear, names she blocked out, could not comprehend. Soon he was hunching against her, between her, then inside her. He grabbed the back of her hair and held on tightly as if holding onto the mane of a galloping horse, her hair unraveling across the quilt. She could no longer sob, no longer breathe, everything turning gray in her mind, when he finally froze, groaned, relaxed, and stood back up.

He kicked his pants away from his feet, unbuttoned his shirt and threw it onto the floor. He did not look at her. He shook his head as if in disbelief. "You are not the woman I married. I don't know you anymore." His voice was now weak, shaky, his anger, his energy now spent.

She gathered enough air into her lungs to move again. She drew up her legs, still dangling over the side, and crawled up to the head of the bed, puffing her pillow to feel its soft substance. She felt deflated, flat, as if his weight had pressed her paper-thin, her only substance being his fluid he had released inside her. She hugged her arms in her fetal position and faced the window.

"And the man I married is only a dream," she murmured.

* * * * *

In the early morning, she awoke with his words still there, as if written on the window she faced. 'You are not the woman I married.' Had she changed? At what point did she become a woman in the first place? When did her smile turn upside down, as if the weight of her world bore down on these muscles?

Was it her wedding night? Did the loss of virginity's blood take with it the naive girl; her dreams of sweet romance (ah, he kissed her lightly, ever so lightly – directly on the lips! – gazing into her eyes as if she was too good to be true); or hearing music around her, like the tune from a gurgling stream in rhythm with the cows' bells in pasture; or birds' twittering meant for her, telling her stories of their flights, and what they saw from their heights.

No, her naiveté did not suddenly harden on her wedding night. She still so vividly remembered the heated flush of her face, when her mother-in-law returned home the next day from a night at her sister's. How Ruby felt terribly awkward and apologetic, as if the residue of his fluids, of her lost blood were visible on her face. That his mother was secretly shaming her for it. She remembered stripping the bed in the early morning, and soaking the sheet to wash away the red circle of guilt. But a light gray moon of a stain remained, man-on-the-moon winking that he knew what they were doing. And a week later, facing her own family. That somehow they were looking at her differently, a knowing smile twitching at the corners of their mouths. How she had trouble looking them all in the eye for months.

Did motherhood bring her into womanhood? Was it her unspoken pregnancy and its public proof of what she and Robert were doing in the privacy of their bed? Why keep it so private, she remembered wondering. What difference did it make if the outcome was protruding obscenely from your belly, as an invisible banner that read, 'Vulgar acts performed here!'

No, she had not changed then, because as the doctor lay her newborn baby in her arms, her first thoughts were the same as when she held her first porcelain-faced baby doll to her eight-year old breast: 'Mine, my own'. Its painted cheeks were etched in her memory as clearly as her breathing babies' warm cheeks were. She felt no different, only that this was the next natural step.

Was it gradual then, this becoming a woman? Was it the days, the weeks, the months, the years, that added bits and pieces of womanhood, like the birds add to their nests, one twig at a time, until one day you realize, as you fly toward home with yet one more twig - can't stop, must keep going! - you realize the round nest is there, intact, precariously clinging to its unpredictable branch, for better or worse, in windstorms, and in sunshine. The nest is holding three babies, their faces turned up to you expectantly, dependent on you for food and protection. You must keep holding on. Is that what womanhood is all about? Just keep holding on, going on, take your duties one at a time, don't look beyond the task at hand. For if you saw the end of the day, and that this day and its efforts only brought night ... and your husband ... in the privacy of your bed ... more pregnancies to labor, more children to feed. An endless cycle. Why ... why would it be worth it all?

"Ruby, are you awake?"

"Yes." She remained still, only allowing breath to enter and exit her body.

"About last night," he said. "I have gotten past my anger and am thinking about some of the things you said to Preacher Paul. You made some good points. I watched in disbelief as someone else spoke passionately through my passive wife. I was disjointed, somehow unassociated with the only woman I've ever known, in the only home I've ever known. Odd. Very odd. Where did these ideas come from? Ah yes, the parade of women! Well, I must put that all behind us now. You did go a bit over the edge though, when you directed your disfavor of wrongful doings toward Preacher, then toward I, but ... well ... in all fairness ... I reacted inappropriately."

He was apologizing. Now she was in disbelief. She felt her spirits lift in spite of herself. Perhaps...

"Robert, could we talk sometime about – all that?"

"I think I've heard all there is to say, haven't I? There is more?"

"Much more."

He breathed in deeply and let his air out slowly. "Perhaps some day soon."

She saw a glimmer of hope through shimmering tears, a small light of promise coming into her dark passage, just as the window in the dark room promised her a bright day.

* * * * *

She paced between the windows of the dining room and the parlor. She didn't want to walk over to Aimee's until the others began arriving – it wouldn't be fair to Aimee to arrive early only to interrupt Aimee's last minute preparations. She could hear from here, the boys' heavy thumping from their third story bedroom. Bess was with them and was probably putting in a gallant effort at playing with them, but as they worked up momentum, their wrestling would undoubtedly become too rough for her. The boys' room would become too warm soon, at any rate, and they had permission to come downstairs but not outside, until Ruby returned from next door.

Finally the horse's hooves of a buggy could be heard coming down the street, and mercifully it stopped in front of Aimee's house. Ruby reached for her hat in the entrance way and then waved it away. It was hardly worthwhile – what was that rumbling sound? Whatever it was it was getting louder. She walked out onto her verandah in time to see Thomas's black metal beast pass by and stop in front of Aimee's house.

Mercy, these automobiles are loud! It seemed to create an uproar all around, from the birds in the trees to the dust on the street. The machine paused and then moved forward past the hitching posts, apparently not wanting to block where the horses would be tied. The engine stopped and all was right with the world again, with the sound settling quietly. The birds picked up their song once more.

Ruby approached as Thomas was assisting Cady from the passenger side. Lizzie stepped out from the back seat. Cady's appearance slowed Ruby's steps down. Cady was bent over slightly, her thinned frame leaning heavily on a cane.

Ruby gave her a small hug, her heart squeezing at the feel of Cady's bony shoulders. "I had heard you were ill, Cady, but I had no idea ..." her voice trailed off. She felt an odd sense of betrayal, as if Cady had decisively kept a secret from her.

Cady waved her off and smiled. "I'll be back to smelling the roses in no time. I look worse than I feel."

Thomas shook his head, his hand clamped firmly on Cady's elbow. "Don't let her fool you, Ruby. She shouldn't be out today, but she doesn't listen to a word the doctor or I say to her."

Ruby saw no bright smile lighting his eyes today and his dark blue suit only seemed to add to his somberness.

Cady patted his hand. "This is far enough, Thomas. I can walk the rest of the way with Ruby and Lizzie." She looked up at him with beseeching eyes, as if to say, *don't make a fuss, please.* "Thank you, darling. I'll see you in two hours, then?"

He looked unwillingly to let go, but relinquished his hold over to Lizzie.

"Don't you worry, Mr. Pickering," Lizzie said. "We'll look after her, won't we, Ruby? We won't let her do more than lift a tea cup!" Lizzie winked and nodded at Ruby.

Ruby gave her a supporting smile and flanked Cady's other side. She smiled shyly at Thomas. "Cady will be fine with us, Mr. Pickering. She is at her best when leading our little group to victory!"

This led Lizzie into a hymn of "Victory in Jesus, my Savior forever, He sought me and He bought me with His redeeming blood..." as they stepped slowly up the walk to Aimee's front door.

A thought suddenly occurred to Ruby that Lizzie must sing to comfort herself, since only in tense times did Ruby see Lizzie do so. Ruby looked back to see Thomas still standing there, hat in hand, watching, concern written all over his face.

Ah, to have this kind of love given to you! I envy you, Cady, for even at your worst, you have the best. She felt a bit ashamed for thinking so, but when she looked over at her house and up to her bedroom window, she felt as empty as her window's inner room.

Phyllis and three ladies Ruby did not recognize were on the front porch – why Phyllis was in britches! Ruby couldn't believe her eyes.

Phyllis looked down at Ruby approaching the steps to the porch and stifled giggles behind her gloved hand. "Ruby, your eyes are as big as saucers! Don't ever tell a fib, Ruby, for your face tells the truth no matter what you say." She turned toward Aimee. "Have you noticed that about Ruby? Every emotion is visible – you know how some wear their hearts on their sleeve, well with Ruby—" and she patted her cheek to indicate where.

Ruby blushed as she and Lizzie helped Cady take each stair slowly. "I apologize, Phyllis. I'll try to remember that next time I speak with my husband."

They all laughed and Ruby blushed more deeply.
Here lately I've been blurting without thinking –
"As I was just explaining to Aimee," Phyllis continued, "my buggy wheel broke yesterday in that huge pothole on Main Street. I do wish they would fill that in!" She placed her hands on her hips, evidently comfortable with her appearance.

No corset; her sagging breasts only covered with a red undershirt and a man's white shirt tucked into brown britches with a black belt, her stomach protruding shamelessly.

"Are our taxes only going to politicians, I ask? Why, just the other day I asked our mayor – Cady do you need some help coming inside? You are looking better today, I declare. No, Ruby, to answer your expression's question, I'm dressed to ride on my black mare. She needed the exercise anyway, so I gave her a good run. Can't very well do that in a dress, now can I?"

"No, of course not, Phyllis!" Ruby answered. "To be honest with you, and how else can I be now that I know." Ruby patted her own cheek, attempting to show her good humor, "I admire your gumption in doing so. I frankly would never have the nerve, although secretly I long to wear such comfortable apparel."

Aimee was holding the screen door open, shaking hands as they entered. Her bruised face was much better today, facial powder carefully applied, smiling at everyone as if she had not a care in the world. The smell of fresh baking drifted around her.

"Ruby," Aimee said, "I would like to introduce you to Anna, Donna, and Jenna. Phyllis met them while going door-to-door gathering signatures for our petition. They wish to become members and participate in our convention. Isn't that wonderful?"

Ruby shook hands with each, noticing their similar facial features, particularly their large blue eyes and long eyelashes. They must be sisters, she thought. Ruby could relate to their shy and quiet ways, probably uncomfortable around strangers, like she was at her first meeting.

"We are so happy to have you here!" Ruby said. "You can only add strength to our cause! Come in and sign up!"

As she followed them in, she saw how out-of-place their clothing was among the black and white clothing of the Ladies of the Lost Legion. They were dressed beautifully in light colored prints and lace, their varying shades of light brown hair tucked under large hats that matched their dresses. They wore white gloves and held tiny purses carried by gold chains. And to top it off, they each held a parasol.

Well, they either feel uncomfortable, or sorry for us.

Ruby entered Aimee's home for the first time, anxious to see its interior. Surprisingly, the layout was different from Ruby's house in that the staircase was not in front of the entrance, but in back of the room and going up the side. The dining room was on the right of the stairs and a door went into the kitchen from the left of the stairs. Ruby appreciated this design because the parlor was larger this way, but she thought it unfortunate that the room was darkened with heavy green drapes at the windows, and cramped with massive wood furniture, stained in deep cherry or mahogany. The one bit of light was over a low but long hutch to her right. The hutch was filled with cookies, breads, and several steaming pewter pots. It was sitting below the window facing Ruby's house. From this perspective, an unrelated home was next door. A sash pulled the drapes partially back and Ruby could look into her kitchen window from here. She made a mental note to always wear her robe while in the kitchen from now on.

New faces had already entered the room. The one familiar face of Sarah, a stack of papers in her hand, was talking with a group of ladies explaining the purpose of petitions.

This was all so exciting to Ruby that she squeezed Cady's elbow and almost giggled. But her giggle stuck in her throat when she glanced at Cady. Cady was trying to focus on walking, her lips pressed together in pain or concentration, it was hard to tell. Ruby saw a padded rocker by the fireplace and they headed there, where Cady sat down stiffly.

Cady smiled up at them appreciatively, and then extended her hand to the others who approached her, wanting to meet her, they loved her newspaper article, ready and willing to follow her. "So happy to have extra hands and hearts!" she answered. She

visibly gained strength through the smiles and encouragement.
Ruby pulled Lizzie over to the piano, away from the chatter. "Is Cady – is she so ill?" Ruby whispered.

Lizzie moved her lips around in thought. "Cady doesn't wish to speak of it," she whispered back. "But folks are going to find out one way or another, I'm afraid." Her warm hand wrapped around Rub's arm. "She has a disease, honey. It is in the womb. Ate up any chance of her having a baby. Or having a life for that matter."

Ruby suddenly felt smothered, the room too dark, too warm, too much noise. "Oh, Lizzie, no!"

"Now, don't say anything about it today!" Lizzie insisted. "Cady's wishes! Smile and give her the strength she needs. Pray for her honey, she just might make it! It ain't over 'til the Lord says it is!"

Ruby turned up her lips to look like a smile, and nodded. She couldn't think of anything to say, so it was for the best that Lizzie left her there to walk over to another group to say hello.

Soon Sarah had the circle formed, beginning with Cady and working around the room, with extra chairs brought in by Aimee. Some ladies had to sit on the floor. Ruby counted thirteen – imagine, and there were only five that came to Cady's tea in the spring. Sarah, always faithful to their routine, sat on the right of Cady and handed her the minutes from their last meeting. Cady read them aloud, enunciating clearly, her voice reaching out tentacles of strength to the others, belying her own body. Then she asked everyone to introduce herself. Ruby discovered during the introductions that her little group had been very busy. Cady, Lizzie, Sarah, and Phyllis had brought in new recruits. Aimee had gone through a great deal of effort hosting this meeting. Ruby, on the other hand, had done nothing here of late to contribute. Her legion had continued working the cause while she was caught in her personal dilemma.

How inadequate I am. Hardly worthy! Well, I have an idea for the convention that might gain favor, and at least show I am thinking about doing my best.

Her stomach churned, though, in imagining herself addressing all these ladies with an idea that she hadn't yet discussed with anyone.

"Ladies, I have an important announcement to make." Cady said. "We now have *two* guest speakers at our convention! Along with Mr. Whiting, the principal of Parkdale High School, we have the honor of hosting Carrie Chapman Catt! Do you all know who she is?"

Ruby had not a clue, but she noticed that Anna, Donna, and Jenna were quite excited about it.

"For those of you who don't, please let me explain," Cady said, her tone of one a little disappointed that more enthusiasm was not received. "Carrie Chapman Catt has, for the last ten years, been working for the National American Woman Suffrage Association. She actually spoke in the Washington D.C. convention in 1890 and was asked by Susan B. Anthony to address Congress in 1892 on the proposed suffrage amendment. *Congress*, ladies! What courage!"

She leaned forward in her chair toward the group, looking like her old self. "Let me give you a little history lesson. The Susan B. Anthony Amendment was first introduced in Congress in 1878, to grant women the vote. This amendment was necessary because the 15th Amendment in 1870 stated that voting rights could not be denied on account of race, color or previous condition of servitude. Gender was not mentioned, as we all know too well. The Senate only voted on the suffrage proposition *once* in the 19th century, defeating it in—" She leaned toward Sarah. "Can you recall the year, dear? My memory seems to have failed me."

"1887, I believe," Sarah said. Her head remained bent over her notes as she continued to scribble.

"Yes, that's it, 1887. Since then, Carrie has followed others, such as Lucy Stone, to winning the vote through the states, rather than through the federal government. You see, ladies, under the Constitution, each state has the right to determine who can vote. So, Carrie has committed herself to extensive travels through the states in speaking engagements and has now established her reputation as a leading suffragist. Just this year she succeeded Susan B. Anthony as president of the National American Woman Suffrage Association. The *president*, ladies! Unfortunately, she won't be here long, just two nights on her way to New York City to assist in organizing a suffrage organization branch. But she has agreed to speak at our convention!" She clasped her hands to her chin, her face flushed with color. "Now do you see how important this convention has become?"

The room was quiet for a moment, excepting the fans, or whatever else they could find, flipping in front of their faces. It was becoming increasingly warm in there.

Ruby didn't know about the rest of them, but at the moment she was feeling rather intimidated by the convention. Even in this heat, her hands were cold and clammy. What in the world would she do at such an important convention? The thought of her poem she had finished only this morning was sounding puny next to a speech by the woman president. The only time she had stood and spoke in front of a group was at her wedding, and she was told what to say then. Now she was thinking of speaking in front of a great deal more people, with her own words, words that might sound insignificant, or worse yet, foolish, and in front of the woman president! Mercy to Heaven!

"Mrs. Catt was our speaker at The Debating Society in the Women's Christian College in Ohio." All eyes turned to Anna. "My sisters and I," she nodded toward Donna and Jenna sitting on either side of her, "attended this college and were members of The Debating Society. Mrs. Catt was an excellent speaker and I think quite swayed the debate to our side."

Cady's eyes flashed with interest. "You've seen her then? Excellent! What was the debate about?"

"Should women in the United States have equal suffrage with men, of course! Mrs. Catt was perfect!"

"Tell us about the debate, please!" Cady said.

"The debate is rather a formal one," Anna said, "presided by three judges, in this case it was, Honorable William Rankin of the Superior Court of Ohio, umm—"

"The Dean of the Women's Christian College, Mr. Roger Wil—," Donna added.

"And my professor of second-year English Literature, Mr. McDonald," Jenna interrupted. Donna rolled her eyes toward Jenna, but Jenna was too busy smoothing out her skirt to notice.

All three were sitting on the floor, their feet tucked under their skirts. If Ruby had half the material of Jenna's dress, she could fashion two beautiful dresses for she and Bess. The many yards of their full skirts billowed out around them, appearing to Ruby as if their tightly bodiced upper bodies had landed in an abundant pile of fabric.

"Anna and I can give you an account of the *winning* side," said Donna, "but you should know we have a traitor amongst us here, with Jenna, who can give you the points of the *losing* side."

Jenna shot Donna a heated glance. "Thank you, sister, for bringing that out at such an opportune time. But I am not a traitor, only…undecided is all, which is why I agreed to come in the first place."

"Are you certain your attendance is not to collect information to take back to Mildred? I do believe she is organizing an anti-suffrage group, isn't she?" Donna asked.

Was Donna taunting her sister in public? Watching such an open display of family disagreement was fascinating. Ruby and Opal argued, yes, but certainly not in public. This interaction was like watching the school play Bess was in last year.

Cady, obviously sensing that a heated personal debate had already begun, spoke up. "We are an open-minded group here, I believe. To hear both sides is only fair. I see this as a learning exercise that can prepare us for the possibility of an open debate during the convention. Please, tell us what you determined as the pros and cons of equal suffrage for women."

Anna began. "The decision of the judges was based on three points." She counted these off her fingers. "Logical arrangement, force of arguments, and manner of delivery. There were five ladies on each of two teams. One team was for equal suffrage, one against. The judges asked questions that each side had an opportunity to answer. You probably picked this up by now but I'll clarify that Donna and I were for it and Jenna was against it. As part of our force of arguments, our pro side asked that Mrs. Catt be permitted to speak. We argued that her speech was no different than bringing in any other evidence to prove a point. The opposing side objected, but was over-ruled." She gave a flash of a smug look to Jenna and then continued. "After much heated discussion, and I warn you here ladies, the convention may become quite emotional, our final points are thus: Freedom was given to all so to give the vote to the women is the only logical step. A woman should not be deprived of the vote just because other women do not want it. It is a matter of justice. To be allowed to vote would expand a woman's narrow views and her personal interest in her community would increase. Umm—"

"We also concluded," Donna chimed in, "that because it is so logical, many women miss the opportunity to speak out. They become apathetic in thinking that they have the freedom to choose, when in fact they do not. Some shrug their shoulders and say they don't see what the big deal is about. They don't see that in the eyes of the government, they are second-class citizens. If more spoke out, we may have won the vote by now."

She leaned toward Anna and said in a low tone, "Was there anything else?"

"No, that is about all I can think of right now." Anna leaned toward Jenna. "Jen, would you share with the group the opposing points?"

"Well now that you have put me on the spot, I suppose I have to," Jenna snapped back. She sighed heavily. "But I must say, I feel somewhat like a lamb among wolves here."

"Please don't feel that way!" Aimee said. "This is my home and as hostess I will not allow any discord. You are welcomed to voice your opinions because we do believe this is a free country, yes?" She looked around the group, who all nodded with affirmations. "Besides," Aimee added, "I'm certain that much of what you say will address the same issues we have all wrestled with in some fashion."

"Thank you," Jenna said, looking quite relieved. "I don't mean to sound so negative, but this has been an ongoing saga between my sisters and I. So!" She was eager now to proceed. "Let me think. Our first point was that if we are looking for influence in our community, we already have it. Women are mothers and that is the most significant influence a human experiences. Secondly, the vote is an expression of will that represents a physical force of order, which should only come from the men. Women do not possess such a physical force. Thirdly, the female vote is more easily manipulated than the male vote because she is not as educated as the male and may simply vote the same as her husband or brother or father. That means the vote would simply be doubled but with the same results. Or worse yet, only the intelligent women would vote and exert political influence, leaving all other women out. Let's be frank here – how much interest do most women have in politics now? Present company is an exclusion I realize, but nonetheless, only a small group. Overall, women would be no better off than they are now."

"Your points are hitting close to home, young lady," Phyllis called out from her perch on the arm of the sofa, "and I see no need to attack a woman's personal integrity. She doesn't have to be intelligent to know right from wrong. What about her instinct, her gut feeling, her common sense? I've delivered babies from mothers who knew that their baby had died in their womb long before I knew; who knew they were pregnant within days of conception. These are the same women who deliver their eleventh baby during the day and then care for their ill toddlers through the night. I would take a woman with common sense over an educated man any day! You make us sound as stupid as a cow following a cow to pasture, or how about a cow following a cow to slaughter!"

"We do have minds you know!" Sarah said, her eyes squinted in anger at Jenna. "If we do not speak out for ourselves, who will? Men? I think not – I *know* not! Besides, men aren't doing such a good job at voting on their own. For example, you may remember that they almost brought us into another civil war and almost left us without a president, in the election of 1876, split as always between the Democrats of the south and the Republicans of the north. Perhaps the only reason that President Hayes eventually gained respect after that election was because he was recognized and presented with a desk by Queen Victoria. Men argue violently; they know no other way. Their physical force of order, as you call it, is not what I call democracy."

Ruby heard Lizzie humming the hymn *Just as I Am* and it sparked a thought. "Why would it matter whether we are intelligent or not?" she said. All eyes turned to her and she felt her heart beat faster, her face flush. "Well, do men have to take a test before voting?"

Others laughed and Phyllis called out, "Some would be hurtin' if they did!"

"Exactly," said Ruby. "They give their vote, *just as they are!* Should women not have that same right without being graded, just as we are? And if only a few of us go to the polls, can we not speak out on behalf of all women?"

Whew, that wasn't so bad! Nonetheless, she was so relieved when Cady spoke and all eyes turned then to her.

"This is true, Ruby." Cady said. "Men represent the best interests of men, so women should represent the best interests of women, just as we are! That will be the slogan for our convention. Just As I Am! What do you think, ladies? Which brings me to our agenda for the convention. We must get this set today! Thank you so much, ladies, for that lively debate but we must move on! Time is short!"

That last sentence hung in the air for a moment.

"Now ladies," continued Cady, "I have a sketchy agenda here but I need some ideas. Here it is so far. First I thought I would begin the convention with an introduction to the Ladies of the Lost Legion, who we are, what is our purpose, our mission, and what we hope to achieve. Then I would make announcements on who will speak and so forth. The next speaker I have down here is Mr. Whiting. He has shared his speech with me and his words are short, very supportive, and to the point. Phyllis will be next, stating the seven reasons why we fight for our rights. Lizzie has agreed to perform as Sojourner Truth and do her famous speech, 'Ain't I a Woman?' The crowd should be sufficiently warmed for Carrie Chapman Catt, who shall speak last. But following our mission statement, is where I hope to have some of our other legion members volunteer to say something of their own. Do I have any—"

"I wrote a poem," Ruby heard herself blurt out.

Oh, now I've really done it.

All eyes were back on her again, burning her face crimson. She focused on Cady's face. "A-Also, I have in mind a chorus to a possible song. I was thinking ... perhaps ... we could enter the grounds singing this chorus - all of us - something that might be inspiring."

"A song, Ruby? Interesting. May we hear it?"

"Well, I don't have a tune for it yet. But here are the words:

> Women are people, too,
> We are no less than you,
> Equal rights will see us through
> To share where freedom reigns.

Donna sat up straight, her eyes wide. "May I play your piano? I just heard a tune in there somewhere!"

"Certainly!" Aimee answered. She was sitting on the piano bench that she had moved next to the settee. She picked the bench up and returned it to the piano that was set against the wall leading into the dining room.

Donna and Anna both stood up, their eyes bright with interest. They picked their way through the group, holding their skirts in closer to allow more room to maneuver. Anna suddenly stopped and turned to Ruby. "Can you write those words down?"

"Certainly!" Ruby stood and looked expectantly at Aimee.

"Oh, you need a pencil and paper, don't you?" Aimee said, and rushed over to a large rolltop desk, rolling its cover back, exposing a paper mess. "Sit here, Mrs. Wright and write!"

Ruby did so, listening to the piano keys strike minor chords, its player and Anna repeating some words of the chorus. Hearing her words being treated with this enthusiasm was exhilarating. She walked her paper and pencil over to the piano.

Anna snatched both out of her hands. "Thank you! Okay now, here it is, Donna! I'll repeat the words. You need a C in that. There you go. Oooh, I like that tune." They began earnestly working through chords and writing them on the paper.

Ruby stood by, quietly watching her birth of words evolve into a life of their own.

Jenna suddenly appeared at the piano. "You know what you could do is, add another verse, based on what we talked about today. You know, the slogan. Something like,

> Women are not as lambs,
> Take me just as I am!
> Let me speak for all wo-men
> And vote where freedom reigns!

"Oooh, I like that, too!" Anna cried. "Let me write that down. And we need an ending to this, perhaps repeating the last two lines, but instead we could say, Voting rights will lend a hand, and then end with Ruby's last line, To share where freedom reigns."

Others gathered around, adding their suggestions of, "while singing we could walk through the crowd in single file", "we could carry candles", "or flowers", "all dressed in white", "oh no, black and white!" Soon they were all around the piano, including Cady on her cane, all singing the two verses. Ruby could hear harmonies of alto and soprano.

She could not believe her ears. She had never felt such fellowship; what did Cady call it, yes, camaraderie. She closed her eyes and opened her mouth and sang out loud. If the convention never happened, it didn't matter at this moment. She had never been happier.

*****

Ruby's eyes opened, a thought flew in, and she froze in fear. Today was the convention. She lay still in the darkness and listened; the birds were not up yet so she must have woken up in the middle of the night. Too early yet to get up. Her mind began its journey through the words of her poem, yet again. She had it memorized by now; she had repeated it so many times. Oh no! What was the last verse! Her heart picked up a few extra beats. She repeated the verse before it, and the last one then came to her. She closed her eyes and prayed, Please dear Lord, help me through this day. I can't even imagine what it will hold. It looms far bigger than I am and I don't know where to begin! She heard a little inner voice say, *Then begin where you know.* Yes, of course, she would take this one step at a time. For now she will quietly arise and move about her morning in the kitchen – she knew what to do there. The fear of the unknown is always bigger in the dark, so she will bring in light. She will go into the kitchen and turn on the gas lamp, light a fire in the stove, and let her day begin there. The light will chase away the dark. She felt better so she wiped her cold clammy hands on the sheets and arose. None other stirred but her.

By the time the others rose and came thumping, mumbling down the stairs, she had prepared their breakfast of biscuits, milk gravy, and fried green tomatoes, started a pot of green beans and ham hocks for dinner, baked a rhubarb and strawberry pie, and baked a skillet of cornbread. Her apron showed remnants of all the ingredients, so much she had dropped or spilled, and her shaky hands were stained with strawberries. A small blister had formed on her finger from where she had clumsily stuck her hand in the oven to gage its temperature. Dirt was on her feet where she had walked to her garden barefoot to pick the vegetables. She couldn't seem to focus on one task for very long; the cornbread was missing some ingredient but she couldn't remember what she might have forgotten. Her mind went from flour, to poem, to crust, to song, to slicing tomatoes, to imagining many eyes on her, to imagining Robert's eyes on her. Then she remembered no one would be at home for dinner. The beans would have to sit until suppertime.

She was certain she quite literally jumped out of her skin in surprise when Victor came in to the kitchen behind her, asking the same question he asked every day, "What's to eat?"

Her husband's eyes raised in question when he saw her disheveled appearance but he said nothing. He ate little and his only words were a request for apple cider vinegar mixed with water to settle his upset stomach. He seemed as distracted as she did. She knew he knew the convention was today; the ladies had posted signs around town stating so. Cady's husband, Thomas, had announced it in the newspaper. Carrie Chapman Catt had added credence to the convention, so Ruby was certain the topic had come up in Robert's shoe shop, but he made no mention.

Nor did she. They had spoken no more about women's rights since the morning after the preacher's visit. Nor had he made any more physical demands upon her person. It seemed to Ruby, as she watched him drink down her apple cider concoction, that his emotion was all spent. His non-intrusiveness had allowed her to move him into the background, as if he were part of the furniture she must wash and care for. Now for the first time in two weeks, she wondered what he was thinking. Then she remembered his eyes during the July Fourth parade – would he have that same look by the end of today? Pushing his thinking out of her mind, she turned away from him and walked back into the kitchen. There was enough to be terrified of, without thinking of his reaction. *That* she would deal with *after* the convention.

She poured water into the dish pan, observing the trembling of her hand in doing so. One step at a time. Robert call out goodbye, and when she heard the front door close, she yelled for Bess, Jonathon, and Victor to get dressed. She heard them clamor up the stairs.

"Mama!" Bess cried.

Ruby ran from the kitchen to the bottom landing of the stairs and looked up.

"What is it, Bess? You scared me!"

"Mama, come upstairs!" Bess cried again, and then she whispered, "I'm bleeding!"

"Mercy!" Ruby whispered as she hastily climbed the stairs, her eyes examining Bess's face, gown, legs, feet, for signs of red. Bess grabbed her mama's hand and pulled her into her bedroom and closed the door behind her. Without modesty, Bess pulled up her gown and pulled down her pantalets. Sure enough, blood was inside.

Ruby sat down heavily on the bed. "Oh my little Bess, you are not so little anymore," she said sadly. She felt she had lost her child in that very moment.

"What is wrong with me, Mama?" Bess sounded frightened.

"Nothing ... and everything," Ruby answered and then smiled as she patted Bess's cheek. She should have known this was coming. She had spotted a few brown pubic hairs just this last Saturday during Bess's bath.

She sighed. "Well Bess, some call it a woman's curse, but I say you will be happy to see this, more times than not."

Bess was studying the blood more closely. "I am *supposed* to bleed?" she asked, looking incredulous.

"Sorry, Bess, Mama is talking in riddles. Yes, you are supposed to bleed every month, and will do so, unless you are married and with child - carrying a child in your stomach - well, actually the word is pregnant, although you are not to say that in public, though only the Lord knows why since women have loads of babies. You won't bleed when you are pregnant. But otherwise you will for many years. So let us start your womanhood off by showing you how to layer rags and cotton and pin them to your pantalets. I'll explain more to you then, and afterwards you must get dressed. I'll prepare you a cup of lavender tea to ease your tummy."

Bess was the first one downstairs. Her hair was not braided today, instead the top half pulled back into a barrette, its long brown length meeting the tied waist in the back. She was wearing her longer white-laced church dress and stockings. Ruby studied her for a moment. Somehow Bess looked much older, her lips more pronounced, her cheekbones more defined, her face more drawn. Yes, she could even see two small mounds on her chest. Did that happen overnight? It would not be long before she must introduce Bess to another curse – the corset. She didn't ask Bess why she was dressing up. Somehow she knew that Bess wanted to dress the part that she was feeling. She was a woman now. Hmmm, a woman now. Ruby studied Bess closely. It was time. Yes indeed, it was time. Bess will attend the convention.

Aimee's mother had agreed to watch Ruby's children at Aimee's home with their own. One step at a time, Ruby was getting closer to the City Hall Park. Step by step she, Bess, and Aimee walked there. By then, Ruby thought surely she would faint from her nervousness in this heat. She threw herself into whatever needed to be done, just to keep her mind from thinking ahead. Time flew. The City Hall bell tower bonged one o'clock, then two, then three. Three o'clock already and people were beginning to gather for the four o'clock starting time.

Tears came to Ruby's eyes when she saw Thomas drive in with Cady in his automobile. They had all worried that Cady would not be able to make it – and oh what a shame that would have been, since without Cady, the convention, no, not even the Legion would have happened! Aimee and Ruby stood together and squeezed hands as they watched Cady exit the car and stand up straight. Her eyes were shining as she looked up and saw the streamers and banners around the top of the gazebo, the signs from their Fourth of July march stuck in the grassy dirt around the bottom of the gazebo. She waved at Phyllis who was handing out flyers to people as they approached, laughing and talking as if she knew them all, flyers that read her 'Seven Reasons Why We Fight For Our Rights'. Cady waved at Sarah who was, along with two unknown gentlemen, putting the final touches on a booth they had put together a few yards away from the gazebo, with a sign across it that read 'Sign Our Petition Here!' Anna and Donna called "you-hoo!" to Cady, their skirts and blouses in satin and lace, but black and white no less, gathering the women together, passing out papers to each with the words and musical score to the song Ruby and they had created. Jenna was not with them.

A stranger stepped out of the automobile's back seat.

"Aimee, that must be the woman president!" Ruby whispered.

The woman walked around the automobile and joined Cady. They approached Ruby and Aimee and the other women gathered around, too. Cady introduced her as "Carrie Chapman Catt, president of National American Woman Suffrage Association. We are so pleased she could be here!"

The women applauded and Ruby felt quite privileged to be here. To think if she hadn't agreed to attend her first tea at Cady's home, what all she would have missed! She would be in her kitchen, thinking in darkness, and not seeing more clearly through the light of others who had so much to offer! She loved Mrs. Catt's large intelligent eyes – they looked so kind, as if you could tell her anything and she would not be shocked but nod in understanding. Mrs. Catt wore the colors of the Legion, in a black and white wide-striped dress, and Ruby realized this subtle significance was a sign of respect that added prominence to their cause.

Anna immediately came forward, Donna following behind, introducing herself, saying "do you remember speaking at the Women's Christian College in Ohio?"

Ruby backed off shyly, having nothing to say, but watching in awe. She had never met anyone famous before and just being there as a spectator was enough.

Eventually she saw her group of women gather at the back of the crowd and Donna was beckoning to her to join. She saw Cady and Mrs. Catt walk into the gazebo and sit on the backbench. This was it! Ruby's heart jumped to her throat and she could barely breathe as she walked through groups of people standing about. She tried not to meet their eyes as some eyed her suspiciously, others curiously, and she heard one whisper, "there is one of them!"

Donna handed her a music sheet and Lizzie draped a white

satin sash over her head and onto one shoulder that read down the front in black letters, 'Women's Right to Vote'. "Made these myself!" Lizzie whispered to Ruby's questioning look.

Ruby started at a drum roll right behind her and turned to see Frances, a lady she only met briefly at Aimee's tea, with a snare drum secured around her neck with a wide ribbon that read, "Women's Vote" written repeatedly down its length to where the drum rested below her waist.

"Ladies, in line, please!" Anna called out.

Ruby grabbed the hand of Bess. "Come on, Bess, it is time you learned to march and sing for women-kind!" Bess fell in line behind Ruby and they all followed Anna's lead in marching in step, the drum keeping time.

The sound of the drum brought more people into a tighter group around the gazebo, many craning their necks to see what was going on. Ruby's eyes darted from behind Lizzie's shoulders and guessed there must be at least a hundred people or so, probably a good deal more on the outskirts of the park milling about. After a few minutes, Anna turned to their formation and yelled, "One, two, three, sing!"

> Wo-men are people, too!
> We are no less than you!
> Equal rights will see us through
> To share where freedom reigns!
>
> Wo-men are not as lambs!
> Take me just as I am!
> Let me speak for all wo-men
> And vote where freedom reigns!
>
> Voting rights will lend a hand
> To share where freedom reigns!

They marched through the crowd, singing loudly, proudly, marching in time with the drumbeat. Most were facing the crowd boldly, not needing to read the music sheet, the song already in their hearts. Around the gazebo they marched, splitting into two groups, one on each side. The drums, the song, the affect met their purpose; people crowded in around the front of the gazebo.

Ruby saw Thomas on her side of the gazebo, a megaphone in hand, eyeing the crowd of mostly men as if they were carrying weapons. When all was quiet, he handed the megaphone inside the gazebo to Cady, who then walked to the front railing without assistance. She faced the crowd, shoulders back, chin up, her stature of one defying defeat. She lifted the megaphone to her mouth.

"Ladies and gentlemen! Welcome to Annan's first Women's Rights Convention! The purpose of today's convention is to urge men to vote in November in favor of a proposed amendment to the state constitution to give women the right to vote. We come in peace and ask that you open your minds and hearts."

Her voice seemed to carry to the very length of the park and echo through the trees. Ruby realized now why her first thought that morning froze her in fear. She felt that way again. Many of these faces watching Cady were not friendly. On the contrary, some were sneering, others shaking their heads. Why, she wondered for the umpteenth time? What were they asking for that was to be mocked and ridiculed so?

One face stood out in the crowd. His face was not sneering, his head cocked to one side, listening attentively, his deep-set blue eyes watching Cady closely. His head turned as someone bumped him in the crowd and his side to Ruby revealed a short black ponytail. He was in the front row, close to where Ruby was standing, and his friendly, and yes, even intense, interest somehow comforted her. Ruby looked for other friendly faces in the crowd and found a few varying expressions; some were smiling, others nodding, one lady hid a yawn behind her glove. She saw two men whisper and both laugh loudly. She couldn't see much beyond the first two layers of people standing quite close to the gazebo. Her eyes drew back to the man with the ponytail, the ponytail man, she smiled to herself. She couldn't help but stare – something about him. Was he part Indian? Certainly not all Indian with those eyes and small straight nose, but his blue-black hair and square jaw were certainly Indian traits. Was his skin naturally dark or did the sun darken it? He was dressed casually but certainly not in buckskin, of course there was that leather vest he was wearing –

Ruby jumped at the change in voices in the gazebo. Phyllis was up there now reading off her 'Seven Reasons'.

Shame on you! You must concentrate more on what is going on.

Fear gripped at her again. She was next! She reached across her chest for her throat and could feel her heart beating against her forearm. How in the world was she to get up there and face this crowd at such close range? She instinctively wanted to run but her feet were frozen into the ground. Her eyes searched the crowd again, and again rested on the ponytail man. She focused on his eyes, his folded arms, his tilted head. He shifted his position, straightening his arms and hooking his index fingers in his belt loops. As he did so, his eyes shifted to Ruby. Her cheeks burned in embarrassment so she looked down at her hands, only to see them shaking.

Before she could think clearly, before she could calm down, she heard her name announced. Her little group was applauding around her and opening the way to the gazebo. Her shaky legs carried her up there, although for the life of her, she didn't know how. She could hear the wood panels of the flooring beat her footsteps as she walked across to where Cady was standing, applauding, her megaphone clamped under her arm. Cady then handed this to Ruby with a warm smile and wink. Ruby attempted to smile back but her bottom lip quivered in other directions. Cady squeezed her elbow and then left her alone to face the many eyes. Ruby suddenly wished she had brought her written poem with her, for then at least she would have something else to look at, some words to read rather than reading these many expressions on so many faces. She clutched the megaphone with two hands and looked out. There was a sea of hats and bonnets, many more that she could see from this raised platform. She felt lost, alone, and oh so afraid, her heart beating loudly in her ears – could they hear it?

She was floating, she was fainting, oh she needed an anchor, when she saw in the corner of her eye, the man, the ponytail man, step forward into her view. She met his eyes and he smiled and nodded as if to say, *Everything is fine and I want to hear what you have to say.*

She reached out to the railing with one hand and held on.

"Cat got your tongue, little lady?" she heard from the crowd and with it followed some snickers.

She glanced back over to the ponytail man, and he nodded and smiled again. She returned his smile shakily, and slowly raised the megaphone to her mouth. She was amazed at the voice that came out the other end of it. It didn't sound like her own, and so much louder, bolder. Hearing herself talk so, gave her added strength, and the feeling of fainting finally subsided. From her inner self, from her heart, her words came:

> I've cried for my babies,
> I've cried for my soul.
> I've cried for my kinfolk,
> I've cried for more coal.
>
> I've worked for my husband,
> I've worked for my home.
> I've worked and I've cried
> On my own, all alone.
>
> I don't claim to be a saint,
> I abhor the name of whore,
> I am a good woman,
> Please open the door.
>
> A door to my own children
> A door to own my own home.
>
> A door to a freedom,
> Of vote, of choice.

More than a cry in my home.
To be community's voice.

Let my voice and my hands
Reach to others in need.
Give me the right to be counted,
Good deeds, to feed, not just breed!

Women have a right to be equal.
People are both women and men.
Revolution was fought for *all* freedom!
Not just men!
It's not sin!
We *all* win!

Ruby lowered the megaphone and relief flooded over her as the applause sounded around her.

I did it, I did it!

She turned to meet Cady's wet eyes and embrace. "That was beautiful, Ruby. Thank you so much!"

Mrs. Catt stood from the backbench and extended her hand to Ruby. "Well done, young lady! I know how difficult it is to stand before such an audience and you are very brave to do so! We need more women like you!"

Ruby walked out of the gazebo fighting the urge to collapse on the grass and clap her hands in glee. Instead she smiled happily at the ladies there patting her back. She glanced out of the corner of her eye to see the ponytail man, his arms folded, grinning broadly at her – what nice teeth! Didn't Mrs. Catt just say she was brave? So she turned and looked boldly into his face and smiled back. He tipped his hat to her and she gave a quick bow.

Her attention was pulled to Lizzie now who was at the front and Ruby folded her hands together to settle them, and knew she could better concentrate now in hearing Lizzie's emotional 'Ain't I a woman?' She looked down at her feet and could swear they looked further away – she felt somehow a great deal taller.

Suddenly her arm was jerked roughly and she turned to see Robert glaring down at her. "You ready to go home now?" he whispered, but his tone was more like, *you'd better be ready.*

Ruby's eyes darted around to the other ladies who only looked uncomfortable and backed away to give them more privacy.

"I-I am surprised to see you here, Robert," Ruby whispered back.

"I can just bet you are. And you are going to be even more surprised as to why I'm here, if you don't leave. I suggest you go now!"

She peered at him closely. "What do you mean?"

"There are a few of us who came here who believe we cannot stand idly by and watch our women folk being corrupted. The only reason we waited this long was because you got up on that damn stage! Here I am trying to protect you while you make a spectacle of yourself! What are you trying to do to me? I'll never be able to hold my head up in this town again!" He jerked her arm again. "Now come with me, Ruby." He paused and looked down between them. "My God, Bess is here! Are you trying to corrupt my daughter, too?" His whispering had become louder now.

She let him lead her a few yards away from earshot and then she stopped. "Robert, she is my daughter, too - can't we talk about this?"

"No." He continued to walk, holding her elbow. He jerked his head behind him. "Come on, Bess!" he growled. He pulled Ruby's elbow hard to catch up to him.

They walked to the outskirts of the crowd, Lizzie's voice becoming fainter as they walked further.

Oh, I am going to miss so much! Oh, and I'm going to miss Mrs. Catt's speech!

She decided to try again.

"Robert, please stop and listen to me."

"Do as I say, Ruby. You are in enough trouble as it is. You have disobeyed me again." His eyes were looking straight ahead, still walking, still gripping her elbow.

"Robert, I want to stay! Please let me!"

"Let the lady stay."

They both turned abruptly to the voice. It was the ponytail man. Had he followed them here?

"Pardon me?" Robert asked.

"Let the lady stay," the man repeated. "She is asking for freedom, just like in her poem. This is a free country, isn't it?"

"I am her husband and you have no right to interfere!" People walking by turned to watch. Robert gave a furtive glance about him. He let go her elbow. "Of course, it is up to her what she wants to do. What do you want to do, Ruby? Stay here or go with me." He was working his jaw muscles in a way that told her he was clenching his teeth.

"Let us both stay, Robert," Ruby answered. "Please just listen to what the women have to say."

"Of course," Robert answered. Ruby saw the ponytail disappear into the crowd. Robert stood there for a few moments, breathing in deeply. "Do as you like. I have other things to do." He left her standing there looking after him, trembling and confused. Now what am I supposed to do? Follow him?

From out of the crowd walked Opal toward her. Ruby was so happy to see her she rushed to her and gave her the biggest hug ever. "Opal, you are an angel from heaven - what are you doing here?"

"Well, as far as Mama and Jesse are concerned, I am here to deliver your dresses to you. They are over there in the wagon." Opal pointed behind Ruby, to the street. "Bess, what are *you* doing here?" she asked with a quick hug. She straightened and looked at Ruby with a knowing smile. "Ruby, I had a strong feeling that you would somehow be involved in this Women's Rights Convention so I came to see for myself. I was hired as a seamstress for three sisters who just moved into town a month or so ago and they told me a little about it. They wished to recruit me but I told them I would have no part of it. I came only to see you – but was I ever shocked to see you step forward with that megaphone! You could have knocked me over with a feather! You have become so audacious! Your poem, Ruby! I was so moved by it!

Where ever did you get the courage to do that! I was shaking in my boots watching you! I didn't know you could write poetry! My sister of secrets!"

"Well—" Gunshots stopped Ruby short and she clutched both Bess and Opal in fear. From a distance they saw a man on horseback riding through the park, a gun pointed toward the sky, the horse aimed at the crowd gathered in front of the gazebo.

"Opal, that is Preacher Paul, and oh mercy, Opal, that is Robert there walking beside him!"

They could hear the preacher saying loudly, "Now, we are not here to harm anyone. We are God-fearing men. Good Christian folk!"

"Ruby, there is brother Ernest, and-and brother James – why there are several men from our church! What are they doing here?"

Ruby glanced over toward the gazebo but, with distance and many people in between, could only see its pointed roof from here. No sound came from it.

The crowd had backed away, forming a half-circle where the horse, its rider, and his brethren stood. Preacher Paul had their full attention now.

"For those of you who don't know me, I'm the pastor at the Clover Baptist Church. Now what I've come here to say is, what these women are doing here, is wrong! Wrong in the eyes of God, and it is my *duty*," he pointed with the hand not holding the gun, toward the heavens, "to stop this wormwood, as prophesied in Deuteronomy, before it eats our town of everything good and pure!" He leaned toward his brethren. "Now you go ahead and hand out these papers to these good folk."

Ruby saw Robert and the others approach the people looking on, handing them each a paper. Some looked dazed in what was going on and only stared at the paper as if it were a strange creature. She watched Robert go deeper and deeper into the crowd.

"Sir, you have no right to disturb this convention!" All eyes turned toward the sound of the voice coming through the megaphone from the gazebo.

Ruby went up on her tiptoes, bracing with her hand on Opal's shoulder, but there were too many people in front of her and taller than her.

"If you wish to be heard, you should do so from your own pulpit!" Ruby recognized Cady's voice and her chest swelled with pride.

"Let the preacher speak!" Came a deep voice from the crowd. Ruby slumped down full on her feet – the voice sounded like Robert's! She saw some heads nod, others shake.

"Sister, I appreciate what you are saying there," the preacher yelled, pointing toward the gazebo, "and I'd be more than happy to preach to you this Sunday morning! Might do you a lot of good! When was the last time you stepped foot inside a church, missy?"

Laughter rippled through the crowd.

"That is enough, Paul!" Sheriff Porter came into view, mounted on his own gray mare, his rifle in plain view, hooked on his saddle. "This is a public place and you are disturbing the peace."

"Are you as a fellow man, going to stand by and let these men-haters destroy our families?" Preacher Paul called back. Ruby could see, even from this distance, that Preacher's face was flushed with anger.

"As the sheriff of this town, I say they are breaking no laws and doing no wrong. Let them be and have their say. You'll have your own soon, I'm sure." Sheriff Porter placed his hand on his rifle. "But it won't be here."

Preacher Paul raised his empty hand, his other hand was hanging loosely by his side, still clutching the gun. "As I said, I'm not here to cause any harm. I've said what I have to say and I'll say no more. Just let these boys finish passing out their papers and then we'll be on our way."

Sheriff Porter shifted on his saddle. "They're not disturbing the peace but you are. I'll have to ask you to leave – now."

"Now sheriff, you and I go way back. We've been friends for a long time. As God is my witness, I don't understand—"

"*Now*, Paul." Sheriff's tone was deeper now, more foreboding. Preacher Paul shook his head in disgust and turned his horse around, away from the crowd. Ruby saw Robert and the others emerge from the crowd and trail after him.

Humph, not even a backward glance to me!

"Where is Papa going?" Bess asked.

Opal tugged on Ruby's sleeve. "You must follow after him, Ruby! Go!"

Ruby stepped toward the departing group of men, now quite a distance away. She stopped. "I can't."

"Why not? He is your husband, Ruby!"

The excitement, the heat of the day, was suddenly wearing heavily on Ruby. "I'm very much aware he is my husband, Opal!" she snapped back. "But, mercy, I've come here to be part of something I believe in, and, God help me, I believe in those women up there!" She pointed toward the front.

She raised her skirts a bit and started back around the edge of the crowd toward the gazebo. "Come on, Bess," she said.

She paused and looked back to see Opal looking back at her, her face looking hurt and ready to cry. Ruby motioned with her finger to Opal to follow her but Opal only shook her head.

"I'll wait here and give you and Bess a ride back to the house. I-I have your dresses here and all." Opal pulled her large hat down to shade more of her face, folded her arms across her heavy bosom, and squinted her eyes toward the male voice of Mr. Whiting coming from the gazebo.

"Fine, fine, fine," Ruby muttered, as she continued around to the front, Bess quietly in tow. Well, at least hopefully something someone will say here will soak into Opal. She can be so stubborn!

Ruby arrived to the side of the gazebo just in time to see the ponytail man enter the gazebo and whisper something to Cady and Mrs. Catt. They both looked surprised, both heads nodding.

"Our women teachers," Mr. Whiting was saying, "are learned, strong-willed leaders in our school. As the principal there, I do not make a decision without conference with my teachers, most of which are women —"

"Did you say 'which' or 'witch'?" a male voice shouted.

Laughter rumbled through the crowd.

Mr. Whiting peered at the crowd over his glasses, the stern look of a teacher silencing his students. He continued. "All my teachers understand the issues and bring forth their recommendations. I have a high regard for these women. My experience tells me they have the thinking ability to cast an intelligent vote for our leaders. I, for one, will gladly sign their petition to state legislature asking that women be given the right to vote!"

The ladies around the gazebo applauded and patted him on the back as he exited the gazebo. With theatrical flare, he walked to the booth where Sarah and Aimee were standing, and signed the petition with flourish. He raised the pen in the air and they all applauded again.

"Don't let them get to you!" called out the same male voice from the crowd. A few laughed but no more was said.

"We have an unexpected guest with us," announced Cady through the megaphone. "A Mr. Jeremiah Bluemountain who wishes to speak briefly to the convention. Mr. Bluemountain?"

Ruby watched in wonderment as the ponytail man stepped up onto the platform. He waved away the megaphone. He leaned forward on the banister railing to where his whole upper body was leaning out toward the crowd.

"You'll hear me well enough, I think," he said, his voice projected clearly and with deep resonance. "I wasn't planning on saying anything; I'm not any good at speeches. Except that I felt I had to say something after I heard the raucous caused by that preacher over there." He pointed to where Preacher Paul had been. "I'm sure he is a good man, trying to do what is right, but he is fighting the wrong battle. I come from good Christian folk, too. My daddy was a coal miner, my mommy was a Cherokee Indian. Being half-Indian I've seen my share of prejudice from the white man, but I've never understood it, especially where women are concerned. I don't know the preacher's background, but where I come from, women worked right beside the men. I've seen them hunt the deer, drag the deer in with their horse, skin it, cook the meat, tan the hide, sew it with sinew into clothes. I've seen women fight like she-wolves to protect home and children. I've seen no difference between men and women except that I've seen women squat in the woods, have their babies, and then walk back, the babies nursing at their breast. What man can do that?"

"We planted the seed," yelled a male voice " – what woman can do that?"

Ruby squirmed at this frankness and glanced to where Cady and Mrs. Catt were sitting, but their faces remained sculpted. She half-expected some women to walk away but their faces showed the same intense interest that she felt.

Jeremiah ignored the interruption in the same fashion as Mr. Whiting did. "And I'll tell you another thing. My daddy fought for the Union Army in the war. When he came back, he told me stories about how women fought in the war dressed like men. Their sex was not found out until they were wounded and the doctors would end up telling the truth. Some of these women were released with an honorable discharge! And he told me of women who didn't fight but stood along the roads where the weary soldiers traveled and handed out bread and cheese. Those soldiers that fell, the women were there to pick them up and nurse them back to life. Daddy told of countless homes he walked by or stayed at, where men were laying all over the yards and it was the women, not doctors, who were stepping around them, dressing the wounds with their own dresses they had cut to rags.

"I'm talking on longer than I meant to, but let me say this: Women have *spirit*! Heroic spirit, the Holy Spirit, the spirit of our Creator. And that preacher says they are *wrong*?" He shook his head. "They are asking for no more than what a man has, gentlemen! Why would we deny them, when we depend on them for helping us with everything else?" He paused for a moment. He nodded his head once. "As my mommy used to say, Wi-na-de-ya-ho, thank you for this day."

His eyes met Ruby's as he exited, and she nodded once and smiled. He returned her smile and it washed over her like a cool rinse. He didn't rejoin the crowd but stood closer to where she stood.

"First, we hear from women," said a male voice from the depths of the crowd, "then a darky, and then an injun. What next - are we going to hear from a child? Maybe that little girl?" Eyes turned to Bess. Ruby turned pale from his accusatory tone, putting her arm around Bess protectively. For the first time today, she wondered if she had done the right thing in bringing her.

The ponytail man, she knew now as Jeremiah Bluemountain, looked at Ruby, raised his hand and shook his head slightly, as if to say, *let it go*. He folded his arms across his chest and turned to Cady who was announcing Mrs. Carrie Chapman Catt.

"Mr. Bluemountain gave me the perfect lead-in to my topic today," said Mrs. Catt clearly and distinctly into the megaphone. She had no pause, only the sort of confidence that comes from someone who did this a great deal. "I have titled it Ballot for Bullet. One of the objections to women's suffrage is because the man has superior strength. It is said that the ballot is a privilege that must be paid for by military service; and since women cannot and will not fight, they must renounce all claim to the ballot. But extraordinary strength is not required in a soldier's life to be a good warrior. As Mr. Bluemountain testified, there were many women who fought a good soldier's life with an honorable discharge. Approximately 400 women fought in the Civil War, according to the St. Louis Times. Many were turned away or mustered out, when it was revealed that they were women. So it is not that women will not or cannot fight. It is true that women abhor fighting as a business or as a profession, yet they *can* fight, when their lives, their family's lives, or their country demands it. And with the same daring and patriotic fervor as men. But don't get me wrong here. We are not pleading for the battlefield. The army is not a good place for a woman, *nor* a man, only a terrible necessity sometimes. It is when this necessity comes to reality, that we wish to show that women are as patriotic, have as much endurance, and can fight as well as men. From this point of view, women are as much entitled to the ballot as men.

"This objection to women's suffrage, along with many other

objections, is currently public opinion. I believe the public objects to women's suffrage because of custom. Law and custom are the two kinds of restrictions upon human liberty. Yet no written law has ever been more binding than unwritten custom, supported by public opinion. Public opinion says women can't think, nor fight, nor take care of themselves. This world taught women nothing skillful and then said her work was valueless. It permitted her no opinions and then said she did not know how to think. It forbade her to speak in public, and then said she had no orators.

"Therefore, it is the responsibility of women, as mothers, wives, sisters, citizens of our community, to step forward and speak out! Prove this custom wrong and ask that the restraint of law no longer hinder them! And it is the responsibility of men, as law-makers and law-holders to change the law that so binds us!"

Ruby's eyes filled with tears and she wiped these away with the back of her hand. Listening to the words of Jeremiah Bluemountain and Mrs. Catt filled her being with strength and purpose. She was doing the right thing in being here, she could feel it in her bones! She had never before felt proud of being a woman; only that it was a burden, a curse. Now she felt brave, keen, alert. Her arm was still around Bess and she squeezed her shoulder. Thank goodness that Bess was here to hear these beautifully positive words! With this reinforcement, she would be a stronger woman than Ruby, Ruby was sure of it.

She looked to her left to see Jeremiah watching her with the kindest eyes she had ever seen.

* * * * *

"Why do you call yourselves Ladies of the Lost Legion?" Bess asked Aimee from the back seat of Opal's wagon. Ruby's ears perked up, her attention no longer on Opal's difficulty in handling the reins. She was happy to hear Bess questioning what was going on around her. Ruby had wondered about this name too, but had not yet thought to ask.

"Well, let's see," Aimee answered. "In very early history it was written that women were not considered inferior to men, but as the creator of all man. Her name, woman, was derived from womb and man, meaning she was a man and more, because she brought new life forth through her womb. This slowly changed over many hundreds of years through men's hunger for power and control. It was important that women agree and submit to men's superiority, and because we are spiritual by nature, the best way for men to achieve control was through organized religion. Women naturally wish to do the right thing. Man's religious rule told us to submit, be subservient, and bear his children. This religious rule has suppressed our creativity and our equality, and authorized man his superiority. Whether it is Christianity in the west, justifying this because Eve, as the tempter, was being punished. Or Hinduism in the east, requiring obedience of women toward men. Or Greek mythology, where Pandora, a woman of course, opened the forbidden box and caused plagues to attack mankind. In early Roman law, women were described as children. These portrayals continue in our fairy tales where older women are evil and the young maidens are pure and childlike. Remember Cinderella? Snow White? Sleeping Beauty? But look at how we have influenced entire eras when royal blood allowed us to reign. Queen Victoria has been queen of England now for decades and is very much loved and respected. Have you read about Queen Elizabeth of England? She was in the sixteenth century. So, we believe that women have tremendous abilities, intuition, and creativity, but they have been lost to archaic beliefs. Hence, our name Ladies of the Lost Legion!"

Ruby turned to Aimee in surprise. It was the first time she had heard Aimee give an educated answer. "Very good, Aimee! I like that! I hadn't even thought about the fairy tales and here I've been reading them to the children for years!"

Opal pulled in the reins in front of Ruby's home. She shook her head, her body rigid. "So now Christianity is a bad thing, is it?"

Aimee jumped out of the wagon and ran to her own home, throwing out "I'll send the boys home, goodbye, thank-you!"

behind her as she went.

Ruby didn't wish to argue and was getting weary of the day. "Opal, come in and have supper with us, please. It would be such a pleasure to have your company."

Opal had no idea just how much Ruby wanted her company. She had no energy left to face whatever Robert had in store for her. He would behave himself in front of company.

Opal's face relaxed. "Well, it's past seven now - I can't see the ruts in the road very well when it starts getting dark, and if I break another wheel on this wagon, Jesse will tan my hide!"

"I'll have you on your way before dark, I promise you. I started supper this morning before daybreak!"

It wasn't until she turned the doorknob, did it occur to Ruby that Robert might have locked her out. Yes, it was locked and she sucked in her breath a bit. She had a key now, hidden under the rocking chair cushion, but Robert didn't need to know that just yet.

"Opal, peek in the parlor windows there and see if you can see Robert in there." Ruby knew if Robert was sitting in his chair and saw Opal, he would open the door. She saw Opal wave to the window, and sure enough, the door unlocked and opened. Robert stepped aside as they all entered, casting a cold sidelong glance at Ruby.

"Hello dear, we are all home!" she said, forcing cheerfulness she was a long way from feeling. Still avoiding his eyes she asked, "Are you hungry, dear? I know I am! And Opal is staying for supper! Isn't that wonderful?" She rushed to the kitchen and resisted slumping over the worktable. The day had probably only begun as far as Robert was concerned.

Robert was more than behaved; he was on his best behavior. He kept topics of discussion away from the day and only asked about the farm, the family, and Opal's upcoming wedding. Ruby could see that Opal was charmed, given away by her giggles and lively chatter, probably thinking again how lucky Ruby was. Are there two sides to every man, or just Robert?

"Oh, thank you Robert, for reminding me!" Opal said at the

supper table. "Speaking of my wedding, I have Jacob's permission to allow Ruby as one of my newehockers. You remember us talking about that don't you Ruby? That is Dutch for sidesitters, or attendants."

"When is the wedding?" Ruby asked.

"Well, let's see," said Opal, ticking off her fingers, "I have already written a letter to Preacher Paul to take my name off Clover Baptist Church. I will be baptized into the Amish faith in August or September. Fast Day is on October 11 and then Fall Communion is the following church Sunday. My membership certification is requested by the second Sunday after communion." She was speaking very quickly, and paused to take a deep breath. "And then that day, all the couples who plan to marry are published. This means that the deacon will announce the names of the girls who they plan to marry – Jacob thinks we are the only couple so far this year. Normally the girl's father announces the date and time of the wedding, and normally the wedding is at the girl's home, but in our case this will be done by Jacob's father, and the wedding will be at their farm. He is a good man, rules with an iron fist, but a good man nonetheless."

She looked distracted for a moment and then said, "Anyway, Jacob and I do not attend the church service on the day we are published. Instead, I will prepare a meal for him at my house and we are supposed to eat alone. That will be a challenge, don't you think? Can't you just imagine six boys peeking into the kitchen from doorways and windows, while we eat?" Her smile came and went. "So then, normally the girl is supposed to formally introduce her fiancee to her parents when they return from church, but of course, well I suppose I could do so with Mama, Jesse, and Edith, but they already know. We're not married yet and have already broken some rules of the Ordnung!"

Opal's face had no color now, and her bottom lip trembled. She was breathing as if she had just come in from a long walk. "So, no need to worry about your dress, Ruby, because I will make it, as is the Amish practice, with a plain cut, no lace or trim. Speaking of which, the dresses I brought! They are still out in the wagon!"

"I'll bring them in," Robert said, seeming eager to be away, and quickly rose from the table.

When the front door closed behind him, Ruby squeezed Opal's hand. "Are you alright?"

"I'm fine, why?" Opal asked, wiping beads of sweat from her upper lip with her napkin. "I'm just very warm in here. I think I've absorbed too much sun today."

"I'll be happy to be your attendant in your wedding, Opal. I'm honored you asked. I just wish..." She trailed off, not sure if she should finish.

"Say what you were going to say, Ruby. You usually do anyway."

"Well, I wish you were marrying someone of our own faith! Going to church just won't be same without you there! You deserve to be there more than I do!"

Too late, Ruby realized she had opened the gate to a pitiful creature. Opal laid her head on the crook of her arm on the table and cried the most pitiful wails that Ruby had ever heard. She wept as if someone had just died, someone she loved very much.

Ruby motioned to the children to go upstairs. The boys left quickly but Bess lingered around the doorway, half-hidden. Ruby walked around the table to Opal's chair and sat beside her. Opal could not hear her, Ruby was sure, so she said nothing, but hugged Opal to her and let her cry, blinking back her own tears. Why must women make so many sacrifices for marriage?

Robert came in carrying a large oblong box, one that was fabric-covered and had made many trips with Opal to customers carrying their new wedding gowns, evening gowns, jackets and dresses. Ruffles of shiny cotton showed off their rainbow of colors from the top. He stopped at the doorway to the dining room, surveyed the scene, and turned on his heel. She heard the box land loudly on the wood floor by his chair.

Ruby stroked Opal's chignon of curls and sighed. There was so much Opal needed to know, to prepare for. She looked at the world so innocently, thinking that life was either biblical or sinful.

We should have a heart-to-heart. If only Mama had talked to me of such things.

"Opal, would you come upstairs with me and help me hang the dresses? We can have a private chat, yes?" Ruby whispered, not wanting Robert to hear from the parlor.

Opal finally dried her tears. Curiosity crossed her brow and she nodded. She silently waited for Ruby to retrieve the box from the parlor and then followed Ruby to her bedroom. This was her first time in Ruby and Robert's private sanctuary and she looked about in awe. Ruby felt she could read Opal's thoughts, thoughts that were saying, *So this is where they make their babies!*

Ruby didn't know how to begin. She hadn't thought about discussing this until just now and didn't feel prepared. She laid the box on the floor by the wardrobe and lifted up the top dress, to give her hands something to do. Its cream-colored lace was lined with satin and sewn into a tight bodice with fringe across the chest. Ruby smiled at the fringe – it had not been on the dress when Opal wore it, so she obviously thought this might enhance Ruby's small breasts. Light blue ribbon tied at the neck and sleeves, and pearl buttons lined down the front.

"This is beautiful, Opal. Your stitching is impeccable. I'm not sure where I shall wear such a gown. Robert and I don't go out in the evenings nor have we eaten in a restaurant since a day or so after our wedding. But this satin - could you not use it for your nightgown?" She continued in a lower tone. "Would this not be pretty for your wedding night?"

Opal turned from examining the chenille fabric on the feather bed and frowned at the dress as if seeing it for the first time. Opal had adorned her mood once again with a practical persona. It was only when she allowed herself to be stripped down to her bare core, did Ruby ever see Opal's true colors.

"Of course not," Opal said. "Cotton is far more practical. My new nightgown is white, of course."

White for virginity, of course, was there unspoken between them.

Ruby shook the dress gently to smooth the lace and hung it

on a hanger in her wardrobe. "And how comfortable do you feel in wearing a nightgown for the first time with Jacob?" She glanced over at Opal and realized they were both blushing.

Opal folded her arms across her chest and frowned again. "Really, Ruby!" Then her face softened. "I realize what you are trying to do here, Ruby, but ..." her voice faded as she looked down at her toes of her summer slippers peeking out from her dress.

Ruby came over and sat down on the feather bed. She folded her hands in her lap and looked up at Opal, still standing by the bed. She decided to open up to her. Only then could Opal speak openly. "Opal, has Mama talked to you about ... well ... the birds and the bees?"

"No, Mama would never speak of such things, you know that." Opal sat down next to Ruby, curiosity still there on her expression.

"My wedding night was very difficult for me," Ruby said and swallowed. "I didn't know what to expect or what to do. I just don't want you to go through what I went through. Women should share these things, so that they don't feel so odd, so they don't feel they are the only ones going through the ... well ... I must be blunt ... pain ... and such mixed emotions. Relations with your husband should not be something to be ashamed of. After all, that is how babies are made."

"Do such relations hurt?" Opal asked.

"The first time, yes. But it is easier to tolerate as you live together. And childbirth eases the relations all the more so." She sat quietly for a moment, thinking back to her wedding night, to what Opal must face first. "I was not expecting it to be so – personal, shall I say? That I would be so revealed to him and so exposed. And I had places he entered that I didn't know were there!"

"Mercy, Ruby!"

"Now you are sounding like me, Opal," Ruby teased. They giggled some of the tension away.

"Well," said Opal, "we really shouldn't be discussing such

private matters." She was sitting on the edge, as if not sure whether to walk away or slide further onto the bed. "But," she turned toward the screen by the window, "while we are here and being so frank," her chest went up and down heavily into a sigh, "I do have so many questions but I'm not sure what is appropriate to ask."

"I'll try to answer them the best I can, with what little I know."

"Fine. Do you remember our bull we keep in the penned pasture? And how Jesse puts a cow in there for mating? Please forgive me for admitting this, but not long after our discussion in the apple orchard and your reference to a 'husband's needs', I decided to see what mating was all about, so I hid behind some honeysuckle bushes and watched. I had paid no mind to this sort of thing before, but I thought since I was engaged to be married - Jesse didn't see me or he would have lectured me good. Now I understand why that pen is way down below the creek and behind a patch of trees."

Opal began tracing the circular chenille patterns on the bed with her finger. "As I watched, this bull slowly circled the cow, sniffing all around her. She raised her tail and I thought she would swat him with it but instead she raised her tail slowly over to the side and allowed him to sniff there, too. While I realize this was obscene, I was amazed that she simply stood so still, as if this was her place and she could do no other. But then he raised himself up on his back legs and fell over her back, and I saw his red appendage swell and push inside her tail, she bellowed out so! I was horrified and fascinated all at the same time."

Ruby suddenly remembered something and clamped her hand over her mouth to stifle a loud laugh. "Do you know how to spell the name of the bull?"

Opal looked up, wondering. "Ruffenreddy? R-u-f-f-e-n-r-e-d-d-y, I suppose."

"No, it's R-o-u-g-h *and* R-e-a-d-y! I didn't understand it until after I was married. I wondered why Mama would slap at

Papa whenever he called the bull that. Then it suddenly occurred to me. Jesse still calls it that, even though there have been several generations of bulls in there."

"And speaking of Jesse, Ruby, I hear he and Edith in their bedroom, too. Often. Their headboard sometimes bangs the wall in a repeated thump-thump-thump, and I can't help but hear. But I never hear Edith, just sometimes Jesse. His breathing sounds as if he is running very quickly. So I ask myself this: Will Jacob act as this bull? And will I bellow with pain when he forces such a large...thing...it is no wonder a woman bleeds the first time! Must I be on my knees and sit very still? Will this be expected of me often, as it is expected of Edith? You said you didn't know what to expect, but did Robert know what to do? Does God give them such knowledge, or is this a natural instinct, like the birds and the bees?"

"Mercy, Opal!"

"You gave me permission to ask."

"I did, indeed! But now I ask myself why I permitted such discussion!" They both laughed. "Well all right, let me think." Ruby grabbed her pillow and hugged it to her, as if to comfort some of her discomfort. She wasn't prepared for such a detailed discussion. Never had she heard nor spoken such things with another. She spoke softly, looking straight ahead. Eye contact would be too difficult at this time.

"From personal experience, you may be asked to lie down on your back and he will lie on top of you and ... find his way. You must have no pantalets or petticoat on for this but he may or may not allow you to keep your gown on. You may find this uncomfortable but this does not last long. What you saw with the bull on her back, well, I believe it is not the normal human behavior, but may still be required from time to time." She blushed at this, rocking herself a little to and fro, remembering Robert's very recent forced entrance from behind her. "I also believe that although you may find his intimacy painful the first time, you will not *bellow* as you call it, nor will you find his *appendage* as you call it, as large as a bull's. You will see it looks quite different and much smaller, thank goodness!"

She thought for a moment before continuing on. "As far as knowing what to do, I disappointed Robert in not knowing what to do. I was too frightened and it hindered his movements. So it is important that I pass on to you to know to relax as much as possible. As hard as it may be, you must open yourself to him completely, trust in his instincts, so that he may find ... where he is supposed to go, so that he can plant the seed that will give you the child you long for."

She finally met Opal's eyes. "It will all be worthwhile when they lay that first-born in your arms."

"I will try to remember," Opal said. "I have so much to learn! Thank you, Ruby, for sharing such private experiences with me. I must remember to speak so openly to my own daughter."

"And I to my own daughter," Ruby said.

Night was falling quickly and Opal must go. She hugged Ruby at the door and thanked her again "for everything" with a wink. Ruby did not mention the dresses again – she wanted Opal to leave on a positive note, so she simply gave Opal a misty-eyed good-bye. She knew by the determined look on Opal's face, her willful chin, that this was not a crossroads to Opal but a rough bump on a very long road she had begun to travel. She would not turn back.

Ruby re-entered the kitchen to wash the dishes. The boys followed her, jostling each other as to who could get closer to her. They were not accustomed to being sent to someone else's home for the day and they wanted her attention. They bumped her as they wrestled each other and it made her jump more than she should have. Robert's change of attitude had her edgy. She lit the gas lamp on the kitchen's small table by the window.

"Boys, settle down," she said absent-mindedly. She was listening for Robert.

Instead of the stairs creaking his exit from the parlor, she heard the front door open. "I'm going out for awhile," he called out. "I'll be home later."

The front door was closing as she entered the parlor hesitantly, waiting for something unexpected to happen. She stared at the door. Only silence. Through the window, she could make out Robert's dark outline on the boardwalk, walking toward town.

"Now, why in the world..." she whispered.

* * * * *

"Now, what in the world..." she whispered. She approached slowly, watching Sarah pick up pieces of her booth, boards splintered and scattered about. The two clay pots of thick climbing ivy Sarah had so meticulously placed through chicken wire over the booth as an archway yesterday, was broken, dirt and vines scattered. One of the signs from the gazebo had been moved and stuck in the dirt by the broken booth. The sign had been changed with a big red 'F' in front of 'Rights', to read, 'Fight for Women's FRights!'

"What happened, Sarah?" Ruby asked, placing her basket containing her dinner on the ground.

Sarah jumped, startled. "Oh Ruby, I'm glad to see it's you! Seeing this sort of destruction at someone's hands makes me skittish, being here alone." She stood up straight and put her hands on her hips. "What happened here, I believe, is a coward came in the night and attempted to destroy our cause by being underhanded. Look at this! I came early to help you set up and found..." and she kicked at a splintered board, anger showing on her flushed face. "Now I don't know what to do. We announced yesterday that the booth would be open every afternoon for two weeks, to collect signatures. Here you are, our first volunteer to station here, and I have nothing..." she kicked at another board, harder this time. "If I could just get my hands on the man who—"

"Whoa, whoa, just don't take it out on all the men!"

They both turned in surprise to see Jeremiah Bluemountain walking through the oak trees toward them.

He ducked under a branch. "So, we had an enemy in our midst yesterday, did we? Not surprising. Could have been worse - I've seen women shot at for asking for fairer wages at a bicycle factory. Annan is actually a peaceful little town in comparison to what I've seen."

"That's comforting," said Sarah, in a tone of one not impressed. She continued to look at the damage around her.

Ruby was glad Sarah was not looking at her. She could feel her face blush crimson in seeing him. The closer he came, the faster her heart beat. She bent down at the knees and fingered a piece of thirsty vine, roots exposed, pretending to examine its leaves.

"We can have a new booth built in an hour," Jeremiah said. "If one of you can come with me and show me the way to the lumber mill or general store, and tell me how much we need, we can have it up in no time."

"I appreciate your thoughtfulness, er ... Mr. Bluemountain, isn't it?" said Sarah.

"Jeremiah."

"Well, I must be frank here, Jeremiah, and say, I have no money left to buy supplies. What little I saved went into this." Sarah said, waving her hand around to the damage at her feet.

Money? Ruby dropped the leaf. Sarah was putting her money into this? But, of course! Building supplies were not free. Come to think of it, nor were the supplies for the signs, printing for the papers Phyllis was handing out and the petition forms, the music sheets, what else, yes the sashes.

I haven't put in a penny for any of this!

"I think I can swing a few dollars for a good cause," Jeremiah was saying.

"No, I'll pay!" Ruby blurted out, standing up. "I don't have money with me, of course, but I have an account at the Joe's General, and he always has planks in the back of the store for sale."

Jeremiah looked visibly pleased, Sarah looked relieved.

"Well, we'd better get going, then, before people start arriving." Jeremiah said, rubbing his hands together. "Sarah, you might wish to wait in the gazebo over there, and if anyone wants to sign the petition, they can do so there in the meantime."

Sarah nodded in agreement. "Oh, which reminds me, we also need more material for signs. We had left the signs in the dirt over there, and some are painted over in red, with the word 'men-haters'."

Ruby turned cold inside – Robert had used that word to describe them.

"My wagon is over here," Jeremiah said, sweeping his arm toward the street. He bowed slightly. "After you, madam."

Ruby's mind raced around him as she walked past him. Alone with this stranger? A married woman? Is he married? Oh that doesn't matter! In broad daylight where everyone will see! Will Robert see? Oh but I can hardly breathe walking beside him like this! Money! How will I pay? I will have to find a way!"

"Ruby Wright, isn't it? If I recall correctly from Cady's introduction. I'm Jeremiah Bluemountain, pleased to meet you." They shook hands as they walked, her hand disappearing in his large one.

"Bluemountain – must be a meaning behind that name," Ruby said. Oh was that being too forward?

"Well, I come from the Appalachian Mountains of Tennessee. When you see the mountains from a long way off, they look blue. When my daddy died in a coal mining accident, my mommy, in Indian custom, decided to change my last name to what I loved best. Lord, do I love the mountains! I come up here to walk on flatter ground, all open, and I feel naked." He tipped his hat to her. "Pardon the expression."

An image suddenly appeared in her mind of him without his shirt on and she blushed.

I don't know where you are heading, Ruby, when you turn red from your own thoughts, not by what someone else is saying.

Well, the mountains certainly explain his accent, she thought, attempting to improve her thought pattern.

He helped her up onto the wagon. The step was higher than usual, her legs too short, so he had to move his hand from her elbow to her waist and give her a lift. Ruby sat down gathering her skirts around her, still feeling his hands there. Her own were clammy and she wiped them off on her skirt leaving a dirt stain from where she grabbed the wagon seat to pull up.

She was happy now that she had decided to wear Opal's light cotton dress with lace trimmed down the front, lace strips that were sewn from her waist to her hem. It was one of Opal's finest creations and the stitching was flawless. Ruby's black skirt and white blouse she wore the day before needed washing, and so she had an excuse to wear one of Opal's bright dresses. Ruby suddenly recalled Opal wearing this dress the day Ruby was visiting and Opal was going to Jacob's home to visit with Jacob's family – Jacob was not impressed by this dress. Poor Opal - not to be able to wear these anymore!

Jeremiah turned the horses around in the park and they headed down Main Street. She panicked as they neared the center of town – Robert's Walk Wright shoe store was only a few buildings down from Joe's General Store. Why had she only now remembered that? Why was she so scatterbrained today?

"Pardon?" she asked.

"I asked if we were heading in the right direction," Jeremiah said.

"Oh, yes," she answered. Oh no, she answered to herself. She caught sight of his hands holding firmly to the leather straps. Nice hands, she thought. Clean, I love clean hands. "The store is on this street about a mile or so from here." She resisted looking at his face and those blue-blue eyes – blue eyes from blue mountains, she thought. Instead, she smoothed her dress.

"Was that your husband I saw you talking to yesterday?"

Ruby flushed at the memory. *Let her stay*, he had said to Robert.

"Oh, yes," she said in answer again. Couldn't answer with something else? *Cat got your tongue, little lady?* another memory whispered from yesterday.

She glanced from the corner of her eye to his dusty boot propped up on the wagon's edge. Could use mending, perhaps she could ask Robert to mend them for him. Oh yes, he would be happy to mend the boots of a man who supports men-haters!

They entered the business district and she pulled Opal's large white floppy hat down more over her face. She looked down at the people walking by but no one took notice of them. There were many more wagons, buggies, bicycles, and even a few automobiles rumbling along here.

Perhaps no one will recognize her in such a fancy dress and hat – including Robert. She dared not look inside his shop window. They stopped in front of Joe's General and she jumped down, unassisted, and rushed inside.

"Is there a sale on something here today I should know about?" Jeremiah called from behind her.

She waited for him inside, her first direct look into his face. He had that same broad grin from yesterday. She had the urge to stand closer, but of course ... he stepped aside for a woman exiting the store.

"No, it is just cooler here, is all," she answered. It was rather dark inside and it took a few moments for her eyes to adjust. She breathed in its familiar smell of cinnamon sticks, plant seeds, and axle grease. Joe sold it all.

"Well, hello there, newcomers! How can I help you today?" called out Joe from behind the counter. He could have no legs for all Ruby knew; only that very round belly. He was always behind the counter directing young boys to "stock, sweep, and sweat – that's what I pay them for!"

Ruby faced the counter, adjusting her eyes to Joe's dim bulky figure.

"Why, it is Mrs. Wright!" Joe shouted. "I hardly recognized you all dressed up like that! But then you are a celebrity now, aren't you? I'll tell you what I did. Curiosity got the best of me and darn if I didn't walk all the way up to City Park and watch a bunch of women bellyaching!" He slapped the counter. "Ha, just kidding!"

His face suddenly changed as if a serious thought had given him pain. He pointed his finger at her. "But I'll tell you one thing. You'll never see me put my signature on any kind of petition. No, siree-bob. City council would be on me faster than a rattler, raising my taxes and what ever else they can think of. You rock their boat, they'll tip yours over."

He pointed to Jeremiah. "Hey, I saw you up there, too! You're not from around these parts, now are you?" He sounded a little like he was making an accusation.

"Yes, sir, I was there, and no sir, I'm not from here. Where are your wood planks?"

Ruby was relieved he changed the subject to why they were here. She didn't care for Joe; he was always too loud, too nosy, knew everybody's business. Probably would tell everyone that she came in with a stranger from out-of-town.

"How much wood do you need for the booth, ma'am?" Jeremiah asked, as they headed to the back, where Joe was pointing. He was speaking loud enough for Joe to hear. He must have picked up on Joe's gossipy ways.

Out of earshot of Joe, Ruby turned to Jeremiah with her hand to her mouth feeling foolish. "Why, I don't know! Sarah handled that yesterday." Why didn't she ask Sarah before they left? Scatterbrained, indeed!

"Well, I'm sure I can figure it out, Ruby. Don't look so embarrassed. Sarah was doing what she knew how, you were doing what you knew how. You contributed your own fair share. I know – I was watching. That was a mighty touching poem you quoted yesterday. Did you write that?"

"Oh, yes," Ruby answered. There you go again with that answer - say something else. "Well, ever since I built my own house, I've had no interest in such small things as building booths."

He turned from the boards he was examining and raised his eyebrows in surprise to her. "You built your own house?"

"Ha, just kidding!" she said.

They laughed together. He nodded as he turned back to the boards. "Good one," he said.

* * * * *

The arithmetic in Jeremiah's head added up nicely and a new and stronger booth was standing within the hour. Ruby purchased two new clay pots and salvaged what she could of the climbing ivy.

She included a small bunch of dried wild flowers in her purchases and added these to the top of the arbor wiring. They cost more than they should have but what did it matter when Robert's account had already risen to eight dollars when they included thick wooden planks and cardboard and paint for more signs? She had asked Joe for her own account but he had refused to give her one. Somehow she would have to figure out a way to pay for this, and very soon before Robert found out.

Ruby stood back with one hand on her chin, its elbow propped on the other arm across the stomach, and looked at the finished product. She glanced over at Jeremiah. He was in an identical pose. Ruby burst out laughing. He looked at her quizzically and she raised her fingers from her chin and waved them. He did the same. He laughed easily, loved to talk. Ruby felt as comfortable with him now, as she once did in Cady's overstuffed sofa. She felt almost enveloped by him and his soft kind voice, his interesting stories of "back home".

"Why, back home, my daddy and us eight boys built our own log cabin, right in a holler between two hills. We called it Smoky Creek, because the creek that ran behind our place had a mist that rose above it about every morning. Mommy and the two girls helped build the cabin too, when they weren't keeping the garden going and cooking over an open fire all day. We lived on vegetables that summer because no one had time to hunt. First we built a lean-to for Mommy and the girls to sleep in and then we added a little bit to it every day for the boys. That was one long lean-to, I'll tell you. Daddy used it as a pigpen after we got the house built. The cabin had a loft for us boys but it was too cramped for me. I spent my spare time in the hills, stomping around every inch of it, loving every minute of it. Just like some ol' mountain lion. Why, every chance I got I would hunt for rabbit and cook it over a fire, and eat it right then and there, sitting on my haunches. I probably growled eating it, but luckily no one else was around or I would never have heard the end of it.

"I had a girl there, we were sweet on each other, mostly from a distance for a few years, until her Daddy caught us holding hands walking up the hill behind her place. He said he was not going to have any half-breed grandbabies running about his place, so that was the end of that. He whipped her with a switch, and he would have done it worse next time, so she did what her Daddy told her to do.

"I left home shortly after that to look for work. There was no way I was going to work in a coal mine and spit up blood like my Daddy. I moved into town and got a job at the bicycle factory. I called it Wheel and Deal because the owner sure knew how to sell those bicycles! He even made up a bicycle race, offering the winner twenty-five dollars, man or woman. So, there were women in the race alright, wearing those knickerbockers that came out a few years ago. He was clever because he must have sold twenty-five bicycles for the race and at five dollars a piece, so you can add that up I'm sure and see that he made a good profit. And to beat all, he marked the ten-mile path through the most rugged brush and rocks, so naturally some of those bicycles fell apart, and don't you know they went back and bought new ones from him?

"But he was also a crooked man and wouldn't pay good wages to his workers, particularly the women. I got paid more than women who had been there for years. It wasn't fair and I told him so, so he lowered my wages to theirs. He added coal to the flames then, I'll tell you. So we organized ourselves a little group and did what you did here. We made some signs and paraded back and forth in front of the factory, declaring unfair wages.

"The women there listened to one strong-willed gal, Dellafay, and if she told them to miss work and hold a sign instead, that's what they did. At first we didn't get the attention we wanted – there were gunshots fired at us from the hill beside the building. That was what I was referring to earlier. We couldn't see who it was, but it doesn't take much brain to figure out who it was. But the good side is that word got to the town newspaper and they sent a reporter to talk to us and Dellafay told him we demanded a town meeting. He put our story in the paper, and then the mayor agreed to the meeting. The reason he agreed was because his wife insisted. As it turns out, the mayor's wife had been reading up on women's

Good Woman

rights and this was just the sort of thing she was looking for. So, she sent a telegram to Mrs. Catt, asking that she speak at the meeting. Mrs. Catt was so good, she got a standing ovation – well from the womenfolk anyway. Mr. Kinsley was told that if he didn't increase his wages, no one would buy a solitary bicycle from him. And if that didn't work, he would be tarred and feathered! Well, it worked but I didn't get to stay to reap what I helped sow.

"That meeting is how I met Mrs. Catt and that is why I am here. Mrs. Catt asked that I escort her, first by train to Syracuse, and then by wagon these last forty miles or so. She had so much to carry, books, clothing and all, that we couldn't rent a buggy. We'll take the wagon back to Syracuse tomorrow or the next day, and then head on to New York City by train. I'm a volunteer escort, I guess you could say, but she makes sure I have enough to eat and have a roof over my head. She gets paid little or nothing for this and she and her husband put a lot of their own money and time into traveling all over. Her husband will meet her in New York City, when he gets to feeling better, and then she will get me a train ticket to go back home.

"I sure miss my mountains. As Joe says, yes-siree-bob. Now that Daddy and Mommy have passed on, I'm going to take over the home-place, and farm what I can. I'm a pretty good carver, too, so maybe I can make some money selling my carved birds and such. Instead of Wheel and Deal, I can Carve and Starve!" He laughed loudly at himself, Ruby joining him.

He was so easy to work with, holding boards for him as he nailed, explaining his measurements to her as if she was as smart as he was and understood it all. She explained to him how she had made cricket benches for her children, enjoying giving him the details, just to see his blue eyes look at her with interest and appreciation. She watched his wet strands of hair falling from his ponytail, she watched the muscles in his arms expand when he lifted the wood. She dared not look at him straight in the face, but she memorized his profile. Sometimes his hand would touch her shoulder; his arm would meet her arm. Out of the blue, an image came to her of the two of them building their own house, working side by side, framing room by room. She shook her head in amazement and then in shame.

He rolled his white shirtsleeves up higher and wiped his brow with a handkerchief from his back pocket. "Let us sit for a spell and take a rest. There isn't a soul in this park now."

Ruby hadn't noticed, so looked around. She had been so engrossed in their work together that she had forgotten. She saw that Sarah had picked up the debris from yesterday's booth and had piled it behind a tree. Earlier, when Ruby and Jeremiah returned with the wood, Sarah had stated that she was departing for the sheriff's office to report the incident. Ruby sensed Sarah's dread in going there – she knew Sarah felt betrayed by the sheriff's office ever since his deputy refused to help her the night her husband replaced her with his housekeeper.

Ruby saw her basket of food shaded under another tree. "Oh, I brought food - we can have a picnic!" she said.

The only seating was the gazebo's backbench so she followed him there. Ruby had taken her hat off to work, and now she realized loose strands were hanging about her neck and shoulders. She attempted to smooth it back with her hands as she stepped up the stairs. The sound of her footsteps across the planks of the wood flooring brought back memories of the day before and she stood frozen in the middle of its round structure, staring at the front and its lawn beyond, where no one stood today, where everyone stood yesterday.

"I was so frightened yesterday, I thought surely I would faint," she said softly.

"I thought you might, too" he replied, his voice as soft as hers. "Where did you get the courage to do that?"

She turned around to where he sat on the backbench, and looked into his eyes, thirsty to drink them in. "From you," she said.

Their eyes locked and his eyelids drooped ever so slightly as if to shade the shine coming from behind the blue. She was the first to look away as she placed the basket between them and sat down.

"Well, this isn't fancy, but there is plenty for the both of us.

Let's see, I have a jar of water, a jar of my twelve-day pickles, and some chunks of corn bread with but—"

"You have corn bread?" he asked, incredulous to this, as if he asked, *you have gold?* He handled a piece as if he had discovered the nuggets himself. "I haven't had corn bread since I left home two weeks ago! Didn't know anyone made it up here." He paused with the piece at his mouth. "May I?"

"I wouldn't dream of breaking your heart with no, now!" she replied with a giggle.

Did I just sound flirtatious?

He munched down, gazing dreamily into the far off. He finished it in seconds. "Good," he said, brushing his hands together to wipe off the greasy crumbs. "What's next?" His hand froze in mid-air over the basket as his eyes spotted Ruby's hair.

With a hair comb in hand, she was combing back the hair around her face, the same comb whose teeth had held her roped bun in place. The rope was quickly running its course down her back.

"Your hair – it's beautiful! May I touch it?"

Ruby nodded.

She felt his hand touch her back and stroke her hair gently. "My mommy had long hair like that and she would braid it and leave it hanging down. You should do that, too – you'll look like my people."

If it were only that easy, to be his people.

She resumed combing. "My hair is a bear to work with, though; too long and heavy, especially in this heat it feels like a horse blanket on my back. It desperately needs a cut."

"Well, which is it, a bear or a horse? You know us Indians, we'll just name you Horse Hair, or Bear Head."

"Wish my head *was* bare, as in b-a-r-e? How much cooler that would be!" She tightened the rope, twisted the rope around her hand, and pinned it down at the nape of her neck with her hair comb.

He watched her closely. "You do that quickly and with such grace, you make it look easy. What is my little horse tail back here, maybe three inches?" He turned his head around for her to look at its back. "One leather tie and it is finished." He turned back to face her. "That's men's work for you, but women amaze me how much they handle every day and still manage to look as delicate as a butterfly and as pretty, too." He smiled at her, his eyes softening, shining again. "You smell of lavender."

She couldn't turn away, even with a blush coming on. "Yes we are pretty tough cookies." She wiped a crumb from his mouth with the corner of the dishtowel she was holding that had covered the basket.

I would do no differently with one of my children.

Three dongs sounded from the City Hall bell tower. "I only have an hour left, and then I must go home. I left the children home alone for the first time—"

His eyes came closer, his lips. "Ruby?" He touched her face and moved his palm along her jaw line, his fingertips awakening her senses. Time suddenly stood still to Ruby. This structure around her became her nucleus, only eternity surrounded them out there, the only sound was his breathing, the only sight was his eyes, like stars brightly shining. She tilted her head and looked at his lips, then looked into his eyes, watched them as they closed, and his mouth was on hers, feeling as soft as a butterfly landing on a flower. Her eyes closed, her lips reached for more, and he brought his mouth fully onto hers. Was it for only a second, or was it forever, she couldn't be sure. But in that space where time didn't exist, she loved him forever, always had, always will.

* * * * *

She walked home in a daze, her feet barely feeling the ground, her fingers gently touching her lips ever so often, her other hand cradling the wild flowers. In her mind's eye, she could still see him.

"Here, Ruby, before you go," and he had walked behind the line of trees to the open meadow beyond the park and picked daisies and other wild flowers, tied them with his leather strap from his hair, and walked back to her with his broad grin, his hair falling forward, touching his shoulders. "My gift to you for a most pleasant lunch. Best cornbread this side of Appalachia! Are you sure I can't give you a ride home – at least part-way?"

She longed to say yes, but she would be traveling along the same road that Robert would be taking, and likely was walking there now. She had enough explaining to do.

Sarah was behind the petition booth now talking with a couple, and people were beginning to walk about the park, likely on their way home from work in the business district. Ruby made a mental note to tell the other ladies that the park was empty during the day and the best time to petition was in late afternoon and early evening. She would tell them tomorrow – no, day after tomorrow, for tomorrow she would meet Jeremiah here again – if Mrs. Catt didn't want to leave! Oh please, Mrs. Catt, stay, stay, she silently cried. The evening, the long dark night and then the morning, it would take an eternity before she could walk back to the park! She would fill up the space by preparing him a linen sachet of her lavender flower blossoms.

She opened her front door to the smell of smoke. The room was grayed with smoke and there was more coming from the kitchen. She could hear her daughter crying, the boys yelling. She ran to the kitchen to see Bess throwing a bucket of water over the stove, flames licking their way out from under the round inserts for pots, the lids red-hot.

"My God, what—" Ruby's words caught in her throat as she saw fire catch onto Bess's sleeve and spread up her arm. Ruby screamed, "Don't move!" as she grabbed the bucket from Bess, and splashed the little remaining water on her. It didn't completely go out and Ruby smacked Bess's shoulder and upper arm to put it out.

Bess screamed so loud that the boys hushed and stood terrified.

"Hush, Bess, it's gone now, Mama got it all, darling, Mama got it all!" She saw the bubbled skin under the charred sleeve and she began to cry. "Mama is so sorry, Bess, Mama is so sorry!"

Aimee ran in from the back door. "What is it, Ruby? I heard the screaming." Her hand was over her heart and she was out of breath.

Ruby was ripping the sleeve open more, to give more air to the burns. "There was a fire," she answered through her tears. "But it is okay, now. Bess is a brave girl."

Bess was sobbing now, but she was no longer hysterical. She didn't want to further alarm Bess by sending for a doctor, but one was needed. "I think Bess needs some salve, Aimee," she said as calmly as possible. "Could you run get Doctor Hughes?"

Aimee nodded and was gone.

"Can you walk upstairs, darling?" Ruby asked Bess. "I need to take this dress off." Bess nodded and they exited the kitchen in small steps and headed through the parlor toward the stairs.

Ruby looked behind her; the boys were following closely, mute, coughing, their eyes wide, red and wet. "Bess will be fine, boys. You go outside now and get some fresh air, away from this smoke. You can come up and see her in a little while."

She looked down and almost stepped on a small bunch of wild flowers tied with a leather cord. Fresh tears came as she stepped over them and slowly walked up the stairs with Bess.

* * * * *

"They will be fine," she heard the doctor say to Robert, his voice coming up from the bottom of the stairs. "The ointment will work and I've bandaged your daughter's arm, and your wife's hand for now. I'll come tomorrow and remove the bandages, to allow the air to heal it."

She heard the front door close and Robert's footsteps coming up the stairs. He stopped at Bess's door and peeked in. Ruby closed her eyes, her arm across Bess's stomach, pretending to sleep. Bess's breath smelled bitter from the elixir the doctor gave her - the doctor mentioned it contained a strong powdered drug, called heroin - but it seemed to work well, for her eyes had closed in sleep for the blessed time being. Robert stood for a few moments and then she heard his footsteps cross the hall to their bedroom.

Ruby's stomach growled as fiercely as her fingers burned but she dared not go downstairs. Breakfast seemed a month ago, Jeremiah a week ago.

Tears tapped softly on the pillow. Oh this is entirely my fault! I shouldn't have stayed so long! If I had come home earlier, this wouldn't have happened. Oh, I shouldn't have left home at all! They are too young to leave alone! But Bess had seemed so grown-up here lately. And she was so happy when she was told she could stay home and look after the boys. She so wanted to prove herself that she had tried to bake a cake; she had helped me bake many times. But she had never stoked the stove before and it didn't seem to get hot enough and she continued adding more coal, some more wood.

Ruby understood completely. She had had her own troubles with that horrible black beast and it was practically as old as she was. She would purchase a new one if she had to beg, borrow, or steal for it! Why was Robert so cheap! He hated giving up anything that belonged to his mother! It is his fault, too!

Bess whimpered, her arm trembling a little. Ruby patted her stomach. If her own fingers burned this badly, what must Bess be going through, with her arm a deep red, skin peeling, deep blisters on her wrist?

Oh I am such a bad mommy, Bess; no, that is a Jeremiah word, I am her *mama* and a bad one at that! Please forgive me, Bess, please forgive me! Oh, I kissed a man other than your Papa, Bess, and I am not a good woman at all!

* * * * *

Ruby sat outside on the front verandah, her wicker rocker creaking with each push, taking in deep breaths of fresh air. After a fitful night, Bess was sleeping again. Robert had left earlier than usual that morning without disturbing she and Bess. Probably got breakfast at the cafe but would likely begrudge her for spending the money. Aimee had come over later in the morning with bread, cheese, and roast beef. She had offered to take Ruby's place at the petition booth so what could Ruby say, but yes, thank-you? It was now noon and Aimee waved to Ruby as she departed her own home and walked down the boardwalk past Ruby's house, toward town, her footsteps on the wooden planks fading...

Ruby's last chance to see him...fading.

She clutched the arms of her chair to keep from running after her, her bandaged fingers stinging in protest.

Back and forth she creaked, Jeremiah, Jeremiah, the rocker cried. Each creak was the sound of her heart slowly breaking. She felt so lonely, knowing he was so close and yet...fading...

After today he would be gone forever and she hadn't said goodbye. Or said come back. Or keep in touch. Or touch her face again. She had so much to say and yet could say nothing. Nothing. These balusters might as well be my prison bars, she thought, glaring at the railing's invisible locks. She reached inside her apron pocket, found the leather tie and once more held it between her fingers, searching for solace there. The wild flowers were drying upside down in the cellar.

"Mama!" Bess called from inside.

Ruby stood up slowly and shuffled toward the door, believing surely she had grown ancient since the day before.

She tried not to breathe in much of the stale smell of smoke, as her shuffle continued toward the kitchen. The walls and stale air seemed to squeeze around her. She longed to be back outside, where her rocker could take her nowhere fast, but at least it was facing toward town.

"Mama?" Bess called again from her bedroom.

"I'm coming up with lunch – be right there," Ruby answered.

"I have to use the pot, Mama!"

"Coming!" Ruby sliced some roast beef and bread, and hurriedly carried the plate and a glass of milk upstairs with one hand. On the way, she made a mental note to ask the iceman to bring more ice for the icebox tomorrow; ice was melting quickly in this hot stuffy kitchen. She had so much to do here, and yet had not the energy to do anything. It was because her left hand was burnt and bandaged. But she had to be honest with herself; if the accident hadn't happened, she wouldn't be here doing her duties anyway.

She helped Bess to the chamber pot, wiped her behind, brought in a bowl of cool water and washed her face and legs to cool her down and then spoon-fed her, all the while feeling restless, her good right hand doing the tasks at hand clumsily. What was it Edith called her boys when they were restless inside the house? Antsy, that's it. She was antsy to get back outside.

"Bess, do you want to go outside and sit in the rocker for awhile?"

"Maybe later, Mama. That awful stuff the doctor gave me makes me sleepy. Can I come down later?"

Ruby nodded and left quickly, heading for the front door, and its light beyond.

"Mama, what's to eat?" Victor called from the kitchen. He and Jonathan had come in from out back. Ruby turned and re-entered the kitchen. Their muddy hands and britches told her they had been at the creek, probably looking for frogs again.

"Go back out and wash up at the pump, boys. I'll make you a picnic of goodies that you can take back to the creek with you." Their whoops made her feel guilty. She wasn't doing it for them; she just wanted to be back on the front verandah, alone with her thoughts.

Finally on their way, she breathed a sigh of relief as she returned to her verandah and sat back into her rocker. She looked up at the blue sky. So blue...I'm feeling blue without you, blue eyes...oooh, another song, from out of the blue, she thought with a sad smile. She listened to the quiet around her and to the steady clip-clop of a distant horse. She closed her eyes and felt his lips on hers – oh to be kissed on your mouth so completely! Their lips were pressed like two pie crusts sealed together, the cracks no longer there, to make the perfect pie. She licked her lips for the sweet taste.

From the sound of it, the horse was coming closer. She opened her left eye to the road and a man on a horse came into her vision. He was two houses down, peering closely at each house he passed.

He turned his head away from her, looking at the houses across the street. She opened both eyes wide – he had a pony tail! Her heart flew into her throat and she sat frozen, watching in disbelief. And then she was up and running, down her steps and down the boardwalk. She stopped dead in her tracks in front of her next door neighbor's house, one hand at her throat to soothe the beating she could feel throbbing there.

What am I thinking of doing - run to him with open arms?

She could only smile, and so she looked up at him with her best, as his horse approached and he drew back on his reins. He looked down at her, giving her his own, the sun shining blue tones to his black hair. They simply gazed at each other, her not quite believing he was really here. The horse shook its head and snorted and this brought Ruby out of her trance. She stepped down from the boardwalk onto the road and patted the horse's neck. This was as close as she dared get, her hand longing to touch his boot, but touching the horse made her somehow feel closer to him, as if touching an indirect part of him.

"I came as soon as I heard." His eyes were looking at her bandaged hand. "Aimee told me what happened when I asked where you were. I know I shouldn't be here, but—"

Ruby looked up into his eyes and the world around them disappeared. "I am happy you are here."

He swung down from his horse in one graceful movement and Ruby suddenly found herself face to face with him. There was not enough air between them to breathe.

Touching her bandaged hand lightly, he asked, "Does it hurt?"

She glanced at it, not quite remembering why it was bandaged. "Not anymore."

He grinned broadly at her, and she let out a soft laughter that felt so good. There had been nothing but pain since she had left him at the park yesterday, and now the pain was all gone. She had the urge to grab his hand and run through the fields beyond the houses; run with their hair blowing freely behind their backs. Running...freely...

"Your daughter? How is she?"

"Much better, thank you. It will take time for her to heal, but heal she will. May I - may I invite you to join me on the verandah? I can make a cool drink – I think I have some lemons and there should be some ice remaining—"

"I don't think that would be proper." He broke in, but he wasn't glancing around at neighbors' windows. His eyes didn't leave her face. It was as if he was trying to memorize her features. "I'm not here to cause problems for you, Ruby. You have children; you would have to make explanations. You might have to lie and that would only make something ugly out of something beautiful. That is how I will remember you – something beautiful." He took in a jagged breath. "We didn't say goodbye yesterday, and I can't leave without it. I can't explain it." He touched her chin with his finger. "And I know, to be the proper gentleman, I should apologize." He leaned his arm against the saddle and looked beyond her, his eyelids drooping heavily ... dreamily. She loved that look about him. She etched every line of his face, hair, shoulders, his arm against the saddle, the deep reds and greens of the horse blanket underneath, his clean white linen shirt, his chest moving with each breath, she etched all this into her memory and branded it there.

"There is no need to apologize," she said softly to his lips. She hardly sounded like herself, and yet she felt more like herself than ever before.

"It felt so right, didn't it Ruby?" He said, encouraged by her words, her tone. He tilted his head down and looked for more support.

"It did, Jeremiah." She felt a surge of happy blush in saying his name.

"I love it when your eyes shine like that," he said. "No wonder you were named Ruby – you glow like a gem! You ever been told that before?"

"No, but then I've never felt like this before." She was out of breath; as if they had in fact ran through the fields and only just now paused.

"I made something for you." He turned to his saddlebag,

unbuckled the flap, and brought out something hidden in his large hand. He opened his palm to her. A wooden carving of a dove sat there looking at her. Its head was smooth and round, its feathers etched in careful detail on its sides.

"Mommy believed that when a dove rested at your home, it brought love and peace. That is what I bring to you."

She picked the dove up carefully, as if grabbing it might startle it into flight. "I will treasure this always, Jeremiah." She could see herself dying with this in her hand. "I wish I had something for you."

"Yesterday was the best gift you could give me, Ruby. I can understand what a sacrifice it must have been, to be there. I'll never forget it, or you."

"Jeremiah, how can I say goodbye?" Her vision blurred and she looked back down at her dove, wishing her heart were made of this wood.

"This can't be goodbye forever, Ruby. Let's think of it that way. I can't stand the thought of it." He patted the horse's side as if it had just given him an idea. "I know what I can do. I'll come back through on my way home from New York City. I don't know how long it will be but when I do, do you think, Ruby, that maybe we could meet again in the park? We could just talk – there's nothing wrong with that, now is it?"

"I would love to sit again and talk with you, Jeremiah. That would be wonderful!" She felt a tremendous relief at not having to face forever. "This is not goodbye then. What a horrible word! Let us just say, what was it your mommy used to say, win-na-de..."

"...ya-ho," he finished. "Win-na-de-ya-ho."

"Thank you for this day," they said together.

* * * * *

"I love you," she whispered to the dove, and gave it a small kiss on its tiny beak. She laid it back in her lap and continued rocking. She looked down the street to where he had, only minutes before, tipped his hat to her, mounted his horse, and rode away. She had watched until he was completely out of sight and the dust had settled back down. She continued to watch now, as if he would magically appear again. Why not? Wasn't the last appearance only a dream? She could dream again. But she had her dove to prove she wasn't dreaming. She clasped it to her heart and rocked some more. She heard the distant clip-clop of a horse. She sat up straight, her eyes intensely squinting toward the sound.

Finally she sat back, disappointment bearing down on her heart. Buggy wheels, too, not just a horse. She watched, disinterested, as Doctor Hughes pulled up in front of her house, stepped down carefully from his rickety old buggy, and tied the horse to the hitching post.

"Well, Ruby!" he called as he walked up her walk. "Next time you see me, I just might have one of those horseless carriages. Just think of how much quicker I can make house calls! We must move forward and not look back. That is what I always say."

And next time you see me, I just might be on the back of a horse behind an Indian! I guess that would be moving back in time.

She smile sympathetically at his tired face. His duties must seem as never-ending as hers, for there are always people sick and dying.

She followed him inside and up the stairs, asking him silently, so tell me, doctor, how do you mend a broken heart?

Before joining him in Bess's bedroom, she entered her own and hid her dove in the back corner of her wardrobe, her recently enhanced trousseau easily hiding it.

His visit was brief. He had several others to call on before supper, he explained. Bess bit her bottom lip and whimpered a little as the bandages came off. Ruby turned her head and clutched at her stomach when she saw some spots had stuck and the doctor must pull.

He talked kindly to her as he did so, to distract her. "Bess, I saw you with your Mama at the women's rights convention, and I couldn't believe my eyes, how grown-up you've become! You were standing there so straight and almost as tall as she! My, my!

It won't be long; this town will see Bess Wright standing in that same gazebo, demanding women's rights! I can almost see it now."

Bess's eyes grew large and she forced a smile through her tight lips. "Did you sign the petition, Doctor Hughes?"

He laughed good-heartedly. "See what I mean, Mrs. Wright? She has started already!"

Bess remained solemn, looking at him expectantly.

"I take no political position," he said to her. "I heal both women and men. We all have our place in this world and that is mine. But I try not to judge others for doing what they must do. Your Mama has courage and I see that same sort of courage in your eyes, Bess. Your arm will be healed in a few weeks and you can shake it at any man, I assure you! Now let us see if your Mama has the same courage as you just showed me, when I take *her* bandages off!"

Just as the doctor flapped his reins and pulled away, Aimee came into view. So many callers today! She waved at Aimee walking up her walk. She joined Ruby on the verandah.

"Goodness, it is terribly warm today!" Aimee said. She waved away Ruby's offer for a cold drink. "I have to get home," she answered. "But first I must tell you what all happened today!" She opened a folded fan from her handbag and waved it front of her face, her strayed blond hair in frizzy curls moving slightly in the hand-made breeze. "First I must apologize. Mr. Jeremiah Bluemountain showed so much concern for your accident, and then said he had something to give you, I felt I had no choice but to agree to give him your address. When he left in such a hurry, I grew concerned that it may not have been the appropriate thing to do."

Ruby saw curiosity, not concern, on Aimee's face. She didn't blame Aimee for wondering. She tried desperately not to blush, as she said as off-handed as was humanly possible, "No need to apologize, Aimee." She wished to hear more about him; just hearing his name was exciting. Her mind scrambled to think of another question about him. "So, why was he there?"

"You tell me," Aimee answered, shrugging. "He arrived shortly after I did, and quite honestly, from a distance I thought he was stalking something, the way he was watching, hunting for...I don't know. Maybe it is because he looks so...Indian. I finally recognized him from the convention and remembered he did a good job speaking on our behalf. At least I thought so, didn't you?"

Ruby could only nod.

"Well, then Sarah told me about how you and he had built the booth we were standing at – I thought it looked different, larger somehow, but thought it was my silly imagination, until she told me what happened with the old one. Anyway, she said Mr. Bluemountain was very kind to do so and told me he was escorting Mrs. Catt to New York City. You should know that Mrs. Catt has been holed up in Cady's home ever since the convention. Cady collapsed that evening and hasn't been out of the house since, so Mrs. Catt stayed a little longer than planned to keep Cady company. Cady seemed in fine health at the convention, but perhaps she found some inner strength to keep her girls strong. Perhaps our cause is what keeps her going...I don't know. Sarah asked that we pray for her. Where was I? Oh, yes, well, when Mr. Bluemountain approached me, asking for your whereabouts, and well, I know I shouldn't say this but," she leaned toward Ruby and murmured, "I was quite taken back by him. He has very nice eyes and a soft accent – he must be from the south somewhere."

She was quiet for a moment, curling a strand of blond hair at her temple, around her finger. "So, did he?"

Ruby flinched slightly in spite of herself. "Did he what?"

"Did he come by?" Ruby could feel Aimee's eyes studying her closely.

"Oh Aimee, I just feel terribly guilty about the whole thing!" she blurted out. She would tell her what nagged at her heart but she would not tell her everything in her heart.

"Guilty? Why?" Aimee's expression of concern hadn't changed.

"Because if I hadn't been there building that booth with Jeremiah, fighting for women's rights and all, Bess would not have been here alone, fighting for her life!"

Aimee stopped twirling her hair and she sat up straight. "Bess is fighting for her life?" She glanced in the parlor window.

"No, not now. She is much better. But it is my fault she is burned in the first place, and if I hadn't returned home when I did, well I shudder to think."

"You think it is your fault because you weren't home? Oh, come on, Ruby, accidents happen! And you can't go on blaming yourself when—" she stopped when she saw Robert coming up the steps.

Ruby hadn't seen him coming either, so engrossed she was in her discussion.

He nodded toward Aimee. "Good day, Aimee," he said coldly. He looked at Ruby and his eyes squinted in what she recognized as anger. "Ruby, did I hear correctly that you weren't home yesterday?"

Aimee jumped up and winced, patting around her skirts as if she had a bee under there. "Well, I must go. Good day, Robert, good day, Ruby." She ran toward home.

Robert's eyes hadn't left Ruby's. "Ruby?"

Ruby raised from her chair slowly and faced him, her judge and jury.

"Yes, Robert, I was not home during the afternoon."

"This has gone on long enough, Ruby. Get inside and get upstairs now."

"It is supper-time, Robert, and I must feed the children."

"How are you going to cook with a burnt hand, Ruby?" his tone was harsh and accusing.

"Aimee kindly brought over some food."

"Then place it on the table, and go to your room! I'll ensure the boys eat." He followed her inside. "Take some food up to Bess, first."

She obeyed, praying he did not make a scene in front of the boys, or raise his voice to where Bess could hear.

"Mama, can I go outside now?" Bess asked as Ruby sat on her bed, with her plate.

"Not now, dear. Remember when the doctor took the bandages off, he asked that you stay inside for a couple of days, to keep the dust and bugs off. I wish we could go outside." Ruby meant it sincerely.

She stayed with Bess, nibbling off her plate, until evening darkened the window. Perhaps she should sleep in here again, she thought. But that would be so cowardly. She had to face him sometime. She imagined him dragging her from Bess's room but shook that off. He would not do that in front of the children. She tensed as she heard him go up the stairs with the boys, the boys calling out goodnight to Bess's closed bedroom door. She opened the door and answered back, blowing them kisses. She glanced across the hall to where Robert stood at their bedroom door. He snapped his fingers and jerked his thumb to his inner room. She held up a finger for him to wait a moment and turned to Bess's bed and kissed her goodnight. She longed to stay with her and hide behind her daughter. She squared her shoulders and lifted her chin as she walked toward him, determined to have a civil conversation with him.

He closed the door behind her. He slapped her face so hard that she saw spots before her eyes. He was breathing hard. She put her hand over her mouth to silence her cry. He slapped her other cheek, harder this time and she tasted blood. She raised her hand to block a third strike and he grabbed her wrist and pulled her arm behind her back. There were no words. Only heavy breathing, and choked sobs. He took hold of her bun, and yanked hard, combs and pins tapping lightly onto the floor. He pushed her onto the bed and fell on top of her back, smothering her deep into the feather mattress.

"No more, do you understand me?" he whispered into her ear. "No more or I will surely beat the living hell out of you!" He jerked hard at his handful of hair at the nape of her neck. "Do you understand me?"

"Yes!" came her muffled cry. She could not breathe and she panicked, kicking her legs. He lifted himself off and she raised her head and turned to her side to breathe in air. Blood dropped off her chin and onto the white chenille bedspread. She jumped up, clamping her bandaged hand to her mouth and ran over to the washbowl. The bandage was turning red. She poured some water from the pitcher into the bowl.

Robert stopped pacing and watched her through the mirror over the bowl. "My God, you are bleeding," he said, his voice low and shaking. He joined her at the washbowl and grabbed a washcloth. He clutched her chin, causing her to flinch, and turned her face to face him. "Hold still," he uttered. He dipped the wash cloth into the water and roughly wiped her chin, and then around her mouth. "The inside of your lip is cut." She winced with pain and drew back her head. "Hold still, I said!" He continued to wipe but more gently now. He poured water into a glass. "Rinse." She obeyed and spit red into the bowl. He turned her shoulders to face him and wiped some more. "I want you to listen to me, Ruby. And listen good."

Fine, I'll listen but I don't have to look at you. She focused her eyes on his square chin.

"You are no longer permitted outside this house, without my permission. You will remain here and look after the children as you were intended to do."

She raised her eyes to his; they were examining her mouth with concern, but his lips were pinched and stern. He let go her chin and threw the washcloth into the water. She stared down at the water slowly turning pink.

"I'm going downstairs to read awhile. You stay here." He turned his back to her and headed toward the door.

To see his back turn from her, cut her off, what was he thinking? To leave me here, to imprison me? From deep within her gut, a low ember caught flame and she felt the heat quickly spread throughout to her very fingertips and toes.

"Robert, talk to me!" she cried through clenched teeth, spewing through her swollen lips.

He paused at the door and looked back, his heavy eyebrows raised in surprise. "Why should I? I no longer trust you." He turned back to the door and twisted the knob.

How dare he! She snatched the washcloth from its reddened pool and threw it at his back with many years of pent-up anger to back it up. It slapped loudly in the middle of his back and he arched as one would in being attacked. He turned and looked down at the weapon, now a limp rag at his feet.

Fear seized her heart but it was too late now, so she raised her chin and stood her ground. She faced him, hands clinched in fists. "Talk to me, I said!" she spat out again.

He picked up the rag and rolled it into his own fist. "Fine," he said. "Fine!" He came toward her and her body steeled itself for the blow. He shook the fist at her. "I'll talk to you! I'll tell you this! My shop has lost a good deal of business, did you know that? Of course you didn't! And do you want to know why?" He was up in her face now, his cheeks splotched, his brown eyes glazed with anger. "Because of you, Ruby! Ever since the parade, I've had to deal with comments in town about how I can't control my own wife, my own household, so how can I manage a business? Some men stopped buying from me altogether, saying they go into Syracuse now, where they can trust the merchant to know what he is doing. And the jokes about your women's group parading yourselves around town. Here is one for you: What is black and white and read once a month? I'll give you a hint; it is not the standard punch line, newspaper. The punch line is, marching women on their periods! Understand, r-e-d? Ha, not so funny, is it? Jokes are one thing, which I hear plenty of, but there's more. Do you want to hear more?"

She backed away a few feet and nodded.

He began pacing the floor. "Of course, a parade was just getting your feet wet, wasn't it? You had bigger ways to disobey me. You had to go on a public display and air out our personal problems into a damn megaphone for the whole town to hear. About how you have cried for your children! Yes, you should have cried for your children! Hell, you haven't even spent time with your children, I bet this entire summer! Your idea of spending time with them is to drag Bess to a convention so she can watch her mama berate men with a bunch of bitches! You should be crying for them!"

He raised his hands up in the air. "And that's not all, Ruby, no that is not all. You may be quite proud of your convention but let me tell you what it did to *me*." He stopped and looked at her. "You remember me, don't you Ruby?" He jerked his thumb to his chest. "I'm one of those men you hate. Well, I'll have you know that I lost my biggest contract because of *you*!" He pointed his finger at her. "For years I had a contract with the textile mill for steel-toed boots. After your public outcry in a God-forsaken convention, the owner of the mill comes to me and says he didn't realize that my wife was part of the petticoat rebellion. That's right, *petticoat rebellion*! You are a laughing stock! He said that, thanks to this group of women, he has several women now crying for better work conditions, and more money. It may run him into bankruptcy. He blamed *me* for what *you* are doing out there and canceled his order. I now have a stock of one hundred and twenty-eight pairs of boots and no buyer."

He walked back to her, his bottom lip trembling. "Let me explain that to you in simple English. That means that I have a hell of a lot of money spent on stock, but no money coming back in. Do you see what I mean, Ruby, do you?"

He turned away and she stared at his white shirt – at the large wet spot blotched with red. His shoulders were lower now, his head down, his energy spent.

She felt stronger somehow, as if in relinquishing his words to her, he was relinquishing his strength to her.

"Robert, how would I have known this, except that you – why, I had no idea!" She touched her sore, swollen lip wishing this of all nights she could speak clearly. She shook her head. "You and I live in two different worlds. You don't know mine any more than I know yours. But my world is much more confining. Sometimes the walls are closing in on me, Robert. I don't mind my chores, I just want to do more! Don't you see? I could help you in other ways, too – I could earn wages, if you are having financial difficulties-"

"This is exactly why I didn't want to tell you, Ruby," he said, his voice tired now and void of emotion. "Now you look at me as a man who cannot provide for his family. And I can. And no wife of mine is going to go out of this home and work."

He sighed, shaking his head. "Let me put it to you this way. I've thought a great deal about this here lately. I've given you everything Mama and Papa worked for, this house, this furniture, and I've given you everything that I have, money for food on the table, clothes on your back, the children. All I ask from you is that you maintain what you have been given. That is all. If you don't remain inside and do what you are supposed to do, what God intended you to do, what you made an oath to do when you married me, then by God, I will divorce you. That is my right as a man. I will divorce you and you will have nothing; no home, no husband, no children."

He threw the tightly clenched rag into the bowl, water splattering the mirror. "Anything else you want to talk about?"

Divorce...no children. She sat down hard on the bed and shook her head. She could think of nothing else to say.

PART III
Fall's Spiraling Leaves

 Maple leaves fall around her, golds and deep reds, on this densely wooded hillside. One red lands softly on one of her two thick braids, braids dangling long below her breasts. Her horse snorts loudly, jingling the harness that straps her head, chewing at the bit in her mouth. She receives a pat on the head, but a pull at her reins, for they must climb faster. She must keep up with him. She looks ahead to see his backside walking beside his own horse, watches how nimbly he steps over a rock that she must soon climb, his sheepskin coat adding thickness to his broad back and arms, the thick piled collar pulled up slightly against the strong wind, his ponytail long now, dangling down his back. She does not see him speak but she hears his voice in her mind, saying, "Don't stop, Ruby, you must keep moving." She bends her uncovered head against the wind and pushes forward up the steep incline. On they go, across a small plateau, and down the other side. They reach the bottom and come to a clearing. A wide fast-flowing river is revealed. A hundred yards across and on its other shore, sits a log cabin, smoke breathing life up its chimney, a mist shrouds behind it. Somehow she knows that this mist rises from a creek back there. She walks along the shore of the river but cannot cross. She sees the cabin clearly but it is so far away. She longs to be there but her steps only take her farther away. She stops. The mist thickens to fog and stretches across the surface of the brown water. The fog reaches their shore in front of him and he walks into it, is absorbed by it and slowly disappears, his horse's back end disappearing last. "Don't stop, Ruby," he says again. "But how do I get to the other side?" she cries out to him. "How do I get there from here? How do I—"

"Ruby, wake up." He shook her shoulders. "Wake up, you are whimpering."

She blinked her eyes trying to clear the mist. The bed creaked as he arose and she heard him yawn. He walked around the bed and into her vision, where she saw him arch his back, stretch and scratch at the crotch of his long underwear as he walked across the room and behind the screen. She listened as his urine splashed noisily into the chamber pot.

"It is daylight, my dear," he said. "Is today a holiday that I am not aware of? Yes, of course, this is your sister's wedding day, on a Thursday no less. May cost me dearly, missing a day in the shop. Why can't they get married on a Saturday like everyone else?"

She had explained this before –wasn't he listening? She sat up and dangled her feet over the side of the bed. "Opal said Saturdays are not used as wedding days because the Amish believe it would be sacrilegious to clean-up after the wedding on a Sunday."

She rubbed her eyes. She felt so weary, she could easily have slept through the morning, she was sure of it. Or at least long enough to finish the dream. It remained with her, as if the mist now surrounded her. Oh why did he wake her just when...her mind played back his tall straight back walking through the trees, the fallen leaves shush-shushing below his feet—

"Ruby?"

She raised her head. He was standing beside the screen looking at her.

"Please prepare my bath for me. The children must also be bathed before we depart. Laziness will not get us there on time."

He was right, of course. She had to get moving ... get moving. *Don't stop, Ruby, you must keep moving.*

Her hands touched her chest, half-expecting to find braids resting there. Her hands continued up to her shoulders, where her hair rested lightly there. She pulled this back behind her ears. It would be a very long time before braids would rest on her chest. Twenty-eight years of growing hair, only to be snipped in a moment, its one solid braid cut below the neck and left dangling, limp, from her hand. She had handed her dead appendage to

Aimee, now her only tentacle to town, who sold its three-foot length for enough money to pay off Robert's account to Joe's General for the booth lumber and supplies. As far as Ruby knew, Robert never found out about the charge.

"I'm still not quite accustomed to it," Robert said, as he put on his robe.

She tilted her head to him questioning.

"Your hair," he said.

First time he has mentioned it, she thought in surprise, and feeling a bit uneasy. His only comment was on that first evening, after several quizzical looks at her face and smaller, tighter bun. "You look different somehow. Can't quite put my finger on it." She had explained to him then, that the summer was too hot, her hair too heavy, too many headaches. This was not a lie, she told herself, even though she knew, deep down, she probably would not have cut it for those reasons alone. "A woman's hair is her glory," Robert reminded her. She simply nodded. She had had no regrets; her head feeling lighter, cooler, even her thoughts less cluttered somehow. No regrets until this morning's misty dream.

She put on her robe and slippers and headed down the stairs, mentally counting how much time she would need in preparing the baths and breakfast. A kettle of water took twenty minutes to heat, she needed two for each bath, well there wasn't enough time to heat fresh water for everyone, so the boys would have to bathe in their father's water. She and Bess would bathe in cold water. How many eggs remained in the icebox? She opened the front door, counting her blessings that Jesse had left a basket of eggs next to the milk bottles. Without Jesse and his gifts of eggs and milk from the farm, meat products here would be scarce. Thank goodness she had sufficient vegetables dried and canned for the winter, although not as much as she had preserved last year. She had to admit that her attention to the world outside her home this summer had taken its toll on her domestic productivity. But this was a small price to pay, for growing in other ways, she told her guilty conscience. Besides, she consoled herself as she opened a jar of stewed tomatoes, we are definitely not starving. There was just enough flour for a few biscuits, and scrambled eggs finished the setting.

Robert raised his eyebrows when he sat down at the table. "Fry some bacon, Ruby."

"There is none."

"And why is that?"

"Because your weekly allowance for food barely covered the essentials. And we are now out of flour." She split a biscuit between Bess and Jonathan, and bit her tongue for her accusatory tone.

"And whose fault is that?" he asked, his voice raising.

"I'm sorry. I'm not blaming anyone, Robert."

He dropped his fork noisily onto his plate. "I certainly am, Ruby! I'm blaming you for this predicament. I warned you that money would be tight. We can give thanks, children, to your mother, for her public shenanigans this summer, bad behavior that cut my shoe contracts in half." He folded his hands together in mock prayer and closed his eyes. "Thank you, Ruby, for this food we are about to starve on."

Jonathan giggled and his older brother elbowed him, knowing better that his father was not joking.

Bess immediately stood up and began spooning eggs into everyone's plate except hers. "There is plenty of food, Papa. I'm not very hungry."

He squinted his eyes at Bess. "And I suppose you weren't very hungry last night when your mother served chicken gizzards? And the night before with eggs and potatoes?" He looked around at the group who had become pale and quiet, picking listlessly at their food. He tapped his fingers on the table and finally sighed. "Bess, you will eat eggs with the rest of us. We will all eat. We will all go to the wedding where we will all eat a delicious Amish feast. We will survive and soon enough my business will pick back up. Your mother needs to lose some weight anyway." He smiled and winked at Victor. "Enough said. Ruby, more coffee please."

She hurried to the kitchen and brought back the pot, feeling hurt from his stings. Think of something positive, she thought. She remembered Jesse's note on the milk bottle. "Oh, yes, and now that fall is here and harvest is over, Jesse will soon bring over back bacon and beef from the killings. Then we will have our own feast!"

"Excellent. More charity," Robert answered, his sarcasm stinging again.

What does he want me to say, she wondered. She left the room, her appetite gone now, and put water on the stove to heat for bathing. She would remain quiet and out of his way.

She preferred it that way, anyway.

Finally on their way out of town in Jesse's wagon, Ruby brought her cape around her tighter. Although tucked tightly between Jesse and Robert, she still felt chilled – their stony faces not making things warmer. They spoke to one another only when necessary. It was a cold November morning and the wind was pulling the few stubborn yellow brittle leaves from their clinging branches. Her eyes followed one as it swirled through the air like it was trying to take flight, only to inevitably spiral helplessly, down, down, to the ground, lost forever. As the wagon slowly passed, her head turned to follow its movements, the wind scattering it about the others on the ground, but never again to fly.

A withered leaf landed on her dark blue dress and she smiled a weak smile as she brushed it off. Opal saw to it that Ruby would blend right in with the wedding party. Ruby's dress was plain cut with a cape, no buttons, only snaps. Her Amish cap was white, to signify her as a married woman. Ruby was glad it fit around her head snugly and likely would hide her shorter hair in its small bun – Opal told her it was against the Amish religion for a woman to cut her hair. As instructed, Ruby wore no jewelry and she would carry no flowers. She shivered as much from nerves as she did from cold, as she thought, just because I look like a duck, doesn't mean I am one.

As promised, Jesse dropped them off at Jacob's home just before eight o'clock and then rushed off. Jesse had picked them up on his way home from his milk run and still must look after the horses and chores before changing and returning for the wedding. Ruby and Robert, their three children tightly surrounding them, stood self-consciously looking about in the barnyard, not certain where to go. Jacob's family farmhouse was simply large and rectangular in size. The house was dwarfed by the larger white barns and sheds on each side.

A young family pulled up beside them, the girl clutching a baby tightly as her husband helped her from the wobbly black buggy, her dress looking much like Ruby's. The girl and her husband both wore black high-topped shoes and his suit and broad-brimmed hat were black. They nodded shyly at Ruby and Robert and led the way into the side door of the house and into the kitchen. The children slowly walked away from the adults and began their slow dance of shy communication with the other children milling about.

As one of the bride's attendants, Ruby was supposed to greet guests in the kitchen with the others, but once there and knowing no one, she stood silently to the side and watched with uncomfortable curiosity. Every wall in the huge room was filled from top to bottom with non-ornate cabinetry and cupboards. Lower shelving and the long wood-planked table were heavily laden with more food than she had seen in a long time. Her stomach growled as she named what she could see from her station, for there was roast chicken with bread stuffing, coleslaw, applesauce, cherry pies, fruit salads, tapioca pudding, loaves of bread, sweet potatoes, peas, pumpkin and lemon sponge pies, and cookies.

The aromas of the food quickly mingled with human scents of many darkly clad relatives and church members, as the room filled and overflowed into other rooms. All women were dressed similar to Ruby, excepting the unmarried girls, who wore black caps. The men and boys all wore black straight-cut coats without lapels, and suspenders, black socks and shoes, black or straw broad-brimmed hats. Ruby noted that their shirts held the only buttons in the room. The married men had beards but no mustaches. Ruby recalled ashamedly when, the week before, Opal had brought over Ruby's dress, and Ruby had blurted out, "why these costumes?" Opal had stiffened at its rude implication, and Ruby had stiffened at her own callousness. Ruby silently endured Opal's patronizing tone as she explained that these were not costumes, but an expression of their faith. She added that the Amish believed their distinctive clothing encouraged humility and separation from the world (separation, indeed! was Ruby's next thought which she wisely kept to herself). Once among them, Ruby had to admit that at least there was no distinction between the poor and the rich. All were equal. And looking no different, she gradually felt no different, and no eyes were standing her out in the crowd. She could blend right in and watch without being watched. She now pitied Robert who looked so out of place in his only light brown three-piece suit, one with lapels of course.

He had disappeared earlier and she eventually found him in what was pointed out to her as the church room that was built on one side of the house. He was sitting stiffly, back erect, on one of the long wooden benches, fidgeting with his brown felt hat between his hands. She supposed that there must be at least two hundred people spread between the kitchen and this room. She glanced about and was relieved to see the familiarity of her own kinfolk standing off to one side at the front of the room. She finally worked her way to Edith, Jesse, and Garnet who all stood huddled, united, visually attempting to blend in with their clothing of solid dark fabrics, but their eyes told Ruby that their minds did not understand their surroundings.

"It is so good to see you!" Ruby said as she gave them each a tight hug. "Have you seen Opal?"

"Oh, she left at four this morning," Garnet answered, shaking her head and waving that question away. "She had to get here early to help with the cooking. They'll have two meals today, dinner and then supper later on. Jacob says to expect to be here past ten o'clock tonight. With all the food we have to eat, I'm not surprised. Right now Jacob and Opal are meeting with the minister somewhere else in the house, for...counseling, I do believe. I'd get lost here, there are so many—"

Someone starting a hymn cut her off. They looked around to see everyone else seated, including the children lined in the back rows. They quickly sat down on the nearest bench, clearing their throats and blushing in embarrassment. Ruby was glad Opal was not here in the room to see her family making a spectacle of themselves. Others joined in singing a song unfamiliar to Ruby, and without a piano, without hymnal books.

Ruby suddenly wondered in dismay where she should be sitting as a bride's attendant, but there was no way she could distinguish the other bride's attendants from the other women. She spotted Robert again, Amish folk closed in on both sides of him. At the very least she knew she should be sitting beside Robert, who would likely remind her later on that her place was beside him.

After the third song, Ruby finally saw Opal and Jacob enter the room, following the minister, all faces solemn. Opal's hands were folded in front of her, her head was down. Opal's dress of sky blue complimented her complexion and light brown hair peaking from its cap and Ruby's eyes welled with tears of love and pride. Opal looked so young. But pity soon squeezed her heart, in place of pride, for as Opal walked closer to Ruby, Ruby saw that Opal's eyes were tired, her lids heavy. Her beautifully creamed complexion was now blotched with flush and white, accentuating the dark circles under her eyes. It was subtle but Ruby knew her sister, and her eyes now overflowed with tears of sorrow. Opal sought Ruby's face as she approached the front bench and when their eyes met, Ruby forced a bright smile, nodding, her eyes saying, *I'm here for you.* Opal's pinched mouth relaxed and turned up into a quivering smile. She turned toward the front, squared her caped shoulders, and with resolve, sat down beside the cleanly-shaven Jacob.

Ruby had not seen Jacob as an adult. She studied the groom from her vantage point behind and to the side, noting his broad shoulders, dark brown hair neatly clipped around his collar, his sharply pronounced nose, the serious set of his thin mouth and rounded jaw line. He would be strict and structured, Ruby guessed, but hopefully fair. He and Opal would live here in his parents' home, Opal had told her, until next spring, when they would build their own home on part of this five hundred-acre farmland. There was obviously plenty of room. Until then, their weekends would be spent visiting their relatives over the winter months, and Ruby already looked forward to their January visit. Who would Opal be, then?

Ruby had never sat through such a long service. The minister said prayer, read scripture, and gave a sermon, much of it in German dialect. After more than two hours, he asked Opal and Jacob to step forward. He spoke lowly, Ruby picking up bits of questions on their marriage to be.

Ruby couldn't concentrate on any of his words. Memories rushed in and flowed out, like waves on the shore. She and Opal were children again in their bedroom darkened by night, fascinated by the fireflies released from their jarred captivity, flickering in the darkness. They were lying in their shared bed watching their narrow walls expand into a black sky, studded by blinking, moving stars. "Imagine, sis, we are looking into eternity," she would whisper to Opal, "and these pinpoints of light are showing us the way to heaven." Opal would answer by taking her thumb out of her mouth, say "yes, I see," return the thumb, and continue watching until she slowly drifted off to sleep. Did they think their childhood would go on forever? No, only she was the dreamer, Opal was the practical one. Opal the practical one who said to Ruby, in the apple orchard, that love comes with time and children. How do you know a man before marrying him, she had asked Ruby. Opal considered marriage a necessity for blessings, but remember, Ruby said silently to Opal, to give yourself to him is to lose yourself to you. Against her will, she imagined Jacob on top of Opal tonight, smothering, pushing, taking, and she losing her girlhood to his needs, opening, clenching, giving. Yes, good always comes out of bad, and so children will come. Opal had quoted Sarah in the Bible, when Sarah found she was with child, 'God hath made me laugh'.

Ruby closed her eyes and prayed silently, "Please, God, let her laugh and be happy. Help her to open to him, to submit, to give, but let her keep enough for herself."

Ruby looked at the back of Opal's cap and longed to see once more those beautifully plaited braids held artfully against her head with her comb of opal stone. She recalled Opal's tears as she washed Ruby's hair, crying "God will know me in that church, as well as mine...won't he?" As Opal said herself, this farm was only a few miles down the road, but might as well be a thousand, for it was, indeed, a different world. Goodbye, my little sister, she silently sent words to Opal, for you will be no more tomorrow. Tomorrow you will be a changed woman, for good and bad.

Through her blurred vision, she looked about her to other women wiping away their own tears.

* * * * *

"Some bright morning when this life is o're, I'll fly away. To a land on God's celestial shore, I'll fly away..." she sang softly and drifted off. She listened to the only sound remaining, her rocker creak, creaking, as she pushed with her feet back and forth leisurely. A cold breeze blew through the verandah, and she tucked her gloved hands under the blanket.

Let the neighbors talk. I can sit out here every day if I want to – it's a free country ain't it? That's what Lizzie said, oh so long ago. Ages ago. Was it only this summer? Oh, Lizzie, Cady, Phyllis, Sarah, how I long to meet with you again...and Jeremiah. She looked down the empty street. No horse plodding along, its rider sitting tall, looking only for her. Oh but there is my dear friend coming up the boardwalk. Aimee, what would I do without you?

Aimee approached Ruby's verandah with a confidant smile. She was dressed in a long black wool coat, her blond head donned with a red fox fur hat, her hands tucked into a matching fur mitt. Her husband's promotion to bank manager had faired well for Aimee. Ruby tucked her blanket more tightly around her faded housedress.

"I was hoping to find you here!" said Aimee, lifting up her skirts to climb the stairs.

"Where else would I be? Good day, Aimee!"

"Indeed, you are here every day," Aimee said as she sat down on the wicker settee. "I worry about you, Ruby. You sit out here every day that I know of, rocking and looking lost. Is there anything I can do to help?"

"You already do help me, Aimee. Your visits mean more than I can tell you. What's the news from town?" Ruby looked at Aimee closely – there was something different about her face ... ah, that was it; Aimee was beautiful without the bruises.

"I have good news and bad news. Which do you want to hear first?" Aimee asked.

"Good, of course. It softens the bad."

"Very well, then. We now have two hundred eighty-eight signatures on our petition. The mayor has agreed that since that is more than fifty percent of the town adult population, *counting women this time*, he will press it forward to the state legislature. Thanks be to women like Carrie Chapman Catt, other towns are petitioning as well. If we get enough petitions to gain notice at state-level, word is they will bring in a bill to allow women to vote. We can then vote for our governor. Then we go for the federal vote, and eventually vote for our president! It may take some time, but like time, we are marching on!" Aimee finished breathlessly, her cheeks pink from the cold and excitement, her frayed blond curls around her forehead bouncing.

Ruby couldn't help but envy Aimee's shining blue eyes, eyes shining because she had a mission, a cause, and she was winning! She fought too, but no longer felt a part of it. The convention had been more than three months now. They were all so far away...across the river.

She smiled and sincerely put forth an effort to sound happy. "That is wonderful news, Aimee. It was all worth it then!"

"That's what Cady said, too! It was all worth it. Which brings me to the sad news, Ruby." Aimee took a deep breath and excelled slowly. "Cady is dying."

"No, Aimee, no!"

"I'm afraid so. She was doing well for a while but then recently collapsed while out collecting signatures door-to-door. Can you imagine?"

"Why was she not collecting them at the petition booth?" Ruby asked. "It is still standing, surely!" Her heart squeezed even tighter as memories she had rocked to sleep came alive and she saw him, white shirt sleeves rolled up, pounding nails into boards that she held steady.

"Oh that is the frustrating part about all this!" Aimee said, her eyes now squinting in anger. "You must remember Anna, Donna, and Jenna, the three sisters? Well, Jenna set up her own booth just fifty yards from ours, her own booth petitioning *against* women's suffrage! Working against women, working against her own sisters, can you imagine?"

Ruby shook her head in shock, but then raised a gloved finger. "Wait a minute! I do recall her sisters accusing her of just such a thing at your afternoon tea, do you remember?"

"Yes, I do. Well, there have been shouting matches, I hear, that were quite unlady-like, between the sisters. Cady was quite dismayed about it, and so hired two men to move our booth to her own front yard. That was a bit out of the way, though, so she and some of the others were going door-to-door. It was just too much for her, Ruby. She had fought so hard. But the word she is sending out to us all, is that it is all worth it, and to not give up!"

"We must go visit her, Aimee! Will you go with me? Perhaps tomorrow?"

"Will it be alright - for you to go?" Aimee had never asked Ruby why she remained at home, but had seen enough to understand why.

"Yes," she answered simply.

With, or without, Robert's permission, she would go.

"Yes," Robert answered that evening, much to her surprise. "You may go for one hour, day after tomorrow, since that is your marketing day. Go for your visit, do your marketing, and then stop by the shop so that I know where you are."

Ruby resisted clapping her hands with glee in front of him. She merely nodded and said thank-you. But her heart soared freely and *that* he would not see. She was going for an outing with Aimee, to see Cady and Lizzie!

"As for tomorrow," he continued and paused, placing his fork slowly on his plate and wiping his mouth with his napkin, "give particular attention to your house duties. Here lately, there is something gloomy and untidy about the place."

She nodded again, completely agreeing with him.

Still sensing a renewed freedom, she felt brave enough to go knocking on Aimee's door the next day. Aimee's mother answered the door, stating in a practiced voice but with a worried frown, that Aimee was in bed with some sort of virus.

"Can I come in and see her?" Ruby asked.

"No, no," Aimee's mother answered hastily. "Aimee wouldn't want to see anyone – looking like she does." She gave Ruby a you-know-what-I-mean look, and Ruby turned away sadly.

What a shame – she looked so beautiful and happy just the day before. Aimee clearly has no warning of when he will strike. Hopefully the bruises and swelling would be down enough to go out tomorrow.

But Aimee's mother only answered the door with the same story, the next day. Ruby walked the long walk to Cady's home alone, kicking at small piles of yellowed leaves, wondering, why is life like falling leaves? Just when you think life is picking you up, it only knocks you down to the ground.

The booth was there by the gate to Cady's home proudly displaying a sign that read *Petition for Women's Vote*! Ruby's reaction to seeing the booth took her by surprise. She approached it with reverence and held on to its small counter to prevent a public spectacle in falling down and worshipping it as an altar. It represented so much: to those whose pen was poised as they stood in front of this, listening to her dear legion of friends as they stated their mission, it represented hope for more rights to all women. Sorrow and regret flooded over her as she realized she had missed her opportunity to stand beside them. She stroked the heads of the imbedded nails with her gloved finger, yearning to touch any essence that remained there from his own touch so long ago. And yes, it represented so much more to her: deep, secret hopes to be touched again, gently, gentle yet reaching deeply into her being to a place she knew not existed before...him. She dared not think his name, not here in public, it only belonged in her own secret chamber.

And now this booth stood here alone, only as an artifact of what was. Would it ever be again? The cold wind blew against her and she shivered. She looked up at Cady's home and almost cried out, *Is everything dying around me?* Of course not , life goes on – was that her mother's voice or her own? She almost smiled in spite of herself.

Take one step in front of the other, until you reach Cady's side, and think of someone else other than yourself! You've spent too much time on your own, and now it is time you reach out to comfort another.

Cady looked like a miniature doll to Ruby, propped up in a large four-poster bed. Her hair was brushed long down the front of her gown. She smiled as Lizzie announced that Ruby had 'come a-callin'. Lizzie offered Ruby a chair on Cady's side of the bed, and she sat down on the other side and resumed her knitting. Cady was thinner, smaller, giving her larger eyes a protruding look but she was sitting up and smiling and Ruby was grateful for that. Ruby noticed many books stacked on Cady's bedside table and a book and Cady's spectacles on the bed. The book was titled *The Woman's Bible*. Ruby suddenly wished she could ask Cady questions; there was so much she knew that Ruby wanted to know. But where to begin, when Cady was at the end?

Instead Ruby reached for Cady's frail, freckled hand and squeezed tightly. "I've missed you," she said.

"And I you, Ruby. We all missed you. Aimee has been giving us news. Bess's arm has healed nicely, I hear. Your family is doing well, I hope?"

Ruby nodded. "The children are in school, Robert is at the shop. The usual." She paused. "I just want you to know, well, I thought about you and the legion, and wondered how you were doing every day since I stopped. I just wish I could have been more a part of it. Thanks to you and the Ladies of the Lost Legion, this summer was the happiest summer of my life!"

"And the most challenging, too, I imagine?" Cady said softly. Ruby felt Cady's eyes searching her own, so she cast her eyes down and let go of Cady's hand. She did not wish to bear her soul here; her tears were too close to the surface as it was.

"Yes, well, whenever one is forced to look at life differently, it does create some challenges," Ruby answered, trying to sound philosophical. "I used to accept life as it came, thinking this was what was meant to be, but you opened a window for me. Now I know that when a small group of women get together with a purpose, we can make a difference. We should be able to vote soon!"

"Soon? I'm afraid not." Cady's voice now sounded resigned and tired. "Yes, we have gained support. Support through hard work by you and the others in gathering petitions, marching in the parade, boldly speaking out in the Women's Convention. You made sacrifices, I know. But these are very small steps in the large scheme of things. We've moved forward but only in inches, for we are only one small town. We must reach out to many women, and gain favorable support from men as well, men who must agree and vote to give us the vote. I believe they fear that giving freedom to the minorities takes some freedom away from the majority. We must fight fear. You must understand this can take years to achieve what we set out to do. Do you have those years?"

Ruby realized that Cady's blunt question was seeking honesty; she had no time for superficial answers. Ruby decided to provide blunt answers, shock or not. "No, I do not. Until they change some property and custody laws, I am bound by marriage and am now forbidden by my husband to continue. We have suffered financially, all in the name of my speaking out for women's rights. Rather a vicious circle, isn't it? I need to fight for women's rights, but I can't fight, because I have no rights!"

"Yes, I understand completely." Cady's expression remained unchanged.

Perhaps my marital woes aren't such a guarded secret, after all. Or worse yet, perhaps this is common?

"You did your best, under the circumstances, Ruby. Take pride in your contributions. You have planted good seed in many minds, and those that take and grow will pass their seed on to others and eventually society's way of thinking will change. You will live to see it." I will not, was unspoken between them.

Cady pulled out an embroidered bookmark from her book. "This is my favorite quote. I don't know where I saw it, but I remembered it and stitched it here to keep in mind. Read this." She handed the bookmark to Ruby.

"'Happiness held is the seed…happiness shared is the flower.'" Ruby read aloud the neat, cross-stitched letters. She handed back the bookmark. "It is pretty and it makes sense, coming from you. You've shared so much with others, and your contributions are far greater than mine. You've planted a whole flower garden!"

"Thank you, but I wish to remind you of a visit you made here in the early spring. You couldn't imagine how you would help, only that you wished to. If you had seen in the future what you are capable of doing, you wouldn't have believed it then, would you? And your duties are not over yet. There is another major contribution you can make."

"Oh, please…don't ask." Ruby said. "For if you ask, I will do my utmost to do it, and then I must answer to—"

"You can do it from where you are. You have much more influence than you realize. I taught school enough years to know that a child's mind is open, inquisitive, and largely unjudgmental. Your own children are your hands to the future. Open their minds to the oppression of women, to the oppression of the Negro, to the oppression of the minorities. Teach them to fight for change, when change is right. Do you understand what I am trying to say?"

Ruby nodded, tears surely coming now. Of course she understood but somewhere along the way she had forgotten. The face of Bess came back to her asking, "Could we talk about that sometime?" Hadn't she asked Robert that same question? He had given her the same answer that she had given Bess; "perhaps someday". Descending order of power just as Preacher Paul preached about and it was up to her to stop its pattern. She also knew that mothers had tremendous power in their homes; her own mother-in-law still controlled the household and she had been dead a long time now.

It was time Ruby marched home and seized her rights. It occurred to her that she had been so self-involved, so self-pitying, she hadn't yet taken the time to reach out to blessings right under her nose. Hands to the future, as Cady said. She reached her own hand to Cady's again and squeezed. She could say nothing.

"And now I have an invitation for you," Cady said. She paused and closed her eyes, both hands moved to her stomach, and she breathed in deeply, her mouth tightly closed. Lizzie laid down her knitting and moved quickly to Ruby's side of the bed. She poured some dark liquid from a bottle into a teaspoon.

"Miss Cady, open your mouth and take this."

"But it makes me so sleepy, Lizzie, and I don't want to sleep."

"It eases the pain, though, honey, so take your medicine. That's it, that's a good girl."

"Should I go now?" Ruby whispered to Lizzie.

"No, Ruby, not just yet," Cady murmured, her eyes still closed. "I must finish what I was about to say."

Lizzie's brow was furrowed deeply with concern as she stroked Cady's arm for a few minutes. Finally, Cady opened her eyes and smiled weakly. "It is better, Lizzie. The pain has passed. You fuss and worry too much. But I don't know what I would do without you." She dabbed at her mouth with a handkerchief, its lace trim noticeably shaking in her hand. Lizzie returned to her chair and resumed knitting.

"Ruby," Cady said, her voice stronger now, "today I received a letter from Carrie Chapman Catt, in New York. She is now heading back home to Iowa and will visit here on her way through. I am expecting her on or about the eighth of December, so, I'm hoping to be up and about by then. I plan to host a ladies' tea, with Lizzie's help, of course. Do try to come."

From the corner of her eye, Ruby saw Lizzie shake her head slightly, worry etched on her face.

"Of course I would love to come, Cady. I'll see what I can —" It suddenly occurred to her that Jeremiah would likely be escorting Mrs. Catt. Her face felt flushed at the thought of possibly seeing him again.

"Ruby, don't fret about it," Cady said, concern creasing around her eyes as she watched Ruby's blushing face. "Do what you must do."

PART IV
Winter's Empty Garden

Ruby and Aimee walked the three miles into town to St. Mark's Catholic Church, Ruby's hands clenched tightly together under her cloak. Gray clouds hung low and ominous, threatening more snow than the several inches already on the ground. The walk took longer than it should have by the time they picked their booted way through the snowdrifts.

The organ pipes had just finished a mournful tune when they took their seats toward the back. Ruby's eyes tried not to follow the end of the isle to where the oblong ornamental casing was displayed. She tried to focus above it to where the organ player sat, but to no avail. Her eyes fell on the top half of the lid, raised to reveal Cady's head and chest. The reality of it all came crashing down on her and she burst out crying. Aimee's arm came around her shoulders and held tight.

Why, Cady, why? You had all the answers before, so tell me why?

It was then that some of Cady's last words arose through the rush in her ears and the memory of them whispered to her, *don't fret about it, Ruby,* and just as suddenly, the tight squeeze on her heart subsided. The tears still flowed freely but she was somehow relieved from releasing them. The service had ended and everyone was now filing by to say their final farewell to Cady. Through her blurred vision, Ruby saw Phyllis at the front, leaning over to kiss Cady's forehead. She saw Thomas on the front pew, his head hung low, immobile.

Aimee stood and walked into the line, but Ruby stayed back.

She wanted to be last. Finally she had her opportunity. The closer she came to the front, the more she clutched the object in her hand. She reached Cady's side and longed to hold the same hand she had held only such a short time ago, but the hand would be cold now. Instead she clutched the side of Cady's eternal bed and felt the satin padding. She stared at Cady's closed eyes, her freckled face, her sealed lips, her freckled hands, one folded over the other.

"Goodbye Cady," she whispered. "I promise you that the seed you planted will continue to grow. If not through me, then through my own. Goodbye to happiness I have known."

She dropped the carved dove down into the satin where it rested by Cady's side.

* * * * *

At the entrance to the church, Ruby hugged Lizzie, Phyllis, Sarah, and Aimee. They all looked like lost sheep without their shepherd. To her own surprise, she told Aimee that she wanted to go for a walk alone, in the park. She wanted to say her good-byes there, too.

"Alright," Aimee said, sounding unsure that Ruby could make this decision, "but please be careful walking through the snow."

Head down, concentrating on where to place her next step in the slippery snow, Ruby almost stepped out in front of a horse and buggy slowing down in front of the church. The loud "Whoa!" from the driver did not attract her attention in that direction. She jerked her foot back and turned down the sidewalk, away from the church, away from the crowd, wanting only to be alone with her thoughts. She faintly heard exclamations from the church steps and wondered, only for a moment, who had arrived. It didn't really matter and she kept walking, vaguely aware that her steps were more a waddle. It was a long walk down Main Street to City Park, and she had to walk with vigilance. There was no wind and the cold air felt fresh on her face and in her lungs. Walking on her own gave her a sense of freedom and of comfortable solitude. The darkness around her, her black cloak covering her, she was almost invisible to passers-by.

She reached the business district and glanced over to the storefronts, her husband's own Walk Wright closed in darkness. Joe's General had a potted spruce tree by his door and it was decorated with Christmas tinsel, popcorn strings, and small nut wreaths. It all looked so different this time of night. Shutters were closed, as if the buildings themselves were sleeping. The few who walked here were talking in low tones as if afraid to wake them up. So different from the summer she remembered here, where so many people and horses were noisily walking about. Where she and ... he ... actually walked into Joe's General in the broad daylight and she made her own purchases, eventually using her own resources – her hair – to pay her contribution to the cause. It was hard to imagine now, but on this same winter street, another warm summer holiday lined it with many people, and she, Ruby Wright, had paraded bravely down its middle carrying a sign, as if she had every right to. No one could stop her, no not even Robert. She had had her say, made her stand, proved her point, before he blocked her way. But she had accepted that now. She had had her day in the sun. She had no regrets, and she would not fret, just like Cady said. *Do what you must do.*

She rounded the bend and saw the gazebo dimly white in the moonlight, over in the City Park. Once upon a time, she stood in front of more people there than she could have ever dreamed of. Was that the same Ruby that waddled along here alone at night? Where in the world did she get such courage?

"Ruby?"

She jumped at her name, at someone knowing her here. She stopped and her heart swelled at the voice's familiarity. She turned around slowly; half afraid she would be right, half afraid she would be wrong. He was following behind her, his hands shoved into the pockets of his sheepskin coat, his collar up.

"I can't believe it is you," she said.

"I thought the same thing about you, when you almost stepped out in front of my horse. I thought it best not to call out to you until we were some distance away. I hope you don't mind that I followed you."

He stepped closer to her, facing her, his cloudy breath warm on her face. In the night light, his teeth flashed a broad white smile. "How are you?"

Here she was saying good-bye to the memories, and now she must face her most beloved ghost alive. It was more than she could handle for the moment and she felt she might faint into his arms if he continued to stand so close. He was taking her air from her lungs with that smile.

"Let's keep walking," she said and turned back toward the park.

He joined her at her side. "Mrs. Catt and I made the journey from New York City as soon as we received the news. We weren't planning on coming through for another week. She was going to visit Cady on her way back to Iowa. She thought the world of Cady, saying Cady was one of the strongest suffragettes she knew. But I see we have made it too late for the funeral. Mrs. Catt is in the church now, paying her last respects."

"The burial is tomorrow, if you wish to go there." Ruby wished to speak no more of Cady. Somehow it seemed too personal, too raw right now. "How did you like New York? I hear it is a very exciting place to be."

"Well, if you like cities, I guess it would be exciting. Too many people for my liking. Exciting to me is stalking a eight-point deer through the wooded hills behind my cabin." He kicked away a mound of snow in Ruby's path. "I spoke at a few women's meetings, though. That was exciting, I guess."

"I'm not surprised. You are very good at public speaking. You have a natural way about you that makes people listen."

He looked down at her and grinned. "Do you think so? That means loads to me, hearing it come from you. Mrs. Catt says a good orator is like a Johnny Appleseed, planting seeds in fertile ground along the way."

"Cady talked that way, too. I will miss her dearly."

Reflection brought stillness, and there was quiet around them for a few moments.

"Are you sure you want to keep walking?" Jeremiah asked. "You're taking steps through the snow as carefully as one walking through piles of dung."

"I don't wish to fall."

"I'll pick you up."

"I'm heavier than I used to be."

He stopped and held her arm to face him. He touched the heavy protruding cloak at her stomach, and saw it was not all wool. He patted its hardness and asked softly, "You are carrying a child?"

She could only nod.

"When will it be born?"

"In March."

He dug his hands into his pockets and looked away. He gazed out at the distant gazebo, saying no more.

"Will you walk with me there?" Ruby asked. "That was where I was heading."

He could only nod. He held her elbow as they walked through the park's bare-branched trees and stepped into the circular wooden frame.

They turned to face the front of the gazebo and gaze out to the smooth white lawn. "I had hoped to see you," he finally said.

"But not like this," she said. She looked up to see him shake his head.

He still held her elbow. "I had this vision of me sweeping you off your feet and riding you off on my horse. Wrong of me, some would say even sinful, but I have such deep feelings for you. I don't know where they come from, but they don't go away. I don't know what is keeping them alive."

"I dreamt about you once," she said without reservation. We only have these few moments together and I must share what little I have to give you.

He turned to face her, now holding on to both her elbows. "Tell me about it," he said.

She drew in a deep breath, not sure if she could talk in such a close proximity to him. Somehow their space became one and all else swirled away. How does he do that? She raised her chin and met his eyes.

I may never travel this road again so I must travel it with strength. Above all else I want these memories of him to be without regrets.

"I was walking, following behind you through the woods, each with our horse." She closed her eyes to bring back the memory, one that emerged from where she had buried it. "Oddly enough, you have the same sheepskin coat on." She opened her eyes to him. "How did I know you wore this coat? You said to me, 'don't stop Ruby, keep moving' so I did. I followed you a long way until we reached the shore of a river. Across the river and on the other shore, I saw your log cabin, with the mist rising behind it. The mist reached for you and you disappeared into it. I longed to reach the other side but could not. I could not find the way."

He was watching her intently, his head tilted, listening, seeming to hear not only her words but the spaces in between. He nodded. "I understand," he said.

He reached into his pocket and with his other hand reached for her own. "Every creature deserves a mate of its own kind," he said and placed a carved dove into her gloved hand, a dove slightly smaller than the first one. She recognized this immediately for she had held that dove so many times. "Keep this with your other, and some way you will find a way," he said.

She stroked its head, almost wishing this gift had not arrived, for she knew she would spend many a lonely day holding it, and wishing for something that will never be. Better to be buried with its mate, but too late now. It would go home to live a lonely life with her. She had not the heart to tell him this.

She looked up and met those beautiful blue eyes, now a dark velvet in the moonlight. "Thank you." Her arms wrapped around his waist as close as her stomach would allow and gave him a hug. "I will always love you," she said to the soft suede of his coat. This felt as natural to say as "have a good day".

"I love you, too," he murmured above her bonnet. "That

scent of lavender you have. Every time that scent comes my way, I think of you. I guess I always will."

The baby's kick brought her back to reality and she pulled away. "I must say good-bye - that is why I walked here - so you must help me to be strong."

"I will." He lifted her chin with his hand – how was it staying so warm un-gloved, the pragmatic portion of her mind stepped forward and asked, some practical thought to keep her grounded. She watched, frozen in time, as his face came closer, closer, as if in slow motion, yet over in a moment, a kiss brushed softly across her lips, yearning for more, yet wishing this one had never happened. Just another branded memory to hold, heavy in her head and heart. She opened her eyes and turned toward the opening to the gazebo involuntarily, her body knowing what she must do. She heard her feet go down the steps, yet she felt above it all. She felt his hand once again on her elbow, but somehow she was detached, floating.

"We are really saying good-bye this time, aren't we?" she asked, dazed. The reality brought her feet hard to the ground and it was all too painful, too cold. She shivered. First Cady, and now this. She began to cry, her heart surely breaking this time. First it was tears. Then as they walked closer to road, farther from their meeting place, it became sobs. His arm came around her, to comfort, to hold, but it only brought a tighter clench around her heart. He walked her most of the way home in dark silence, holding tighter when her step sometimes slipped in the snow. At one corner of the street, enough light from the half-moon shown down to draw her eyes to the sheepskin trim on the front of his coat. She followed it up to his chin, to his nose, to his forehead. The wan light gave him the appearance of a stone sculpture, one of a grim warrior. He looked ahead as if looking far beyond, not aware of her gaze. She worried not if others saw them, how could they see, when she was in her own sad world with him?

One street away from home and she stopped and placed a hand on his chest to go no further.

"I may be back," came his soft voice from the darkness. "Next year I will be traveling with Mrs. Catt from town to town and doing more public speaking."

Ruby could say nothing more. What more was there to say, her mind asked, numb, frozen in time. She reached for his hand, and kissed the top of it. She held its warmth to her wet cheek and then little by little walked away, still holding his hand, still holding until it was only his fingers, fingers sliding away until there was nothing left to hold.

She dared not look back, but in her mind's eye she could see him still standing there, she could hear him say, *Don't stop, Ruby, you must keep moving.*

She rounded the corner to her street and walked into strong wind that whipped her cloak around her legs. Her velvet bonnet lifted and tugged at its strings tied below her chin. Tears froze on her face. She bent forward, tucking her chin down, and pushed against the wind, pushed her feet against the higher snowdrifts. Snow was coming down hard now. How long had it been snowing?

You must keep moving, Ruby. She pushed forward again, aware that her legs were heavy and stiff from her wet woolen stockings. Snow and wind blew around her, through her, blowing up her skirts, billowing them out like a storm-swept sail. Her teeth chattered, her fingers and feet frigid with cold. She lifted her feet higher and higher to trample through the rising white, but she knew she was moving in slow motion. The wind chilled her lungs as she breathed in heavily, her body losing strength. I must keep moving, she silently repeated over and over again. She slipped and almost fell, and heard a small cry escape her lips. She visualized falling here, unable to get up, like a turtle on its back, and icy flakes quickly and quietly covering her from sight. She could very well freeze to death, for beside her were empty lots and no one was out now. Behind the lots were open fields and wind blew freely in from the side now too, pushing and pulling her as if she weighed no more than a rag doll.

After a long dark moment, she looked up to see houses, light flowing from their windows and out onto the lawns with promises of warmth. Enough light to illuminate her short spurts of breath clouding out from her mouth like smoke signals. The boardwalk began here, and she was able to get better footing on the wooden planks. Several houses down she could see her own home. She trudged on and soon she could see a bright light coming out from the parlor window.

Robert must be in his chair reading. He will not be happy with me, for I am later coming home than he had agreed to.

Fresh tears warmed her cheeks and she sniffed loudly, with no means to a handkerchief. It was then she realized her hand still clutched the dove. Knowing this brought her no real comfort, only a heavy weight, as if its lines were etched with sorrow. She watched the snow blow around her feet and join a snowdrift on the edge of the cobbled street. Hesitating for only a moment, she let go the dove from her stiff fingers. It fell into the soft snow and sunk deeper until it was completely covered.

At a snail's pace she made her way up her walk, feeling surely that if it had been one more house, she wouldn't have made it. She paused at the railing to her steps and looked up at the door. If he didn't answer – well this would be a turning point in her life. She didn't know where it came from, but suddenly she sensed some inner resolve. She was going to make changes, whether he opened that door or not.

She approached the door and turned the knob. It was locked. She wiped at her eyes and nose and then knocked. She waited.

The lock clicked and the door opened. He reached beyond to where she stood and grabbed her arm as she stepped in. He closed the door behind them. He looked down at her red, swollen face and ever so slowly his arms circled around her and he held on.

* * * * *

She awoke long before dawn and moved her heavy bulk as quietly as possible into the sewing room across the hall. Tonight was Christmas Eve and she awoke with a gift idea for sachet dolls that just might work. She lit the gas lamp on the table by her sewing machine, and looked around the tiny room, hands on her lower back to ease the pressure there. Soon she would move her sewing to a corner of her bedroom and this would become a bedroom for the new baby. In its own time, of course. The baby would sleep in its cradle by her bedside for several months. The cradle sat here for now, waiting expectantly. She ran her hand over the hand-carved spokes of its hood, a hood that protected the baby's head but allowed a mother's watchful eye from any angle. She wished once again that she had known her father-in-law who had created such beautiful woodwork. Its miniature headboard matched her own bed's headboard, etched with roses, leaves, and long winding stems. The same cradle that Robert had slept in, and his three older children had slept in, was again brought down from the attic, washed and padded with cotton stuffing sewn into cotton muslin, awaiting its next bundle to hold and protect.

She sat down and began the task of making a narrow pillow to go inside a perfect find - an embroidered pillowcase. She had found four of these pillowcases wrapped inside a yellowed tablecloth, when she was cleaning out the dining room hutch last week. The tiny stitching was definitely her mother-in-law's. The pillowcases had never been used, but they would be now - four would be perfect for four sachet dolls, one each for Bess, Opal, Garnet, and Edith.

A surge of energy in the last few weeks had allowed her the type of housecleaning that was long overdue. Aimee said she was "nesting" for the new baby. But she was going deeper than her normal surface work, cleaning out drawers, closets, and cupboards. She was throwing away, moving, or using items that she hadn't dared bothering before. Now it was time to make better use of her mother-in-law's things; better yet, they were now her things, for her mother-in-law couldn't very well take them with her, now could she? Why did Ruby ever think these things were not to use, as if expecting the old woman to come home any day now, was beyond her comprehension now.

The baby kicked hard and rolled over. "That's right, flesh of my flesh, out with the old and in with the new," she whispered down to it, patting the baby's outer covering.

She used leftover cotton and muslin from the cradle's mattress to make the pillow and its stuffing. She measured so that the pillow would be approximately nineteen by seven inches. She stitched the two long sides together and one short end together. In the open short end, she shoved in cotton stuffing. She picked up a handful of dried lavender blossoms from its bowl, and breathed in its heavenly fragrance. She found some stems among them, and she ran her fingers along the stems to dislodge the buds, and discarded the stems. She added the blossoms to the cotton stuffing and tied it with red velvet ribbon she had taken from her mother-in-law's ancient robe. She placed the inner pillow inside the pillowcase, up to the top, rearranging the stuffing so that more would be at the top for the head, and then some at each side for the arms. She tied more red ribbon a few inches in from the top seam of the pillow to make a neck, and ribbon on each corner piece to make the wrist of the hands. Another longer piece she tied in a bow further down to form the waist. She fluffed its skirt, the embroidery hanging nicely in the front, as if on the hem of a dress, its edging scalloped. She was pleasantly surprised with the results.

Reaching for another pillowcase to begin another doll, she heard Robert call her name.

She walked to the doorway of their bedroom, scratching her stretched stomach. The only good thing about being pregnant was not wearing a corset. Of course her stomach was still as tight, and she couldn't bend from the waist either way.

"Yes, Robert?"

He was putting on his robe. "You are still in your nightgown, Ruby. Please be decent and put your housecoat on."

She stepped inside to where it hung on a peg on the bedroom door.

"The holiday is here," he said. "My favorite time of the year. I wish to bathe and be fresh to celebrate. Please prepare my bath for me."

She nodded and headed toward the hall, slipping her arms

through the sleeves of her housecoat. Robert followed her, calling up to the boys' room to come on down. He tapped on Bess's bedroom door. How odd to be coming down now before she has prepared his water and called him. She heard the boys' bare feet thumping loudly down their third-story stairs, whispering.

She entered her kitchen, by then all of them trailing behind her. She glanced behind her, her face in a scowl.

Mercy, do they expect me to have breakfast ready with a wave of my wand?

She opened the stove's door.

"Move aside. I'll start the fire," Robert said, pushing her aside with his elbow. She almost fell over, more from surprise than from physical contact.

"I'll pump the water," offered Victor.

She stepped back in confusion and onto Jonathan's foot. "Oww!" he cried out.

"Sorry, Jonathan, Mama is not accustomed to so many helping hands in my kitchen."

"I want to take a bath!" he shouted.

"You do?" Ruby asked. "This is another surprise. No arguments? That is a nice Christmas present for your mama."

Jonathan pulled her toward the scullery. "No arguments – I want to take one now!"

"Mercy, Jonathan, I've never seen you in such—-" she stopped and stared open-mouthed. There sat, as pretty as you please, a white oblong tub with ornately curved claw legs, just like she had seen in the magazines. She heard the others gathering behind her.

"Yep, she's surprised, alright," called out Jonathan proudly.

"I don't believe it," she said to no one. She wished her awkward bulk would allow her to step in and stretch out in its long embrace. One must feel as protected as a cocoon in one of these.

Bess squeezed passed her mama through the entrance to the room and touched the rim of the tub. "A bathing tub! Look how deep it is, Mama!" she said, her face looking more to Ruby like her own than ever before. "Where did it come from? It is not even Christmas yet!"

"Dad, Jonathan, and I carried it in last night," Victor said, his voice sounding deeper to Ruby, more grown-up with this secret revealed. "It was hidden in the stable until Mama went to bed."

"I was concerned," Robert said, "you would be up ironing or baking until all hours of the night, but you went to bed earlier than usual. I had time enough to install piping to drain water through the floor."

He was standing close behind her. She continued to stare at the tub, blinking at such bright white.

"It is an early Christmas gift," Robert continued, "but I wanted to take the opportunity to bring it home in the wagon I rented for tonight's trip to the Christmas Eve service."

She continued to stare and blink. "You rented a wagon?"

"It is a long trip to walk in your delicate condition, especially in this snow."

"Oh, Mama," Bess said, "do we have to go to church in a wagon? My new dress you made me will get dirty sitting with these boys." She folded her arms and looked at her brothers like they were stray dogs.

"Sit beside your mother, then," Robert spoke up quickly, his tone conciliatory. "I needed the wagon to bring home the tub, and the wagon is cheaper to rent than a buggy. We may not travel in style, but we certainly will bathe in style. That should make your mama happy, yes?" He placed his hands on her shoulders.

This is my first very own possession, this piece of furniture!

She was equally amazed at Robert's warm handprints through her housecoat.

* * * * *

"It is so kind of you to have us here for the weekend, Ruby. I hope we are not imposing," Opal said, sliding out of her coat in their entranceway.

"She says this every weekend, at every home we go to," Jacob said solemnly. He was standing off to the side, his jacket still on. Ruby noticed he was growing a beard, but his mustache was shaved. He remained unsmiling as his shook Robert's hand, nodding his head once.

"Of course you are not imposing, Opal!" Ruby said with a hug. "Januarys can be so drab, and you've given us something to look forward to. I sincerely hope you have dressed warm, though, for my beastly stove cannot keep up with this frigid winter."

"I'm still not accustomed to moving about as we do," Opal said. "Last night, Friday night, we went to his uncle's home. After breakfast today, we visited his sister's home for the noon meal. Usually we go to a third place for supper, and travel elsewhere to spend the night. I pleaded with Jacob that we stay at your place for supper and overnight. After all, you and Jesse are the only two relatives I have to stay with. Jacob has relatives all over."

She hung her coat on a peg on the wall, and began unbuttoning Jacob's jacket. "I'll hang that for you," she said to him. He remained still as she stepped behind him and slipped it off his shoulders. She hung his coat up next to hers and then grabbed the leather suitcase he had carried in and set down. "Where can I take this?" She seemed to Ruby jittery and ill at ease.

"You and Jacob will sleep in our bedroom."

"Oh, no, Ruby, we don't wish to take your bed!"

"It is all arranged. Robert and I will sleep in Bess's room."

"I will sleep in the boys' room." Bess said. "I don't mind," she added hurriedly, but not convincingly. Even so, she was quite excited about Opal's visit. She gave Opal a hug. "Aunt Opal, would you please braid my hair onto my head the way you had yours at the women's convention? I want mine just like that! Mama doesn't know how."

Opal cast a furtive glance toward her husband, and shook her head solemnly. "Oh no, Bess, Aunt Opal doesn't remember how to do such things. I'll pin your hair like mine is now, how's that?" She removed her white prayer cap and turned her head for Bess to see.

Bess moved her head to see Opal's plain rolled bun at the nape of her neck. Disappointment was written clearly on her face. "No thank you. Mama can do that for me easily enough."

Ruby understood it was as difficult for Bess as it was for her, to see Opal dressed so plainly in her dark blue dress covered with a cape and apron. Black high-top boots now replaced pretty slippers that not so long ago were donned to match bright fabrics. Did Opal miss those dresses tucked away in Ruby's wardrobe? Ruby knew she herself missed them, for she could no longer wear them. Instead she wore the only dress she had for public viewing. One she had made when pregnant with Bess, now a faded black calico fabric sewn with a fifty-eight inch waist, and a larger than normal white apron to cover its front. She had attempted to dress it up a little by adding the same calico print as pockets and ruffles on the apron. She smoothed down its front now, realizing she was the pot calling the kettle black.

Victor and Jonathan came forward then and gave Opal an obligatory hug around the neck. They liked her well enough but were disappointed that Jesse and the boys were not there, too. No one embraced Jacob – he seemed too distant, too much still as a stranger.

Opal's eyes darted again to Jacob, who jerked his head toward the stairs to the second floor. Opal and her case made the climb, Jacob following behind.

"I'll have supper on the table by the time you come back down," Ruby called up the stairs.

"Thank you," Opal answered. Jacob turned to Ruby and nodded again.

Ruby rushed to the kitchen, now feeling as uncomfortable as Opal. She sliced the roast pork thinking how much forward she looked to this visit, and now it seemed as if something had so soon gone wrong! Robert was none too pleased, as it was, saying he spoke to strangers all day in his shop, and his home should be his place of refuge. Nonetheless, he had finally consented to the visit, Opal being Ruby's family. Ruby shook her head at it all. She did not envy Opal's first year of marriage. Opal had much to learn about her husband and his habits. She obviously wanted to please him, but he looked none too pleased.

Bess joined her and picked up the knife to slice the bread.

"Mama, I love Aunt Opal. Did I say something wrong?" She thought for a moment, frowning. "Oh no, I mentioned the women's convention!" she said in a loud whisper.

"Oh yes, I hadn't even thought of that," Ruby said, bringing on her own frown. "He would be upset that she was there. Of course, she was not participating. She was against the convention, as a matter of fact. We must make mention of that during supper, Bess."

"And then Papa will be mad. I can't believe I said something so stupid!"

"Well, Bess, since you resemble me, you'd better get used to blurting, because you will say something stupid more than once in your life. You'll just have to learn to clean up after yourself. But please don't let that hinder you in speaking your mind, if you feel strongly enough about something."

They were bringing in bowls of steaming potatoes and turnips, when Opal and Jacob entered the dining room. Jacob sat down where Robert indicated, and Opal stood behind his chair.

"Opal, please, have a chair," Ruby said, setting down the bowls.

"In a moment, Ruby." She bent down to Jacob. "What would you like? Pork?" He nodded. She laid a slice on his plate. "Potatoes?" He nodded and she spooned a generous helping to him. She did this with the turnips, corn, and bread, until there was no more room on his plate. She cut a small chunk of butter and placed this on a tiny saucer next to his plate. "I always loved these little butter pats," she said.

"Another of my mother-in-law's legacy," Ruby said, sitting in her own chair, trying to keep her own attention diverted by helping the children fill their plates. She resisted from handing Jacob a bowl of food to help himself.

Jacob leaned forward and looked at his butter pat closely. Its miniature size was further diminished in his large-knuckled fingers. He shook his head. "Such things of the world are unnecessary. You will pray for forgiveness, Opal, in coveting your sister's trappings."

Opal turned pale.

"No need," Ruby said, "I considered it a compliment."

Opal shook her head at Ruby, as if to say, *please don't say anything more.* She took her own seat beside him.

Robert cleared his throat and gave Ruby his stern look before returning his concentration to slicing his pork.

Jacob ignored her as he bent his head. "Let us pray!" he commanded. "Oh merciful God," he said, not waiting for the others to prepare. "We come to you today with repentant hearts and willing minds. We wish to erase all that is worldly and live only in God's grace. I wish to stress only humility, family and community, and separation from the world. For you, dear God, intended that we work and toil in this green earth, feed our own, raise our families simply without need of gadgets and goods that do not serve your purpose. The fruits of our labor are around this table and on this table. Guide us to do what is right as we strive toward eternal life with you. Amen and amen."

His head remained down as he proceeded to eat in large rushed bites.

"Um, sir? May I call you Uncle Jacob?" Bess asked, her large eyes searching his face with earnest. She was leaning forward over the table, her hands still clasped in prayer, one of her two brown braids curled on her plate.

Jacob smiled for the first time. "That will be fine." He continued chewing.

"Uncle Jacob, I-I want to apologize for saying that Aunt Opal was at the women's convention. I-I mean, she *was* there, but she didn't want to be. She was only there to bring Mama and me home."

Ruby felt a surge of pride at her daughter's resolution.

He nodded. "Your aunt explained that to me upstairs." He took a long drink of milk. "But tell me why such a little girl as you, was at such a place as that?"

Bess sat up straighter. "Why, I'm twelve years old! My birthday was in December."

"You are too young to understand that it was a place of

iniquity."

Ruby froze, her fork to her mouth. She stared at him in disbelief. He would not meet her eyes. Her face flushed red.

In my own home, at my own table, he would say such a thing! Now Robert had an ally, for sure.

She looked out of the corner of her eye at Robert, expecting his glare to be directed toward her, waiting for him to join in judgment. Instead, he was directing it toward Jacob. His cheek had a small rash patch she recognized as anger.

"That may not have been her place to be, but it is not your place to tell my family where they ought to go!" Robert said.

Jacob nodded, still chewing. "You are right. It is not my place."

He finally raised his head to raise his cup. His head jerked toward the kitchen. Opal jumped up and asked Ruby if the coffee was made. As they headed together toward the kitchen, Opal sounded in forced merriment as she complimented Ruby on the delicious pork and asked if it came from Jesse's pigs.

"Yes, it did! It is so good to have fresh meat again!" Ruby said, her voice sounding to her ears of mocking happiness.

She heard Jacob ask Robert incredulously, "You do not have your own livestock?"

She did not wait to hear his answer as she said loudly to Opal, "I've made some potato candy for dessert!"

"Potato candy!" Opal said merrily in return. "How do you make that?"

She decided to talk over any conversation in the dining room. "Well, I cook the potato with the skin on, let it cool, peel it, mash it, add butter and vanilla. Then I add sifted sugar until the dough is stiff. Roll the mixture out like pie dough, spread crushed peanuts on top and then roll it up. Then I cut it in slices and let dry for a day. Shall I serve it?"

"Please do!"

They returned to the dining room bringing pasted smiles and a sugary dessert to sweeten the sour faces. They were received with a scowl and a frown.

Only the children enjoyed the fruits of their labors.

The next morning, after breakfast, Opal called Ruby up to her bedroom. Opal's face was pale as she closed the door behind them. "Ruby, I am so sorry."

"For what?"

"For this." Opal pulled back the sheet to reveal a red circular stain and several smears. Could it be Opal only lost her virginity last night? Surely not two months after they were married! Could it be that Jacob demanded his needs be met, while she is on her monthly bleeding? Either question she could not comprehend nor say out loud. It also revealed to her the lack of privacy Opal was afforded in her new life.

"Accidents happen. It won't take me long to wash," she said. She snapped the sheet back in place before Opal died of embarrassment.

She was glad she had a gift basket in hand to hide the uncomfortable moment. She handed this over to Opal containing jarred pickles and tomatoes, lavender sugar, and a sachet doll. "My gift to you. I missed you terribly at the Christmas Eve service, and at Jesse's for Christmas Day dinner."

Opal raised the red flannel covering. "Thank you, Ruby." She held up the jar of lavender sugar. "What is this? It looks like lavender buds in sugar."

"Good guess," answered Ruby. "You must store this for about a month, shaking once or twice weekly, then strain out the flowers. It is delicious sprinkled on fresh-picked berries, or on top of cookies."

"You and your lavender, Ruby! Is there anything you can't do with lavender?"

"It doesn't prevent more babies," Ruby answered, patting her stomach.

Opal picked up the sachet doll, slowly brought it up to her nose, closed her eyes and inhaled its fragrance. She smoothed its embroidered skirt, and closely examined its stitching. She handed it back to Ruby. "I have no need for such things," she said. "Give it to Bess."

Robert, Ruby, and the children joined Opal around the buggy

in their back alley by the small stable. Jacob hitched only one of his horses to his buggy. Ruby heard a horse whinnying inside the stable. She noticed that the stable's door was no longer hanging loose from a broken hinge, and new boards were patched to its walls to replace rotted wood and gaps between. She opened the door to a large brown mare eating hay.

"Our gift to you," Opal said softly from behind her.

"Mercy!" she said, looking at Jacob. He continued working the harness.

"Jacob breeds and breaks them," Opal explained.

That is no surprise, Ruby thought.

PART V
Spring's Rebirth

Blue! The paint is actually sky blue! Ruby could hardly believe her eyes. She squatted with a grunt – it seemed years since she was able to bend from the waist - and stirred the blue contents with a branch. Yes indeed! What a beautiful change this would make to the dreary gray walls! And this would blend so nicely with the whitewash. Whitewash that would soon cover all this dark dreary mahogany wainscoting and staircase. She also planned to tear off the dining room's heavy wallpaper printed with exaggerated golden damask patterns as soon as the baby came, when she had more strength and less clumsiness to climb the ladder.

She leaned on the settee for support to lift herself and face the parlor bay windows. For now, she would begin here in the parlor - oh dear, those heavy red flannel curtains must come down. She could make more bath towels and washcloths from them, and use pieces to wrap gifts, as she had done with the matching dining room curtains at Christmas. So much more light now came through the dining room window, immodestly covered with only the white lace under-panels. Robert never noticed the curtains missing. She loved the white lace under-panels – what she needed was more lace! That was it! Then she could drape a lace valance over the top. Lots of bright white to lighten the room! Didn't Robert say himself one time that it was gloomy here? Yes, whitewash and sky blue and white lace. She looked up the staircase. Yes, blue walls up the staircase and into the hallway, and paint blue right into the bedroom. Now for the other two second-story bedrooms...lavender, that's it! Didn't Opal ask if there was anything she couldn't do with lavender? Well, it was true it couldn't prevent babies, but the color certainly could surround the baby. And Bess loved lavender, too. She clasped her hands together, so excited with her newfound creativity. She would brighten and color it all, yes indeed! These walls would feel so much more like her own, with her own touch and design.

She paced the floor, thinking. She grabbed the banister landing post for support as she unconsciously waited out another small contraction. Ah, but she would need a great deal more paint. She could not afford nor carry more than this small tin of paint she brought home from Joe's General.

And she would need Robert's permission.

Hmmm, she would have to think this over carefully.

The tightness in her tummy subsided and she stepped back and looked at the wall below the staircase. The mahogany wainscoting stopped midway up and the remainder of the wall was painted gray the rest of the way to the kitchen's doorway. On that wall was the oval mirror and small stand below it.

I know what I can do. I will paint this small wall today and we can both see for ourselves.

Not wanting to think twice about it, she reached up to the oval mirror and released it from its hook. A light gray oval shaped shadow remained on the wall, from the mirror's many years of hanging in this same spot. Ruby paused to look at herself. She wished she hadn't. Her face was puffy and pale. Strands of brown hair dangled around her ears from the windy walk home from marketing. She looked closer – that was not just brown, but gray strands, too! Not wanting to see any more, she propped the mirror against the back wall.

"No matter," she mumbled, "the baby is due soon and much of this puff will fall away. I will soon look human again, instead of like a cow."

Her thoughts turned to blue. Sky blue. She crouched down to the paint again. Yes, blue is a beautiful color. Blue skies, blue eyes, blue mountain. Was that why ... ?

"No matter," she mumbled again. "I'll paint the ceiling blue, if I have to. Let me look at the ceiling and think it's the sky. If it makes me happy, I promise not to fly. There, that's poetry for you, Robert."

Letting out a loud sigh, she reached for her new paintbrush, longing so for change, change from gloom to bright light. She felt she were in a deep well, looking way above her at the light and fresh air. If only she could climb her heavy body up a ladder to the top, she could breathe and move freely again.

She brought her cricket bench in from the kitchen to stand on to reach the top of the wall.

She attempted a jagged deep breath for strength and dipped the brush into the thick liquid.

Well, this will be taking my first step on the ladder.

* * * * *

She heard the front door open. She brushed the flour off the front of her white apron – oh dear, some blue paint was smudged on the tip of her protruding stomach. Her arms did not reach much beyond her front pouch and a great deal of her painting time was spent standing in a slightly bowed position, her buttocks extended behind her. She was thankful more than once that no one was there to see such a sight.

She glanced at the wall as she walked from the kitchen to the parlor. Yes, the paint was almost dry now. Her spirits lifted just seeing the light difference it made.

She knew before seeing him, what he would be doing and would be saying.

"How was your day?" Robert asked as he struggled with the knot at his neck. His brown eyes were squinted; his thick neck was flushed from this difficulty.

"Fine, thank you, and yours?" she answered, as she tiptoed and gave him the token peck on his long brown sideburn.

He leaned his shoulder against the entrance wall and sighed the sigh of the man returned from the jungle who had narrowly escaped the claws and jaws. Nonetheless, she envied this know-how and fresh air he brought in with him every day. "The order for work boots arrived – I got the contract with the textile mill, this time, by the way, so I am back in business again – but unfortunately, as luck would have it, too many size sevens came in the shipment. A number of the men came in ready to purchase and I had to send some of them away with a promise. Hopefully they won't go over to Joe's General and buy his cheap hardtops. The leather will crack in weeks, I warned them."

He pulled his daily newspaper out of his jacket pocket and headed toward his chair. He stopped short and pointed toward the mirror propped on the floor against the wall. "Why is that there?" he asked.

She swallowed hard and her mind reached for the next higher step on the ladder. Her arm swept toward the blue wall. "I thought I would make a change...bring in some light...isn't the color beautiful?"

He stared at the wall, blinking as if it were too bright for his eyes. He sat down heavily into his chair without meeting her eyes. He opened his paper. "Take it off," he said.

"But don't you like it? You have to admit it—"

"I liked the way it was."

"Robert, the way it was, has been that way for years. It needs a fresh coat of paint."

He looked back up at the wall. "It doesn't match the rest of the walls." He met her eyes accusingly. "What were you thinking?"

"Well, I want to paint the rest of the walls blue, too." And whitewash the mahogany. That comes later, one step at a time.

He turned a page of his newspaper and hid behind it. "I liked the way it was," he repeated. "It will remain so. Do you think that because my finances have improved, you can spend my hard-earned dollars frivolously?"

She had to sit down. Another contraction was tightening her stomach like a drum. She picked up the cricket bench and brought it over to the settee. She sat down and propped her feet on the bench.

"Robert, I was thinking about that today. Can you please

listen to me for a moment?"

He sighed audibly and lowered his newspaper enough to eye her irritably, as much to say, *Well?*

"You are right, of course. Painting the house would not be cheap, but I'm willing to do it myself. Some now and finish after the baby is born. But I can pay you back the money."

He lowered the newspaper to his lap and opened his mouth but she jumped in. "I have an idea." She tapped her heel on the bench. "This cricket bench would be ideal to sell in your shop. You could prop people's feet on it to try on a shoe; or you could sit on it to assist. When they ask about the bench, you could tell them they are for sale. I've made four of these already, this one, and the children each have one. They use them all the time. I could make them here, perhaps in the stable. You wouldn't have to tell anyone your wife made the benches. For all they know, you made them. That doesn't matter. The important thing is, I could earn some extra money and help you out."

"If you want to help me out, Ruby, you could do a better job at what you are supposed to do. When Mother was alive, you could eat off the floors. Now, only the mice can eat there, and keep quite fat at that." He sniffed, seeming pleased with this. "Enough said. End of discussion." He raised his paper again. "Is supper ready yet?"

She slipped off the first rung of the ladder into darkness again.

Her stomach felt like her washing tub wringer was attached to her navel, cranking her skin tighter and tighter. She sucked in her breath and silently waddled toward the kitchen, holding in what was trying to come out.

* * * * *

She desperately wanted a bath. Out of the ordinary, this being late evening in the middle of the week, but she wanted one just the same. Somehow she needed to cleanse herself of ... the paint ... his words? Too tired to think more about it, she put the water on the stove to heat. She carried the cricket bench to the scullery beside the tub. The soap was on the shelf above her and she inhaled its lavender scent. Edith had only recently sent this to her. They had made an agreement. If Ruby provided the lavender blossoms, Edith would make the soap.

Hmmm, these would sell quite easily and we could split the money.

She shook her head.

That's right, Ruby, set yourself up for another letdown.

The bath was finally prepared. She slipped off her nightgown, stepped up on the bench, clutched the side of the tub, carefully brought her legs over its side and stepped in. Holding on to both sides of the tub, she squatted down into the water and sat down with a grunt. She inched her way down into a lying position. The warm water came up over her legs, arms, and breasts. She closed her eyes, enjoying her moment of rare pleasure. How wonderful to be able to stretch out. No more squatting in a round washtub!

"You forgot your soap."

She jerked to the sound, her eyes opening wide in surprise. Her arms immediately folded across her breasts. She glimpsed over to his leaning stance against the doorframe and looked away.

"Robert! I-I thought you had gone to bed hours ago!" She looked down at her massive mound, wishing she had something to cover up her monstrosity. And its fuzzy patch below. A patch she herself had not seen in some time. To think he was seeing it was appalling, especially in a room other than their bedroom. How indecent!

He entered the room and picked up the soap. "Sit up. I'll wash your back."

Ruby obeyed, not quite knowing what to expect. She relaxed a little - at least in this position she did not feel so exposed. She heard his knees crack as he knelt behind her. He moved the soap up and down her back.

"I woke up, wondering where you were," he said. "Do you know it is past midnight? What have you been doing?"

"Ironing."

"You should have been ironing today, instead of painting.

Then you wouldn't be up all hours of the night. You need to think of the baby. Speaking of which..." he reached around her, moving the bar of soap over her punched-out navel. "Lay back down, the way you were."

He was making her uncomfortable and she only wanted to be alone again. Holding in a sigh, she closed her eyes and did as he told her. She didn't want to see her naked mound rise up as her head lay down. The soap traveled down the slope of her stomach to her breasts. She winced at the massage of her tender nipples - would he know they were enlarged because they were ready for suckling? Likely not. The soap traveled back over the slope and down its other side, landing on her patch. The soap moved around in a circle and then slipped down between her legs and through her patch, gently, up and down, repeatedly. A flush moved over her warmer than water. She licked her lips and tasted salt from perspiration on her upper lip. Afraid to lose the moment, she remained perfectly still. There was a small roar in her ears, like listening to a seashell. The tide subsided and she opened one eye to see him standing up, tightening his robe belt.

"Come to bed," he said brusquely.

She found herself alone again. The tingling sensation was still going on down there. Should she touch where he had just been? Her hand moved toward it and stopped. What was she thinking? Shameful!

She rinsed the soap off, and with great difficulty lifted herself back up onto her feet. She waited for a moment while a wave of dizziness passed over her. It would have been nice if he had stayed to help her. *And See You Like This?* She probably looked worse standing than lying down, her hips being broader than they were before. She reached for a broad strip of red flannel and dried herself off very slowly. She had a sinking feeling Robert wouldn't be asleep when she came to bed, but she could take her time.

In due course, she entered their bedroom and made her way carefully to the bed in the dim light. She quietly laid back her covers and slipped into bed, lying on her side as close to the edge of the bed as possible, her belly practically hanging over. There was silence from the other side and she breathed a sigh of relief.

"Don't move," she heard from behind. She felt the bed sink in behind her as he scooted over close. He was tugging at her nightgown, raising it above her knees, then up to her hips.

"Robert, you might hurt the baby—"

"Don't be silly, I won't hurt the baby. It has been months. I can't wait any longer. Your husband has needs. Lift up."

She lifted up her lower hip to allow the gown to slip up above her buttocks. His hips, his patch of curly hair, his manhood, was pressing against her buttocks. His knee nudged between her knees. Holding on tightly to her shoulder and hip, he pushed until she opened. He found his mark and entered. He moved slowly at first and then rapidly, bouncing hard against her. She kept her head down, chin on her chest, hand clutching the edge of the mattress until he finished with her.

When he finally let go, slipping out of her, away from her, her first thought was, *I hope he didn't hurt the baby's head.* She stroked her stomach, saying silently, *It will be alright, baby.* It did not respond. The baby had been quiet for a few days and this meant it was saving its strength for the difficult travel through the canal to its new life on the outside. Boy or girl, she hoped it had a hard head.

She listened to the steady breathing of her husband telling her he had fallen quickly to sleep. A human lay beside her, and another inside her, yet she felt lonely.

* * * * *

Melancholy. That was it. She was suffering from melancholy. She watched Robert walk away to his shop; the children walk away to school. They had another life out there to look forward to and she envied them. She watched this all from her parlor window feeling left out, out of touch. She stood watching until there was nothing left to watch. The sun suddenly came out from behind a cloud and shone brightly into her window, its rays warming her face and beckoning her outside. It had been so long since she had sat on her front verandah. She wrapped a heavy shawl around her shoulders and exited her door. The air was fresh, still a bit too cool, but tolerable to sit for a while. She sat down in her rocker and winced at the tenderness between her legs. She snorted - men's needs indeed, as if women have no needs! She looked up and down the street, surprised to see much of the snow had gone. Small patches of snow only remained in the shade of trees. It looked so different from only a day ago, so clean, everything coming to life again.

She sat rocking quietly, letting her mind rest, her eyes roam. Buds on the trees, crocus and tulips were budding next door – flowers so soon! Nature was truly amazing in its ability to spring to life as soon as the sun offered the slightest warmth. I guess we all crave it, need it, she thought as she brought her shawl around her.

Her eyes followed the tulip bed to the boardwalk. There, something lay on its side, looking oddly familiar. She stood up and walked to her railing, squinting here where the sun's rays reached her face. Something drew her away from the railing, down her steps, down the boardwalk toward it. Was it a dead bird? She got closer and stopped. No, not a dead bird, but a wooden one. Laying in a slush of melting snow. The snow had drifted high that night she let the dove go. What was she thinking – that it would fly away? That it would stay forever hidden in a snowdrift? Seasons change, all that was, goes away, and life begins again. She picked it up and wiped it clean with her shawl.

Wooden, just like my heart, we belong together.

She took a fleeting look around to see if anyone was watching from their window – no, no heads were peeking around curtains. The view sparked a familiar memory ... mercy! This was the exact spot where she and *he* spoke last summer.

How ironic that I would let go and then find this dove in the same spot.

She walked back to her verandah, the dove tightly held in her hand, deep in dream. He had given her flowers and two love doves and she had given him nothing. If he were coming here today, what would she give him? A song was the reply. Quietly rocking, her mind conjured up images. A haunting melody played there and she hummed her first verse as the words came to her.

> Spring of flowers, in a meadow
> And you there beside me.
> Lying in the tall grass, your arms around me,
> Your sweet fragrance filling me.
> And you whispered, "Oh I love you,"
> This is where I want to be!
> Sweet dove, sweet dreams!

Dreams, yes, that was all. She sighed as she played out the inevitable words.

> Eyes are misty, you softly kissed me,
> Anticipating what can be.
> Clouds are shading, oh God it's fading
> I'm slipping to reality
> Then I realized I was only dreaming,
> Four gray walls surround me.
> You're a lost love, but at no cost, love.
> You're only my fantasy.
> Sweet dove, sweet dreams!

Tears warmed her cheeks and she got up to go inside. No need to show the world her melancholy mood.

Fluid warmed the inside of her pantalets. She froze. Her mind switched from fantasy to reality in a flash. Delivery was nigh. She opened her door, but was seized with a gripping contraction. She bent with the pain, squeezing her carved dove until surely its wings would splinter. She paused until the pain subsided.

"Mercy, not out here," she muttered. "Robert would die!"

She dropped the dove into her apron pocket and looked around. She must get help. She tottered over to Aimee's house. No one answered her door. No, not even Aimee's mother. Oh, what rotten luck. She headed back to her house. To go to another neighbor was out of the question. They were strangers and to reveal such a personal crisis to a stranger would be mortifying to Robert. Besides, she told herself as she re-entered her parlor and sat down in Robert's chair out of breath and her heart racing, if contractions are far apart, it could be tonight or tomorrow before the baby comes. The endless hours of dark pain of past deliveries came rushing over her, and she closed her eyes tight to block it out. She knew she must endure this; she had no choice. She watched the mantel clock and timed her next contraction clutching the arms of the chair. Fifteen minutes apart. Another long wait.

Suddenly it occurred to her that she might be wetting the seat of Robert's chair. She raised herself with one hand, holding under her stomach with the other. She looked down. Yes, there was a small round spot. Hopefully it would dry before he got home. She tried to think clearly and not panic.

Ruby, you will go upstairs, take off this eternal housedress and apron, and lie down on the bed. You will read a book and time your contractions.

She felt better being told what to do and did just that.

Another contraction met her in bed. A cry escaped with this one. Someone must go for Doctor Hughes. No, not Doctor Hughes, a midwife, she wanted Phyllis. She hadn't thought of this before –why did it occur to her now? It didn't matter. She felt comforted by the thought of another woman, an experienced one at that. She would have to get word to Phyllis...but how? Sometimes she could hear Aimee's carriage pull into its back yard stable. Or sometimes Aimee could be heard outside playing with her children, or working in her garden. Ruby made it to her window and opened it to her back yard. She breathed in the fresh air, longing to be in healthy sorts and out of doors. She trudged back to her bed.

Ruby picked up her book again. *Sense and Sensibility*, by Jane Austen. She smiled weakly. Ironic she would pick that up since she needed some sense to plan better. She attempted to concentrate on its words, but the words eventually blurred with the pain, and got lost when her eyes shifted to the clock on her bedside table. She read the same paragraph over and over. Her mind drifted; what if the baby is stillborn like her mama's two babies? What if she died in childbirth like her mama's sister? She could bleed to death before someone came home. Fear seized her heart as tightly as the baby seized her womb, and she scooted off the bed, and holding onto the bed, she lowered herself onto her knees.

"Dear Lord," she prayed out loud, "please forgive me for not wanting this baby when I first found out it was growing in me. It was wrong of me, Lord. Please don't punish me. It has now become a part of me. I want this baby with all my heart. It doesn't matter if it is a boy or a girl, just as long as it is a healthy happy baby. If You do that for me, Lord, I'll be good, I promise. I'll be a good mother, a good wife, yes Lord, I will be a good woman. One that You and Robert can be proud of. I ask this in Jesus' name, if it be thou will, amen and amen." She wiped away her tears with the sheet and climbed back into bed. Sleep came and allowed her rest for ten blessed minutes.

By noon she had accepted the fact that this was going to be a very long haul. Some food to keep her strength was needed. She took the stairs one step down at a time, holding on tightly to the banister with both hands, her swollen bare feet creaking the wood with each step. A path she had taken thousands of times from her bedroom to her kitchen now seemed out of place, ridden with heavy panting, groaning floor planks, loud clock tick-tocks. Breakfast dishes on the dining room table were from another time, a long time ago. She looked around the kitchen as if for the first time, looking for recognizable food. There were cold biscuits in a pan on the stove. One in hand, she walked around the dining room table, plucking leftover ham from the plates and tucking it into the biscuit. She ate this promptly before another contraction could come on, washing it down with leftover milk from one of the glasses. She feared she would choke on her food if one did. Without a backward glance, she walked from the dining room into the entranceway and back up the stairs.

"To hell with my duty of dirty dishes," she muttered between clenched teeth.

The afternoon was crawling at a maddening rate. Despite the cool air blowing in from the window, her gown was wet with perspiration. Her strength was ebbing away. She shifted her heavy mass around on the feather mattress trying to find a comfortable position. She finally found some small relief when she propped pillows behind her back and raised her knees up to where her feet were flat on the bed. When the next contraction came, she spread her knees shamelessly and cried out. The pain lessened somewhat in her lower back in this position.

Suddenly Bess appeared at her doorway.

"Mama?" Her voice was shaky, ready to cry.

"Bess ... you are an angel ... Mama is ... having a ... baby," Ruby called out. Another cry escaped her lips.

Bess ran to her bedside. "What can I do?" She stroked the top of Ruby's hair back.

"Pour me some water to drink from the pitcher there, and then wet a cloth to wipe my face. It will help to cool me down."

Bess wiped her mama's face carefully as if it were made of soft snow. "Do you need me to go fetch Papa?"

"What I need is a midwife, but Phyllis is on the other side of town." She studied Bess's oval face for a moment. Yes, she can handle this. "Take the horse and ride to Papa's shop, no, better yet, send Victor. I'd rather have you here with me. By horseback, your Papa can get here faster. I'll send him to the midwife's house, from here." She pulled the sheet over her legs, thinking of Robert coming home. "Close the door, your papa would not want the boys to see me this way."

Soon Ruby could hear the stable doors open in the back, and the horse clip-clopping away, down the alley. "My little man," she whispered.

Exhausted, she drifted off to sleep. She was aroused by voices out in the hallway; Jonathan arguing with his sister outside her door.

"I want to see Mama," he cried.

"No, not now, Mama is having a baby," Bess replied.

"I want to see Mama just for a few minutes!"

"Let him in," Ruby called out weakly.

Bess opened the door and Jonathan ran to the bed before someone could change her mind.

"Sit here on the bed with me and tell me—" A hard one came this time, harder than before, causing her to bear down and clench the sheets. She was sorry her children must witness this, but she had no choice. She heard herself whimper.

"Jonathan, what are you doing here. Leave the room!" bellowed his father from the doorway. Jonathan jumped at the voice and ran from the room, crying.

"Doctor Hughes is on his way here," he said to Ruby from the doorway. He did not enter the room. "I stopped by his office on the way here. I'll listen to no more nonsense about a midwife. Midwives are unwashed and inept. Bess, stay with your mother. I'll be downstairs."

The doctor soon arrived and sent Bess out of the room. "We've been through this before, Ruby, so you are not to worry. I must examine you now to see how much you have dilated." He washed his hands at the washbowl and sat down on the edge of her bed. "Now, lie down flat. That is a good girl." He raised the sheet only enough to move his hand between her legs.

Ruby flinched when he reached her center. His fingers probed, entered. Pressing hard with his other hand on her lower stomach, his fingers pushed farther inside her and she bit her lip to prevent another cry. Another man, other than her husband, sitting in her private sanctuary, touching such private places, how could a woman ever become accustomed to such a thing?

He finally withdrew his hand and returned to the washbowl to wash. "You are not dilated as much as I had hoped. How long have you been in labor now?"

"Since this morning. Contractions are every five to ten minutes. I-I can't take much more."

"Don't be silly, of course you will take more. Women always do in childbirth." He poured an amber liquid from a bottle into her glass. "We need to induce labor. Drink this. I'll wait for a little while downstairs and then I must go. Mrs. Preston is also in labor."

He held the glass patiently while she panted and prayed through yet another one, the pain in the lower back, back again. Lying flat, she was unable to move.

"Raise your head, Ruby." She tried but it wasn't enough. "Here, I'll help," he said irritably. "Women have babies every day, Ruby. You can't quit now."

He brought the glass to her lips. The liquid tasted strongly of alcohol mixed with some bitter herbal taste.

"But what will I do if you go?" Ruby said. She was now afraid to be alone again. Her mind had recalled every horror story ever told to her, of dead or deformed babies, or healthy babies lying in a mother's dying arms, her life taken to give life.

"Doctor Hughes, did you know that pregnancy causes more death than any other disease, except tuberculosis? Twenty-five thousand women die every year from pregnancy and labor."

So there, smarty-pants, I'm not just another dumb woman in labor. I even said the word 'pregnant'.

He looked down his nose at her through his spectacles. "Now who told you such a thing?"

"I-I can't remember." Someone from her Legion group had said that, but she couldn't remember whom.

"Sounds like a wife's tale. Women talk too much. And worry too much." She received a pat on her head – like a puppy dog. "You will be fine. You will have the baby, with or without me."

Fresh tears streamed down her face.

"Don't worry," he said to her tears, "If this doesn't work, I will come back later on tonight, I promise."

In an hour he returned to her room and re-examined her. "No change. You are dilated only to five fingers. Five more to go. I must go now to Mrs. Preston. I'll check in on you later tonight."

"Thank you, doctor," Ruby said stiffly and sniffed. She had decided in that hour that she would give him no more tears. "Would you please send Bess up here, on your way out?"

"Your husband thinks you should be alone."

"That is the last thing I need," she snapped. "I'm sorry, but

I need Bess."

"I'll ask."

Bess soon appeared. "Papa says I can only stay a moment."

"Help me sit up, Bess. Lying down like this is killing me...thank you, sweetie."

She pulled Bess close to her and lowered her tone. "Now I must ask you to do something very important for me. It may not be forthright but I can't lie here in this pain, waiting for men to decide what to do with me. Only another woman would truly understand. Here is what you must do, Bess. You must go next door to Aimee's. She should be home by now. Give her a message for me. Tell her I am ready to deliver, but am suffering difficulties. Ask her to go to Phyllis. I need Phyllis here. She is a midwife, a very good one, but your papa must not know she is a midwife. He must be told she is a concerned friend here to help. Do you think you can slip out of the house without his knowledge? Perhaps out the kitchen door? Yes? That is a good girl, Bess. Only you are not a girl anymore, but a woman now and I know I can depend on you. Come back upstairs and report to me, as soon as you return."

"What if Papa won't let me back upstairs? He has his chair turned toward the stairs and is watching the stairs like a hawk."

Ruby felt the grip rise up again and she tensed. Anger was rising with it.

Stop controlling me! Stop telling me what to do and when to do it! Obey, Obey! As if I had not a mind of my own! It is his fault I am in this pain, yes his fault! Bastard! I hate him!

She brought the sheet up to her mouth and bit down. She must prevent these words from falling from her mouth. Bess must not know these thoughts. She was bent over Ruby very close now; washing Ruby's face with a cool cloth, worry puckering her smooth brow. A brow someday to be wrinkled from all the puckering it will do.

Finally, Ruby felt it safe to speak as the wave settled down again. "We must insist! This is a woman's situation where women should take charge! Be strong, now go!"

Bess ran from the room. Ruby watched her go, thinking Bess was probably now more afraid of her mama than of her papa. She was asking Bess to do things, contrary to her teachings: To lie, to sneak away, to disobey her papa.

Perhaps I am delirious, perhaps I am going mad, but I don't care! I cannot take this anymore! I know! I will call Robert up here and distract him, so Bess can get out! Why didn't I think of that before?

"Robert!" She tried to yell, but her voice cracked and it came out a squeak. She tried again, louder this time. She heard nothing. She threw her book at the door and her aim was good. It made a loud bang. Bess reappeared at the door.

"Mama, are you okay?"

"Send Robert up here, please!"

"Oh, of course," she suddenly smiled as if she now understood. "Papa!" she called down the stairs. "Mama must see you right away!"

Robert appeared at the door, newspaper in hand. Bess waved from behind him and disappeared.

"Robert ... read to me!"

"Pardon?"

"Read to me, now! Keep me distracted!" And I will keep you distracted.

"I should not be in here at such a time. It is quite inappropriate."

"Robert, for God's sake, you put this baby in here! By God, you can help a little in taking it out!" Mercy! Where did that come from? But it was true!

She bit her lip, waiting for his anger.

He stood frozen for a moment, studying her. And then a strange smile moved across his mouth. "Yes, I hadn't thought of it that way. I suppose you are right." He hesitated for a moment inside the room, and then scooted a chair over to the bed. He sat down, opened the paper, cleared his throat, and began reading.

"'President William McKinley was once called the 'advanced agent of prosperity'. Now in his second term, he is now being criticized for supporting imperialism and the full dinner pail. It is said McKinley keeps his ears so close to the ground that it is full of grasshoppers. Could this be why the United States has now annexed the Philippines, Guam, and Puerto Rico? Reliable sources say—"

Heavy panting pulled his eyes away from his reading to Ruby. She sat, chin on her chest, sheets clenched in her hands, eyes and lips pinched tight. He was silently watching her but she didn't care. Cries came at the peak of the pain, sounding in her ears like a trapped mouse.

The newspaper rustled, and he cleared his throat again. "Politics are more than you can understand. Let me find an article that might keep you more distracted ... oh, yes, here is one you will enjoy. This lady spoke at your women's convention, I believe. I wouldn't normally bring this to your attention, but this is a special circumstance that warrants—"

"Just read!" she gasped. Damn, he talks too much!

"Very well. 'Mrs. Carrie Chapman Catt will speak at the local chapter of the National American Woman Suffrage Association, N-A-W-S-A, in Buffalo New York, on March 25, 1901. Mrs. Catt is the president of this association. She succeeded the infamous Susan B. Anthony as president last year. Infamous because she was arrested in 1872 for attempting to vote for Ulysses S. Grant in the presidential election. The history of these activists, calling themselves 'suffragettes', has not provided the results they seek. During the Civil War, activists such as Anthony and slave-born Sojourner Truth, lectured and petitioned the government for the emancipation of slaves with the belief that, once the war was over, women and slaves alike would be granted the same rights as the white men. They made a serious error in this assumption, for when the war was over, suffrage of women, and that of the Negro, was treated by the government as two separate issues. The Negro vote, particularly in the South, would produce the immediate political gain that the women's vote would not. Abraham Lincoln declared, 'This hour belongs to the Negro'."

Robert lowered the paper, his eyebrows raised to Ruby. "Isn't this the same president you declared to Preacher Paul as your hero?" He clicked his tongue. "Pity. Abe betrayed you, too."

Ruby forced a small smile. "Please continue."

"'Women activists were enraged at this. To fight this, Elizabeth Stanton and her colleagues established the American Equal Rights Association in 1866. Again they met defeat in 1868, through the ratification of the Fourteenth Amendment, as it defined "citizenship" and "voters" as "male" and raised the question as to whether women were considered citizens of the United States at all. They were defeated again in 1870, in the Fifteenth Amendment that enfranchised the black men. The Amendments stressed the activists to the breaking point, and they split into two factions, the National Woman Suffrage Association, and the American Woman Suffrage Association. Finally, in 1890, these two groups merged again to form the N-A-W-S-A. Through N-A-W-S-A, Mrs. Catt hopes to win support for equal-suffrage rights, not only at state and federal levels, but at international levels, hoping to incorporate sympathetic associations in thirty-two nations.'"

Robert flipped to the next page. "Well then, it sounds like these women are having trouble getting along. I'm not surprised. In how many ways does God have to tell them they are wrong? Stubborn wenches."

Tension was building and this time she might blow. "I think I've had enough reading for now. Would you please be a dear and check on the boys? I think they are in their room."

He stood up, noticeably eager to go. "What about supper?"

In between pants, she said, "Go...to...hel—go to Bess. She can make do."

In her conscious mind, she knew it was only several hours later, but in that dark passage of time, it seemed like days. She was crying out loudly now and she didn't care who heard. The baby seemed stuck there somewhere between her bones and flesh, pushing, crushing, but not moving anywhere. She could hear sounds, footsteps, doors opening, closing, but they all seemed far, far away.

She opened her eyes and Phyllis magically appeared. She stroked Ruby's forehead, Ruby's arm. "I'm here now Ruby, and everything will be all right. I'll stay with you and we will do this together, honey. You've been in labor a long time, haven't you?"

Ruby nodded.

Phyllis lifted a basket onto the bed. "I told your husband I had gifts here for you." She winked and smiled. "It wasn't a lie. You'll be happy I brought these, when all is said and done."

She brought out a long rubber hose attached to a rubber bag. Next came a piece of plastic sheeting, with small holes in one end that looked to be a part of a shower curtain. She placed this under Ruby's buttocks. "I'm going to give you an enema. Elimination can bring with it the body's natural desire to eliminate the baby. It works and it avoids embarrassment while you are pushing very hard. A bowel movement is not what you want to deliver!"

"Mercy, Phyllis!"

Phyllis giggled. "Sorry. You are in no mood for my silly humor. What I need to do first is to help you relax. You have broken blood vessels in your face from the strain. You need a more peaceful environment here for you and for the baby. Tension can slow down or stop the labor. The baby does not want to come out into a bright and noisy world."

Phyllis lit a fire in the fireplace. The gaslights were turned down very low, and a candle was lit on the bedside table. The alarm clock was placed in a drawer of the bureau. "Don't worry about the time. Nature will take its course in its own time."

She brought out a small vial. "Stick out your tongue." Four drops of liquid landed there. "Homeopathic medicine to calm your nerves. It has clematis and impatiens in the oil." She sniffed and drew back a little. "Have you been in the drink?"

"No, of course not. Doctor Hughes was here earlier and gave me a concoction that tasted much of whiskey."

A scowl formed between Phyllis' eyes. "It wasn't an elixir made from powdered heroin or opium, I hope. Such powerful medicines are not good for you or the baby."

Out of the basket came a glass jar. "Good, this is still warm. Drink my herbal tea, Ruby. This will warm you and settle your stomach. Have you eaten?"

Ruby shook her head. "I'm not hungry. But my family – I don't know if they have eaten—"

"Aimee is feeding them now. She brought over chicken and dumplings that they seem quite satisfied with."

"Bless her heart ... bless yours. I am so glad you are here."

The tea was so soothing and warm, Ruby could already feel her shoulders relax, and her hands were no longer in a tight fist.

"You are more comfortable sitting than lying down, aren't you? This is perfectly natural. When the baby begins its journey out, you may wish to squat on the bed. A bit barbaric, I know, but gravity aids your delivery that way, and takes the pressure off your back."

Another contraction was coming.

"Ruby, listen to me. Breathe deeply, in and out, quickly, like a dog panting, over and over. Don't stop. That's it. I'll massage your shoulders. There you go. Do you feel you need to push? No? Then we will just ride the next few out."

Ruby was asked to roll over onto her side for an enema. Ruby did not question nor hesitate. Modesty had flown out the open window by now.

"You have a scar here, Ruby. Did you tear with your last delivery? I thought so. You should have been rubbing olive oil on your perineal area for the last few weeks."

"What is that?" Ruby asked, trying not to think about the uncomfortable insertion.

"The perineal area is between your anus and vulva, or vagina, or whatever you want to call it."

"I-I don't call it anything."

"Yes, these are women's deep, dark secret places that they themselves do not dare go to. Let us call it our secret garden then, shall we? All done." Ruby felt the tube leave her. "Where is your chamber pot? Can you walk? Yes? You'd better hurry!"

Ruby made her way behind her screen, and made the difficult squat to the low pot, just in time. Why were women taught to be modest and dress from head to toe, when there are times like these when she must bare it all, and these disgusting sounds, to so many!

The door open and Bess spoke to Phyllis. "Papa wants to know how much longer you will be here to visit."

"Tell your papa," Ruby called out, "I have asked Phyllis to stay and keep me company until the baby is born. Tell him it is almost time and to keep the boys occupied. Is Aimee still here?"

"Yes, she is helping me wash the dishes."

"Tell her to come up when she is finished. She brought some things I need." Phyllis said.

"And Bess?" said Phyllis. "I think you should be here to see this miracle of birth, too. We can all share in a new life coming into the world, together."

"I would love to," Bess whispered, "but Papa says it would be indecent."

Ruby finished with her chore and waddled over to the door. She bent over with a newly found pain and intense desire to push. "Robert," she called out in a trembling voice, "Bess will stay here with me. I need her to help. It is almost time! Please leave it to me!"

"I should go get Doctor Hughes," he called up the stairs.

"No, no, the doctor is busy." She slammed the door and turned the skeleton key in the lock.

Holding her stomach, groaning, she walked back to the bed. She felt like she had been riding a horse all day. "Sorry about Robert, Phyllis."

There was a knock on the door. "It's me. Aimee." Phyllis opened it to Aimee, Bess trailing behind looking worried.

"I brought a bag of blankets," Aimee said. "I had them warming by the stove downstairs."

"Good," said Phyllis. She took one out and laid it over Ruby's stomach. "Did you bring the boiled shoe string?"

"Yes, it is in the Mason jar that Bess is carrying. Bess said the jars had been sterilized for canning."

Ruby grunted out, "I'm a little behind in my canning."

"No need to apologize for Robert," Phyllis said to Ruby. "His suspicions toward midwives are becoming more common nowadays. Breathe now, remember, like a panting dog."

Phyllis began massaging Ruby's shoulders again, until Ruby relaxed. "The sad thing is, midwives deliver approximately fifty percent of the babies, with a lower mortality rate than obstetricians. Yet guess who is criticized? The first official act to limit the practice of midwives was a law passed right here in our own state in Rochester, New York only four years ago. Here in Annan, we are required to have the personal care of twenty women before a permit is granted us. On the other hand, some doctors leave school without once witnessing a birth, yet he is permitted to deliver.

"Bess, in my basket there, I have a jar of orange juice. Give a drink to your mama. It has lots of pulp to give her strength."

Bess brought the jar to Ruby's lips. "What does midwife mean?"

"It means, 'with woman'. We believe in remaining with the mother, keeping her as comfortable and relaxed as possible, and have patience with nature. We do not believe in surgical instruments or forceps, nor use medicines that would induce labor rapidly. It's just not meant to be. I know several women whose uterus ruptured because their bodies were not naturally prepared.

"Massage your mama's feet, Bess.

"Women have been birthing since our creation. It is a natural elimination process, and only natural remedies should be used. Unfortunately, with our newly trained obstetricians, they are considered highly trained, with modern techniques. To keep themselves in business, they accuse the midwives of being untrained grannies. We are stupid and superstitious. On the other hand, I read just recently that some physicians say they cannot understand how an intelligent man can take up obstetrics, which they regard as about as serious an occupation as a cat sitting in front of a mouse hole, waiting for the mouse to come out.

"Ruby are you having another hard one?"

Ruby could only nod – everyone seemed dreamlike, only this seizure seemed real.

"Do you need to push? Yes?" Phyllis moved the blanket down over Ruby's knees, and raised Ruby's gown above her hips.

She fluffed Ruby's pillows behind her back. Ruby raised her knees so that her feet were flat on the bed, to give her more support. She pushed, the strain burning her face, her yell unavoidable. Phyllis spread Ruby's knees and looked in between. "That's it, Ruby, I can see the crown of the head."

Ruby could barely catch her breath; the bearing down was so strong. "I can't do this anymore! I have no strength!"

Phyllis grabbed her hand and squeezed. "You're doing fine, honey. Your body will find the means to push."

"Now!" Ruby panted. She pushed again with all her might, her hands and legs trembling from the force. She was certain her whole insides were trying to come out this small exit. She spread her knees further, vaguely aware that Bess was lying next to her, holding her other hand, Aimee was standing beside Phyllis, wiping Ruby's forehead. They were all speaking in soothing tones. It seemed no longer a secret garden down there, but a stage to watch and witness.

"Quick," Phyllis said, "Aimee, get me some cloth strips and blankets. She is tearing a little. Bess, there will be blood, but come over here and see the baby's head. Don't be squeamish. Aimee, go to Ruby's other side and when Ruby pushes again, grab her leg and push toward her like this." She bent Ruby's leg at the knee and pushed against it. "Ruby, when you feel the urge to push again, hold it to the count of ten. I'll count. The head is almost out. You are doing good, honey. Push hard!"

Ruby had no choice. She bore down and screamed out. The sound was primitive, savage. She felt an intense burning, something was tearing she knew. She took a deep breath and pushed again, not wanting to stop, wanting this out once and for all. "O-o-o-out!" she yelled.

Phyllis removed the blanket that was over Ruby's legs and said, "Look, Ruby!" Ruby looked down to see the top of a small round head. She panted loudly, pushed again, then saw shoulders, its chest, its—

"Vulva," she croaked.

"Yes, Ruby, it is a girl!" Phyllis cried. She had a fresh blanket under the baby, holding it as it slipped the rest of the way out. She held the baby up for all to see, spotted in mucous and blood.

"Oh she is beautiful!" Ruby said hoarsely.

Phyllis raised Ruby's gown up further and laid the baby face down on Ruby's stomach. "We'll leave her there for a moment so that gravity assists in draining the fluids from her mouth and nose. You must unbutton your gown, Ruby. You need to breast-feed immediately. You are bleeding quite heavily and the sucking action will stimulate the uterus. This will cause it to contract and close off the blood vessels. We need to reduce this bleeding right away."

She threw the blanket back over Ruby's legs. She no longer was smiling but was seriously moving in quick motions. She placed the baby at Ruby's breast.

"Hand me those strips of cloth, Aimee." She threw the blanket back over Ruby's legs. Her knees were still up and Ruby could no longer see below. She only knew Phyllis was working and wiping. "Here is the afterbirth," she heard Phyllis whisper. "I need more cotton for the bleeding. I'll need to pack her."

Phyllis was pushing and massaging Ruby's stomach. Ruby barely noticed the pain Phyllis' movements caused her below. It seemed far away now, barely detached. An intense relief flooded over her. Attached at her breast laid a splotched little thing, its hair smeared to its head, its little fists (yes, ten fingers!) waving angrily at its new world, its little mouth trying to cough, cry, suckle. How does it know to suckle? Its legs (yes, ten toes!) were pumping up and down reminding her of Victor's legs at Christmas when learning to ride his new bicycle. A totally new creature that she carried inside her and then pushed into living. Such a miracle! It was as if the first three babies came to her in other ways and this one was a new experience.

She nearly stopped the hands coming at it, hands that tied a shoestring tight around the umbilical cord, and then scissors came into view cutting off the remaining cord from the baby's body.

"Do this," Phyllis said. She gently stroked the baby's nose from the bridge down to the nostrils. "Do this several times while nursing to clear the mucous."

Ruby felt sweet pain as the baby latched on to her nipple, tugging hard at invisible strings attached deep in her womb. A warm blanket came down over her shoulder and partially over the baby. She saw Bess's finger come into view, as it slipped into the little fist, and the fist held on.

"My very own little sister," Bess cooed. "No more dolls for me, Mama, because I will have a real live doll to dress up."

* * * * *

Her eyes opened slowly, trying to blink away the blurred vision. The room swirled, shifted, and then settled into place. Into view came Robert, sitting by her bedside holding her hand, studying her fingers carefully as if their lines and knuckles held the answer to his question. It was all so quiet.

"Robert?" her voice came out in a hoarse whisper. "Where is everyone?"

He looked up, startled, as if surprised to see her. He squeezed her hand. "How are you feeling?"

"I'm not sure. I can't lift my head, it feels too heavy. Where is the baby?"

"She is asleep here in her cradle. Do you remember anything?"

"Of course. I remember the delivery quite clearly, and then ... nursing the baby and ... that's about it."

"Soon after, you fainted. You lost a good deal of blood."

"Is the baby alright?"

"She is fine. Aimee nursed it early this morning, and it went right back to sleep and has been sleeping since. It is now noon."

Aimee nursed the baby? But of course. Her youngest was only two, and Aimee would still be breast-feeding him.

The baby stirred and squeaked. Robert peeked in. "I think she is looking for her next meal. She must have heard her mama's voice."

Her milk 'let down' as her mama called it, and filled her breasts.

"Have you held her?" she asked.

He shook his head, his brown curls sticking out around his

collar. She made a mental note to trim his hair soon. He needed a shave too.

"Help me sit up. I'll need to nurse. Hold her for a few minutes before giving her to me."

He lifted Ruby under her arms to a sitting position, and fluffed pillows behind her. She saw then that he was wearing the same brown trousers and white shirt he was wearing yesterday. Yet, there was something different about him…she grunted softly at the burning pain below, and sat still until the room stopped rocking.

He cleared his throat, hesitated at the cradle and then leaned over and carefully slipped his hands under the bundle. It suddenly occurred to Ruby that he had never done this before. His mother had been there for the last three and she never allowed him to pick up the baby on his own. She recalled how his mother would ask him to sit down, and then she would wrap the baby tightly in its blanket and hand it to him, each time instructing him on where to place his hands.

His mother was not here now and he must do this on his own. Another thought came to her - one that took her totally by surprise. Robert was growing up. Had he struggled the last two years without his mother there telling him what to do? Ruby knew she had experienced a sense of liberation once his mother passed away, but Robert … perhaps he had felt lost.

The baby came up from its bed, legs exposed and kicking, the blanket underneath dangling. Robert was awkward, but he was holding her head. He sat back down stiffly in his chair, watching the baby carefully, as if she might squirm away.

"Hold her to you," Ruby said. "She needs to feel your warmth."

He brought his arms back enough so that the baby touched his stomach. All Ruby could see were little legs and arms beating at the cool air – and a smile play around Robert's lips. She watched as his arm slowly, carefully slid under the baby, to where the baby's head rested in the crook of his arm. His other hand found the blanket and wrapped this around her.

"She is a cute little thing, isn't she? Were the others this …

perfect?" he asked.

"Each in their own way. Where are they?" She unbuttoned her gown down the front, noticing that this gown was not her own.

"Downstairs cooking dinner."

"Where are the boys?"

"Bess insisted the boys help her cook. She is becoming quite a grown-up lady."

"Phyllis and Aimee – have they gone home?"

"Phyllis stayed until Doctor Hughes arrived, sometime around four this morning. He examined you and said you will be fine with a few days rest in bed. I was not pleased with his late arrival and told him as much. But he assured me he could not have done better than the midwife who was here." He squinted one accusatory eye at her before returning his attention to the baby.

"Oh dear ... I am sorry, Robert."

He shrugged. "I don't blame you, Ruby. It likely saved your life, and the life of this little one." He handed his bundle over to Ruby.

She folded the blanket snugly around the baby and lifted it to her breast. The baby hungrily moved her head back and forth until her mouth found her connection. Ah, there is that sweet tugging again. What did Phyllis call it, yes, stimulating, that's it. Never did she feel as close to her babies, as she did when breastfeeding. To be able to give and nourish from your body, like no man ever can. What a beautiful moment that men will never share with their little ones. For the first time, she felt sorry for Robert.

Robert was watching with interest. "Your face softened doing that. You look happy. You hadn't looked happy for ... quite some time." He scooted his chair over closer to her bedside. He cleared his throat. "I prayed that another child would bring you back ... your smile. Well, to be quite honest, I thought I was losing you. First, to another man."

Ruby's heart leaped to her throat and she glanced up at him, afraid. He was bent over, elbows on his knees and inspecting his hands, rubbing hard at the permanent shoe dye stain in his cubicles.

"But then you explained he was Cady's husband and he was giving you a ride home."

Ah, the ride in Thomas' steam automobile – why that was last spring! Her heart settled back down to where it belonged.

"And then to those high and mighty women and their damned cause! I had to fight for what was mine, you see. I had to bring you down to where you belong - with me. I did things I'm not proud of, but you left me no choice - even to the point of destroying some ridiculous women's booth! But ... last night, and all through the night, as I waited and watched from my chair downstairs, I feared losing you to something worse - death. I'm partially to blame, for it is my child that would have killed you. Only then did I fully realize," he paused and looked at her, tears wetting his brown eyes, tears she had never seen before. "I love you." He sniffed and shook his head. "I know I've never said that before, but, there, I've said it." He sat back looking relieved and more comfortable now that that load was off.

"And I've been thinking about something else, too. As I sat there in my chair, turned toward the stairs, I had my feet propped up on that home-grown cricket bench of yours. So here is my decision: make your cricket benches and I'll take them to the shop and see if they sell - as long as this hobby doesn't interfere with your duties, of course. And I won't allow you to peddle them around like some pathetic door-to-door salesman. My shop should give you a sufficient market. Are we in agreement?" He reached over and patted her tummy gently.

His face softened and blurred through her own tears. "Can we seal the bargain with a kiss?" she asked softly.

He smiled almost shyly. He looked behind him at the door and when sure no one else was watching, he half stood and leaned toward her cheek. She remained still until his lips were too close to turn back. Her mouth turned to his and she grabbed his neck with her free hand, pressing her lips to his. His eyes opened wide in surprise at close range with her own eyes. His neck tightened but she didn't let go. He closed his eyes tightly and relaxed his head. "Hmmm," he murmured and kissed back. She let go then and he sat back down, both of them blushing bashfully.

She took a deep breath - could it be possible? Could happiness be found ... here?

"Thank you, Robert. The boys could help me set aside a place in the stable, if you could buy my supplies."

"I can live with that, if I can live with you," he nodded his head slowly and licked his lips. "I can live with that."

* * * * *

With the baby suckling at her breast, she paced between the parlor windows and the dining room window. The birds were calling her outside. She would have to go, that is all there is to it. She pulled the baby's blanket up to cover her exposed breast and baby's head, and opened the door. A warm fresh breeze greeted her, moved around her, soothing her. She breathed in deeply and headed for her rocker.

She sat and took in the panoramic view around her verandah, giving thanks for the warmth and peace surrounding her. Tiny, green buds along the tree branches were promising summer leaves. Birds were chirping to her from their branches that it was time to build their nests for yet another season. She believed this to be true for humans, too, and her nest would be blue! And this railing, yes, could be changed from brown and green to sky blue and lavender! Why not? Finally, her own home.

She hummed a strange little tune, thinking it to be one of her own. Then she remembered it was the tune to the song they sang at the women's convention. She sang out softly to the baby, "Women are people, too. We are no less than you—" As if on cue, a buggy stopped in front of Aimee's house and Phyllis and Aimee climbed out.

"You-hoo!" she called out to them, causing her bundle to startle from its contented feeding.

They waved and walked over. "My, my," Phyllis called out, coming up the stairs. "You look as pretty as a painting sitting there. Your color has all come back! Last time I saw you, you were as pale as the sheet you laid on." She peeked under the blanket. "Oh, good, her head has rounded out nicely. She wasn't too long in the birth canal. Some babies' heads come out oblong from their poor mother's long labor. Look at all that dark hair, Aimee! She is a little doll!"

"Oh, she is, Ruby," Aimee said. "What did you name her?"

"Cady."

Phyllis smoothed the blanket. "Of course, that is as it should be."

Ruby looked up to see both Phyllis and Aimee in tears. Her eyes joined in. They all smiled wistfully. Cady's spirit re-born whispered around them.

Aimee brought out a handkerchief from her sleeve and dabbed at her eyes. "Speaking of which, we just came back from a most interesting meeting! Mr. Thomas Pickering, Cady's husband, has graciously offered his home, the back parlor of it that is, to the Ladies of the Lost Legion for a classroom. He said he would gladly do so in memory of Cady. Anna approached him with the idea. She wishes to begin classes to teach women how to campaign and lobby for suffrage. She and Donna went to Buffalo and were taught from none other than Mrs. Catt. It is a beginning. Mrs. Catt wishes to eventually conduct a school for suffrage workers, teaching local women lobbying techniques on how to build the support necessary to achieve suffrage in the states. The battle may be over, but the war has just begun!"

Her excitement was contagious. "It sounds like the Legion is as alive as ever!" said Ruby. "I am so happy to hear this. Are you both taking the classes?"

"You bet," said Phyllis, "and so are you."

Ruby looked up from under low lashes, tears now escaped and running. She shook her head ever so slowly. "No, I'm not," she said softly. "But I will send someone better. Bess. Bess will be there to represent my family of women. She is still young enough not to be affected by how other people ... or the church ... thinks ... she should act, or how her husband thinks she should act. I will give her the freedom to think on her own. I will see to it she does not grow in the shadows here, but out in the sunshine. And so will little Cady. They will have the same freedom as their brothers here at home. That is my battle. And I will prepare them to fight the women's war out there. That is all I am armored for. But it is enough. I have found peace with this."

They nodded in understanding.

She swallowed hard, feeling shrunken under their looks of pity. She changed the subject. "How is Thomas fairing now?"

"I understand he will be traveling a great deal now," Phyllis answered and sniffed. She stroked the baby's head. "He has accepted a job as an international reporter, rather than remain here in his office job at the newspaper. I think he just wants to go where Cady's memories aren't."

"Will Lizzie remain in their home?" Ruby asked.

"Yes, thank goodness! She has nowhere else to go. This home was her lighthouse in a storm, she said to me once. Cady once told me that she and Thomas brought Lizzie in, badly beaten. They had found her stumbling along a dirt road in Georgia and she never would tell them what had happened. But they had a good idea. You see, Thomas is originally from the south, grew up with money on a large plantation, and he knew that many of the single slave women freed after the war, stayed on working where they were, for lack of livelihood anywhere else. Once men returned from the war, and freedom talk died down, these poor women were treated as slaves again, beaten, raped, had their master's children, while they helped deliver their master and mistress's children. Anyway, Thomas and Cady were visiting family down there after their honeymoon, when they found her. That was fifteen years ago and Lizzie has been with them ever since."

"Poor Lizzie," said Ruby, but a bright light blinked in her mind. "A lighthouse...how descriptive."

She looked over at Aimee, her arm still in a sling, her exposed wrist badly bruised, her glove likely hiding more bruises. If a woman had a place to run to in the storm... "How many bedrooms does Thomas have?"

Phyllis cocked her head in question to Ruby. "I'm not quite

sure. Five or six bedrooms, I think. Why?"

"If Thomas is willing to give up his back parlor for women's suffrage, do you think he would do the same with the bedrooms? After all, he won't be there much."

"I suppose so," Phyllis said, scratching her head in confusion. "Though that request definitely takes advantage of his generosity. I don't see your point, Ruby. The ladies taking their training there would have no need to sleep there as well."

"No, but women seeking refuge would. Women who," here Ruby could not meet Aimee's eyes, "well, like Sarah for instance, when her husband forced her out. Think how much more emotionally lifted she might have been, if she could have gone to a 'lighthouse' for support. Or women who have been abused, like ... Lizzie. A place they could go to where understanding women would help them, give them food and clothing."

It suddenly occurred to Ruby that she was in a situation like that once. "A place to sleep in a warm bed," she added. "The lighthouse could provide her protection from the storm, until it blew over. Like a husband's drunkenness for example." She felt compelled to add this last statement to get the point across to Aimee.

Aimee sat down on the settee carefully, as if the weight of what she was thinking was too much to hold standing. She nodded slightly, as if afraid to topple over her thoughts. "Ruby, that is a marvelous idea. I-I could certainly volunteer my services there ... gladly ... it would indeed be a haven for abused women. As long, of course, as it remains a secret that – well – husbands don't know about. Phyllis, your thoughts, please?"

Phyllis remained standing, her arms folded across her stomach, her eyes darting back and forth between Ruby and Aimee. Her expression was of one in deep concentration, as if sizing up the width and breadth of this idea.

"Of course, it must remain secret," Ruby quickly answered, nodding her head to Aimee. She didn't want this suggestion to die with Phyllis, before she had the chance to add more wood to the fire. "So naturally, women volunteers would be required. Volunteer work, cooking and bringing in washed and ironed clothing, I'm certain I can obtain Robert's permission to do that. After all, that is all women's work! And Lizzie! Lizzie would always be there to welcome women in at all hours."

Phyllis nodded once, as if she had now decided. "I will talk to Thomas Pickering tomorrow. This may be the perfect opportunity to personally protect our own, until the day comes when we can change the law to protect us. We could call it the Lighthouse for Ladies...no, that sounds too much like a boutique, or home decorating. Lighthouse for Women, that sounds more serious somehow."

She pulled out a man's pocket watch from her skirt pocket. "I must go now to check on Mrs. Campbell. You must know Mrs. Campbell, Ruby. The Campbell family goes to your church. Her name is Sarah. She is expecting their ninth child any day now. Poor thing is exhausted, her last child is only eleven months old."

She bent to Ruby's cheek and gave her quick peck. "I'll stop by later on this week and let you know the outcome of my discussion with Mr. Pickering."

Aimee rose slowly, her eyes misty now and still on Ruby. "I must go home, now, too. My mother tires easily nowadays – four growing toddlers takes it toll, I know. I hope I don't end up with nine."

She squeezed Ruby's shoulder. Their eyes locked in understanding. "Thank you, Ruby. You are a dear friend."

Ruby nodded. "I'll be here, if you need me." She could say no more, she hated so to see them go.

She listened to their laughter as they said their good-byes on the boardwalk and she longed to laugh with them. Phyllis rode off in her buggy and Aimee's front door slammed shut. The birds had quieted down, and the baby had gone to sleep.

Her memory tugged at her mind and she finally allowed the doors to open. She let her mind wander back to long ago last summer. Ah, but she had such good times with them! The afternoon teas, the talks, the long walks, the march, the songs, the harmony of women meeting, publicly speaking! Women coming together for so many different reasons, yet with a common goal. Her heart swelled with pride at what she had achieved, except that ...

... except that her freedom had led her to ... *him*. And for what, she silently cried, licking the salt from her tears.

He brought me love too late to give him my life. Robert brought me love too late to give him my heart.

Or was it too late?

Wasn't it Robert who had been carrying home a gallon of sky blue paint every Friday for the last four weeks? And didn't he say just this morning that while he was at Joe's General, Joe was showing him a new-fangled stove, one with a temperature gauge?

Ruby looked down at her baby's peaceful face, her own life's milk still white in the corner of its mouth. Its high forehead reminded her of her mother-in-law's.

"As your grandmother always used to say," she murmured, "life is an endless cycle. Birth, death, and rebirth."

With her free hand, she brought out the weathered wooden dove from her apron pocket and looked into its tiny brown eyes. What she saw were warm chocolate drops.

I bring home to you peace and love, his memory whispered.

That he did.

About the author

VANESSA RUSSELL is a writer of fiction, poetry and song, all of which she has woven into her first novel. Her first profession was as a technical writer with the United States Air Force. Born in Texas, Vanessa has made her way slowly north, next living in Kentucky and then Ohio, and is now settled in the woods of Ontario, Canada with her husband and son.